FATAL
INTRUSION

Selected Short Fiction

The Rule of Threes

The Broken Doll

Scheme

Cause of Death

Turning Point

Verona

The Debriefing

Ninth and Nowhere

The Second Hostage, a Colter Shaw Story

Captivated, a Colter Shaw Story

The Victims' Club

Surprise Ending

Double Cross

Stay Tuned

The Intruder

Date Night

JEFFERY DEAVER

FATAL INTRUSION

A NOVEL

ISABELLA MALDONADO

THOMAS & MERCER

Text copyright © 2024 by Gunner Publications, LLC, and Isabella Maldonado

Published by Thomas & Mercer, Seattle

www.apub.com

Amazon, the Amazon logo, and Thomas & Mercer are trademarks of Amazon.com, Inc., or its affiliates.

ISBN-13: 9781662518713 (hardcover)
ISBN-13: 9781662518720 (paperback)
ISBN-13: 9781662518706 (digital)

Cover design by Caroline Teagle Johnson
Cover image: © Grant Faint Images / Shutterstock; © diyun Zhu / Getty

Printed in the United States of America
First edition

To the men and women of HSI,
who work around the clock and
around the globe to keep us safe.

MONDAY

CHAPTER 1

Walter Kemp was not about to let her escape again.

"Come out, come out, wherever you are," he muttered in a sing-song voice.

She couldn't hear very well, but still he treaded carefully, unwilling to blunder through the dense woods and scare her off. He wanted her calm and unaware until he was good and close, so he had to be stealthy.

And deceptive. He tossed a pebble deep into the lush foliage to further disguise his position.

On the outskirts of San Diego, the secluded park felt far from civilization. And from prying eyes.

"You can't hide forever," he whispered. "Not from me."

Walter, a solid man in his sixties, wasn't the least stiff or winded by the hunt. He was nearly in the same shape as thirty years ago. A bit less hair, but so what? There were more important things in life.

Like what he was presently up to.

She had slipped away from him, forcing him to spend the past half hour stalking her. When he found her this time, he wouldn't let her out of his sight until he was finished.

A slight rustle to his left caught his attention. Was that her? He squinted in the direction of the noise.

She peeked out from behind a bush, and his heart hammered with excitement. She was every bit as beautiful as when he had first seen her.

Catching sight of him, she froze. No matter, she couldn't get away. "I've got you now."

She hadn't been his first, and she wouldn't be his last, but she might be the loveliest.

He reached into his vest, thick fingers fumbling over the finely machined metal and plastic. One of the tools of his trade. Slowly, carefully, he raised his hand and took aim. He would have only one chance.

She opened her mouth wide as if to scream.

He pressed the button and held it down. At the rate of thirty shots per second, the Nikon captured ninety images—in stunning forty-five megapixels—of the *Lampropeltis zonata pulchra*, also known as the San Diego mountain kingsnake, before she slithered into the underbrush.

Walter had pictures of several males but had been on the hunt for an elusive female for weeks. Only careful study had allowed him to spot the subtle difference in the subcaudal scales—those under the tail—and the slightly shorter proportion compared to the overall body length that indicated the sex of the reptile.

Unlike with many other species, where the females weren't as brightly colored as the males, all San Diego mountain kingsnakes sported alternating bands of red, black and yellow covering their bodies. The vivid display that mimicked a venomous coral snake was an illusion to scare off potential predators. This species was harmless to everything except the small mammals and lizards in its diet.

Mission accomplished, Walter covered the expensive lens and tucked the camera back into his vest. Now unconcerned about making noise, he tramped back to the trail that led to the lot at the park's entrance.

He would much rather be walking in nature than attending yet another ground-breaking ceremony. At first, many years ago, real estate development had been exciting. His life's passion. He had started off with a small loan and slowly parlayed it into an empire.

Things had begun to look different after over three decades in the business, however. He'd reflected on all the formerly wooded acreage he had eviscerated to turn into suburban havens, and he had started changing his practices. Last year he took up the cause of affordable housing and had been working to improve blighted areas of the community that had fallen on hard economic times. He lost money on every project but felt he'd gained back some of his soul. In addition, he could look his only child—an adult son—in the eyes again. If he was blessed with grandchildren, he would be giving them a better world.

Walter made it to the parking lot, thinking about how his son's high school science project more than a decade ago had led them to bond over the study of reptiles and amphibians. They had both volunteered at the local herpetological society, though only Walter remained a member.

He was nearly to his car when a soft clatter drew his attention. He glanced down to see a small white ball roll past his booted feet. Mesmerized, he watched its progress as it rattled along the asphalt and disappeared under his car.

Hurried footsteps pounded up from behind, startling and unnerving him. As he turned, the blade of a heavy-duty shovel crashed down onto his head.

He cried out in shock and pain.

Stumbling, he threw his arms up in an attempt to protect himself, but another devastating blow drove him to his hands and knees. The agony was beyond anything he'd ever felt. It gripped his entire body, dulling his thoughts and slowing his reactions.

Darkness closed in as his sluggish brain tried to make sense of what was happening.

"Why?" he gasped.

Or maybe he just *thought* the word.

Then he pitched forward, as if in slow motion, falling face down onto the oil-stained surface of the deserted parking lot.

He sank deeper into oblivion, unable to lift his leaden arms. He managed to turn his eyes upward. The shovel was about to come down in another vicious arc, and he knew this would be the last blow.

Someone was killing him . . .

An instant before the tool struck and the void engulfed him, Walter Kemp found himself looking not at the face or torso of his attacker, but at the hands, in clear plastic gloves, gripping the shovel firmly.

Specifically, at the bold and carefully inked tattoo of a black widow spider that graced the man's pale inner wrist.

His last image before the world went dark.

———

Dennison Fallow swung the shovel with all his considerable strength. The satisfying *thwack* of metal against bone, followed by an ominous crunch, told him his work here was done.

He paused to study his handiwork. Good.

The Push, deep within Fallow's soul, was satisfied.

For now.

The man lying at his feet hunted snakes, but this time he'd been the one hunted. And by a far superior predator—a spider.

Various species of these creatures employed many clever means of ensnaring their prey. Some wove a web and patiently waited for an unsuspecting victim to get caught. Others constructed trapdoors or disguised themselves. Today Fallow had attacked in an ambush, like a wolf spider, among the most aggressive arachnids in the world. They don't bother with webs. Or disguise. They charge their prey like a mountain lion.

He continued to watch Kemp for several minutes, making sure the man's chest had stopped rising and falling. One could never be too careful.

That thought reminded him of the shovel he still gripped tightly. Though he'd worn gloves, he'd make sure he removed all traces of his presence from the handle and the shaft, because he was going to leave it behind at the scene.

After all, how could you tell a story without setting the stage?

II
TUESDAY

CHAPTER 2

Selina took another sip of the aptly named Zombie Reanimator, the house specialty at the Wicked Brew Coffee Shop across the street from Montelibre Polytechnic Institute's Perris campus in Southern California.

She'd been holed up in the corner of the café most of the afternoon, putting the finishing touches on a chemistry thesis due tomorrow. Her professor, who by all accounts had neither a heart nor a soul, wouldn't grant her an extension under any circumstances. According to campus lore, he had failed a student who missed the final exam, despite knowing the young man was in the hospital after a car crash, and had refused to change the grade until the university chancellor intervened.

Although Selina suspected the tale was more campus folklore than fact, she would not test the hypothesis by submitting her paper late.

"That looks pretty intense." The male voice was smooth and deep.

Selina jumped and sat upright. Her startled gaze met the pale-blue eyes of a stranger seated at a nearby table.

"Chemistry," she offered, somewhat flustered by the unexpected interruption. "My thesis is on covalent bonds."

"I prefer biology." He scooted his chair closer. "But the subjects are related. When you think about it, one can't exist without the other."

She estimated him to be in his early thirties, too old to be an undergrad and too young to be a tenured professor. Was he involved in post-doctoral research? She darted a glance at the folded newspaper in his hand, noting a nearly completed crossword puzzle—done in ink and without any errors.

Smart and—she sensed—supremely aware of his abilities. Interesting.

No wedding ring either.

The pressed tan cargo pants and close-fitting shirt were a notch above the jeans, rumpled T-shirts and faded hoodies favored by most of the café's clientele. The shirt was a curious shade—an attention-getting red, a hue only somebody with self-confidence could get away with. His gray tweed sport coat didn't obscure an athletic physique. The navy-blue baseball cap bore no logo, and what hair was visible beneath it was light colored, contrasting with the dark three-day growth that shadowed his lower face. His glasses, with round tortoiseshell frames, were stylish. He wasn't Hollywood-leading-man handsome but had an undefinable appeal.

He glanced at her tote bag. "Any chance you have a pen I can borrow?" He held up the paper. "Naturally mine went dry just before I was done."

Rather than carrying around the ubiquitous backpack seen everywhere on campus, Selina favored a worn gray shoulder bag. Instead of a hundred zippered—and irritating—slots, the tote had one giant compartment that held everything, including her laptop.

"Sure." She picked up the bag and opened it wide to peer inside before plunging her hand deep into its dark recesses. "Got to be one somewhere in this black hole."

He smiled.

Engrossed in digging through the student-related detritus at the bottom, she didn't realize he had moved closer until his warm breath fanned the side of her face. She snapped her head up to see that he too was examining the contents of her bag.

She straightened, subtly pulling the tote closer. "I'll find it."

He raised his hands, palms out, in a disarming gesture. "Hey, sorry. Just trying to help."

The boyish grin seemed genuine. Was she being paranoid? Her fingers clasped a long, cylindrical object, and she pulled it out.

"It's a plastic cheapie," she said. "You can keep it."

His smile widened. "Much appreciated."

He took the pen from her outstretched hand and turned to the puzzle. "Seven-letter word for wide-bodied tree." Speaking only to himself, not her. "Sequoia." He gave a half smile of satisfaction, jotted the answer and stood. Tucking the newspaper under his arm, he turned toward the door. "Good luck with your . . . bonds," he said over his shoulder.

And then he was gone, pushing his way outside to the sidewalk.

Selina set the tote back on the chair beside her, still thinking about the brief encounter. He had seemed friendly, then ended their exchange abruptly. Had he been about to ask her out before she got possessive about her bag? He wasn't bad looking and seemed intelligent and polite.

And he was single.

Probably.

Then she glanced up and saw him standing outside, looking back at the café. Their eyes met, his narrowing a fraction. Still smiling, he inclined his head briefly and walked away.

Turning back to her schoolwork, she reflected that however appealing he was, the chance of a date would have come in at somewhere south of zero. One look at the small black-and-red tattoo on the inside of his wrist had made the decision for her.

Spiders had always creeped her out.

CHAPTER 3

Special Agent Carmen Sanchez could not acquire a good head shot through the grimy window.

Her .40-caliber SIG Sauer P229R pistol was up to the task—as was she—but the pane of glass would deflect the hollow-point slug enough to send the round who knew where, potentially wounding or killing one of the hostages.

"I know what you're thinking, Sanchez," the California Highway Patrol lieutenant said through the transmitter bud in her ear. "And you'd damned well better not do it." A brief pause followed. "Those shots are for snipers with spotters and big-ass long guns."

But the sniper and spotter and rifle weren't in place yet, and the hostages were in danger *now*. Jason Powell was currently holed up inside a ramshackle minicompound in the town of Ario, located in the Mojave Desert. He was backed into a corner, desperate, armed and mentally unstable.

Carmen had arrived at the scene less than ten minutes earlier. She'd pinned her long black hair up to keep her field-to-target view unobstructed and surveyed the area carefully.

Normally an agent with the Department of Homeland Security would not be among the first to arrive at a standoff in the middle of nowhere, but she had been on Powell's trail for two days when the call for assistance came out from the Ario police chief that he'd been spotted here. She'd made a beeline, beating the cavalry by half an hour and doing her own recon.

The California Highway Patrol was just setting up, and Lieutenant Kevin Albright, who headed the Mojave-area office, had taken charge of the scene as the incident commander. Carmen, however, was a DHS special agent assigned to Homeland Security Investigations. A federal HSI agent did not fall under Lieutenant Albright's command, a fact that seemed to be causing him serious heartburn.

"And you're too close," Albright added, his sharp words carrying through her earbud. "Powell has a shitload of iron in there. M4s, Glocks, SIGs. You go down, I've got to risk my people to drag you out."

Albright and several CHP troopers had established a command post about two hundred feet back. The lieutenant was surveying the scene—and Carmen herself—through expensive binoculars.

She had been the one to advise the Ario police chief, Gregory Smits, about Powell and his armory before taking up a forward position behind a crumbling concrete wall fifty feet from the compound. Apparently Smits had briefed Albright when he arrived, and now the lieutenant was regurgitating the very intel she had already provided.

"And a case of C-4, Semtex and some other high explosives," Carmen said. "This guy's a genius with IEDs."

Exactly her earlier words to Smits, which he had undoubtedly used in briefing Albright.

Her comment, blunting the man's know-it-all attitude, was met with a few choice expletives, and she knew he had gotten her point.

"I'll maintain position until your SWAT team is in place, Lieutenant," she added. "But if I see a way to end this before then, I'm going to take it."

She weathered a barrage of threats from Albright that included everything from filing a formal complaint with the DHS Secretary to throwing her in jail.

Unfazed, Carmen ignored the diatribe and continued to study the compound, noting every square inch within sight. When Albright ran out of steam, she picked up her narrative as if he hadn't spoken: "And tell the tac team Powell loves to use fishing line for his booby traps. Nearly invisible. As for bargaining, the negotiators should know he has a history of faking surrender before an attack. One of his favorite tricks."

There was a long silence. She imagined Albright deciding she may have useful intel after all and that he should pass along the information to the teams before they engaged.

"What else can you tell us?" Albright's tone had grown distinctly less hostile.

"Powell's a conspiracy theorist and a recluse. He used to be on meds, a lot of them, but he became anti-pharma. Now he's also anti-technology, anti-capitalist and anti-government too. Last week he planted a bomb at the corporate headquarters of a tech company in Glendale, protesting one of its acquisitions. Negotiators tried to talk him down, but he kept ranting about Big Tech forming a cabal to control the world."

"We received a DHS bulletin about an unknown subject protesting a merger, but I didn't hear about any bangs."

"That's because the robots managed to cut the blue wire or the yellow wire, or whatever, in time," she said. "But Powell got away while they were rendering safe."

"Why the hell am I just hearing about this now?" Albright had gone back to hostile, which seemed to be his default setting. "His name and face should have been plastered on a nationwide APB."

"We didn't have his name yet. He was just a DomTerr unsub. Powell's been living off the grid and restricting himself to the dark web for years. He wasn't in any face-rec or DNA databases, and it took us until this morning to ID him."

"You have eyes on the hostages?" Albright asked.

"Hard to see through the window, but it looks like a man and woman. Both appear to be White and in their forties. Scared but unharmed."

"Hold on a sec," Albright said. He carried on a one-sided conversation through what would be his phone. He returned to Carmen. "Okay. We just got a call—a married couple fitting that description was carjacked just north of Glendale yesterday." He paused. "I can't make any vehicles. You?"

She scanned. "No."

"He ditched their wheels somewhere nearby and forced them to walk here. Man, in this heat."

A shout from inside the building ended their discussion. Squinting, Carmen saw the male hostage on his feet and moving forward, arms lifted, railing against their captor, Powell. With surprising speed, Powell spun his assault rifle and smashed the stock into the man's ribs. He collapsed out of her line of vision, but she could see Powell shoulder the weapon and train the barrel downward, evidently pointing at the man. The imminent threat—and the woman's wail of terror splitting the air—spurred Carmen to act. With no viable target through the window, she decided to take a chance on the plan that had been forming in her mind.

She stood.

"Where are you going?" Albright said, the alarm in his voice evident through the transmitter.

"Pay Powell a visit."

Albright surely would run the scene by the incident commander playbook. Secure the perimeter and start negotiations. That could go on for days. However, Powell wasn't a typical hostage-taker; he was like a cult leader. He had followers, fanatics. As soon as they learned of the standoff, they might pay a visit and start sniping at the officers from the nearby hills. Suicide attacks were a distinct possibility.

This had to end now.

Disregarding the lieutenant's protests, she strode to her SUV, a chunky, black Chevy Suburban, and opened the liftgate. It took mere seconds of digging through her nylon equipment bag to find what she was looking for.

"Sanchez, no! The tac unit's suiting up and getting bomb gear ready. They'll be good to go in less than ten minutes."

She jogged back to the wall and surveyed the compound again, noting angles and lines of sight. Crouching, she started forward.

"Stand down," Albright bellowed. "That's an order."

She veered to the left, circling around behind the building, ready to respond if Powell appeared in either of the greasy windows—logical shooting nests.

"The instant you try to breach the back door, he'll tap 'em," Albright muttered. "And it's got to be wired with C-4 up the ass. You'll get everyone killed—including yourself. Stand. Down." His voice rose to a shout. "Now."

Staying low, she trotted to the back door and removed the canister she had retrieved from her SUV. She twisted the nozzle and placed it on the ground facing a small vent. Unlike the others, Carmen had been close enough to hear a low hum coming from the main building. She realized that Powell would have come up with a way to deal with the heat. This was, after all, the Mojave Desert. Temperatures inside the closed building would be fatal—unless he'd devised a way to cool the place without county electrical service. Easy for someone who had spent years living off the grid.

She hadn't spotted a generator, so Powell must have installed solar panels or lithium batteries to power a unit. Either way required some sort of airflow to and from the outside.

Keeping below window level, she scuttled around to the front corner of the building and pulled out a roadside flare from her waistband at the small of her back. She popped off the plastic cap, turned it over, and struck the rough surface against the end to ignite the flare.

The sizzling orange-and-yellow flame was impressive.

"Holy shit, Sanchez," Albright said. "Are you setting the damn building on fire?"

She tossed the burning flare to the ground near the front door and darted back to her previous position behind the wall before interrupting Albright's tirade.

"Give me four, five minutes, Lieutenant," she said. "And this will be done."

"Yeah, right. Like Waco. Where everybody died."

She offered no reply. The newly arrived tac team members began their deployment, creeping around the perimeter in stealth mode. The hiss of the flare was the only sound to break the thick silence of a desert on a windless day.

She gasped when a gloved hand slammed down on her shoulder, then spun her around. She had to tilt her head back to take in the giant, decked out in full tactical regalia. Albright had obviously sent the largest operator he could find to shut her down.

SWAT team members didn't speak when setting up for entry, and the giant did not break protocol. He didn't have to. The message was clear in his dark eyes, which were narrowed to angry slits: she was a rogue agent who had likely just caused the deaths of two innocent captives.

Even at five seven with a solid, athletic build, Carmen was no match for a man more than a foot taller and probably eighty pounds heavier. The giant shoved her to her belly, put a knee on her back and muscled her wrists together, zip-tying them.

"You can't be serious," she called out, loud enough for Albright to hear over the comm.

No response.

"You do not want to do this." Though Carmen's voice was low and threatening, it had no effect.

He jerked her to her feet and frog-marched her toward the command post, his right hand fiercely gripping her left biceps. She didn't resist. He was just following orders. Besides, her work here was done.

They got twenty feet before he stopped in his tracks and pivoted. The tactical team would be on a different frequency, and she could not hear the transmission. But he'd apparently been given new instructions.

He loosened his grip and Carmen jerked her arm away. She turned to peer at the compound.

The two hostages, followed by Jason Powell, were filing out of the building with their hands in the air. Powell held no weapon.

"Stop where you are," the tactical team leader, a wiry woman in her mid-thirties, shouted at them. "Lift your shirts and turn around in a complete circle."

Rather than converge on the threesome, the SWAT team was making sure none of them were wired with explosives set to detonate when they were close to the police. All three of them complied.

"Walk backward toward my voice until I tell you to stop," the team leader continued.

The tac supervisor was taking no chances. Powell could have rigged an IED with a proximity sensor to detonate when anyone approached, or he could have wired the entire building to blow with a timer. Given either of those possibilities, they were making sure everyone involved put distance between themselves and substances that detonated at thirty thousand feet per second.

Her captor's sausage-like fingers returned to Carmen's arm. She wasn't out of the penalty box yet. Blowing out an impatient sigh, she watched the rest of the team separate the hostages from Powell, who was pushed to the ground, sending up a plume of dust.

"You're all tools!" he shouted as rough hands patted him down. "Nothing more than armed tax collectors in the service of big government and big business. How does it feel to be *used*?"

She had researched Powell and had read some of his rambling manifestos but hadn't heard him in person. The frenzied delivery was unsettling, even if the messages weren't original.

"The government sold us out," he continued, voice rising in volume and tempo. "DrethCo merging with Brakon? Oh, you'll see! That'll be it!" He gazed around, wild eyed, a manic grin on his face. Spittle flew as he shouted, "Learn history or be doomed to repeat it. Look at Hitler, look at Stalin. This is a hundred times worse!"

As Powell continued to rant about conspiracies, corporate greed and privacy breaches, Lieutenant Albright, a broad-chested, muscular man roughly her height, strode toward the giant who still held Carmen firmly in place. He stopped close to her. The grim satisfaction etched on his features told her he was enjoying her predicament.

"Show's over," she said. "You can let me go now."

The lieutenant jabbed a finger at her. "You got lucky, Sanchez. But the only place you're going is in the van next to Powell. Your supervisor can bail you out of jail. Reckless endangerment, assault, criminal negligence. And that's just for starters."

This was getting tiresome. Time to explain. "No one was ever in any danger. The canister was filled with mercaptan." When both Albright and the giant continued to glare at her, she elaborated. "It's a harmless chemical added to natural gas to give it that sulfur smell so people will know there's a gas leak. It doesn't burn or explode, just stinks. I lit the flare so Powell would smell the gas, see the smoke, and get the hell out." She added coolly, "Which is pretty much what happened, wouldn't you say? Now cut the ties off."

"Bullshit. He could have started killing hostages the instant he smelled the fumes," Albright shot back.

Her arms and wrists were starting to ache from the awkward position, but she refused to show any sign of discomfort. "After we identified Powell as a suspect this morning, my office pulled up background intel. Someone fitting his description carjacked a food delivery truck less than five miles from here two weeks ago and a nearby gun store was burglarized that night. Got away with two hundred pounds of food and water. And all the weapons I told Chief Smits about."

"What does that have to do with killing hostages?"

"Because if he did, he knows we'd come in shooting. And he'd die. You don't stockpile stores of food and ammo if you don't plan to use them. Means he isn't suicidal. He found this compound and fitted it out. He's on a mission, and he's just getting started."

Sounds of a scuffle drew their attention to the arrest team.

"We're all slaves of big business," Powell yelled as they lifted him to his feet. "They control our reality. Don't you fools see that? Can't you tell what Dreth's up to? Don't you understand what that merger will do?" He struggled as two tac members led him into the transport van and secured him inside. "You've taken the blue pill," he shrieked as the rear doors started to close. "Wake up!"

"That guy is making zero sense," Albright said. "Unless he's laying the groundwork for an insanity defense."

Carmen decided she was done playing nice. She directed a sharp glare at the giant, then Albright. "Either Mirandize me and put me in the van, or cut off the zips, Lieutenant." She spoke quietly, aware a soft voice conveyed far more menace than shouting. "I haven't broken any laws. But you two? You're forcibly impeding a federal agent engaged in the performance of official duties. Obstruction of justice." She paused to let the implication sink in. "I'm quoting from US Code Title 18, Section 111. Oh, and you're both armed. That puts you in the 'enhanced penalty' section of the code. I think the max sentence for that is twenty years."

Their gazes locked for a long moment. "Cut her loose," Albright finally said.

The giant whipped out his SOG locking-blade knife—coincidentally the same model Carmen owned. He sawed through the ties, gripping her arm more tightly than necessary. She let it slide, distracted by the cell phone buzzing in her pocket. She gave the big man a cold smile, rubbed her wrists and dug out the mobile. A quick check of the screen indicated Supervisory Special Agent Eric Williamson—her boss—was trying to reach her.

Albright opened his mouth to deliver what she assumed would be a lecture about command and control at crime scenes when she held up an index finger, lifting the phone to her ear with her other hand.

Which had the delightful side effect of infuriating the lieutenant even further.

"Yes, sir?"

"I just spent the last five minutes convincing the CHP commissioner that I do not have a rogue agent working for me," Williamson said in his characteristic baritone.

Despite a tense, life-endangering standoff, Albright had found a few minutes to run a complaint up his chain of command—with lightning speed, she noted. Apparently keen to eavesdrop on the ass-chewing she was about to receive, Albright had deduced who the caller was and had hung around to watch her squirm.

"Sir, I—"

"I explained to him that you were following up on a lead regarding a bombing suspect in Glendale," Williamson cut in. "And assured him any actions you took were authorized by me." He paused a beat. "Tell me I won't regret vouching for you, because now my ass is on the line too."

"Thank you, sir." Aware Albright could hear only her side of the conversation, she smiled for his benefit. "But I really don't need a commendation. It's reward enough to know the hostages made it out safely."

Williamson chuckled. "I take it one of the local CHP officers got their feathers ruffled and is presently in the audience?"

"Oh, absolutely. It was touch and go for a moment there."

"How long do you need to keep this up?"

"Just about done here," she said, grasping for something else to needle Albright with. "And thanks for sending the jet. Flying commercial can be *such* a pain."

Albright spun on his heel and trudged toward the command bus with the giant in his wake.

"I'm free to talk now," she said to Williamson when the two men were out of earshot. She proceeded to fill him in on the takedown and her trick with the gas canister, rounding out the account with an overview of her interactions with Lieutenant Albright.

"I'll take care of his complaint," Williamson said. "But he had a point. He was the incident commander. It wasn't your show."

"But, sir, I—"

"That being said, it took some fast thinking to end a standoff that could've lasted for days, weeks maybe, without a single shot fired, or anyone getting hurt."

Never comfortable with compliments, she changed the subject. "You should've heard Powell's rants. He's obsessed with big business conspiracies. The Glendale headquarters he tried to bomb? They're merging with some other outfit, and he probably sees it as data mining on steroids. That seems to be the flavor of the week. But whatever his cause, he's not alone. There are more and more like him every day. They jump on the internet, and in sixty seconds they've started a movement."

"I remember when the bad guys used landlines and were only after money," Williamson said. "Now it's all about causing chaos and disrupting lives—and ending them too." He clicked his tongue. "*That's* why they need to okay my proposal."

Over the past few days, her boss had made cryptic comments about the chain of command in Washington taking forever to review a memo he'd submitted weeks ago.

The placeholder title, Project X, only added to the mystery of the plan, whatever it might be.

Like many massive federal agencies, the Department of Homeland Security's internal structure divided and subdivided its personnel and resources into ever-smaller sections like Russian nesting dolls.

At the innermost core, she and Williamson were part of the National Security Division, which was a subsection of Homeland Security Investigations. Their stated mission was to detect, disrupt and dismantle threats to national security, but few people seemed to understand exactly what they did, which could be both useful and problematic.

All of which meant Williamson had a lot of obstacles in his path to get anything done. He seemed impatient for results, and she wondered what her boss was trying to accomplish.

"You going to share more, sir?"

"Until it's official—"

"It's need-to-know," she finished for him. "And I don't need to know."

His silence confirmed this.

Her cell vibrated with a text. Williamson was saying something else, but his words faded into the background as she read the message. The phone nearly slipped from her suddenly weakened grip.

Still staring at the words, she whispered, "There's a problem. My sister."

Williamson's deep voice was filled with concern. "Selina. What happened?"

"Somebody attacked her on the way home from a coffee shop in Perris. I have to go."

...She disconnected, gripped her weapon to keep it securely in its holster and began the sprint to her bulky Suburban, moving as fast as she could through the fine and uncooperative sand.

CHAPTER 4

Two hours later Carmen Sanchez held up her creds at the front desk of the California County Medical Center in Riverside. After a brief exchange, the receptionist directed her to a corridor on the left.

The hallway was painted a sickly shade of green made even more unappealing by stark fluorescent lighting. As she jogged over the ancient linoleum, Carmen glanced ahead, her eyes landing on a sign.

← MORGUE

A young orderly was pushing a gurney in that direction. On it sat a black body bag—presently occupied.

"Dios mío," she whispered.

She sped up, leaving the man and his passenger in her wake.

A voice from behind startled her. "Can I help you?"

She turned around to find a male nurse regarding her with a sympathetic expression and blurted, "I'm Selina Sanchez's sister. She was brought in earlier. The stabbing?"

On the frantic drive to the hospital she'd managed to coax a limited account of the incident from the Riverside County call center. The dispatcher, clearly reluctant to release information over the phone, had described the attack as vicious, with dozens of knife wounds to the victim.

"I was here when she came in." The nurse shook his head as if he had just finished mopping up the blood. "Follow me."

He started to the left. In the direction of the morgue.

Carmen walked fast, even though she was exhausted, and light-headed, after the whirlwind journey from Mojave.

They continued down the grim hallway . . . and *past* the morgue. To the Critical Care Unit.

When they turned the corner, Carmen spotted her sister and raced ahead to pull Selina into a bone-crushing hug.

Her dark eyes wide, Selina barked a gasp of surprise. "What the hell, Carm?"

"Mi'ja," Carmen whispered. "I was so worried . . ."

The image of the body bag on the gurney flashed back to her, cutting off her words.

His mission completed, the nurse turned and went back to his duties.

Carmen pulled away to examine her sister, who seemed unharmed with the exception of a small bandage on her forehead, near her left temple. She wore a slight scowl indicating she did not appreciate public displays of affection.

At least not from her big sister.

During the drive from Mojave, Carmen had dictated her initial statement about the Powell takedown to her admin assistant over the phone. She'd also tried to contact her sister, but each call had gone straight to voicemail.

Her assistant forwarded a bulletin from the Riverside County Sheriff's Department reporting the assault, which included attempted murder, but few details. Carmen's mind had reeled at the mention of a near homicide. Selina was the only close family she had. Their parents had died some years ago and only extended family remained, all of them far away from the Southern California towns where the siblings lived.

"How is he?" Carmen asked, eyeing the patient in whose room Selina had been sitting. She figured he must be the victim with the multiple stab wounds the nurse had referred to earlier.

Her sister's eyes glistened with welling tears. "Critical. He'll live but he may lose the use of his left arm." Her voice grew strained. "All because he was trying to help."

Selina went on to explain that the man had heard her yelling and run to her aid after she'd been attacked by someone who'd previously approached her in her favorite coffee shop. She described him as a White male in his thirties with an athletic build. When asked about distinguishing marks, Selina mentioned a spider tattoo on the inside of his wrist.

"The psycho stabbed the guy who tried to help me a half dozen times before I managed a knee strike to the side of his leg." She gave Carmen a knowing look. "Like you taught me."

In preparation for an undercover assignment years ago, Carmen had been trained in an elite Russian fighting technique called Systema. The rigorous skill was too complex to teach in whole to her sister, so she'd drilled Selina in a few select defensive tactics instead. One of them targeted the common fibular nerve on the side of the thigh slightly above the knee. Called a peroneal strike, the blow caused a temporary loss of motor control, numbness and tingling down the leg, which lasted anywhere from thirty seconds to a couple of hours.

"Sounds like you saved each other," Carmen said quietly. "Sorry to hear he's not doing well."

"I had to keep pressure on his wounds so he didn't bleed out," Selina said. "Otherwise Spider Tatt Guy would have been the one in the hospital. At least he was limping when he got away. Hope it hurt like hell." Her gaze returned to the unconscious patient. "I have to do something to help him."

Carmen glanced around. "Has his family come by to see him?"

"The police notified his brother over the phone. He's flying in from Chicago. There's no one else." Selina turned back to her, suddenly enthusiastic. "I'll help him with medical and physical therapy bills."

"Lina, you're a student working part-time. How are you going to—"

"Crowdfunding." Her excitement grew. "I'll get his brother to set up an account and I'll do the rest."

"And I'll be the first to donate," Carmen said, also grateful to the man who had stopped to help a stranger. "But right now, I need to know what happened. Give me the whole story." Carmen's unit was tasked with pursuing and catching dangerous people.

And Carmen Sanchez was now in hunting mode.

She listened—both clinically and with alarm—as Selina told her about the stranger in the coffee shop who started off friendly but ended by giving her what was, in retrospect, an eerie gaze from the sidewalk after he'd left.

Then she described the attack itself. "I was walking home along a side street between two buildings, and this little white ball rolled in front of me. When I looked down at it, he came rushing out from behind a dumpster." She absently stroked her shoulder. "Felt like a rhino slamming into me."

Carmen hadn't heard of an MO like that before. "White ball? Like a marble?"

"Maybe. I don't really know. I went down and he came at me holding a rope. I think he was going to strangle me." A frown. "Carm, it was identical to the one I use."

Carmen stilled. "Your competition rope?"

Her sister, who was a rhythmic gymnast, used a multicolored nylon rope in her floor routine.

So he knew she was a gymnast. That fact was troubling as hell.

"Did the police find them? The rope and ball?"

"I don't know. They said they'd look for them." Selina added, "Oh, and I scored a bonus."

"Tell me."

"His cell phone. It went flying out of the side pocket of his cargo pants when I kicked him in the leg like you showed me. I grabbed it before he noticed it was gone."

"Lina, great!" Despite her excitement, though, Carmen had to be honest. "May not be that helpful. It's almost impossible to open a screen-locked phone."

Selina smirked. "Not this one. He had it unlocked. I'm thinking he used it before he jumped me. I went into the settings and turned off the screen lock."

How many people would have shown such presence of mind in similar circumstances? "That could be a gold mine." She moved to hug her sister again.

But Selina eased out of range.

Carmen forced herself to give her little sister space. Things had been cool between them since their father's death. Apparently it would take more than a homicidal maniac to mend the rift.

The account of the attack left her deeply concerned but, as an investigator, also aroused her curiosity. Spider Tatt Guy didn't fit any known criminal profiles she was aware of.

"Is there a lead detective you talked to?"

Selina pulled a business card out of her pocket and handed it to Carmen.

DETECTIVE RYAN HALL
MAJOR CRIMES BUREAU
CENTRAL HOMICIDE UNIT
RIVERSIDE COUNTY SHERIFF'S DEPARTMENT

Carmen took a picture of the card with her phone. She wasn't surprised the case had been turfed over to the main homicide unit out of headquarters. The local Perris RCSD station would be too small to handle an attempted homicide.

"Okay, Lina." Carmen lifted a brow. "Keep going with the details."

In addition to self-defense, she had taught her little sister how to be a good witness. Most people panicked during a crisis and had trouble providing usable information to the police.

Whatever sat between them personally, it was time to focus on the task at hand, and Selina, aware a knife-wielding perp was loose on the streets of Southern California, concentrated.

"I acted scared so he would let his guard down. I even pretended to pass out, so he relaxed and stepped back to see if anybody was around. That gave me a chance to get a good look at him. I memorized everything I could. White, around thirty, light-colored hair under a dark-blue baseball cap. No team stitching. He had round, tortoiseshell specs, and light-blue eyes. He was tall, about six two, and I could tell he was pretty buff even under his gray tweed jacket. Oh, and he had on a bright-red shirt and tan cargo pants. Couldn't see any jewelry or other tats. Taking the spider out of the equation, he was pretty easy on the eyes."

"The knife? Folding blade or fixed?"

"I don't know. Just it was about six inches long and the blade was dark, not shiny."

"And you never saw him checking you out on campus or anywhere else before?"

"No. And I got the impression the police think he picked me out at random. Detective Hall said they'll look for reports of any similar cases."

"Random?" Carmen scoffed. "Not if he had the gymnastics rope. He targeted you. And you could still be in his sights. I don't want you in your apartment until this guy is collared. The police offer you somewhere to stay?"

"No." Selina seemed surprised by the proposition. "The detective didn't mention anything about putting me up."

"Well, Riverside County may not be playing Airbnb but you're not going back to your place," she said firmly.

Selina lifted her hands, palms up. "Then where am I supposed to stay?"

Carmen considered the problem. They didn't have any family in the area. "You could crash at my bungalow for a while." She lived alone; Carmen was allergic to roommates.

"Huntington Beach? That's an hour and a half away—without traffic." Selina's jaw was set. "No way am I letting some psycho make me drop out of college, even for one term. I worked too hard to get here."

Her sister, who was near the top of her class, had refused any financial help from Carmen. Instead, she made up the difference for the tuition and room and board not covered by her athletic and academic scholarships by working part-time at a big Riverside County company.

Education was her number one priority.

"Remote classes?"

Selina scoffed. "How could I do lab work without a beaker or a petri dish in sight? And no way would my hard-ass chem professor excuse me. I'd fail for sure."

"I'll figure something out. In the meantime, we're going to have a little chat with Detective Hall." She added under her breath, "*And his supervisor, if we have to. I need to make sure they're aiming in the right direction.*"

Carmen took her sister's arm and felt the muscles tense under her fingers. She sighed and let go. With a last look at the unconscious Good Samaritan, the two women walked into the corridor and started for the exit.

CHAPTER 5

Not good.

Driving along the highway between Perris and Los Angeles, Dennison Fallow peered through the windshield at yet *another* roadblock barring his way to the safety of his subterranean nest.

Riverside County might be smaller than LA but was a sprawling metropolis in its own right with a population of two and a half million souls. Statistically, a lot of those people did a lot of bad things. And what did *that* mean?

A lot of cops to stop them.

And many of them were currently looking for him, it seemed.

Fallow braked his old, battered black Nissan Pathfinder to a smooth stop—no attention-grabbing skids—and pulled into an empty driveway of a tract house, one of hundreds in this neighborhood. A few minutes' wait, listening to the radio for news about the attack.

Nothing.

He backed out and turned away from the roadblock, then cruised slowly toward a street that would take him to the highway, and eventually out of this portion of the county.

And back to sanctuary . . .

An automated female voice emanating from the replacement phone mounted to his dash told him, "Expect delays. Police activity ahead. You will reach a roadblock in a quarter of a mile."

He'd lost his original burner in the fight with Selina and had immediately found a convenience store to buy a new one. Upon activating it, the first app he'd downloaded was Trooper Snooper. With continuous updates on police activity based on input from fellow motorists as well as police-band radio, the app had saved him untold trouble over the years.

He'd no sooner changed direction than she warned him of another stoppage.

Lord, they were everywhere.

It was impossible to enter a freeway with cruisers posted at all the ramps.

Fallow shifted in his seat and winced at the pain in his left knee. Selina had put a hurt on him. Spinning and punching and kicking. It didn't seem like karate or tae kwon do. Something else. More blunt, more dangerous. Deadly even. Kneading the joint, he wondered if she'd torn his ACL.

No, it didn't seem so. But the limb still throbbed like hell.

He replayed the incident in Perris.

As he'd done with the snake hunter, Walter Kemp, Fallow had rolled the white ball between Selina's feet, drawing her attention. Then he'd plowed into her, slugging her cheek with his fist, sending her sprawling to the ground.

There she'd lain—his for the taking. He'd started toward her with the colorful gymnastics rope wound around his hands, angling it toward her neck. But then, in an instant, she was on her feet, attacking.

She was like the lovely Portia spider, a brown-and-black species. They're jumpers but their preferred means of catching their next meal—mostly spiders—is to curl up motionless as if caught in the other's web. When the homeowner returns, the Portia leaps up and attacks.

Fallow had been unprepared for his prey to fight back, or to be especially fierce, or skilled in self-defense. Her dark eyes were filled with anger and determination, not fear, and she planned her blows with precision.

Fallow was not a small man, and he was strong—to pursue his passion he kept himself in good shape. But she fended off his swinging fists and easily dodged the knife he'd drawn. Then, finally, she'd delivered that devastating kick just above his knee.

He'd had his gun but that was for emergencies only. Gunfire brought cops. And brought them fast.

So, he'd decided to retreat.

Glancing over his shoulder, he'd been stunned to see that far from running away herself, Selina was chasing him down. Fortunately a bystander appeared, and Fallow had stabbed the would-be rescuer six or seven times, opening a few select veins, injuries Selina would have to stanch to prevent him from bleeding out.

And then he'd sprinted, hobbled fast actually, back to the SUV, taking the gymnastics rope with him. He'd chucked it into some bushes by the side of the road miles from the scene.

A disaster . . .

How bad was it?

Well, Selina had seen him. He'd had the hat and glasses, but she'd know his pale complexion and have a rough idea of his face even though he hadn't shaved for days. She could make an educated guess of hair color and, of course, she would have seen his distinctive light-blue eyes.

As for his lost phone, Fallow was always prepared. Anything that might accidentally be left behind at a crime scene or that he intended to leave as a calling card, like the shovel yesterday, he'd cleaned with alcohol spray from a small bottle and a tissue. And for the attacks themselves he wore clear vinyl gloves, which were invisible when seen quickly or from a distance.

So, no chance of fingerprints, but he'd undoubtedly left some DNA. The stuff was everywhere. According to what he'd learned, it seemed as if all you had to do was tap something with a fingertip and, bang, you transferred your entire genetic history, going back to Neanderthal days.

But Fallow had never been arrested as an adult, so his telltale deoxyribonucleic acid was not in any databases that could land officers on his doorstep.

And his old phone's contents?

That was more concerning, but at least they were encrypted.

So not an immediate danger.

Right now his priority was getting past the roadblocks.

He cruised along the four-lane street, lined by tattoo parlors, pawnshops, taquerias beside Jewish delis, stores selling rent-to-own appliances. If the route remained free of police, it would take him straight to safety.

His nest . . .

His eyes swiveled about. He noted no approaching threats on this stretch of asphalt, though squad cars zipped everywhere in the vicinity. The sirens were silent, but the lights were so bright and flashed so insistently they seemed to scream.

Roadblocks meant the police knew what to look for. And Fallow wanted to find out exactly what that might be. He steered behind some bushes near one of the blockades and watched two beefy uniformed officers flagging down vehicles.

They were focusing on dark SUVs with only one occupant.

A security camera must have gotten a shot of him entering the vehicle and speeding away from the alley in Perris where he'd parked for Selina's assault. Fallow knew the danger of video and had planned the attack out of view. But he must have missed one. In any event, it apparently didn't capture any part of his tag number, since the officers at the roadblock paid no attention to license plates.

He'd altered his appearance, no longer resembling the polite gentleman in the coffee shop asking to borrow Selina's pen—which was a ploy to peer into her bag to check for a weapon or pepper spray. He'd ditched the fake glasses and baseball cap and shaved off his beard, using hand lotion as shaving cream, taking care not to cut himself. His head hair was blond. But soon would not be.

The Trooper Snooper app was programmed to report on police presence so drivers could avoid speeding tickets. Accordingly, the reports on roadblocks were not comprehensive. It flubbed the job regarding one that came into view in the distance when he crested a hill. The Yellow Brick Road home had been sealed off.

And worse, Fallow saw a patrol car in his rearview.

Make that *two* patrol cars.

He examined the map on the phone, and an idea occurred to him. There was a place nearby where he might be able to lose them—if he could get to it in time.

The pair of cruisers was closing the distance. No lights, no sirens. But Fallow knew a great deal about the police. They were like spiders too, preferring not to give themselves away until they pounced.

The haven he sought was two blocks ahead.

It was by no means certain he'd be safe there. In fact, it might mean death—his or someone else's—as easily as salvation.

But he was out of options.

He kept to the speed limit—thirty miles an hour.

Only one more block to go.

In tandem, the cruisers drew closer.

Fallow's hand went to the pistol in his waistband.

A colorful glow filled the sky ahead, beacons showing him the way to safety . . .

Or to death.

A half block.

The police cars behind him sped up.

Fallow spun the wheel of the SUV and zipped into a large parking lot. He jammed the pedal down and made for a row of cars in the back, concentrating so hard on not crashing into any vehicles or pedestrians that he didn't dare glance behind to see how close his pursuers might be.

CHAPTER 6

Carmen and her sister passed through security at the Riverside County Sheriff's Department headquarters, and Detective Ryan Hall met them in the lobby to escort them upstairs.

The sandy-haired man, of athletic build, was young to be a gold shield, Carmen thought, but he couldn't have made it to the Central Homicide Unit without some righteous collars to his name. His suit was light gray, and he wore a blue dress shirt without a tie, which told her he was one of those investigators—like her—who preferred fieldwork. Male plainclothes detectives often shunned ties, which gave perps an easy way to control or strangle them if a takedown turned physical.

"Coffee, water?" he asked, the words tilted toward Selina more than Carmen. Both women declined.

Carmen, Selina and Hall walked into the conference room, a brightly lit, scuffed place with a rectangular table that seated twelve or so. No decor to speak of. Four monitors, wall mounted. And the remains of a torn piece of masking tape that had once held who knew what.

Drew Webster, the captain in charge of Major Crimes, greeted her by name. The rotund man in his RCSD uniform sat at the head of a table occupied by two other detectives, both males in their forties and looking nothing alike, except, curiously, nearly identical tans. They introduced themselves to Carmen, who forgot their names immediately.

Webster asked, "How's it going, Agent Sanchez? Bet you're busy in Long Beach."

"We are."

"And Eric, doing well? When you see him again tell him I need to win back that ten dollars. Man has one hell of a swing."

Her boss, SSA Eric Williamson, made it a point to get to know local law enforcement throughout the region. He'd confessed to her that golf wasn't his favorite sport, but he'd made it a point to improve his skills, because forging relationships before a crisis was critical.

"I'll tell him, Captain."

He turned to Selina with an expression of concern. "And are you doing all right, Miss Sanchez? After your ordeal? So sorry to hear what happened to you."

Selina blinked, apparently caught off guard by the direct question. "I'm fine." She walked to the far end of the table, her gaze returning to her phone.

Detective Hall pulled out a chair for Selina, then took a seat beside her. An unexpected show of etiquette in a building populated with no-nonsense people whose sole job was to catch criminals.

Carmen slid out a chair for herself on Selina's other side.

Once everyone was settled, Webster turned to Detective Hall. "Could you walk our colleagues through the investigation so far?"

Hall tapped a remote control and two screens mounted to the wall came to life. "This is what we've got, Agent Sanchez."

She took in an artist's rendering of a man in a baseball cap with chiseled features, round-framed glasses, and what looked like a starter beard. As in all composite sketches, the lifeless eyes bordered on eerie.

A separate drawing beside the first depicted an inking of a black spider with a red hourglass shape on the underside of the abdomen. A black widow. She studied the body art that had prompted her sister to call her attacker Spider Tatt Guy.

Her eyes traveled to the second board. The profile.

Sex: Male

Race: White

Age: Approx 30

Hair: Light-colored, length unknown, probably short (hat worn)

Facial hair: Approx three-day growth, full beard, dark brown

Eyes: Light blue

Scars/marks/tattoos: Tattoo on inside of right wrist in black and red ink, black widow spider (see sketch).

Height and weight: Approx 6'2", 190–220, muscular build

Clothing: Bright-red collared shirt, tan cargo pants, gray tweed sport coat, navy-blue baseball cap w/o logo. Wore clear gloves, probably vinyl. Shoes unknown, smooth sole (no ID via tread marks possible).

Speech: English, no accent

Other distinguishing features: Round tortoise-shell-framed glasses

Weapons: Knife, type unknown. Approx six-inch blade. Dark handle. Multicolored rope similar to what victim uses in gymnastics.

MO: Distracted victim with small white ball (no fingerprints, entered into evidence), then body-slammed and attempted strangulation. When unsuccessful, attempted to use knife.

Hall nodded toward the monitor, then turned to Selina. "The description's solid. You did a great job when we were with the sketch artist. Lots of people get flustered, can't remember much, but you . . ."

Selina emerged from texting to return the detective's smile.

Carmen noticed a flush creeping up Hall's neck, its source the unnecessary comment to her sister. A quick glance at his hands revealed no wedding ring. Hmm. Smelled like he might be getting ideas. A part of Carmen understood that any interest Hall might have in Selina could be useful. Another part of her was castle moat and barbed wire fence when it came to her sister, who had been through a lot in her young life.

Carmen turned her attention back to the room. "Canvass?"

Hall replied, "We checked a four-block radius around the site. No one saw anybody even close to his description."

A decent search, but she would have made it eight blocks. Carmen moved on. "Tell me about his phone."

"Selina managed to turn off the screen lock." Hall glanced at the two detectives behind Webster, apparently taking the opportunity not only to impart information but to offer Selina more praise. "That was quick thinking, especially after what happened to—"

"My sister's smart and knows how to take care of herself." Carmen's pointed interruption was designed to redirect the detective and warn him off Lina at the same time. "What did you find?"

Hall's eyes snapped back to her. "Not much. It's a burner."

A normal cell would have a contract with a provider. A search warrant would require the carrier to turn over the subscriber's name, address and call records. A prepaid was largely useless in tracing the user.

The anonymous phone added to her growing belief that the unsub was an organized offender with experience in criminal activities. In fact, burner phones were not as common—or as easy to set up—as TV shows would have it.

"We're tracing the EID and serial number to the point of purchase," Hall went on. "Might get lucky if there's a security cam where he bought it."

Possibly, but Carmen pictured Spider Tatt Guy buying the phone out of the back of a van in a dark alley in Crenshaw. She asked, "Fingerprints?"

"None. Scored some touch DNA. It's not in CODIS or any other databases but at least we'll have it for comparison if we develop a suspect."

Might not even be his, of course. Cross contamination was a constant problem.

Carmen asked, "How about the phone's contents?"

Webster said, "We got it to Cybercrimes immediately, right, Hall?"

Hall nodded. "They didn't find much. The log shows calls to another burner. No SMS or MMS messages. And there were some encrypted files. The techs are trying to crack them now. I just checked and they're not having any luck."

"And the rope?"

"No sign of it," Hall said. "I've got somebody canvassing sporting goods stores in the area, but he probably paid cash."

No probably about it.

"What's the current status of the search?"

"He was allergic to videos, but he slipped up once. A security cam caught a figure limping two blocks north of the scene. He got into a dark SUV and headed west. We isolated an image, but it was low res. We couldn't get the make or model, let alone the tag." He added, "We put out a BOLO with what we had."

This be-on-the-lookout alert had gone out to all law enforcement throughout Southern California, which meant tens of thousands of officers were now aware of the unsub.

One of the two suntanned detectives at the opposite end of the table said, "And we have strategic roadblocks covering all the freeway entrances ringing Perris."

"Good. Now, the spider tatt?" Carmen asked. "Ever seen that before?"

The one with the better tan but the more wrinkled suit said, "We've got a database for body art. Gangbangers' mostly." He glanced at the screen. "No spiders are an exact match to his."

She moved to the most unusual item. "The white ball?"

"No idea what it is. Crime Scene is going to check it out too."

"What about NCIC?" she pursued.

The National Crime Information Center was a nationwide clearinghouse for all manner of crimes. The system was managed by the FBI but the data was entered by local, state and federal agencies.

Hall said, "Nothing matching his description, all fifty states and territories. And MO? Meeting somebody in a coffee shop, restaurant or bar, then following and attacking? Well, that comes in at tens of thousands."

"Your upload?"

The detective on the right seemed put out. "We follow protocol, Agent Sanchez."

The NCIC is maintained by the FBI, but local law enforcement agencies compile and enter all the data. It's grunt work and takes time. But it's also vital, and, though it wasn't her place to prod Riverside County to do their job, Carmen wanted the details of the attack in the system ASAP in case another agency had come across a similar MO or this unsub.

Webster lifted a placating hand toward his detective. "We'll get it done right away." He directed a meaningful glance at Hall, whose head bobbed up and down briefly.

Carmen sent the captain an appreciative nod, then said, "Let me give you *my* thoughts, if I could."

"Please," Webster said.

"I profile him as an organized offender."

"Really? Why?"

She counted off the reasons on her fingers as she spoke. "He wore a bright-red shirt to draw attention away from his face. He used clear vinyl gloves—at a glance, no one would notice he was covering his fingerprints. He used a burner phone and wiped the case. He asked to borrow a pen and peeked inside Selina's bag when she opened it. Could've been a ploy to gather more intel about his target—did she have a key chain alarm, a knife, or maybe a Taser? He bought the gymnastics rope in advance. So he'd been researching his target. And he distracted her with that marble, or whatever it was, before he moved in. This is not an impulse crime."

"Good," Webster said, looking genuinely impressed. "We'll add that to the profile."

Hall was taking notes on his tablet. He nodded without looking up. "Yes, sir."

Carmen asked, "Will this be task-forced, Captain?"

Taskforcing meant an all-hands-on-deck approach, assembling at least a half dozen people from different agencies and setting them up in a war room, which this place definitely was not.

"We're looking at that now."

She wouldn't let him get away with vague assurances. "What agencies?"

"It'll be all the relevant ones," he said, then glanced at the detective seated to his right. "Won't it?"

"All of them, yes, sir."

Carmen said, "Good. I'm glad to hear that, Captain. Until then, who will be working the case?"

"Detective Hall is very competent," Webster said quickly. "One of our shining stars. Up-and-comer as they say."

She made no response, shifting her gaze to the artist's sketch of a spider on the high-def monitor. Without taking her eyes from the unsettling image she said, "One more thing, Captain. The unsub knows my sister's identity. I want her in a safe house. Do you have one available?"

"Carm!"

Rather than respond to Selina's interjection, Carmen kept her eyes steady on the other end of the table.

After a brief whispered conversation with the right-side detective, Webster straightened and turned back to her. "I'm sorry, Agent Sanchez. I'm afraid we don't."

When she merely looked at him in silence, he added, "We keep them available for, well, more serious situations."

"More serious? Meaning gangbangers diming out other gangbangers?"

"Mostly."

"This was an attempted murder, and it has all the hallmarks of a serial doer."

Webster's brows went up. "You know of other victims?"

"No. Not yet. I'm saying my sister's a witness and he knows who she is. And he's got plans for the future he doesn't want interrupted."

"I understand, but there's nothing available."

"Well, if a place opens up . . ."

"Of course. Detective Hall will contact you."

Hall took the cue. "Right away."

Webster rose. The two detectives beside him followed suit.

"Ms. Sanchez?" he said to Selina, who tore herself away from texting to look up. "I'm sorry for your misfortune. We'll find this guy."

Carmen watched the men leave the conference room before turning to Hall. "Detective, could you show us out?"

"Sure." His face brightened—probably at the prospect of spending a few extra minutes in Selina's company.

As the three headed through the quiet corridors, Hall and Selina shared a hushed conversation, but Carmen paid little attention. She was reflecting on the meeting that had just occurred.

Though she mentally rephrased that to the plural. What had just happened had been a meeting within a meeting, a not-uncommon phenomenon Carmen Sanchez, veteran law enforcer, had experienced before.

Webster's real agenda was to see if this case had anything to do with national security. If so, would she, as an HSI agent, either try to claim jurisdiction or armchair quarterback the investigation? Then, depending on a number of factors, he would have handed it over or dug in and fought to keep it. Webster had learned she wasn't here in a law enforcement capacity, but as a relative of the victim. So it was his case to run, budgeting and allocating personnel as he saw fit. He could push forward, or he could hold back.

Carmen had her own agenda. First, to see if she could score a safe house for her sister. Because, serial killer or not, Spider Tatt was still a threat to Selina. Second, to see how proactive Riverside County would be. The answer was what she'd expect for an assault that hadn't resulted in death. Webster would deploy appropriate, but limited, resources. There would be no task force, and Hall was on his own.

She could hardly blame Webster. Carmen kept her finger on the pulse of crime in Southern California and knew that last year there were 112 homicides in Riverside County and nearly 300 attempts. Combine those with open and cold cases from prior years, sex assaults, Border Patrol liaison cases, terrorism, gang and hate crimes, and Webster's plate was overflowing.

Which led to her third agenda item in the meeting within the meeting: to learn as many details about the case as she could as quickly as possible.

And so, when the trio arrived in the lobby and Carmen made sure nobody was around to hear, she came to an abrupt halt. Hall and Selina did too.

She turned to the detective. "Ryan . . . I'm going to call you Ryan, and I'm Carmen. Good?"

"Uhm, okay."

Selina looked on warily.

"Just so I'm clear," Carmen continued. "You're the only member of the task force investigating my sister's assault."

"I have backup," he said defensively. "And there's Patrol to canvass, Crime Scene, Tactical, Cyber. And Accounting, if I need it."

"Accounting?" she asked, nearly laughing. "Okay, now listen. Here's what's going to happen. I want a copy of the files on the unsub's phone, the encrypted ones. I want it yesterday."

"Carm," Selina said. "Maybe chill?"

"And I want to know what the hell that white ball is," she said as if her sister hadn't spoken.

Hall frowned. "You think it's important?"

"Anything that's unique at a scene is *always* important. I've never heard of a gang hit that involved a little white ball. Do you remember any?"

Before he could answer, she steamed ahead. "You'll upload the cases to NCIC?"

"Ten minutes."

"And if you get *anything*, a witness surfaces, somebody calls a tip line, somebody who looks anything remotely like Spider Tatt gets brought in for public urination, I want to hear from you personally. I'll give you my number."

"I have Selina's . . ." His voice faded. "But, yes, give me yours."

She recited it as he entered it into his phone.

"Priority one," she reminded him. "That drive."

"Okay. I'll call Cyber tonight."

"Or you could go to them in person."

"I could. I mean, I will."

"Now, I can't get Lina into a safe house, yours or ours, so I'll put her in a hotel somewhere in the area under a different name."

"Hello?" Selina lifted a hand dramatically. "I'm right here. And I get to have a say in this."

"It's the only option, Lina, if you don't want to stay at my place."

Selina heaved an exaggerated sigh. "Whatever."

"And one more thing, Ryan. Since I can't get her a protection detail, that means you're going to have to check on her from time to time." She paused to give him a smile that might or might not have been genuine. "But I have a feeling you won't mind that part of the assignment. Am I right?"

He flushed a deep crimson. "I—"

"Good night, Ryan. Lina, let's go." She pushed open the door and they stepped outside into the cool, pine-scented night.

CHAPTER 7

Would there be a gunfight?

Dennison Fallow sat in his Nissan Pathfinder, in the parking lot he'd just sped into, and stared through the rear window. His hand was on his pistol—an efficient, if ugly, Glock.

Probably the same weapon the officers in the two police cars behind him had.

His heart pounded.

Firing at them would hold them off, giving him a chance to escape, maybe carjack another vehicle in the lot. But it would also bring hordes of other cops.

Now the two cruisers came into view at the parking lot's entrance.

Fallow drew his gun, pulled the slide back and let it go, snap, snap, chambering a round.

And the cops . . . continued past.

They hadn't been following him at all. A coincidence.

He sagged against the seat and blew out a noisy breath. He then dropped the magazine from the pistol, worked the slide again to eject the bullet and shoved it back into the mag, which he reseated. Glocks, he'd learned, had sensitive triggers and it was better not to have a round chambered when he carried concealed by cramming the gun in his pocket or—like now—the back of his waistband.

He looked around, and a thought came to him.

Some spiders are social.

Anelosimus, for instance, a spiky reddish variety, live in colonies with as many as fifty thousand residents. They share webs and food and jointly participate in labor.

But such species are rare. The vast majority of spiders are loners, territorial and aggressive to interlopers of any kind, even—perhaps especially—their own.

This described Dennison Fallow to a T.

But there was one venue where he felt comfortable among crowds: casinos. The Lucky Lady, for instance, in whose parking lot he'd sought refuge from the twin police cruisers behind him.

Like the others in Southern California, the casino was always packed with people who'd come here for that chance, however slim, to capture their dream at one of the many green-felt tables or shiny clanging machines placed strategically throughout the massive room.

The two officers were gone but the question remained: Could he escape the dragnet?

He'd formed a plan to do just that, which was why he was here.

The Lucky Lady ran courtesy buses for gamblers without cars, or those wishing not to drive after drinking.

Hitching a ride on one of these coaches was a solid gambit. He would, however, shift the odds in his favor—an appropriate word, given his location.

Odds . . .

He nosed the SUV into a space surrounded by scores of other vehicles. It was now, in effect, invisible. The police lacked the personnel to check every car and SUV and pickup in the lot.

Why would they even search here anyway? And if by some remote chance they did, those efforts would be pointless. Because his vehicle had all the traceability of a ghost. He'd worn gloves every time he'd touched a surface and now, to be extra safe, he took a gallon bottle of oxygen bleach and splashed the pungent liquid in and around the seat, destroying any DNA from shed hair and skin cells.

After donning a gray Greek fisherman's cap, he climbed from the SUV and made his way through the casino's front door. There were no metal detectors, so he entered with his pistol hidden at the small of his back—he'd left the knife in the SUV—and the guards examined only bags and backpacks, of which he carried none.

He was in his home away from home, surveying the huge interior, all glitz and lights and happy sounds of slot machines paying out, of bells ringing, of PA announcements about "mega jackpots" at this table or that.

He had to walk through a maze of slots to get to the gift shop   a ploy to entice visitors to slip a few tokens into the beckoning machines on the way to buy souvenirs. He bought a white baseball cap, a pink sweatshirt with the resort logo on it and a pair of aviator sunglasses, using cash, of course.

He stepped into the men's toilet, aware the restrooms were free of the ubiquitous cameras that surveilled every other inch of the facility. Once alone, he hung his sport coat on a hook in the last stall, where a janitor would assume it had been forgotten. Tossing it in the trash, however, might have raised suspicion.

He pulled the sweatshirt over his head and finished his transformation with the hat and sunglasses. Casinos were perhaps the only places on Earth where an average person could wear shades inside and not draw attention. Serious poker players hid their eyes to avoid giving away their tells.

But Dennison Fallow was not here for poker.

Or blackjack or craps or the sports windows.

He was here for the only game that mattered to him: roulette.

The courtesy shuttle wasn't leaving for forty-five minutes, so he decided to spend that time at a table.

Roulette was relatively new in the history of gambling. People have been winning and losing money at cards for over a thousand years, and more than two thousand with dice.

But roulette, which means "little wheel" in French, had its origins in the seventeenth century—supposedly when the mathematician and philosopher Blaise Pascal created what he hoped was a perpetual motion machine. His brilliance at numbers and lofty thinking did not extend to mythical inventions, but the wheel he created came to the attention of gamblers and soon its popularity soared.

The wheels differed in the US version versus the European, but Fallow liked the fact that in both versions the numbers totaled 666, the symbol of Satan or the Beast or whatever demonic creature you believed in.

Fallow ambled up to one table, where a player was on a lucky streak—or so the heavyset, drunk businessman and the dozens flocking around the table thought. There was no such thing as a streak. Every roll of the ball was the start of another chapter of your fate. And each one had zero to do with the previous.

But Fallow enjoyed the mini frenzy, which gave him the chance to ease close to a young brunette in a skimpy red dress placing tiny bets that mimicked the winner's. Her perfume reminded him of a girl called Katrina, a classmate from middle school.

The scent stirred memories. Of being behind the gym, gazing at the captivating Rorschach pattern made by her blood.

The businessman, puffed up with confidence, placed his entire winnings on a combo called a "street," where you picked three numbers. In his case 34, 35 and 36. If any of those came up, he would win, and the payout would be eleven to one.

The spin, then clatter, clatter, clatter . . . tap.

He lost.

His new friends had no more use for him, and they dispersed.

Fallow bought some chips and sat at a table in the back of the room. For twenty minutes or so he didn't place any bets, but merely stared at the mesmerizing rotation of the wheel and the journey of the ball, known as the "pill," speeding in the opposite direction until it lost altitude like a space capsule returning to Earth and stuttered its way to a number, rewarding some bettors, robbing others.

He then joined in, placing some chips himself.

This calmed him by taking his mind off the terrible incident with the bitch in Perris, the roadblocks and the pursuers. Even losing about eighty dollars didn't bother him. Just being at the table and watching the wheel brought him solace, taking the edge off the Push.

He sometimes wondered why he was drawn to this game where the house had a decided advantage. He'd concluded that maybe, just maybe, looking down at a roulette wheel was somewhat reminiscent of looking down at a spider in the center of a circular web.

He glanced at the clock. The bus would leave soon. After tossing a ten-dollar chip on the table as a tip for the croupier, he stood and walked outside.

A successful escape was not as simple as hopping on the Good Fortune Express bus. The police were not stupid. While most of their efforts would focus on solo men in dark SUVs, one or two might consider that he'd abandon the vehicle and take public or private transportation. They would rightly dismiss Uber and Lyft because riders needed a credit card, and he'd be too smart to leave a trail like that. And taxis no longer cruised the streets, at least not around here.

But a sharp cop might realize a fugitive could blend in with other passengers aboard a casino bus.

So to push those odds further in his direction, he'd find a companion.

He surveyed the crowd at the curbside, waiting for the huge coach's doors to open for the drive to Chinatown, a popular place for gamblers to congregate for shuttles to the various casinos around the area. He spotted just the person who might serve his purposes. The woman was in her late forties with a muffin top of pale skin bulging over faded jeans. Her shiny brown blouse was wrinkled and dotted with a few stains, and an impossibly large fake gold necklace dangled below loose skin at the base of her throat. Her hair was unbrushed, and her skin mottled and dry. This was someone who'd surrendered to the addiction of gambling.

And of liquor too, he could smell.

Perfect.

Fallow returned to the gift shop and purchased a souvenir thermos. Then, in the lounge, he bought a double vodka and, when the bartender wasn't looking, poured it into the thermos. He did the same with another. Then he fished a tiny tablet from his pocket and dropped it in, careful to cover his movements with his hand.

Outside he meandered up to the woman he'd noted earlier and struck up a conversation. He pretended to take a furtive drink as her eyes focused hungrily on the thermos.

He had her.

When the bus doors opened, they boarded together, picking a seat near the back. While they shared stories about their adventures at the tables and slots, he looked around and took another fake slug and offered her the container. Not even bothering to wipe the lip, she sucked down two large gulps.

One minute after declaring Fallow was her new "BFF," she was asleep.

The timing was perfect. As soon as her head lolled against his shoulder, the bus rolled out of the parking lot and arrived at the roadblock barring the entrance ramp to the highway.

Tamping down his disgust, he slung an arm around her, smelling her sour perspiration and oily hair and knock-off perfume that competed with the stench of stale nicotine.

Maybe the officers would simply wave them through.

But no. The roadblock was staffed by one of the smarter cops. The officer motioned the driver to open the door.

Fallow closed his eyes and began breathing deeply as if he were asleep.

Heavy footfalls treaded up the aisle.

Then they stopped. "Sir."

Shit.

Fallow's free hand slid around the gun's grip. He would kill the cop first, then shoot the drunken woman through the neck so everyone would have to tend to her, allowing him to escape—just like he'd done in Selina's attack, with the fool who tried to play the hero.

"Sir," the deputy repeated to the man directly in front of them. "No open containers."

"Oh . . ." The middle-aged, balding passenger stared down at his beer bottle. "I'm sorry. I . . . I lost big today."

"Just keep it out of sight," the officer said, kinder now.

"Yeah, okay, sir. Thank you."

Fallow closed his eyes again. He heard more footsteps and the occasional creak of metal—the floor under the deputy's weight.

In three minutes, all was good. The trooper left, the door gave its hydraulic hiss once more and the bus trundled forward.

Fallow shoved the repulsive woman aside. He could not get a shower fast enough. He examined her face. Was she breathing? He couldn't tell.

And he didn't care.

Taking the thermos with him for disposal later, he moved to an empty seat, stretched out and stared at the ceiling, imagining a roulette game unfolding in his mind's eye.

A wheel of fortune.

And what would fate bring tomorrow?

He couldn't say.

Other than, of course, more death.

CHAPTER 8

With a nod to the young, crew-cut guard at the chain-link gate, Carmen nudged the black Suburban past him and into the lot of the Department of Homeland Security's Long Beach, California, field office.

She carded her way through the outer door, then the inner and took the stairs two at a time. The elevators here were notorious. While every other office building in this commercial chunk of the shirt-sleeve waterfront town was dark, DHS wasn't sleeping. Her part of the facility, which housed several teams assigned to Homeland Security Investigations, was particularly busy. It always was. She strode into a hive of activity with agents and support staff poring over computers or sitting with colleagues in cramped conference rooms amid empty coffee cups and crumpled fast-food wrappers, making it feel more like midmorning than the late hour it was.

Homeland Security Investigations is a little-heard-of but extremely active law enforcement arm of the federal government, with over ten thousand employees in 230 offices around the country and a presence on every continent. HSI uses its sweeping jurisdiction to investigate many forms of illegal transnational activity, including human trafficking, drugs and weapon smuggling, international organized crime, money laundering, technology theft and national security threats.

Like most HSI operations situated near a border, the Long Beach office had extra challenges. For example, Carmen had cultivated contacts in Mexican law enforcement who informed her of an unidentified

American who had purchased explosives in their country before slipping back into the US.

She had connected the intel to the unknown subject, later identified as Jason Powell, who tried to blow up DrethCo's headquarters in Glendale. With her knowledge of the case and her connections, she'd been designated to track down Powell—wherever he went.

Now that he was in custody, instead of heading to her minimally decorated office to fill out additional paperwork, Carmen made a beeline for the northwest corner office in the functional facility best described as Federal Government Contempo.

Supervisory Special Agent Eric Williamson, who oversaw a group of agents assigned to HSI's National Security Division, was large everywhere with the exception of his trim waist. Carmen suspected he worked out now nearly as much as he'd done in college, where he was an all-star quarterback. Or maybe he kept in shape thanks to weekend sports with his four boys. Their pictures, along with those of his elegant wife, a federal prosecutor, filled the credenza behind his desk.

Williamson listened with what appeared to be a mixture of concern and alarm as she described the attack on Selina.

"Your sister's okay, though, right?"

"For now."

"She still at risk?"

"He's an organized offender who targeted Selina specifically. And now she's an eyewitness. So, yes, she's still at risk."

"How are you handling it?"

"Riverside doesn't have a safe house. Or won't free one up if they do. I can't use one of ours."

To put someone in a federal safe house in a case without federal jurisdiction would amount to personal use of taxpayer money. Neither she nor her boss would go near that.

"I got her a room at a bed and breakfast. Under a different name. A detective will check in on her. Because he's a good detective. And because he's sweet on her, I think."

Williamson chuckled. Then the expression changed. "What is it, Sanchez?" He was scanning her face.

"They're not on board. Not the way I'd like them to be."

"Riverside? They're good. Webster runs a tight ship."

"But they're treating it as routine."

"Give 'em a chance, Sanchez. They're just getting started."

"The urgency's not there. You can tell, right? You can always tell."

He didn't respond, even though he was the one who'd taught her that a key component of a successful investigation was unbridled enthusiasm in running down perps.

"This unsub is dangerous," she went on. "It isn't the first time he's done something like this, and it won't be the last."

"You know that?"

"No specific cases, yet. But this guy is methodical. Like he's got some experience behind him."

Williamson had also taught her that intuition was another key component in running a case. She continued, "This guy is trouble. Big trouble. The locals are slammed with other cases. They don't have the resources we do."

"If you're asking me to leapfrog over Riverside, how the hell would that work? He's not a transnational threat to national security. That's the only way I could justify it." Then the big man added mysteriously, "For now, we have to stay in our lane."

She raised a brow. "For now?"

He looked as if he regretted his last words. After a long pause, he asked, "You remember Project X?"

Of course she did. He'd mentioned it earlier that day—at the Powell takedown in Mojave. "What does some program you're trying to get off the ground have to do with this?"

"If I get approval, you'll have a lot more latitude in your investigations."

The comment jolted her. He'd mentioned her specifically in that sentence. Had that been on purpose?

"I can't go into details yet," Williamson continued. "But the proposal is under consideration as we speak. I'm expecting a phone call from Washington any day." Then he delivered the punch line. "So this is *not* the time to freelance." Meaning: don't endanger my baby.

She wasn't ready to give up. "He'll keep going, sir," she repeated.

"If he does, then the Bureau can handle it. They'll work with Riverside and whoever else. They love serial killers. They've all read *Silence of the Lambs* and want to be Clarice."

The FBI, also a federal agency, had primary jurisdiction over homicides only in certain circumstances. They investigated cases of Americans murdered abroad, assassinations of US and foreign officials, hate crimes and terrorist acts and some others. But the Bureau's stellar technological and psychological profiling departments meant agents were often invited to consult with state and local authorities and became de facto investigators.

Carmen Sanchez knew this quite well. She was a former FBI agent. Williamson had recruited her away from the Bureau nearly three years ago. She had been a member of the Los Angeles field office's SWAT team, a part-time unit consisting of field agents who qualified for tactical training in addition to their normal caseload.

Bank robbery is a federal crime investigated by the FBI, and Carmen's team was deployed to a hostage situation at a Los Angeles bank. She and her fellow agents would later learn that the robbers had studied the infamous North Hollywood shootout of 1997 and used similar tactics.

Clad in head-to-toe body armor, armed to the teeth with an array of weapons including assault rifles, and each hauling a backpack with thousands of rounds of ammo, the robbers were prepared for battle.

When negotiations failed and the gunmen selected the first hostage to execute, Carmen was one of the team members shot after making a dynamic entry. None of the robbers surrendered and each was killed in the ensuing firefight. The hostages were saved, but she had been the sole survivor from four-person Entry Team Two.

The incident had left its mark physically, mentally and professionally. Personally too. In a big way.

One of the illegal armor-piercing rounds used by the robbers had penetrated the lower edge of her ballistic vest, perforating her abdomen. She and her husband had often argued about her dangerous career choice before the incident. In the aftermath, the very real prospect of her death—along with her refusal to quit her job—had brought an end to their already strained marriage.

Fortunately her sister had jumped in to help after Carmen's husband left. Selina, who had just gotten her driver's license at sixteen, drove Carmen to physical therapy and doctors' visits. They had bonded during the experience, which made their current rift even more painful.

The most unexpected fallout had come from her supervisor at the Bureau, who was extremely supportive . . . until he wasn't.

When her recuperation lasted months, he began to view her as damaged goods eventually. A liability. And, worst of all, he grew suspicious about how she had survived. As the only female on the team, she was used to having to prove herself, but his subtle questioning of her tactical prowess, and the unspoken implication that perhaps a male SWAT member in her position might have made better choices, left a sour taste in her mouth.

Enter SSA Williamson, who visited during her convalescence to explain that he'd reviewed both the footage captured on the bank's camera system and the after-action report. Reading the subtext contained in her supervisor's conclusions, Williamson made it clear that he intended to poach her away from the Bureau to work in his unit at DHS.

At a low ebb on several fronts, Carmen had welcomed the chance at a fresh start. After four months of transitioning through red tape, she'd started the next year assigned to Homeland Security Investigations in their National Security Division. It had been the right decision, and she'd been happy under Williamson's supervision. What was happening between them at the moment, though, left a blemish.

"If the Bureau can consult, I can too." She gave him a significant look. "If my boss authorizes it."

"You want a green light to wade into the middle of a local aggravated assault case with zero jurisdiction? That's kind of a leap, wouldn't you say, Sanchez?" He narrowed his eyes. "Well, your boss doesn't authorize anything."

"What if it was your sister? Your mother?" She was breathing hard. "Wouldn't you do everything in your power to move the investigation forward?"

"You've just said it," he cut in. "This is personal. I'd never use assets inappropriately for my own family. And I won't do it for yours. Come on, Carmen."

She switched tactics. "Okay, take Selina out of the equation. There's something about this unsub that's different. It's not just an ag assault."

"I heard. Organized offender. Still, it's for Riverside to deal with."

Silence stretched between them. The fact that he was right didn't make his answer go down any easier. Collecting herself, she gazed out the window at the array of loading and unloading cranes that defined the brightly lit Long Beach waterfront.

There was yet another component to the situation, deriving from an incident that had driven the sisters apart years ago—something she had never shared with anybody. And one that she certainly would not reveal to Williamson now.

Selina had never forgiven Carmen for what had happened, virtually disappearing from her life.

Now, Carmen saw in this terrible occurrence a way to not only save her little sister's life, but perhaps an opportunity to return from the sorrow caused by that rift.

Carmen Sanchez was now determined to make both happen.

If she couldn't do it with Williamson's blessing, she'd find a way to work around him.

"Then I'm requesting leave," she finally said, then added, "sir."

He regarded her with an inscrutable expression. "What exactly do you intend to do?"

Her answer was simple and formal. "Look after my sister until there's no longer a threat to her. Call it a protective detail."

Williamson studied her again, not unsympathetically, and was perhaps taking into account that she had not had a vacation in two years, and reflecting on her ingenious and injury-free collar of Powell that morning. He said, "Okay, Sanchez. Request granted. I want a memo on the current case."

She stood. "I'll get it to you ASAP."

Williamson returned his attention to the tallest stack of folders on his file-covered desk. "And Sanchez," he said, glancing up, "keep her safe."

She left his office and headed for hers to collect a few things she needed, reflecting that her real answer to Williamson's question had been somewhat more complicated than she'd verbalized: Yes, she would "look after her sister."

But to Carmen Sanchez those words had a broader meaning: that with or without Riverside County or HSI or the Federal Bureau of Investigation or anyone else, she would do everything in her power to figure out this unsub's game, locate him and—using her cuffs or her gun—make sure he never threatened another soul.

CHAPTER 9

Perris, California, was nothing like Paris, France, but Carmen had to give the proprietors of the Eiffel Tower Inn credit for capitalizing on the name of their small city.

They had decorated the cozy bed and breakfast in a French motif and included items like café au lait, croissants and croques madame *et* monsieur on the breakfast menu.

Crepes too. Lots of crepes.

Her younger sister, however, seemed too distracted to appreciate the floor-to-ceiling Louis XIV red-and-gold wallpaper or the herringbone parquet floors.

"How long do I have to stay here?" Selina asked.

If Carmen had her way, Selina would be on lockdown at her own place in Huntington Beach. The bungalow was small, but secure, with the latest alarm system—not that it was Fort Knox, but the title was held in a trust, so the house was virtually impossible for bad guys to track down.

But Selina had decided to stay in Riverside County, so here she was.

"I don't know," Carmen said. "But I won't consider you safe until we figure out what's going on—and nail Spider Tatt's ass."

Selina's brows drew together. "So, despite what Detective Hall told us, you don't think it's random?"

Carmen eyed her. "Not any more than you do."

Understanding passed between them, and Carmen dared to hope something was thawing. It had been a long time since they'd been in harmony about . . . well, anything.

Selina lifted her chin. "I'm only going along with this because I respect your law enforcement chops, so don't think we're going to stay up watching horror flicks and eating popcorn in our pajamas."

Carmen hadn't planned to mention it now, but time was running short. And it was also a way to test the waters. "I was thinking about holding a memorial for Dad next month." She hesitated. "On his birthday."

"Wait." Selina put her on hold with a raised finger, then began patting down her pockets. "Nope, I can't find any."

Carmen looked on in silence, waiting to see where this was going.

"Damn. I cannot find a single one." Selina lifted her shoulders in an elaborate shrug. "I am fresh out of fucks to give when it comes to our father."

Her sister often hid her pain beneath a thick layer of snark.

"Look, Lina, I want to put the past behind us." She edged closer to her sister. "There's nothing we can do to change what happened."

Selina stepped back, reestablishing distance. "*You* might have forgiven him, but I haven't."

And there it was. The impenetrable wall they couldn't seem to get past.

Their father.

"It's not about forgiveness," Carmen said quietly. "It's about acceptance."

"Yeah? Well, I don't *accept* what he did either."

She looked into Selina's blazing eyes, so filled with pent-up anger and resentment, and wondered whether she would ever see things differently.

Their father's suicide three years ago had been particularly hard on Selina, who turned seventeen two days after he died. Instead of celebrating her birthday, Selina had buried the last vestiges of her child-hood along with her father.

Their mother had died several years earlier after a protracted illness, and Selina hadn't forgiven their father for making her an orphan.

Carmen, who had been thirty years old at the time, found herself not only being a full-time FBI agent and caring for Selina during the last year of high school, but also trying to help her cope with the terrible pain the girl felt—a pain she herself shared. Carmen felt the same anger her sister did, but also realized their father must have been in terrible anguish to leave his two daughters behind.

The intervening years hadn't taken the edge off Selina's caustic remarks, and Carmen understood that her sister had transferred some of her resentment onto Carmen herself—the only available target. She opened her mouth to object to Selina's characterization of their father, but a strange jingling sound interrupted her.

They both turned toward the unfamiliar noise. The antique-style French phone with a keypad in the shape of an old rotary dial trilled again, and Carmen crossed the room to lift the receiver from its cradle. The device felt cumbersome in her hand. She had to tilt it at an odd angle to get the mouthpiece in the right position before answering the call. "Yes?"

"Miss Sanchez?" a tinny male voice said through the landline.

She hazarded a guess. "Detective Hall?"

"I'm at the reception desk," he said. "And I, uh, I'd like to see you . . . if that's okay."

Hall clearly believed he was speaking to her younger sister.

Carmen couldn't resist needling him. "That's fine, Detective, because we want to see you too."

There was a long pause as Hall digested her words, doubtless struck by the "we."

"You're with your sister." Disappointment flattened his tone, but he recovered admirably. "I'd like to talk to both of you."

Yeah, right.

"We're in room seven." Carmen lowered the receiver back into the cradle.

"Who was that?" Selina asked.

By the time she explained, Hall was knocking at the door.

After exchanging greetings, he looked around. He did a quick perusal of her sister but—Carmen gave him credit—didn't let his gaze linger and scanned the room for security.

He went up a notch in her estimation.

But she'd already seen to the matter. The drapes were fully drawn, and the windows locked. A chair had been moved to the door where she'd instructed her sister to wedge it under the knob after she left. And she had plugged Selina's phone into a charger and left it beside the bed, ready in case of emergency.

After his examination of the impromptu safe house, Hall leaned back, half sitting on the low desk. "I checked on the Good Samaritan and spoke to his brother, like you asked," he said to Selina.

Carmen recalled the man who had landed himself in the hospital after intervening in the attack and her sister's determination to help him.

Selina bit her lip. "Will he be okay? I called the hospital, but they wouldn't tell me anything."

"I'm the lead detective on his case, so they let me talk to his treating physician," Hall said. "The prognosis is good. The nerve damage wasn't as extensive as they thought. He'll have the use of his arm and should make a full recovery. His brother made it in from Chicago and he'd like to discuss your crowdfunding idea."

"When people hear the story, they'll donate," Selina said. "You don't see bravery like that very often." She put a hand to her chest. "He risked his life for me."

"I would've done the same," Hall said, then flushed—his go-to complexion, it seemed. "I mean, most guys would. Or, well, that is, *some* guys would if—"

Carmen interrupted his babbling. "Why don't you pull your size eleven oxford out of your mouth so you can give us an update on the case?"

He shot her a look that was equal parts defiant and embarrassed. "In addition to the BOLO, we've put out that composite of the unsub. Every patrol officer in Riverside, LA and Ventura Counties will see it in roll call at start of watch. It'll be on their mobile data terminals in their cruisers, and they'll have it on their phones. And I got all the case info uploaded to NCIC."

Her prodding had been successful.

"No matching cases in the database. That weird white ball? Crime Scene can't catch a source. Can't even find out what it *is*. But we're still looking. This perp is pretty damn smart."

Carmen had already arrived at the same conclusion but was curious to hear the detective's take. "How do you mean?"

Hall pulled out his notebook. "Didn't leave a molecule of trace at the scene. That's rare." He continued reading. "His phone's MIN and serial number? To find the point of sale?"

"And?"

"Bought at a bodega in South Central."

Confirming Carmen's earlier guess.

"And before you ask," Hall went on, "there were no video cameras set up in or around the place. Oh, and the other burner—the one he called and that called him? Same bodega."

Another dead end. Though his initiative impressed her.

Hall wasn't finished. "Those three encrypted files? The geeks at the lab can't open them."

From her days in Cybercrimes, she knew that once inside a phone— the hard part—it was often possible to crack encrypted data. The bad guys got lazy and used simple passwords. She'd opened a file by typing in "PASSWERD."

She hated the idea of critical information both at their fingertips and wholly out of reach.

"You mentioned having access to cyber," Hall said. "Did you mean the Bureau?"

"That's right. Why?"

"One of our people has a buddy in Quantico. He said it would be at least a couple of weeks before they can even take a look. And based on the algorithm, he's not even sure they can crack it at all. Nobody's seen anything like it."

Carmen sighed. "You made the copy I asked for?"

He reached into his pocket and pulled something out. He opened his palm. A small black flash drive sat in the middle of it. "It's all yours, but . . ." He hesitated. "What're you going to do? I mean, if the Bureau can't get to it for a week? You know somebody else with a magic touch?"

Resigned, she plucked the drive from his hand.

And chose not to share that the only individual she knew who might have a touch magic enough to crack the code was the last person on Earth she ever wanted to see again.

III
WEDNESDAY

CHAPTER 10

Professor Jacoby Heron watched the new batch of students amble into the classroom.

Sweats and hoodies and jeans and shorts and running shoes and sandals.

Faces of all shades, hair of all lengths. Eyes drowsy, eyes alert—and nearly all curious about what lay ahead. This was *not* English Lit 101.

Forty-nine students had signed up, some for credit, some to audit. Over the semester, as in all college courses, there would be the gravitational pull to drop out, to skip the assigned reading, to daydream, to doze, to rely on their good buddy ChatGPT to "help" with the one paper he assigned to determine their grades.

And those risks were what Professor Heron was already—in the first minutes of the first class of the first semester—strategizing to defeat.

What he was about to teach them was far too vital to ignore. He had every intention that they walk out of his class with weapons to help them survive in a world very different, and far more dangerous, than that of their parents.

He needed his course, "Intrusion in History and Present-Day Society," to change them forever.

It was early Wednesday morning. He'd been awake past midnight finishing an analysis for one of his clients. He divided his time between security consulting and teaching, but the few hours' sleep was a luxury compared to the old days when Red Bull and adrenaline kept him up for 21/24ths of many a day, pounding away on keyboards.

The classroom was in one of the original buildings of Hewlett College in Berkeley. The structure had a functional midcentury modern style, boxy and metallic and glass. Jake was sometimes asked if the school, not far from Silicon Valley, was named after *the* Hewlett, and he'd answer, "Well, *she* thought of herself that way." The school's founder was not the computer and printer innovator who was Packard's partner, but *Rebecca* Hewlett, the billionaire shipping magnate who'd turned from industry to activism and education. She'd written a single check to get the school up and running.

Jake walked to the podium and organized his notes. Slowly. Taking his time. Understated otherwise, he tended toward the dramatic in front of a class.

At six two, he often slouched, occasionally telling himself he shouldn't, but unable to come up with a reason why not. His straight brown hair was characteristically unruly and the trim beard aged him some, though the lighter strands were blond, not gray. Pale, dotted with a few freckles, Jake had not had a tan since the summer after his senior year in high school—eighteen years ago—when his uncle had tried, unsuccessfully, to instill a love of fishing in Jake and his older brother, Rudy.

This morning he wore his typical attire: black jeans, scuffed brown slip-on shoes, a somber blue sweatshirt over an equally drab gray crewneck. The garb was typical of much of the staff. Hewlett was not an institution of professorial tweed and country club casual.

He scanned the class, mostly senior students, noting some absences and a few hostile looks.

Familiar with the reason for both, Jake could only be amused.

The hall grew quiet under his scrutiny.

"Morning," he began, his deep voice conveying a natural gravity. He skipped the pleasantries and got straight to the subject matter. "Colonial America. Life, liberty and the pursuit of happiness. The world of *Hamilton*. Of redcoats, King George, revolution, all that. But do you know the two greatest concerns citizens wrote about at the time? More than tea tax?"

Blank stares met his penetrating gaze.

"Gossiping and eavesdropping. They obsessed the colonists. Threats to their privacy. Here's a quotation from a visitor from the UK in eighteenth-century America: 'In England everyone appears to find full employment in his own concerns. Here, it would seem the people are restless until they know everyone's business.'"

Chuckles from the class.

"I'm talking about . . . *intrusion*. Which I define as someone or something deliberately entering into a place or situation where they're unwelcome or uninvited. In this course we'll look at human history through the lens of those violations. And learn what the intrudee could have done—and can do—to protect themselves against the intruder."

He waited while students scrawled notes onto paper or typed them into a laptop. He did not allow audio or video recordings of his lectures.

"What types of intrusion will we cover? Crime, for one. All criminals intrude. Then war. There've been five hundred and eighty-eight full-throated invasions by one nation-state against another since the Peloponnesian War in the fifth century BC, and tens of thousands of smaller incursions throughout history.

"Then there's political intrusion. All laws and regulations affect us, and some consider those intrusive. Government snooping? Intrusion. Corporate data mining? Intrusion. And what about religion? When does a comforting sect step so far into your life you find yourself in a cult or a terrorist cell?"

He glanced around the classroom. Everyone took copious notes, but how many appreciated his meaning?

None of them. Yet. He still had some months to bring them around.

"Your personal lives," he plowed on. "All relationships, whether romantic partners, friends, family or coworkers, involve letting someone inside your boundaries. Sometimes that's welcome. An 'alliance,' I call it. Sometimes it's negative. That's intrusion, psychologically—and physically—dangerous. Look at abused spouses and children."

He knew students would have mixed reactions to his words. Jacoby Heron had been called a crackpot more than once. He'd been called pompous and strident and paranoid. Like all those who preached, however, he continued to spread his message despite the repercussions. His mission was to make his students and clients and lecture audiences aware of how quickly people could surrender to threats that were becoming increasingly insidious and difficult to recognize.

He knew these dangers from bitter personal experience.

"We'll start today with a subject dear to everyone's heart. Government overreach. Remember the revolutionary colonists? Do you know who the premier gossipmongers in those days were?" When no hands went up he continued, "Snooping town postmasters. Thanks to them, any letter might as well have been nailed up in the town square for the world to see. Sound familiar?"

Comprehension dawned on a few faces now.

A truly satisfying feeling. All teachers and professors recognized it.

"Exactly like hacking your emails today," he said, spelling it out for the rest. "Let's talk about some of the philosophical underpinnings of the concept of privacy back then."

Forty-five minutes later Jake concluded his lecture and assessed the class. It was a good one, more attentive than most, he decided. He was giving them the URL of his website, which contained the course syllabus, when his voice halted like a seized engine.

The hallway outside the classroom was shadowy. Even a well-endowed institution like Hewlett didn't waste money on unnecessary lighting.

But there was no doubt who he was looking at.

And, as he watched Carmen Sanchez, arms crossed, looking his way, he couldn't help but recall the words he'd recited to his class:

Deliberately entering into a place or situation where you're unwelcome or uninvited . . .

CHAPTER 11

Jake Heron covertly eyed Sanchez as they strode back to his office on the east side of the quad.

They had walked in silence and he had no intention of breaking the ensuing tension. Whatever she'd come to tell him, she should say it. And then leave.

"I'm not with the Bureau anymore," Sanchez finally offered.

"Really?" He deliberately kept his tone flat, hiding a rush of anger. The last time he'd seen her, she'd been dedicated to the FBI, and nothing else.

"Went to Homeland Security Investigations. Criminal side of DHS. You've never heard of it."

"No." His tone suggesting the broader truth: that he didn't care.

While the classrooms and admin building at Hewlett were suburban office park, the quad was botanical-garden quality. It might have been cut and pasted from the campuses of Harvard or Northwestern.

As they wound over a gravel path, surrounded by sumptuous vegetation and thick, swaying trees, he imagined the frost emanating from him withering the lush foliage in their wake.

Despite his resolution not to engage, his curiosity was piqued. "You drove up here?"

The drive from LA to Berkeley took nearly eight hours in heavy traffic on the 101, which was often clogged like a bad artery. A more picturesque journey on Highway 1 required an entire day—and involved the risk of plunging off a hundred-foot cliff into the Pacific Ocean.

"We've got a plane."

An even worse harbinger. Anyone who takes a private jet to pay you a visit must have an important agenda. Which in turn meant she would not be easily deflected.

A voice behind them interrupted his musings. "Asshole!"

He sensed Sanchez tense as she tried to locate the speaker. Did her hand move to her waist, where he supposed a weapon was nestled?

Jake imagined she had as many enemies now as she did with the Bureau.

After finding no threat directed at her, Sanchez apparently concluded the shouted insult was meant for him, and fixed him with a querying look.

He explained that he'd earned the hatred of a number of students and faculty members yesterday when he'd appeared as part of a debate program. He was slated to appear against a young, extremist state representative whose views were inflammatory—to put it mildly.

A contingent of students—and more troublingly, professors—disrupted the event and kept shouting down the man. To their shock, Jake had campus security clear them out of the venue. Somehow, the protesters felt Jake was trammeling their right of free expression because he hadn't allowed them to trammel someone else's right of free expression. It was a shame they hadn't behaved better. They would have enjoyed seeing Jake dice the sad, ignorant man into small pieces.

His barring of the protesters was, he knew, the reason for the first-day absences and glares in his class not long before.

"Here." He pushed open the door of an office building, and they were greeted with the smells of paint and garlic. Art department classrooms and the cafeteria occupied the ground floor.

One flight up he walked to his office door and, from a zippered pocket, removed a key like a length of floppy links for the chain lock. This was among the most formidable securing mechanisms ever invented. Jake could pick most locks, but cracking a chain lock could take up to ten minutes (an average intruder might spend an hour or two or, more likely, give up).

The other offices on the floor were secured by RFID electronic card locks, an amusingly useless form of protection.

She gestured toward the nameplate.

Prof. Jacoby Heron.

"Not 'Jake'?"

"Either." And she cared why?

As they walked inside the dim, musty room, he studied her once more. She appeared little different from the last time he'd seen her, several years ago. Athletic, confident, poised, aware of her surroundings. Undeniably attractive with her long dark hair, brown eyes, and heart-shaped face. Her expression, though, seemed . . . what was it? Guarded. Maybe an indication that she'd seen a great deal on the job, and a lot of it tough to witness.

He recalled the last time they had been in close contact, *physical* contact, those silky tresses brushing his face, her toned body pressing against his.

Four years ago, on Christmas Eve . . .

A scent memory flooded back. Lavender. Yes, he recalled it from that night. He smelled it now. Then Jake shooed the sensation away, lifted a stack of papers from a chair for her to sit in, and he himself settled behind the fiberboard table he used as a desk.

How quickly could he get rid of her? It wasn't a good sign that she slipped off her leather jacket—cut similarly to his brown bomber but in black—and set it on an adjoining chair as she took a seat. She wore attire of the sort he recalled. Black slacks, boots, a dark-gray sweater, what most would call business casual. A few pieces of jewelry—gold chain necklace, two rings, though her heart finger was bare.

And, of course, the large black gun on her right hip.

She looked around. "When I was in college you could fit five faculty offices in here."

The cluttered space was twenty by thirty feet. Ceiling-high shelves were stacked with rows of books, file folders, spreadsheets, articles and printouts. On tables in the back sat computers and their vital organs, cameras, audio recorders, binoculars, tools, drones and drone parts (they tended to crash), bundles of wires and cables, and dozens of battered metal and black equipment suitcases.

"I rent it from the school," he said. "I trade the teaching fee for the space. Run my business out of here too."

In the corner was a twin mattress, covered with sheets, and a pillow and blanket. He occasionally spent the night here. His apartment was fine, a pleasant eight hundred square feet overlooking the bay and featuring a nice view of Alcatraz, but he didn't want to waste time commuting when a job was hot. He had no desire to tell any of this to Special Agent Carmen Sanchez, if that was, in fact, her current job title.

He followed her gaze to the framed photographs on the windowsill behind the table. His uncle John and aunt Marta. Then his brother, Rudy, and his daughter—Jake's niece—Julia, lean and sporting casually done french-braided blonde tresses. One shot was a close-up of Julia, pretty face dusted with freckles, smiling as she held up a gift Jake had gotten for her.

This particular picture took Sanchez's attention for a time.

Finally she looked back at him. "So. You're wondering."

He lifted a noncommittal shoulder.

"I need some encryption cracked. And you're the best in the country."

"Oh, you're *flattering* me? Really, Sanchez?"

He expected more from her, expected she'd be above such a cheap tactic.

His reaction flustered her, and he wondered briefly if her comment had not been a tactic at all but an honest expression of opinion.

But another question arose immediately.

She would have all Homeland's resources behind her—the FBI's too presumably—so she must have been truly desperate to seek him out.

Why?

He fixed his eyes on hers. And waited.

She caught his tacit question. "This one's off the books, Heron," she said quietly. "I'm freelancing."

He was surprised. To say the least. This did not sound like Ms. By-the-Book. "And?"

"I'm a Fed, and this is a local case. Attempted murder and felony aggravated assault under the California Penal Code. I don't have jurisdiction. Riverside County's investigating, but they're short staffed, so it's been back-burnered." Her voice took on a matter-of-fact tone. "And that's just not good enough for me."

"Why *is* a Fed investigating a state crime?"

"My sister, Selina. She was the victim."

Whatever his thoughts about Carmen Sanchez, he had no ill will toward the girl.

"Is she—"

"She's all right, but a guy who stopped to help her ended up in critical care for his trouble."

Sanchez explained about a stranger striking up a conversation with Selina in a coffee shop in her college town of Perris, California. He'd seemed normal at first, though something about him raised her sister's suspicions. And he'd asked to borrow a pen, then peeked inside her bag when she opened it.

Purses and wallets were a favorite target for all sorts of intruders, because they could learn so much about possible victims, their resources and defenses.

"To see if she was armed," he said.

"That's what I think. He followed her, rolled something that looked like a white marble toward her feet to distract her, then attacked. Was going to use a gymnastics rope, like the kind she uses in her routines, to strangle her. She fought back. The Samaritan came by, and the perp stabbed him. Took off while Selina stopped the bleeding."

Sanchez explained that her sister scored the perp's burner during the assault. "She went to settings and disabled the screen lock before it timed out."

"Smart move."

"The phone itself is a dead end. A partial print from the SD card wasn't usable. Touch DNA had zero matches in CODIS, and they couldn't track down any purchase info. Riverside County techs pulled some files off it but couldn't crack the encryption." She pulled a plastic baggie containing a flash drive from her pocket. "The detectives mirrored the contents for me—professional courtesy."

Or professional *intimidation*, Jake thought. Her eyes could be quite . . . insistent.

She slid the bag toward him.

He glanced down but made no move to pick it up. "How freelance are you? You've got to know somebody in Cyber at Quantico."

"Word is it'll take a couple weeks. And even then, this might be beyond them."

Intriguing. They had world-class code breakers.

"I have a feeling he's got more victims in mind. So I need those files cracked. Now."

A flash of the determination he knew so well.

"So this is . . ." He waved a hand.

"Yeah, Heron. I'm calling in my favor."

After all these years.

Fine. Get it over with and send her on her way.

He took the sealed baggie. "Gloves?"

"No. That's not primary."

Which meant the drive wouldn't be submitted into evidence at a trial, so he didn't need to preserve it in pristine shape and avoid getting his own prints on it.

He loaded a diagnostic program—a homemade virus identifier—and began scanning the flash drive. "Got to check it for mals."

She frowned. "It came straight from the detective on the case."

There could be malware infecting a video game loving grandparents gave their grandkids for Christmas. In the fifth dimension of the internet, you trusted no one.

Once the program passed muster, he looked through the data and found the phone's operating system software was standard issue and of no interest to a criminal investigator.

Then Jake identified the three files she'd mentioned.

SD.BLF

P.BLF

JM

Using a text editor, he opened the first one, which began:

我看到山坡上的房子，奶牛正悄悄地跟在后面

The second file was similar.

"Asian?" Sanchez asked.

"Asian *characters*. No meaning to them. This is what encrypted files look like in an editor. The first two use a modified Blowfish algorithm."

He opened the third and they found themselves looking at a block of symbols..

Sanchez said, "Chemical diagram."

"You recognize it?"

"Organic chemistry and I got along pretty well." She lifted two palms. "Something Selina and I have in common. But no idea what it is."

"It's an encryption algorithm. Never seen anything like it before."

"Can you decode it?"

"Me? No. Not anymore. I usually run my own *physical* pen testing—penetration testing—at the facilities and homes of my clients. I contract out the internet work. It's sixty hours a week to stay on top of the hacks and exploits. I don't have time."

"Okay, one of your contractors then."

He scrolled through line after line of code. "Maybe. There's one person . . . she specialized in alternatives." He looked at her. "From the old days."

Sanchez scowled. "With the funny name."

"She had a lot of handles, nicknames and aliases, changed them all the time. 'Aruba.' That's the one she used the most."

"That's it. Is she still in the islands, or has she moved on to a different name and location?"

"No idea." Jake didn't know if the petite, athletic woman was still alive, let alone in business. Hell, she might be in jail.

"Can you ask her?"

Surprising himself, he recalled her secure dark web email address, and sent a brief note, expecting a **404 Not Found** error message.

But no more than thirty seconds later, his screen lit up with a reply in the thread.

Aruba: No shit. It's really you, Babbage???

Sanchez was reading over his shoulder. "Who's that?"

"Me. My handle was Babbage-28. After Charles Babbage. He created the first computer, in the 1800s. The Difference Engine."

Even in this obscure part of the web, real names were never used.

Babbage: In the flesh. So to speak.

Aruba: Need to authenticate.

Sanchez pointedly turned her head. "I'm not looking if you're going to type in a passcode."

Jake chuckled. "No secret code. Just something only the two of us would know."

> **Babbage:** Hot tub. Courmayeur, Italy. On_?

A response appeared quickly.

> **Aruba:** December 1. It was snowing. And we—

> **Babbage:** That's good enough.

Sanchez cut him a look. He ignored it.

> **Aruba:** Holy shit it's really you! How are you? What are you up to?

> **Babbage:** Good. Pen testing. You?

> **Aruba:** Writing script to keep a leash on AI. If it had its way, there'd be no need for humans. But given it's you, Babbage, this isn't a random chat.

He half expected her to end with a wry-faced emoji, but she did not.

> **Babbage:** We'll catch up later. Have a question. Got some files with encryption I've never seen. Any chance you could try your hand?

> **Aruba:** They're clean?

> **Babbage:** Proctoscope.

Aruba: Shoot 'em my way.

He typed and hit Return.

Aruba: Received.

A moment passed.

Aruba: Yeah, weird script. But I'm not surprised.

Jake was aware of Sanchez looking his way. Ignoring her, he bent back to his keyboard.

Babbage: Meaning?

Aruba: With you, the only thing I expect is the unexpected. Stand by.

CHAPTER 12

"You think she can do it?"

Jake absently replied to the question, "Aruba's got access to Fugaku."

Sanchez raised a brow. "Which is?"

"One of the fastest supercomputers in the world. Broke the exascale at one-point-one-quintillion calculations per second. Not consistently, though. Usually, you only get about four hundred and forty petaflops out of it. But that should be good enough for us."

As Sanchez digested the information, he wondered if her time in Cyber helped her appreciate the computing power at his disposal.

A moment later she broke the silence. "I was thinking of that piece you wrote, in the *Journal of Criminal Psychology*." Shouts from outside took her attention for a moment.

Situational awareness . . .

She continued, "About investigators analyzing crime in terms of intrusion."

"You read it?"

She shrugged. "A rainy Saturday, and there was nothing good on Netflix."

His opening paragraphs read:

> The author of this article is a penetration tester, a security specialist whose job is to try to find weaknesses in his clients' computer networks and physical facilities.

This job requires him to get into the mind of a potential intruder and, with the client's permission, breach their security. He thus identifies weaknesses—called "Points of Potential Intrusion"—and offers suggestions as to what steps to take to protect themselves from actual malicious actors.

Having had some experience with law enforcement in the past, the author suggests in this article that the pen-testing process could be turned around and used by authorities to identify offenders. Once a crime occurs (and *all* crimes are intrusions), investigators can become pen testers in reverse and attempt to discover the Points of Potential Intrusion by which the criminal might have accessed the victim or the site of the crime and in doing so attempt to learn information that will lead to the identification of the criminal, and, if it's not clear, the purpose of the crime.

Investigators can also use intrusion as a tool in establishing motive, by determining whether the intrusion was the end purpose of the crime (the theft of a painting from a gallery to sell it, for instance) or a means to facilitate a different crime (kidnapping a gallery guard to assume his identity and then steal the painting).

"It was interesting," Sanchez said.

"You try it out?"

"No. Thought I should talk to you first." She picked up a bright-red floppy drive—a 5¼ incher—that really was floppy. The entire thing held 360 KB. About the size of one small thumbnail photo. He doubted she'd ever seen an antique like that.

She set it down.

"How would you analyze what happened to Selina?" Sanchez asked, interrupting his musing.

Did her Favor—he mentally capitalized the word now—entitle her to more than jailbreaking a few files? He decided to give her whatever she asked for, so he could wrap this whole unsavory situation up as quickly as possible.

Admittedly, though, he *was* intrigued by the curious crime. Those with a talent for picking locks tended to be driven to unlock broader mysteries as well.

"I'll pose my second question first. What was his goal? The attack itself or to facilitate some other crime?"

She said, "Not mugging or sexual assault. He might have had some postmortem fetish in mind, but he was in a public area. No, I think he just wanted to kill her."

"Let's stick with the killing for its own sake. Assume that was his goal. Anything in his behavior suggest he was acting on someone's behalf?"

"A professional hit?"

"Exactly," he replied. "Does she have enemies?"

"None she's ever mentioned. I doubt it. She's . . . the sweetest kid on Earth."

Jake decided not to ask why Sanchez had hesitated at that particular point in the sentence.

"Whistleblower?"

"No. At least she never told me."

"You should ask her."

Again, a hesitation. "I will."

"Does your sister have access to sensitive information at school, a job or from friends? Could she know something about somebody who would silence her?"

"Murdering her for a reason like that?" Sanchez looked skeptical. "She works part-time in Personnel at this big company in Riverside

County. Can't remember the name. But all she does is handle routine employee files. Nothing controversial that I ever hear of. And no boss issue. Her supervisor is a nice guy. As for school? She's just a student. No drama. No political activism or anything. Not her thing."

"All right, Sanchez." He gave her a probing look. "What about you?"

"Me?"

"You've made enemies," he prompted. "You've got solid defenses." He glanced toward her sidearm. "But your sister's a soft target. Somebody could get to you through her."

She shook her head. "I get threats, like anyone in law enforcement. But nobody's on the radar."

He considered the facts. "So we can't answer that question yet: whether he wanted her dead for her death's own sake. Or because he needed her dead to further some other crime."

Sanchez shook her head. "Neither one makes sense."

"Okay, next question, PPI. Point of Potential Intrusion."

"I'm supposed to . . ."

He offered, "You're supposed to identify those, how he got to her. And work backwards. A mugger gets a victim because she's walking down Main Street at midnight on a dark night, with streetlights out in a particular portion of the city. Did he know she'd be taking that street? How? And why at that time? Did he know the lights were out? Had he checked the area before? Did he shoot out the lights or cut the wires? Was he interested in her particularly, which means he knew her or knew about her? If so, how? Get lists of all her friends, coworkers . . . It goes on and on, Sanchez.

"No matter how careful people are, how vigilant . . . there are always weaknesses to exploit."

"PPIs."

"PPIs. That's the vital question. In her case? They know each other?"

"No."

"Contact before the attack?"

"No. Not that she knows."

Jake suggested, "He was in the audience at one of her meets? He would've seen her use the rope."

"Possible. But, again, she didn't remember seeing him."

"Can you track down attendees at the events through ticket sales?"

She laughed. "It's not the NBA, Heron. It's college gymnastics. You walk in, sit down on bleachers, watch the meet and leave."

He paused and frowned. "Oh, don't tell me she posted pictures or clips of herself performing?"

A brief pause. "Don't make that face, Heron. She's a kid."

He scoffed. "All the more reason *not* to post. Social media is candy for intruders. It's the richest PPI we have."

"You don't need to lecture me. I had her shut down Facebook, Twitter or X or whatever it is, Insta and Snap."

"There are others."

"Those are the ones she used."

"So the PPI is likely virtual. Since he was careful in the physical attack, he'd act the same online. Completely anonymous. Proxies, VPNs. You'll never find him that way." He considered other possibilities. "I'm sure you've pieced together a chronology from video clips in and around the coffee shop and the site of the attack. Did you see where he came from, which direction he ran?"

She grimaced. "Part of his organized-offender schtick. He picked a place with no cameras. Got a silhouette of him and a dark SUV. That's it."

"You're doing all the right things, analyzing PPIs. My thinking, you don't have enough facts yet. Keep digging. And keep looking at the question of whether he wanted her dead for her own sake or as an adjunct to another crime."

Sanchez seemed to take this in thoughtfully. Then she lifted her phone and showed him a police composite of a White man with a chiseled face, round glasses, a short beard, a baseball cap. A second drawing featured a close-up of a spider inked on his wrist. Jake studied it for a moment. "Not bad art."

Carmen said, "Earned him the nickname Spider Tatt Guy from my sister. Can you do anything with this?"

"Like what?"

"Facial recognition?"

"Using a sketch? Have *you* ever tried that?"

She glanced around the dim recesses of the place. "I thought maybe you could access some cutting-edge AI program that's still under development. You know, the kind they have at research universities. Stuff that's not out in the field yet."

"Well, I don't. And if I did know a program that could ID a suspect from a sketch like that, what do you think my response would be?"

"Not very positive."

Jake had just written a scathing article about a woman arrested because a police department's facial-rec system wrongly identified her as a drug dealer. The dangers of video surveillance and facial recognition occupied three solid hours in his course.

His computer flashed with an incoming message.

Aruba: Have the first two decrypted. See attached. Parsing metadata. Need to farm out the last file. Algorithm I've never seen. Very cool. Very righteous. Very complex.

A fast laugh from Sanchez. "Just like that? Quantico said it could take weeks."

Jake shrugged. "One point one quintillion."

And the fact it was Aruba doing the cracking didn't hurt.

He responded with a thumbs-up emoji and opened the attachments. They were two pictures, displayed side by side. On the left was of a man in his sixties in a business suit officiating at a ground-breaking ceremony for a real estate project.

Sanchez exhaled a troubled sigh and pointed to the image on the right, a pretty, dark-haired young woman in a red leotard, accepting a medal on a ribbon. In her left hand was a rainbow-colored rope.

"Selina," Jake said.

"She took second place at a competition this spring." Sanchez grimaced. "And, yeah, the picture was on Facebook."

"You recognize the man?"

"No."

"Send it to your sister. See if she does."

Sanchez recited her email, and he sent her the picture, which she forwarded.

A response arrived within seconds. She squinted at the text. "Lina says she's never seen him."

Jake got another message from Aruba, and he couldn't help but think of the hot tub in Piemonte, the glacier at Monte Bianco spreading out before them as steam wafted in clouds. Of the two hours they had spent in the turbulent blue water, half the time had been devoted to debating the advantages and disadvantages of assembly computer language.

He read the message. "She got the metadata. The first picture was taken in San Diego two days ago. Can't be geotagged more specifically than that. Mean anything?"

"No." Sanchez lifted her phone and placed a call. "Mouse. You're on speaker with me and Jake Heron."

A whispered response carried through the cell phone's speaker. "With . . . *Heron*?"

Who was this "Mouse" person and what stories had Sanchez shared with her about him?

"I need you to run the same profile as Selina's attack," Sanchez continued. "San Diego. Victim is a White male, sixties or so. The pic is on its way. NCIC, San Diego and Imperial Counties."

"I'll get Declan on it." The line went silent as they were put on hold.

More than a bit curious, he shot Sanchez a look. "Mouse?"

"My assistant. Her real name is Alwilda. She spends most of her time online. So: 'Mouse.'"

There were worse handles than a user interface device, Jake supposed.

Several minutes later Mouse's lilting voice came through the speaker. "Got something, Carmen. There was nothing in NCIC. But I talked to Homicide at SDPD. Murder yesterday. Walter Kemp, sixty. Lived in La Jolla. Real estate developer. Beaten to death with a shovel, which was left on top of the body."

"A staging token," Sanchez said.

"Could have been what he was planning with the rope." Jake knew that some serial perpetrators left objects as messages. Sometimes the meaning was obvious, sometimes it was left as a puzzle for the investigators to decipher. Sometimes the meaning made no sense to anyone but the suspect.

Mouse said, "They're treating it as lying in wait."

Sanchez explained that this meant it was special circumstances murder . . . and opened up the possibility of a death sentence, though California hadn't executed anyone in nearly two decades.

Jake asked, "Was there a small white ball recovered?"

Mouse hesitated.

Sanchez said, "It's okay. He's consulting."

He wasn't sure what to make of her characterization of his involvement but supposed it was more or less accurate.

Mouse responded. "Yes."

Sanchez and Jake shared a look. The same MO.

Mouse asked, "You want me to contact Riverside Sheriff's about it?"

Sanchez glanced at the picture of Jake's niece once more before responding. "Not yet."

Jake looked at Sanchez. "You understand what you've got?"

"A smart, organized serial killer with no discernible motive who doesn't fit any classic profile." She sighed. "The hardest homicidal predator to catch. And the speed . . . two in two days. Hardly ever see that." She directed her next comment toward the phone. "Mouse, I need to get to SDPD headquarters. When's the next shuttle from San Francisco?"

"Hold on . . . nothing to San Diego but I found a flight from SFO to John Wayne Airport. There's space."

"Get me on it. I'll drive down to San Diego. Text me the name of the lead shield on the Kemp case."

"You got it, Carmen."

Sanchez disconnected.

Jake made his position clear. "If Aruba can decrypt the third message, I'll send it to you." Their eyes met. "Then we're even."

"Then we're even." She reached out and shook his hand, which seemed a strangely impersonal gesture considering the nature of the last contact between them on that fateful Christmas Eve.

When her lavender-scented hair had tumbled across his skin . . .

She eyed him a look that might almost be described as coy. "I liked that line in your article."

He lifted an eyebrow.

She continued, "That you'd had experience with law enforcement." Tucking her notebook away, she walked to the door. "Look, Heron—"

A thud and splash from one of his windows startled them both. Someone had pitched a cherry slushy against the glass.

It sluiced downward like thick red blood.

"The debate?" Sanchez asked. "With the extremist congressman?"

He waved the question away. "It'll die down. The protesters are mostly undergrads. They've got the attention spans of gnats."

"Well, good luck."

And whether Special Agent Carmen Sanchez meant with vindictive students or the rest of his life, Jake Heron had no idea.

CHAPTER 13

Dennison Fallow sat up in his bed and swung his legs over the side, resting his feet on the cold concrete floor.

The unforgiving rectangle of whatever futons were made of was covered with sheets that had gone gray from too many washes with too little soap. The blanket was a threadbare brown that clashed.

He checked the time on his phone. Usually he was up earlier. But the disaster yesterday had taken a lot out of him, and he'd slept soundly until twenty minutes ago.

Wearing a T-shirt and white boxers, he stood and, wincing, examined the bruise on his leg, courtesy of the bitch Selina. The pain bore a double edge, stinging both his knee and his soul—a reminder of his failure.

But, Fallow well knew, failures could often be remedied.

He hobbled into the bathroom, where he grabbed a bottle of over-the-counter pain pills and shook two into his palm. Tilting his head back to dry swallow them, he noted several webs in the rafters of the black-painted cellar ceiling. He'd moved into the house recently and hadn't seen them before. He examined the larger one, a messy bundle known as a "tangled web," though most people called them cobwebs—the first part of the word coming from the Old English "coppe" for spider. These types of webs—made by a specific family of arachnids (the *Theridiidae*)—are particularly sticky, as people learn when they try to sweep one away.

He stared at the mass. Webs fascinated Fallow. Spiders began generating silk when they moved from the sea to the land about four hundred million years ago. The material comes from the creatures' spinneret glands on their abdomen, each producing a different type of silk for a specific purpose—smooth and thick for escape lines, sticky for trapping, tiny for wrapping prey.

He waited a few minutes, but it seemed this web was abandoned. Disappointing.

Fallow loved spiders. They were ingenious and persistent . . . and far more dependable than human beings. He'd taken his recent nickname from them not solely because it was creepy and intimidating—though there was that—but because of his affection for all things arachnid.

This did not extend to comic books and popular films. Fallow had little patience for the superhero whose behavior did not resonate with a spider's heart and soul. As for shooting webs from extremities, only a few spiders did that. The Darwin's bark could fire strands five times tougher than Kevlar up to seventy-five feet.

Fallow's home was thirty minutes away in Santa Barbara, so he was crashing here, in the basement of a single-family residence in Anaheim, to be closer to what he thought of as "the action."

No stranger to basements, Fallow decided this one was not terrible. His bedroom was at the far end of a large open area, walled with fake-maple paneling tacked up do-it-yourself style with mismatched nail heads and sloppy cuts. This main room measured about twenty-five by thirty feet. There were tables and folding chairs, a couch, a huge computer station, a fridge and a micro. Cases of Red Bull, Mountain Dew and coffee pods for a well-used black Keurig. The area, lit with interrogation-ready fluorescent lighting, resembled the man cave or clubhouse that it was.

Finishing up in the cramped bathroom, he dressed in tan slacks and blue shirt with extra-long sleeves. He buttoned the cuffs tightly to cover up his inner wrist tatt of the black widow, the most sensuous of arachnids, with the round, glistening leatherlike body and red hourglass-shaped marking that served as a warning to predators. He knew Selina would have helped the police do a sketch of his face, and she might have also seen the tatt. So in addition to changing his appearance he'd have to keep the spider concealed until he had it removed or redesigned.

One thing more to hate her for.

He sat at the desk beside the futon and booted up his computer to check various feeds. The attack hadn't made the news yet. Rising and stretching, he walked into the basement proper. Other people would be here soon, but for now he had it to himself. From the fridge, he took a pineapple juice box, jammed in the straw and drank the contents. Exactly how *Thomisidae*—flower spiders—dine, squirting digestive juices into their prey and sucking out the interior, leaving a perfect shell.

A glance at his watch. Okay. Time for work.

Returning to the bedroom, he sat at his desk, logged on to a corporate website and entered an employee ID and passcode. He slipped the headset and stalk mic over his head and hit a number key at random.

And Dennison Fallow, who happened to be both a talented killer and an in-demand freelance call center operator, heard a click and said, "Good morning, welcome to American General Appliances customer service. May I have your name please?"

CHAPTER 14

Carmen walked through the double doors of the San Diego Police Department's six-story headquarters, which looked appropriately San Diegan, with its immaculate white and ocean blue exterior paint job.

She showed her creds to the police aide, who handed her a pass and directed her to the homicide pen on the fourth floor.

As she stepped from the elevator, she was greeted by Henri Étienne, a tall, rail-thin detective she'd spoken to briefly on the drive here from her house in Huntington Beach. She looked him over and her first thought was, Where did he get clothes to fit a frame like that?

Wherever it might have been, he'd found a good source or a skilled tailor. His charcoal-gray suit fit perfectly. It was neatly pressed, as was his gray silk shirt and tie. The monochromatic effect complemented the silver at the temples of his close-cut Afro, giving him a haute couture look straight out of *GQ*.

"The drive here?" he inquired politely, the faintest trace of a Caribbean accent lending an exotic lilt to his words.

The 5 freeway could be a parking lot but today had not been bad. She told him this, distracted, thinking of the questions that kept surfacing. Two days, two attacks. Similar, and yet different. Who, why? And was he targeting another victim?

A serial killer who was a smart, organized offender . . .

Étienne escorted her into the Homicide Unit's busy pen. San Diego was idyllic in a lot of ways but was also a short drive to the Mexican border. That in itself didn't spell trouble, but guns flowed south and drugs flowed north and recently a pop-up cartel had started operations in Santa Rosa. The ensuing turf war had bled, literally, into the United States.

Étienne jerked his chin toward the far corner. "That's my office. Coffee?"

The very question brought with it a sense of fatigue. "I could use some. Sugar only. Thanks."

When they reached his doorway, she noticed a man with mussed, straight-cut, longish brown hair, sitting inside with his back to the door. He seemed to be studying pictures of Étienne's family on a credenza.

The detective said, "Your associate is already here."

Carmen stopped walking.

Shit. Who was he talking about?

Was it somebody from Riverside County? Sent by Captain Webster or young Detective Hall? A senior agent dispatched by her supervisor, SSA Eric Williamson, who might have had second thoughts about cutting her free for the renegade op. Had the emissary come to order her off the case? Suspend her? Or, the worst, fire her outright?

But no, there was a worse worst.

Jake Heron swiveled around, apparently just noticing the detective and agent, and stood, giving no reaction as various explanations for his presence flashed through her mind.

Étienne said, "I'm getting Agent Sanchez some coffee, Mr. Heron. Anything for you?"

"You have Red Bull?"

"Um. No."

"Coffee's good. Black."

"Be right back." The detective left for the break room.

Heron continued to study the cramped office. "Your jet only got you to John Wayne. Mine brought me all the way to San Diego." He was speaking absently.

As if her chief concern was how he'd beaten her to the meeting.

He continued, "University has a Lear. A couple of our regents are meeting in Coronado. I convinced them to leave a little earlier than they'd planned."

Carmen crossed her arms and fixed him with a glare that demanded an explanation for his presence in a matter that was none of his business.

The debt had been satisfied. They were supposed to go their separate ways.

He brushed at his beard with the back of his hand—a habit she remembered—and returned his gaze to the credenza, where the detective had dozens of framed pictures. "We can't seem to help enabling intruders. We want the comfort of reminders of family around us, but we give away something to strangers in the process. The pictures, I'm talking about."

She took the chair two removed from his. "This isn't going to work, Heron. You can't be here," she whispered urgently. "How did they let you in? You have a fake badge?"

He was unfazed. "That would be illegal. I told the aide at the front desk I was a consultant. Like Sherlock Holmes. Turns out she's a fan of the movies."

Was he being cute? You could never tell with Jacoby Heron. She had read in his article that humor was one of the most dangerous forms of intrusion. If you made people laugh, you owned them.

She snapped, "Tell me why you came. Tell me and then leave. Did you hear from Hot Tub Woman?"

"Yes."

"Okay. Good. But they make telephones, Heron. And don't say you tried but the call didn't go through."

"I wanted to tell you in person. It's big."

"I'm going to repeat myself. Tell me and then leave."

"The third file? Even Fugaku couldn't get in at first."

"Twenty quintillionzillionfucks of a second. Get to the point."

"It's operations *per* second. But, finally, she got something. The encryption algorithm? Using chemical symbols?" He displayed his phone.

"Right," she muttered. "I remember. Bottom line?"

"The file decrypted into a picture."

She hazarded a guess. "Another victim?"

"It's a picture from an advertisement. Bob's Big Boy."

"The hamburger chain?"

"It's just Big Boy now," Heron said. "The picture is from a while ago when Bob was still involved. If there ever was a Bob."

"Where is this going?"

Heron said, "There was something hidden in the picture."

"You mean like a face or words too small to see with the naked eye?"

"No, what was in the picture itself was irrelevant. I'm talking about something hidden in the bytes that *make up* the picture. Steganography."

Carmen was familiar with the technology. "We learned about that in the Bureau," she said, her anger temporarily defused by the intriguing lead. "They said it's mostly used in spycraft."

Cryptanalyst lecturers in Quantico had explained that a color digital photograph consists of pixels, each made up of three bytes (one for red, green and blue). Even low-resolution pictures can contain millions of bytes. Steganography is the art of manipulating some bytes so they represent a message, which can be read by special software. To the eye the photograph appears normal, even though some bytes are distorted.

"Everybody uses steganography nowadays," Heron said. "Not just secret agents."

"And this picture's got a message inside?"

"Exactly."

Her pulse kicked up a notch. "What does it say?"

"Incoming on your unsub's phone." He recited it from heart. "'Contact in Moreno Valley has the hardware you want. Twelve hundred. Guaranteed untraceable.' And your Spider Tatt Guy texted back 'Good.'"

"Not *computer* 'hardware,' right? Not with all this work to hide the texts. And the word 'untraceable.'"

"Agreed," Heron said. "Probably a gun. He's going to buy one. Or already has. The metadata showed the message was sent a few days ago."

Carmen had a vague idea of where Moreno Valley was. She called up a map on her phone. It was a large commercial and residential district near the east side of the Santa Ana Mountains in Riverside County.

"You flew here to tell me that?"

"And to help you follow up. Moreno Valley's a big place. Spider Tatt got the specific address some other way. Probably on a phone he ditched. We have to narrow it down."

"What? No. You've delivered your message. Thank you. Now head back to your classroom and cherry slushies."

"This is important, Sanchez. A killer using two-layer encryption for a simple text? Nobody does that. And now we know there's a second player—the person who sent the message to him."

She mused, troubled, "A serial organized offender, working with a partner? That's very rare."

Heron continued, "Who is he, and why is he involved? And why this level of encryption sophistication? And who's the gunrunner in Moreno Valley? Answering those questions could be the key to our finding that Point of Potential Intrusion I was talking about."

Our?

Étienne returned with three steaming cups cradled in his long, thin fingers. He handed one each to Heron and Sanchez, keeping the third for himself, and sat down. The detective looked from one visitor to the other. A trained investigator, he would have noted the tension between them.

Carmen said, "Heron stopped by to give me some information on the case. He has to leave now. Are there cabs outside? Or should he call an Uber?"

Before Étienne could respond, Heron held up an index finger. "I've canceled my other plans. I can stay and help." His smile slid from the detective to Carmen. An insincere one, she believed.

Carmen fumed but gave no visible reaction. She sipped coffee, burned her tongue.

Blamed Heron.

Tempting though it was, she couldn't have him forcibly removed. There was nothing to do but proceed with the meeting.

She said, "Tell me where you are with the Walter Kemp investigation."

Étienne glanced from Heron to Carmen, apparently unsure how much to share with a civilian.

Carmen debated but then reluctantly said, "You can discuss the case with him. He's a consultant." When the detective simply stared, she added what he'd told the police aide, "Like Sherlock Holmes."

Civilian consultants were alien to most investigators, the best-known examples being the use of private tracking dogs and time- and money-wasting psychics to find missing persons.

Étienne's eyebrows went up. "Hmm, consultant. Must be nice for you Feds to have budgets for that."

"I'm volunteering," Heron said shortly.

Carmen hid a smile, recalling that Jacoby Heron could be prickly when he felt insulted.

The San Diego detective continued, "We know the crimes have similarities, and that it's the same doer. We found touch DNA and ran it through rapid testing. It matches what was recovered in the Riverside attack. A shame there was nothing in CODIS."

She'd take even a small win. "At least it's confirmed. Definitely the same perp."

"In our case, the murder occurred in an obscure corner of a state park," Étienne said. "No witnesses. No cameras. No cell phone pings around the time of the attack. That part of the county is deserted. We saw in your NCIC profile he got away in a dark SUV. Our canvassers didn't find a vehicle like that in a two-mile radius immediately after the murder."

Heron said, "And an organized perp like this might have used dump wheels."

She was surprised Heron knew the cop slang. Criminals sometimes stole or bought a cheap car for a job, abandoning it afterward and often torching it to destroy trace evidence.

She had to agree with the interloper, who seemed to be willing her to see his potential value to the investigation.

The hell was Heron's game? Concern for public safety, or something else?

She deliberately kept her sister's name out of it when she posed her next question to the detective. "Did you get the artist's sketch from Riverside County?"

Étienne said, "We did. I must say he looked normal. In a Ted Bundy sort of way. Not quite as photogenic as *he* was, of course. The photo will go to all divisions." He shrugged his narrow shoulders. "But you *are* aware of how often composites lead to a suspect?"

Her only response was a humorless laugh. Ten percent would be optimistic. She moved on. "In addition to the pictures of Mr. Kemp and the Riverside victim, Dr. Heron extracted something else from the unsub's phone. He was apparently going to make a purchase in Moreno Valley. An untraceable weapon, I'm sure. Did your Crime Scene team or canvassers find anything about firearms at the Kemp scene?"

"No." The detective's face tightened. "But a doer like this? Armed? That's disturbing." He typed on his computer, apparently adding this bit of information to the suspect profile in the database. Then he turned to his visitors again. "The same but different, I was saying. Different locations, victims with no visible connection, different means of killing, leaving tokens, but not the same one. The shovel with Mr. Kemp and, what was it in the other victim's case? Some sports object?"

"A rope. Gymnastics. Didn't leave it, but we're sure he was going to, after he . . . killed the vic." Carmen stumbled on the word. It was hard to refer to her sister that way. There was a blush of flippancy about the shorthand, which all cops were prone to use. "The unsub got her picture off the internet. Did you see Mr. Kemp's photo?"

"Yes, it was in your NCIC posting. We can't tell where it's from. There was no metadata. His son, Michael, is coming in. I thought you'd want to interview him."

"I do."

Heron leaned forward, ignored Carmen's admonishing look and said, "I'm curious about the ball he used to distract the victims before attacking them. Does it mean anything to you?"

Étienne was quick to respond. "No one here has ever seen anything like that. I was planning to ask his son about it too. He might know."

"Do you have anything else?" Heron asked.

"Not yet. We're still canvassing for witnesses. And looking to see if Mr. Kemp had any enemies. Though they both appear to be random victims of a serial killer."

Random. *That* again.

Carmen was about to take issue with the characterization, but never had the chance.

"It's not random," Heron said bluntly. He was gazing at the ceiling, missing her glare altogether. "They're connected. We just don't know how yet."

Pumping the accelerator of her anger.

Carmen tried to remain calm. "Dr. Heron is an academic. Like a sociologist."

"Sociology?" Heron frowned. "What I do is nothing like sociology."

He'd gone all prickly again.

Étienne looked from one to the other, like he was watching a volley at a tennis match.

"We need more facts," Heron said, steepling his fingers, making him appear even more academic, despite his protest.

Carmen scowled his way. Not because of his comment, but because of the pronoun.

We . . .

A young officer in a pristine uniform stuck his head in the doorway. "He's here, Detective."

Étienne said, "Show him in."

Curly-haired Michael Kemp was in his late twenties, fit and sun burnished. An outdoorsman.

Carmen recalled that his father's hobby was nature photography. Maybe his son had accompanied him from time to time. It occurred to her that if he'd done so yesterday, the man might still be alive.

Or perhaps Michael too would be dead.

The young man's face was hollow with loss.

Étienne made the introductions and Carmen explained what had happened in Perris, leaving out personal details about Selina.

Michael's ruddy complexion darkened with rage. "Someone *else*? Who the hell is this guy?" He glanced from her to Étienne. "And you still haven't caught him?"

"We're devoting all available resources to the case. Believe me."

The words calmed him.

"Mr. Kemp," Carmen began. "Did your father say anything about being stalked? Or followed?"

"No. He would've mentioned it. We were close." He choked back tears.

Heron asked about the mysterious white ball.

Carmen decided not to object. As long as the "consultant" was here, let him pose questions she intended to ask anyway.

Michael told them it had no significance he knew of.

Carmen said, "I understand your mother died when you were young. Did your father remarry? Is he in a relationship?"

Michael discreetly wiped his eyes. "After Mom passed, he gave up his personal life. I was fifteen and her dying . . . I was a basket case. Dad totally stepped up. He became like both parents."

Carmen felt a tightening deep within her at this talk of loss and sacrifice among family members.

With some effort she forced her own memories away.

"Did he have any connection with Montelibre Polytech? The second victim went to school there."

"Not that I know of."

"Business in Perris—California, not France?" Carmen asked.

"Where's that?"

"Riverside County."

"He was a San Diego man. Never went north."

Heron asked, "Was your father online a lot?"

"Not much. About average for most people his age. You know, emails, googling or Bing, the news. Facebook. LinkedIn. He thought a lot of it was a waste of time."

"Did he post on social media?" Heron asked.

Carmen showed him the picture recovered from the unsub's phone.

Michael's jaw tightened. "He downloaded a picture of Dad, then attacked him?"

"It seems so."

Étienne asked, "What was the photo from, do you know?"

"The *LA Herald*'s San Diego edition. Online. The pic was from the ground-breaking for a new housing project. Dad was a well-known developer. Laurel Heights shopping center, the Metropolitan Insurance building? Those were his. He borrowed a little nest egg from his father and parlayed that into an empire, well, a modest one. Then he changed direction. Now he was all about affordable housing and socially conscious community planning. That's what the photo was from." He fell silent and rubbed his eyes to bleed off tears.

Étienne asked if Michael could provide a chronology of his father's last few days.

He rattled off an unremarkable account of shopping, yard work, office hours, meals, Netflix . . . and plans to photograph a rare snake. Normal, except they were the man's last hours on Earth.

Carmen could draw no helpful conclusions from what the young man told her.

"The other victim?" Michael asked. "Are they . . . I don't think you said. Were they . . . were they killed too?"

"She'll be fine," Carmen said. "A man who tried to help her was injured, but he'll survive."

"Well, that's good. Thank God for that."

Carmen looked at the detective. "I don't have anything else."

When Heron shook his head, the detective said, "I think that will do it, Michael. I'll let you know if we find anything. Thanks for coming in. We're sorry for your loss."

Carmen gave him one of her cards. "If you or anyone you know can think of anything that might help, give me a call. Or the detective here."

Michael's eyes were red but no longer tear-filled. They were fierce. "Anything I can do to help you find this son of a bitch . . ." His voice hardened. "Just ask."

He turned on his heel and left.

Carmen got to her feet, and Heron followed suit.

Before leaving, they exchanged business cards with Étienne. Carmen stole a glance at Heron's.

JACOBY HERON, PhD
INTRUSIONIST
PERSONAL, CORPORATE AND GOVERNMENTAL SECURITY SOLUTIONS

The detective was staring down at it too. "Sherlock Holmes," the man chuckled as he tucked the card away next to hers in his shirt pocket.

CHAPTER 15

"It'll be a mistake."

"What?" Carmen asked, as she and Heron walked from the SDPD headquarters into the cool, overcast day. These were their first words since they'd left Homicide.

"I shouldn't go back to Berkeley. You need me."

"Need you?" she scoffed. "Things have changed. This is no longer just about my sister. I'm going to talk to my boss, get the case green-lighted. Then I'll have resources. So, no, I don't need anything else from you."

"Yes, you do."

"You and your hot tub friend gave me Moreno Valley. You gave me a possible weapon. You gave me your professional opinion. Appreciate all the above. We have each other's phone numbers." She pointed to a sign that said RIDESHARE PICKUP. NO PARKING.

"What I can help you with can't be done over the phone. It's beyond that."

She studied his body language and sensed deception. He was holding something back. "What exactly *are* you bringing?"

"What do you mean?"

Answering a question with a question. Huge red flag. "Bringing to the table. Give me something specific."

"I don't have anything specific yet. Call it a hunch."

She wasn't buying whatever he was selling. "You're not a hunch kind of guy, Heron. Coders don't do hunches. They do data, they do algorithms."

"Call it a hunch based on data. Of which we need a lot more."

"For your PPIs."

"That's right."

Well, she didn't do hunches either, especially not when their source was somebody she had a problematic history with. And who had blustered his way into *her* investigation.

"Here's where we say goodbye, Heron." She turned and strode to her vehicle.

Once inside, she started the engine, dropped the transmission into gear and sped from the lot. She looked in the rearview and saw Heron leaning against the wall, head down, tapping his phone to summon a ride.

She glanced back at the windshield just in time to slam on the brakes and skid to a stop at a red light. She cursed, unsure whether the obscenity was aimed at Heron for getting under her skin, or at herself for letting him.

Her phone buzzed with an incoming call. She hit the speaker icon without checking caller ID, fully prepared to disconnect if it was Heron pleading his case again.

"Sanchez here."

"Good news, Carmen." Mouse's voice was bright with enthusiasm. "We looked up what you wanted, Declan and me, and we have a hit."

"What I wanted?"

"About the dealers?"

"What dealers?"

"Arms dealers. In Moreno Valley."

She had never known her assistant to be deliberately obtuse. "What are you talking about?"

Mouse paused. "What you asked for."

"Remind me."

"An hour ago. Mr. Heron called. He said you were busy but needed us to look up any NCIC reports or Riverside County Sheriff's records about illegal gun busts in Moreno Valley. And intelligence about runners. I—"

A honk blared behind her. The light had turned green.

She spun the wheel hard to the left and the bulky, black Suburban made a sloppy, skidding U. She sped back to the police department.

"Stand by a sec," she said, a bit harsher than she'd intended. "Need to pull over."

Mouse would figure she was trying to be safe, but safety was the furthest thing from her mind right now—justifiable homicide was a bit closer to the mark. Moments later, she manhandled the ungainly SUV into the headquarters lot and screeched to a stop. She beckoned Heron with her right index finger, using the left to jab the button that lowered the passenger window.

Heron tucked his phone away and bent down, brushing his floppy hair to the side.

She didn't trouble to hide her anger. "What the hell did you do?"

Before he responded, Mouse's voice came through the phone's speaker. "Um, you all right, Carmen?"

"I'm fine. Answer me, Heron."

"Did she find a name?" he asked.

It was not lost on Carmen that he had answered a question with a question. Again. Time to set him straight. "You're not a LEO. It's bad enough you *intruded* your way into SDPD. You can't ask my assistant to do research. That's a crime."

"Is it?" Heron seemed genuinely curious.

A fierce sound welled up inside her and issued from her throat like a growl.

"Did I do something wrong, Carmen?" Mouse sounded worried.

"No, you're good. I should take you in, Heron. I could swear out a warrant for misuse of government resources. I know the US attorney down here and she'd prosecute you in a heartbeat."

"Can I . . . You mind?" He pointed at the phone and said, "Hi. Mouse, it's Jake. What did you find?"

"Hi, Mr. Heron."

Carmen bristled. Heron wasn't just elbowing his way in, he was staging a coup.

"His name is Alex Georgio," Mouse said. "Apparently he's the go-to for black market weapons in that part of Riverside. And, you were right, twelve hundred is the going rate for a cold gun—one without a serial number."

Carmen stilled, listening.

Heron asked, "What about electronics?"

"You got that right too. I called Alcohol, Tobacco and Firearms, and the ASAC reported back that they've never been able to jam Georgio up with a major felony case because his phones and computer accounts are too secure. I used the word you told me to say, and he laughed and said, 'Exactly.'"

Heron said, "Righteous."

"Yeah, the codes on all his devices were totally righteous. In the past, they tried sending in undercover agents to do buy-busts, but he never took the bait. Um, Carmen. Is everything okay?"

"It's fine. Text me this Georgio's address."

"He moved to a new place—also in Moreno Valley. ATF is tracking it down. I'll send it along as soon as I hear back. Should be anytime."

"Be sure to send it to *me*. Only me."

"Will do. And Carmen? The boss wants you here."

"Tell him I'm on my way in. And thanks, Mouse. Good job."

Heron began, "Appreciate your—"

She disconnected before he could give her assistant any more assignments.

They eyed each other a few seconds and broke away simultaneously.

Carmen popped the lock. "Get in the fucking car."

He climbed in, set his gear bag on the floor, slammed the door and buckled up.

She pulled into traffic, still fuming. "Aren't you going to cancel your Uber?"

"Never called one. I knew you'd be back."

CHAPTER 16

Fallow knew the answer before he asked the question. "Do you have your warranty number, Emily?"

"No," came the voice from the other end of the line. "But I don't need it. I know my rights. You're going to try to say I don't have it so you can't help me." Her strident voice abraded his ears like sandpaper on rough wood.

Emily was one of *those* customers—ones sometimes referred to as "Karens" in social media.

Sitting in his comfortable desk chair in his makeshift basement home office, Fallow responded pleasantly, "No problem, Emily. I'm happy to look it up. What's your last name?"

"Why should I give it to you?"

"I'll need to know which warranty you have."

Silence for a moment.

"Halcomb."

"Thank you for that information, Emily. While I look it up, why don't you tell me what the problem is?"

"My dishwasher broke. The day of my daughter's sweet-sixteen party!"

"I'm sorry you had a problem with one of our products, Emily."

"You don't *sound* sorry."

"Ah, here's your record. I'm afraid the warranty has expired."

She seemed prepared for this news. "That's not my fault. Nobody told me it was going to expire."

"Well, Emily, it does look like last March we called and left a message about renewing."

"That's a lie. No one ever called."

"I'm sorry for the misunderstanding, Emily. But I'm afraid there's no current warranty on file."

"That's it. I want a supervisor."

"Of course, Emily. I'll transfer you."

He forwarded the line to another call center operator. They took turns pretending to be supervisors, of which there were none in the company call center service department, at least none who would talk to complaining customers. He believed this was true of nearly all consumer corporations on Earth.

Fallow handled a few other calls, then took a break.

He was distracted.

The run-in with Selina had shaken him.

He'd been left frustrated.

More importantly, the *Push* was unsatisfied.

And when the Push wasn't happy, well, *that* was a problem.

He drank another juice box and thought about the Push, recalling the first time he'd told another soul about the force that drove him.

Four years ago, in a psychiatrist's office in Santa Monica, Dr. Stillman had asked him, "So, what do you call it, Dennison?"

The question confused him. "What do I call what?"

"The drive to act out physically to relieve the tension, the pain inside. Like scratching the itch or rubbing the sore tooth. Some people call it their 'Urge,' with a capital 'U,'" Dr. Stillman explained. "Some call it their 'Curse.' The ones who are less subtle but more scientific call it their 'Compulsion.'"

"Oh. The Push. I call it the Push."

"'Push,'" Dr. Stillman repeated and seemed pleased.

Dennison Fallow, who had a long history with shrinks, had learned that a flash of approval during a session had as much value as a penny in a gutter.

"That's a good term for it," Dr. Stillman continued. "Like there's an entity inside you, actively pressing you to do things."

"That's right."

Dr. Stillman was well under six feet, but broad. He wore gray slacks, a white dress shirt and a light-blue sport jacket that wouldn't button even if he tried hard. His face was kindly, a TV doctor's face. And he had a shrink's carefully barbered goatee. "When were you first aware of the Push?"

"I guess when I was around twelve."

Thinking of middle school, of Katrina.

Behind the gym.

Her blood. A lot of it.

"You've been fighting against the Push all these years. It must be so hard."

If the man only knew . . .

"And all you want is for that itch to go away. For the Push to stop."

This was his fifth session with Dr. Stillman, and despite his cynical thought a moment earlier, he was—maybe—beginning to warm to the man.

Dr. Stillman had looked at him for a long moment, exhibiting no more emotion than Fallow himself displayed. Did the doctor think he was a hopeless case? All the others had come to this conclusion.

But then Dr. Stillman smiled. He wrote a name and address on a prescription pad. He pushed it forward. "Go see him. He's a specialist."

Fallow's lips had grown tight. He was twenty-six years old and had been fighting the Push and its relentless instruction to hurt and hurt and hurt for more than a decade. It was exhausting.

He glanced at the name. Charles Benedict.

"He's a good man. He helps people when traditional therapy fails."

"You're saying I need a therapist of last resort?"

"No, Dennison, I'm saying you need a specialist. That's all."

"I'll think about it."

"That's all I can ask."

The next day, after a very enjoyable and calming visit to the marvelous Spider Pavilion at the LA Natural History Museum, Fallow had impulsively looked at the slip of paper the doctor had given him.

A specialist . . .

And he had called this Benedict and made an appointment.

Never realizing at the time that the consequences would be . . . well, "consequential" was a massive understatement.

Both to him and, as it turned out, to Mr. Benedict himself.

He now forced his attention back to the task at hand, in the bedroom office of the house in Anaheim. Back to the headset and computer.

Fallow hardly needed the $22.50 an hour he was paid by American General Appliances to field warranty questions. But there was a reason he signed on as a part-time flex-hour work-from-home employee.

The company had compiled an extensive database about its customers—the result of artificial intelligence data scraping mostly. He could learn plenty about people like the dishwasher-betrayed Emily Halcomb, 25458 Arroyo Verde Court, Los Angeles. He could see if the family bought dog food for a potentially dangerous defender of the homestead.

If she or her husband had purchased guns or ammunition.

If her husband's job might require him to travel.

If they had invested in a security system and, if so, what type?

His job, in other words, gave him all the relevant information needed to make an informed decision about whether to pay her a visit.

Emily passed the test handily. He shivered with anticipation, looking forward to spending an hour or two with her, along with some duct tape and a blade.

Dennison Fallow did not have a sense of humor. But he appreciated irony and how clever it would be to slice off the digit Emily had used to tap each number on her phone, following the automated system's instructions.

Press 3 to be connected to our service department . . .

What a fun thought.

Doodling a picture on a Post-it Note of Emily missing a finger, her blood and tears cascading, he scanned the data sheets about her.

The poor thing.

Who had about forty minutes of pain-free peace until he started in on her.

That was how long it would take Fallow to get to Emily Halcomb's split-level in San Fernando Valley where, according to social media, she'd just returned from her Wednesday yoga class.

Fallow practically salivated with anticipation. The Push was like a dog straining on a chain.

He sent a text to the director of the call center operation to say he was taking the day off.

The man texted back his approval. There was a long list of freelancers, like Fallow, working from home. One of the reasons he liked the job so much. He could take off whenever he chose.

And pursue whatever he wanted.

Or whomever.

Ah, Emily . . .

He collected a filleting knife, the gun he'd gotten for emergencies, the vinyl gloves and other tools of the trade from the top drawer of the battered dresser.

But as he was assembling his kit, he received a text. From the message, it seemed Emily had a few more hours on God's green earth.

There's a problem. Be there in thirty minutes.

Fallow stared at the screen for a moment.

He wasn't happy, the Push wasn't happy. But if this particular sender identified a problem, it was wise, no, it was *vital* to take him seriously.

CHAPTER 17

Carmen Sanchez sensed an impending explosion.

Her boss, normally calm as a spring breeze, seemed to be working his blood pressure up to stroke level.

"The last we talked, you were going to play bodyguard for your sister. Now, you're, what? *Running* a case we already decided you—and therefore *we*—have no jurisdiction over?"

She was prepared. "In order to protect her as best I could I just wanted to nail some facts."

He scoffed. "And in what universe did you think about the optics of getting a civilian involved in a murder investigation?"

"Didn't have a choice, sir." She refused to back down. "No federal resources." A risky thing to say since he was the one who'd refused to provide them. So she tempered it with, "And Riverside wasn't stepping up."

Keeping a lid on the anger—barely—he pointed at the monitor resting on a credenza beside his desk. "You had this Heron call your assistant and put in a request for information?"

So that was how he'd learned about the man's involvement. It would have stayed under the radar if Heron hadn't enlisted Mouse. She had called someone at BATF, who had no doubt called Williamson to verify Mouse's status before divulging information about the Moreno Valley gunrunner.

Minefield here.

And, as with real mines, the best thing to do was sidestep.

"I'm dealing with a fluid situation, sir."

Why had Heron pushed forward without her knowledge or consent?

Hotheaded. Impatient.

She'd been called such things too, but she never let those qualities steer her outside the boundaries of the rules. His blundering had placed Carmen squarely in the hot seat. She couldn't explain that the request had come from him alone without getting him arrested, so she had to weather an ass-chewing she intended to pass along to him. With interest.

"I checked into Jacoby Heron," Williamson said. "Quite the character."

"Whatever's happened in the past, Dr. Heron is a renowned expert. That's why I called him. And he got results when the locals couldn't. It's because of him we tipped to the gunrunner. Who I really ought to be checking out—"

"I'm not finished."

"No, sir. Heron can also access one of the fastest supercomputers in the world. Performs eleven bazillion calculations per second or something."

"You think we don't have supercomputers?"

Their equipment probably didn't stack up, or Aruba would have hacked *them*. She lifted her hands in a disarming gesture. "I was out of options." Meaning Williamson's refusal had forced her to look for outside help.

"In my college days, what you did is called an end run. Okay then. Not okay now."

"Yes, sir."

A long moment passed.

"Jacoby," Williamson muttered. "What the hell kind of name is that anyway? He cracks some secret files, and it looks like you two discovered a potential serial killer. Congratulations. Our conversation earlier: Riverside isn't muscular enough for you? Okay, I'll call the SAC in the Bureau's field office and she'll open a file."

She'd prepared her argument in advance. "And that'll be exactly the wrong approach."

He crossed his massive arms. In this instance the gesture wasn't a defensive body language move. It was purely assertive, if not intimidating. "Explain."

"Under other circumstances, yes. But not here. The Bureau will assign a case agent. They'll read my files, then bring in San Diego PD and Riverside County Sheriff's. The agent will spend about a week getting up to speed on both investigations. Meanwhile, the Behavioral Analysis Unit will psychoanalyze the unsub using criminal and geographic profiling."

"I'm not seeing a problem."

"Time, there's no time," she blurted. "We have to move *fast*." Then told herself, ironically, to slow down. "While all that's going on, more victims will die." When he raised a skeptical brow, she added, "There was only one day between the first and second attack." She preempted his next question. "And, yes, I believe San Diego was the first, because we haven't found anything like this in NCIC or anywhere else. That tells me our guy is just getting started and there won't be a long cooling-off period before he hits again."

"Let's say for a second that your assumptions are correct. We keep coming back to the fact that HSI has no jurisdiction. That doesn't change just because you want it to."

Now for the tricky part.

She eyed him closely. "Project X."

He blinked. After a moment—during which her heart pounded fiercely—he said, "Tread carefully, Sanchez."

But sometimes in this business, in this *world*, you couldn't.

She said, "Okay, I don't know exactly what it is. But you've dropped hints. Isn't this unsub the sort of actor you have in mind? Maybe the

DHS' definition of national security is too narrow. You want to expand it. To be more . . . creative."

In theory HSI was meant to investigate transnational actors and schemes. She guessed from what she'd heard that Williamson believed the phrase in the title of the umbrella organization "Homeland Security" should be HSI's guiding principle: protecting citizens whether or not the threat originated in a foreign country.

The wave of anger—at her throwing his own secret initiative back at him—roiled through his face.

Damn.

But then he calmed. "I'm not agreeing, I'm not denying. I am, however, going to ask you another question. Have you thought through what *else* that means?"

Oh.

She said, "If there's a win, if I nail the unsub, it's good for the project. If there's a loss—if I screw up—it may never get off the ground."

Which could effectively waste six months of her boss' life and nail-strip his chances for advancement, as well.

"Observant, Sanchez." He rocked back, debating.

Carmen felt a sense of desperation. Mouse had texted her the illegal gun dealer's new address. It was the only lead, and she *had* to get there.

She doubled down. "Look at how much farther along the case is now than it was an hour ago. A solid lead."

"You don't even have enough for a search warrant."

The cryptic text on the unsub's phone was compelling, but she agreed that it didn't rise to the legal definition of probable cause. The courts had set the bar high for invading a person's home to dig through their personal belongings. There were, however, other options.

"A bit of recon could solve that problem."

"You want to put eyeballs on the place?" he said. "Do a trash run?"

Nothing prevented an agent or officer from surveilling someone's house, if they watched from a public space. And anything discarded in the trash was considered abandoned property—fair game for plunder.

"If I see evidence of a crime in plain view, we'll get a warrant. If not, we find another way. But we have to move fast. He could—"

"Sit back, Sanchez. You're on the edge of your chair. You're going to fall off."

She sat back.

"Even if I buy your low opinion of the Bureau's velocity, that has nothing to do with your civilian."

She realized Heron's presence could be as big a threat to Project X as what opponents in Washington might see as the National Security Division of HSI overstepping its jurisdiction. This concern she couldn't counter.

Williamson took another look out the window at the stellar display of dock and ship lights. Every color imaginable. Hypnotic.

After five seconds he said, "I want to talk to this guy."

She hadn't bargained for a direct meeting. Who knew what Heron might say or do? "Sir, I can tell you anything you need to know about—"

The man's massive index finger stabbed the intercom. "Show Dr. Heron in."

CHAPTER 18

Arachnids are infinitely patient.

A quality Dennison Fallow did *not* share with the creatures.

Neither he nor the Push.

As he waited in his bedroom office to meet with the man who had texted him to warn of the "problem," he lay on the bed looking at the raftered ceiling. Romeo was hard at work building a web in the corner to entice Juliet, unaware she would mate with and then eat him. Fallow believed the girl surviving to kill again would have made a more satisfactory ending to Shakespeare's play (minus the cannibalism, of course).

Emily Halcomb, the expired-warranty lady, would be home soon.

She was likely to be alone for a time after returning from yoga. A shower, coffee, email . . .

However long the delay until visiting Emily, though, Dennison Fallow would make sure the Push was satisfied.

He had to.

He rose from the bed and lifted his knife from the dresser. He removed it from its scabbard. There were fine blades that folded and locked open. But for the kind of work he had planned with Emily, he preferred a fixed blade. This ten-inch kitchen knife was the perfect length for today's business. He tested it against his thumb. A gentle rasp resulted. He picked up an empty ceramic mug from the desk beside his computer and, turning it over, rubbed the blade's cutting edge in a circular motion against the raw porcelain on the bottom rim. As good as a hundred-dollar knife sharpener.

After several honing strokes, he conducted another test, easily slicing paper. His standard for sharp.

Then he heard noise in the basement proper.

Was it the texter from a half hour earlier?

He stepped through the doorway and found that no, it was someone else. Poley, a man about eight years younger, was sitting in front of a bank of computer monitors at the far end of the main basement room, playing a first-person shooter game.

When they'd first met, Poley had explained his nickname was short for Napoleon, his legal given name. Fallow later learned the real reason others called him Poley was his close resemblance to a roly-poly bug.

"Yo, dude," Poley said by way of greeting. "I thought of a new game they should make. 'Call of *Doody*.' Instead of bullets guess what you shoot?"

Fallow watched Poley plunge his hand into a box of Lucky Charms and shove a fistful into his mouth. Disgusted, Fallow was once again struck by how much Poley resembled the chubby, scuttling, ravenous creature that had been the true source of his nickname.

An image that had simply never gone away.

Poley chortled in a high-pitched voice as he mowed down a series of avatars in the game. He stopped shooting long enough to call out to Fallow, "Oh yeah, those two dudes are coming in later. Just so you know."

"Dudes?" Fallow asked.

"Yeah, Trey and Doobie," Poley said, apparently under the impression Fallow wanted to know who the two individuals were, rather than why the idiotic word had been used to describe them. "I told you about them before. They're cool."

Ah, cool *dudes* . . .

The sound of footsteps on the stairs drew his attention to a pair of toned, tanned legs slowly descending from the kitchen.

It was Poley's mother.

When she stepped onto the floor, the woman ignored her son. Instead, she addressed Fallow in her husky alto voice. "Dennison."

Jennifer was late forties but might have passed for a woman ten or twelve years younger—not that she seemed to care one bit about things like that. High cheekbones, flowing auburn hair, a figure like the hourglass on a black widow's torso.

And that voice.

Today she wore a pink spandex top and a distressed black denim skirt with a silver chain belt. Never stockings. A tall woman even when barefoot, she favored black patent leather shoes with two-inch heels. She and Fallow were eye to eye.

She carried three juice boxes and two twelve-ounce water bottles.

"How are you feeling?"

Last night after returning here from the casino bus stop in Chinatown, he had walked upstairs and knocked on her bedroom door, asking for a painkiller for his leg. She'd dug through a full medicine cabinet and provided what he needed.

"Stiff," he said. "But it's okay."

"More meds?"

"No."

"Water?"

He stretched out a hand to accept the proffered bottle. Jennifer played den mother, replenishing the snacks and the beverages for the "den-izens," of the basement, she joked, a double pun: the basement and his name.

The door to the property's backyard creaked, pulling his thoughts away from Jennifer and Poley and Emily Halcomb's fingers. A man in his thirties entered, wearing a tailored black suit and white shirt.

It was the texter.

Gaunt and narrow-faced, the man had slicked-back ebony hair that contrasted eerily with his pale complexion. He wore thick glasses with round frames that matched his hair in both shade and gloss. Unsmiling, he scanned the room until his gaze settled on Poley, who seemed to squirm under the scrutiny.

Poley shut off the game without saving it and quickly got to his feet.

"Crumbs," the newcomer said.

Poley snatched a can of compressed air and blew off the workstation. "Now leave."

"Sure, I guess." He disappeared up the stairs. Jennifer seemed amused by her son's hasty retreat. She nodded, with a smile, to the man who had just entered. He greeted her similarly—minus the smile. She left, trailing Poley up to the first floor.

The man lifted his chin, wordlessly commanding Fallow to wait.

Insulted, Fallow shot him a glare but, even though the knife and the gun were heavy in his pockets, and he was larger than the suited man, he felt an odd sense of powerlessness.

And so he waited.

The man neatly hung his suit jacket on a hanger and placed it on a rack near the stairs before heading to the computer station. He sat, shut down all three computers, and cleaned the keyboards with alcohol spray as if the previous user had a communicable disease. Then he rebooted.

Lightning fast, his fingers danced over the center keyboard.

Fingers . . .

Fallow thought of Emily. The Push nudged.

Patience, he thought.

The Push ignored him.

Without looking up from the keyboard, the slim man said, "So. Last night. You lost your phone." His voice was low, but soft for a man's. That made it creepy. "You think somebody has it?"

Fallow chose not to explain or elaborate, either of which could be interpreted as a sign of weakness. "Yes."

"Hmm."

The man's name was Tristan Kane, but he was usually known by his online handle: FeAR-15, the latter letters and numbers—an assault rifle—echoing his love of first-person shooter games. "FeAR" for short.

"The police have it?" FeAR asked.

"We should assume so." Fallow heard the unease in his own voice as he spoke. "But your encryption programs? You said they were . . ."

FeAR stopped typing and leaned back, looking up at the black ceiling. Unlike Fallow's, the lenses of his glasses were real. Spending eighty hours a week staring at computer screens for twenty years had to affect your rods and cones.

FeAR was possessed by his own Push. His was not about watching someone's life bleed away or removing appendages. He wielded a different kind of power by executing untraceable cyberattacks, then turning himself into bits and bytes that vanished into the ether.

These skills led him to boast he was "more omnipotent than God."

Though, Fallow had wondered, wasn't omnipotent as powerful as it got? But you didn't call out FeAR for *anything*. Not if you were smart.

After a moment the hacker said, half to himself, "I used two algorithms. The first was a Blowfish and DoD base. Possible to breach, but I'd put it at level eight. The other one, for your messages? It was righteous. Better than Signal. My own creation. Based on chemical formula schematics. *And* I used key files. A 1337, however, might be able to manage it."

Fallow cut through the self-aggrandizing technobabble. "Could someone crack into the damn thing or not? And what exactly is a 1337?"

"I'll translate for you," FeAR said as if talking to someone particularly dim. "A world-class hacker, like me, is called 'elite.' The term was shortened to 'leet.' In hack-speak, letters are substituted for numbers that resemble them. 1 for L, two 3s for Es, and 7 for T." He finished with exaggerated patience. "Got it?"

The sarcastic words took Fallow back to a dark place. A memory that carried with it a fist in his gut, and arm muscles growing weak as yarn.

What have you done this time, Dennison? They called from the school . . .

But Fallow was no longer that little boy. He leaned close and muttered, "I speak English. I understand English."

"I was explaining that a twenty-year-old script-kiddie couldn't get in. Ninety percent of law enforcement couldn't get in—not for a couple of weeks at least. But there *are* a few 1337s out there. And with enough brute-force computing? It could be done."

Fallow sighed. He'd deleted every message on the phone except one. One that could lead to a place he did not want anyone to go.

A clatter of the keys. "If I'd known you'd be careless, I would've built a better wall."

"You've never lost a phone?" Fallow shot back.

"No," FeAR replied evenly. "I haven't."

A scoffing sound slipped from Fallow's throat. He returned to his bedroom, collected the rest of his gear and pulled on a jacket.

Sadly, the visit to Emily Halcomb and her precious digits had to be postponed.

He had a more pressing mission: he, and his gun and freshly sharpened knife, would have to beat any *elite* hackers—he refused to use FeAR's pretentious 1337—to Moreno Valley.

CHAPTER 19

Federal agencies generally made Jake Heron break out in figurative hives—this was true of anyone who targeted the dangers of intrusion as a profession, and no one intruded better than Washington, DC. But if the price of admission into this game was time on the hot seat, he'd willingly pay it.

Admittedly, he'd bypassed Sanchez and instructed Mouse to conduct research. Time was short and it had to be done, but he understood that feathers had been ruffled.

He cast a sidelong glance at Sanchez as he entered her supervisor's office. She seemed ill at ease, and might actually be squirming.

He hovered politely while Sanchez introduced him to her boss and Jake took stock. Appearances could be deceiving, but he believed this particular book could be judged by its cover. From the perfect razor cut of Williamson's Afro, down the length of his well-tailored suit, and ending with his gleaming shoes, every detail about the man spoke precision and efficiency. And the eyes . . . Ah, Williamson's eyes saw everything.

Initial greetings offered clues as to how much of an intrusion risk the person you were meeting presented. Jake could tell a lot from a person's handshake. Like everyone, he despised the clammy limp fish variety, but some people—usually of the male persuasion—overcompensated for their own perceived inadequacies with a bone-crushing grasp. Others tried that stupid trick where they attempted to show dominance by rotating their hand into a superior position before releasing. Those guys might as well wear a sign around their necks that said SMALL PENIS.

Williamson's grip was firm, dry and without unnecessary pressure. Confident.

And those with confidence were the best suited to intrude—if they were so inclined. Defenses tended to fall quickly, under a cool, unwavering gaze.

The large man studied Heron before he spoke. Then he offered, "You've been helping Agent Sanchez investigate her sister's assault. And now this other attack, the San Diego homicide."

"Correct."

"You've accessed some . . . sophisticated equipment in the process."

"It was my—" An almost imperceptible shake of the head from Sanchez stopped him midsentence. Apparently she hadn't mentioned Aruba. ". . . my choice to find appropriate computing power for the situation. We academics, especially in Silicon Valley, have the best cutting-edge technology."

A true statement, but a completely generic one that made no mention of who had used the supercomputer and in which distant country it was located.

Williamson frowned. "Don't be clever with me, Professor. Investigations are confidential. Anyone you bring into the middle of it—even for number crunching—is a potential liability."

The boss had figured out someone else had to be involved. Williamson went up a notch in Jake's estimation—a fact he would keep in mind going forward.

"SSA Williamson," he began, recalibrating his approach, "Agent Sanchez can tell you that this perp is unique. My area of expertise makes me particularly qualified to help find him."

"Intrusion. I've read." Williamson cocked his head. "Interesting you brought up your background. It's the last thing *I* would have mentioned if I were you." He tapped one of the sheets of paper in front of him.

Jake refused to show any outward reaction to the pointed remark. "Government files don't always tell the whole story, now, do they?" he countered.

Williamson's eyes narrowed a fraction before he then moved on. "Tell me more about this so-called area of expertise."

"Clients hire me to look for risks of intrusion—digital and physical. Computer servers and corporate or government facilities. It's called pen testing. Penetration."

"How does that work?"

"Just what it sounds like. I hack into my clients' computers and break into their headquarters and research facilities and houses."

"And you steal information."

"That's right."

Williamson said wryly, "And you give it back."

"If I don't, then I don't get paid."

"And you'd go to jail."

"That too."

The supervisor scanned his face carefully. "I'm curious. Do you *always* find a vulnerability in your clients' computers or buildings?"

"No . . . I always find a *lot* of them."

"And none of your clients are ever as tightly buttoned-up as Fort Knox?"

"No. And, for the record, even Fort Knox isn't Fort Knox."

"And that singular skill of yours will be useful in this investigation because . . . ?" Williamson pursued.

Jake mentioned the conclusion he and Sanchez had come to in San Diego. "This unsub of yours is guilty of intrusions—assault and murder. The first step toward analyzing a crime is identifying the Points of Potential Intrusion. How the victims were selected and targeted. That'll lead to the perp's motives and eventually identities. We need to keep looking for PPIs. They're there, and I can find them. It's what I do."

He had used first-person pronouns as a reminder of the importance of his continued involvement.

"There's another issue. It's also not clear what he's up to exactly. Is it intrusion for its own sake, such as thrill killing, or to further another crime? I want to find that out."

"Why with our agency, though? You could go help out Riverside or San Diego. Now that it's serial, they'll probably call in the Bureau. Your pen-testing skills would be an asset. You're cyber, they're cyber. Match made in heaven. Go hunting for PPIs with the Hoover-istas to your heart's content."

A blunt—and *confident*: "No."

Williamson cocked his head. Sanchez stirred.

Prepared to push his luck to the breaking point, Jake said, "I won't work with the Bureau. Or anybody else." He tipped his head toward Sanchez. "Only her." His tone—and expression—said that this was nonnegotiable.

Her eyes narrowed slightly as she apparently tried, as she'd done earlier, to figure out his angle.

Williamson seemed to be performing his own calculations, realizing Jake couldn't work miracles, but he could add significant value to the case. By agreeing to his terms and cutting out the Bureau, he would have to expend political capital to put Sanchez in charge of working with local authorities, with all other federal agencies taking a back seat.

Or Williamson could simply pull the plug and get back to other business, handing the case over to the FBI and local cops.

The tension in the room hummed like a transformer during an ice storm.

Williamson eyed each of them in turn. "Something going on between you two?"

Sanchez spoke first. "Active dislike bordering on open hostility," she said, then added, "but we trust each other."

A bizarre way to characterize their relationship. Well, that history was . . . complicated.

"I'd rather work with someone I trust than someone I like," Williamson said.

"No danger of liking, sir," Sanchez assured him.

Ditto, that.

Then she added, "I'll take responsibility for him."

Jake thought she sounded like a kid asking for a puppy. Promising to replace chewed-up slippers and make sure the water and kibble bowls were filled.

The image amused him.

After another long pause, Williamson leveled a hard stare on his agent. "I'm still turfing this over to the Bureau." He put up a beefy hand to forestall her objection. "Relax, Agent Sanchez. Let me finish. But before I do that, I need more facts. At this point, we know shit. We need to find . . ." A look at Jake. "The Points of Potential Intrusion."

Sanchez said quickly, "I'll find them, sir, and wrap them up with a bow to deliver to Quantico."

Williamson's gruff facade melted. Clearly, the two of them had forged a solid rapport. A man who worked alone, Jake found this—momentarily—enviable.

"For once, can you play nice?" Williamson asked her. "I keep getting emails from CHP about the Powell takedown in the Mojave. I had to pay for the tac team's uniforms because your little stunt got, I'm quoting, 'stinky shit gas,' all over them."

Jake couldn't even begin to guess.

"Don't fuck with any policies or procedures," Williamson finished.

"I won't, sir."

Apparently satisfied, Williamson glanced at his computer, where apparently Jake's life history was probably on full display. "And you, Heron. Don't break any criminal codes."

Jake gave no visible expression, other than a shallow nod, but he was exhaling a mental sigh of relief.

The strategy had paid off. Pushing Williamson with an unwavering "No" was just the type of behavior expected from a renegade like him. Which put the senior agent's—and Sanchez's—suspicions to rest.

And neither of them had a clue what a mistake they'd just made. He'd been concerned the subject of the chemical formula encryption algorithm would come up. Williamson, with his probing dark eyes, would cross-examine him about the code and somehow deduce a fact that he would find particularly unsettling: that Jake Heron had, pure and simple, lied to Sanchez about it.

"Breaking laws?" He adopted an innocent expression. "Wouldn't think of it."

While also hearing in his mind her words earlier.

We trust each other . . .

Williamson grunted. " Points of Potential Intrusions, hmm? Well, next steps?"

"The gunrunner," Sanchez told him.

The big man's baritone voice bordered on impatience as he said, "Then get your asses over to Moreno Valley. Now."

CHAPTER 20

She had kept up her part of the bargain.

Carmen Sanchez had cut a deal with Captain Drew Webster of Riverside County Sheriff's Department. Give me a clone of our unsub's phone and I'll share what I find.

On the drive from Long Beach here to Moreno Valley, she'd done just that, dictating Mouse a detailed email to send the captain, copying Detective Ryan Hall, about the encrypted messages they had cracked and the likely connection between the Spider Tatt Guy and gunrunner Alex Georgio.

And, what's more, she took the extra step of alerting him that she was driving into Webster's territory to conduct surveillance.

He hadn't responded. Hall had, but only to ask that she let him know what she found before adding that he'd just checked on Selina, and she was all right.

This was the preferred outcome anyway. She wanted the op today to be lean, just her and Heron. More bodies would only increase the risk that Georgio might tip to their presence and go to ground or burn evidence. Or both.

And start shooting, full auto mode.

There was always that.

Checking GPS.

They were five minutes away from the gunrunner's house.

Some portions of the Moreno Valley, in western Riverside County, were stylish, some comfortably middle class. This neighborhood was modest, made up of small one-story houses, many of which could benefit from a fresh coat of paint—pastel, in keeping with the block's predominant color scheme.

They saw a woman jogging on the opposite side of the street. A dog walker held a leash in one hand, and a laptop tucked under his other arm, probably on his way to an outdoor café to work on the patio, while his ruddy Irish setter sat at his feet or lapped water from a bowl most restaurants in California readily provided for patrons with canines. Farther down the sidewalk, two retirement-age women racewalked in that odd rolling gait. A pair of teenagers set up makeshift ramps on the sidewalk. Wooden planks propped on milk crates weren't ideal for practicing skateboard jumps, but the kids were apparently prepared to risk a few broken bones in the pursuit of airborne exhilaration.

She flashed to a memory of Selina coming to her, crying, and displaying a small patch of missing skin from a Rollerblade mishap. The girl had hugged her fiercely after she treated the wound. Carmen forced the memory away.

Before parking her Suburban on an adjacent street, she'd driven around the block where Alex Georgio, the gunrunner, lived. There were no trash cans at the curbs to raid, so she scoped out places for them to conduct surveillance of his house unobserved.

"Let's go," she said to Heron.

He grabbed his gear bag from the back seat and together they strolled up the street toward the target house.

"We'll have to blend in," she said.

"Blend? You bought jogging suits and Nikes?" Heron asked. They were both in what could be called tactical outfits—black jeans and leather jackets, his brown and hers black.

He seemed serious. And she supposed pen testing involved the use of various disguises and costume changes.

"No. I mean blend in literally. In the bushes." She pointed to clusters of privacy hedges planted decades ago to prevent people on the sidewalk from seeing inside people's houses. Now untrimmed and overgrown, they formed a barrier obscuring Georgio's residence from the street and neighbors' homes. It was probably why he'd chosen this place, perhaps unaware the dense greenery would also hide anyone who cared to snoop on his house.

Heron said, "Blending in involves wearing disguises to look like employees or locals. You mean MOPS. Minimally observable points of surveillance." He clearly liked the foliage. "I tell my pen-testing clients to cut down every tree and bush for a hundred yards around their facility to screw up spies."

"The urban-blight look," she said sardonically. "The employees must love you."

He blinked as if the concept of happy workers was wholly alien.

She held up her phone. "Put yours on vibrate. Keep it on. How's your battery?"

"Ninety percent." He adjusted the ringer and slipped the unit into his inside jacket pocket.

"First, we see if anybody's home. If it's Georgio, we watch. I need to catch him in *any* offense. Fed, state, felony, misdemeanor. Anything I can use for leverage to get him to ID our unsub." She displayed her phone. "Here's his picture."

He glanced once at the nondescript bearded, dark-haired man, of a complexion and bone structure suggesting Eastern European roots. He nodded when the memorization was done.

Heron rifled through his gear bag. "I'll get glass on the front."

She shot him a questioning look.

"Glass. Pen tester term for binoculars."

He turned and she gripped his arm. "Find a hole in the hedge you can see through but stay on public property. That's critical."

"Got it." He walked to the front left side of the house and vanished into a thick growth of shrubbery, both feet on the sidewalk.

It was a good—and legal—location for observation.

Carmen herself took up a position on the opposite corner, the back right, working her way into the sour-scented bushes. She pulled aside a branch, giving her a view of the back door and what seemed to be kitchen windows. A light was on in the room and another—with frosted windows, probably the bathroom. But there was no movement or fluctuation in the light, which would indicate life inside. She glanced at the stand-alone garage. The door was down and there were no windows, so she had no idea if a car was inside.

The big question: Had Spider Tatt Guy already bought the "hardware" mentioned in the text? If not and they were able to collar Georgio now, that might keep a firearm out of the unsub's hands. One could hope.

For ten minutes she stared from window to window.

Nothing. Frustrating. Had Heron seen any signs of movement? She hit speed dial.

Four rings. Then voicemail.

Goddamn . . . What part of "keep it on" had he missed?

Or had something happened to him?

It wasn't hard to imagine a scenario in which Georgio had surrounded the property with some kind of invisible security system that had alerted him to their presence. Then he'd use a silenced pistol to eliminate the threat before grabbing a go bag and fleeing out the front.

Carmen pulled her jacket aside and gripped her Glock as she began to pick her way around the outer perimeter of the yard, keeping out of sight as she went.

Unbidden, an image of Heron ignoring his assignment and speaking on the phone with Hot Tub Woman popped into her head. Was that why he couldn't take her call? Then she chided herself for the ridiculous thought—and wondered why the hell it had come to mind.

Focus.

She looked around for threats. Saw none.

She walked around the corner to the spot where Heron had made his surveillance nest in the hedge.

He was gone.

CHAPTER 21

Shielded by the overgrown foliage separating the yard from the street, Jake crouched at a side door that opened onto a small garden on the side of Georgio's house. A door neither he nor Sanchez had seen initially.

He had spotted something inside the bungalow and wanted a better look. The front door was closer, but also visible from the driveway, which was the only place not concealed by dense plantings. He couldn't risk a delivery person or a visiting neighbor calling the police to report a prowler in black jeans and brown jacket, wearing blue nitrile gloves, picking a lock.

Some things you could explain away. Others, not so much.

Jake selected a tension wrench, a three-ridge rake and a hook pick, clamping the latter two between his teeth. He started with the wrench, inserting the tip into the bottom of the keyway and holding it in place with one hand while he used the other to slide the rake in just above the wrench. After a few failed attempts, he switched to the pick, pushing up the first pin inside the lock until it set, then proceeded with each of the other pins until he could turn the plug.

After a quick glance over his shoulder, he twisted the knob and eased the door open to find that it led to the family room. The house had a security alarm, but his radio frequency scanner had detected no RF transmissions between the main panel and the window and door sensors, which told him the system wasn't active.

The other potential risk?

Large, aggressive dogs, a favorite low-tech deterrent of gun and drug dealers. Heron's penetration kit included an irresistible bacon-flavored dog treat loaded with acepromazine, enough to make the most hostile attack dog drowsy as a baby at bedtime.

But no canines charged.

He'd just stepped across the threshold when he was jerked backward by the jacket collar.

"Jesus," he muttered.

"What the hell, Heron?"

He turned to Sanchez, whose red face, clenched jaw and rapid breathing let him know he'd crossed more than just a threshold. "The last thing Williamson told you was not to break any laws. Less than two hours later and you're committing burglary. So intrusion is okay if it suits your purposes?"

"You don't need a warrant if you have probable cause, right?"

"Wrong. To enter without a warrant, we need *exigent circumstances*. Lock the place up again and—"

"Is that exigent enough for you?"

She followed his gaze to a spatter of blood on one of the white-painted walls.

"And there." He was pointing to the floor. A crimson pool. And it was moving, creeping along the hardwood floor from the den or living room into the hallway.

She smoothly drew her Glock from its holster. "Get behind me."

Edging inside, weapon ready, she barked, "Federal agent! Show yourself! Hands up."

Silence.

She crossed the family room and peered down, then moved forward into the hallway. "It's Georgio."

She made no attempt at resuscitation. To say Georgio's throat had been cut would be a gross understatement. Someone had sliced open the front of his neck from ear to ear. Nearly a beheading.

Jake recalled reading somewhere that an average adult male had about five liters of blood in his body. It looked like about four liters of Georgio's was on the floor in an expanding puddle.

Swinging her weapon from door to door, she called over her shoulder, "Outside, Heron. The sidewalk. Call 9-1-1 and tell them there's a 187—homicide—at this address. And watch your back. We have no idea where the doer is."

Jake, though, decided he wouldn't go all the way off the property, but remained in the side yard so he could hear if she ran into trouble. Not that he could do much about it, armed with only a lockpick set. To avoid startling potentially trigger-happy armed guards, pen testers never carry weapons.

He had barely started to call the emergency line when a woman in yoga pants and a loose-fitting tank top came running up the front walk toward him, waving her arms.

"Someone stole my dog," she shouted. "Have you seen an Irish setter?"

Jake's pulse, already elevated, kicked up another notch. "Sanchez!" He turned to the woman. "What happened?"

"I have an electric fence." She pointed next door. "The collar's lying on the ground, and he took one of my leads. My baby . . ." Her face was tight with alarm.

"What's going on?" Sanchez came up behind him, holstering her weapon. Apparently the house was free of knife-wielding attackers.

"Remember the dog walker?" he said to her.

She nodded.

"Wasn't his dog."

"Oh, hell." She let out a frustrated groan. "That was *Georgio's* laptop he was carrying. He walked right past us! Did you get a look? Clothes?"

"Dark, I think. That's all."

"I'm going to get my dog back." The woman broke into a run, heading back toward the street.

They both rushed to intercept her, catching up at the head of the driveway. "No, ma'am. Leave it to us. He's armed."

"What?" she wailed.

"There." Heron pointed up the street, two blocks away.

The Irish setter, red-plumed tail wagging, was alone and unharmed, tethered to a stop sign at the corner by its leash.

"The dog was window dressing," Jake muttered as the woman dashed toward her dog.

"You make the call?" Sanchez asked.

"Not yet."

"Do it—"

Her words were cut off by the roar of an engine near the dog. A dark sedan raced away, blowing past the stop sign.

Sanchez raced to the Suburban. "Call in the 187, Heron. And tell them an officer is in pursuit."

CHAPTER 22

Carmen yanked open the driver's door and flung herself inside. The short run to the SUV had cost her precious seconds, but she might still be able to catch the fleeing suspect.

She stuck her cell phone in the cup holder and tapped the screen. She'd told Heron to call 9-1-1, but the locals needed real-time information only she could provide.

"Nine-one-one. What's your emergency?"

"Federal agent requesting assistance. I'm attempting to locate a vehicle headed eastbound, East Alessandro in Moreno Valley. The driver is a person of interest in a homicide."

She peeled out into the street, all eight cylinders spinning the tires fiercely, sending a plume of smoke and gravel rooster-tailing behind the Suburban.

"Please identify yourself."

"Agent Carmen Sanchez, Department of Homeland Security." She didn't add the Investigations part. Even those in law enforcement circles weren't always familiar with it, but everyone had heard of DHS.

"Suspect and vehicle description and last known location?"

"White male, approximately thirty years old, driving a dark four-door sedan. Couldn't tell the make or model. California tags. No number. He should be considered armed." She glanced up at the street sign after several skidding turns. "Now headed east on Dracaea . . . Can you alert CHP? Suspect may be heading toward the 215."

"Ten-four, Agent Sanchez."

It was what she would have done, taken the entrance ramp. Not only could he hide in the wide freeway's traffic, but he could exponentially increase their search area quickly.

She took a right turn, working her way toward the nearest ramp, not far north.

"Agent Sanchez, is this vehicle related to the homicide just reported on Witchhazel Avenue in Moreno Valley?"

"Affirmative." She spotted the sedan in the distance. "I have the suspect vehicle in sight, heading south on Day."

Odd. Why wasn't he going north toward the closest ramp to the freeway?

She accelerated as much as she dared in a residential zone, determined to keep him in view without spooking him into doing something reckless and getting innocent bystanders hurt or killed. She'd have backup soon enough. Officers with ram bars over the grilles of their cruisers for PIT maneuvers. Tire-shredding spike strips too.

"Any further on the tag?"

"Negative."

"Make, model?"

"No."

"Number of occupants?"

"Appears to be one."

"Driver's name?"

"Unknown."

Carmen kept up a running commentary of their progress to the call taker, who relayed the information to all area law enforcement on multiple channels, while she began to close the distance.

Suddenly the unsub's vehicle shot forward and skidded onto another street.

"He's made me. Now heading west on Alessandro." She skidded into the turn and floored the pedal. Oh, no you don't, asshole. I'm on you like glue.

"He's coming up to the 215 ramp . . . no, wait, now he's *past* the ramp. He's . . . okay, north on Sycamore Canyon. I clock him between eighty and eighty-five."

The hell was he going this way for? There were fewer side roads along the route. The rugged peaks of the state park loomed ahead and to the left. The only thing in this direction was . . .

She scanned.

Riverside West High School.

What was he—?

She learned the answer even before the question formed in her mind.

The sedan suddenly swerved to the left, veering into oncoming traffic.

Directly into the path of a school bus.

"Suspect vehicle crossed the double yellows. He's headed right for a school bus. Half mile north of Alessandro on Sycamore Canyon. Riverside West High."

The dispatcher's voice became a distant drone as Carmen watched the sedan's driver engage in a deadly game of chicken. Was the man suicidal? He'd probably die in the crash, but how many children would end up hurt or worse?

The bus driver blasted the horn. Tires screeched. The sedan continued in a straight line. At the last second, the bus veered to the side of the road, attempting to avoid a head-on. When the unwieldy vehicle's right-side tires slid off the pavement, the driver desperately tried to maneuver back onto the road, but physics took over. Carmen looked on in horror as the top-heavy bus tipped onto its side with a thunderous crash. Momentum carried it down the sloped gravel shoulder, where it rolled onto its roof and came to rest in a ditch, upside down. Steam—or was it smoke?—billowed upward from under the hood.

"I need EMS, fire and backup," Carmen told the call taker. "The bus is off the road. It's flipped. Maybe burning."

"Rescue is en route. ETA six minutes."

The perp's sedan shifted back into its lane and accelerated away.

Every instinct urged her to give chase and nail the man who had butchered Alex Georgio and Walter Kemp and had attacked Selina.

But there were other victims to think of now. Those kids and the driver in the bus. Six damn minutes till the cavalry arrived?

Cursing, she stomped on the brakes and pulled over. She jumped out and raced to the bus as visions of bodies lying crumpled and bleeding filled her mind. She dropped down and crawled to one of the forward side windows that had begun to slide open. The driver, a man in his mid-forties, was struggling to climb out, blood pouring from his nose.

Carmen hurried to help him, then looked inside.

The bus was empty.

The driver looked at her with shocked eyes. "He just . . . he was just . . . there was nothing I could do. My God, if I'd had a load of my kids."

"Come on. We shouldn't be this close."

He lurched to his feet, allowing her to lead him to a grassy spot a safe distance away. She realized the clouds from under the hood were steam, but that didn't mean there was no fire risk. As the driver sat down, cross-legged on the grass, and stared in mute disbelief at the horrific tableau, she called in the last known direction of travel of the sedan, still unable to provide a better description or tag.

Sirens wailed in the distance, approaching fast. But not fast enough. She glanced at a map on her phone. By now he would have cut back to the freeway, invisible amid the millions of cars in the Los Angeles traffic system.

Free to escape.

Free to target yet another victim.

And who would be the next to die?

A question that had been nagging, unformed, in her mind bubbled to the surface. Why had he not taken off the instant he walked past them, in the guise of a dog walker, when she and Heron arrived at the gunrunner's house?

At least thirty minutes had passed between that moment and his fleeing.

Then the stark answer struck her.

The unsub had stayed near the scene to learn what he could about the two chasing him.

His pursuers were now his prey.

CHAPTER 23

Carmen held up her credentials. "Who's in charge?"

Simple question. No simple answer.

She'd arrived back at the murder scene to find a half-dozen law enforcement officers having a discussion in Alex Georgio's front yard. Typical of incidents in congested locales like this, it was jurisdictional hash. The men—yes, all men—included the chief of and other personnel from the Moreno Valley Police, deputies from the Riverside County Sheriff's Department and officers from the California Highway Patrol.

And now, adding to the mix, of course, was a Fed. And one with an attitude that suggested maybe *she* was the one in charge, even if no legal justification for that existed.

The CHP supervisor, a lean man who was possibly a former drill sergeant in the military, spoke up first. "We're only here to get more info about the suspect and that dark sedan to update our BOLO," he said. "Had my people canvass for witnesses or video—you know, Ring, Nest cameras. But nothing."

She wasn't surprised. Spider Tatt Guy seemed to go to great lengths to stay clear of video.

"Case's ours, I guess." The words came from the chief of the Moreno Valley PD, a burly balding man with a broad, freckled face. Adding to the official overlap, Tommy Delaney was also the captain in charge of the Sheriff's Department's Moreno Valley station. Strange, but not the first time she'd heard of such a joint assignment.

Also present was a blustery MVPD patrol sergeant, who leaned forward to study her ID closely, a classic case of chest bumping. "Homeland Security Investigations?" His heavy brows drew together. "Don't you guys handle border shit?"

She sighed and stashed the slim leather case back in her pocket. "That's another branch of Homeland." Looking from one to the other, Carmen said, "We're pretty sure this incident's related to a recent homicide in San Diego and an attempted murder in Perris. A serial doer."

That got everyone's attention.

"The Perris assault's being run by Ryan Hall, gold shield at RCSD homicide. I called him. He's on his way."

Delaney was nodding. "I know him, sure." It seemed he wanted to add something like, He's kind of young for this, isn't he? But he said nothing. Technically, Hall, being from the main office, was his superior, whatever his age.

They didn't have to wait long. A Sheriff's Department unmarked arrived and lean, gray-suited Ryan Hall climbed out, adjusted his weapon and ducked under the perimeter tape to join them. After a brief exchange of introductions, he turned to Carmen and lifted an eyebrow. "The scenario?"

This was a somewhat different side of Hall. More professional. More confident.

After all, he tracked down killers for a living, and he wouldn't have earned that job by being uncertain.

She explained to him and those assembled that they'd learned the suspected serial doer in San Diego and Perris had bought a weapon from Georgio, or was going to. He had probably grown concerned that the gunrunner would dime him out or had incriminating information about him, and he'd come here to kill him and steal any records leading to the unsub.

And he'd succeeded on both counts.

"Then he got away," she concluded. "North on the 215 probably." A glance at the CHP supervisor. "One of how many dark sedans?"

The man squinted. "Twenty-five billion, as of today."

Carmen gave a grim chuckle.

Hall tipped his head toward the house. "Crime Scene? They cleared the place yet?"

Delaney said, "They okayed us going in, we wear suits." He nodded at the CSU van, whose back doors were open, displaying a box of white Tyvek coveralls among other gear. The gruff Moreno Valley sergeant dug out a bag and handed it to the detective.

She stuck her hand out. "I'll take a set of those too."

The sergeant didn't move. An awkward silence ensued. She might act like she was in charge, they'd be thinking, but the Fed versus state distinction was still front and center and the homicide here fell solely under the California Penal Code.

It was Hall who deflated the tension. "Captain Webster said we're supposed to comply with any requests Agent Sanchez has. The Sheriff's Department and she are working jointly on the investigation. We're treating it like a task force."

She frowned toward him, and he nodded, confirming just between them what he'd told the others.

Damn. Webster had come around. He hadn't responded to her email earlier, but her keeping the promise about the encrypted files meant something to him. He wasn't the sort, she understood, to give her a call and make nice. He was more comfortable sending messengers, like Hall.

Fine with her. She got the results she wanted. The multiagency jurisdiction game is like chess, and while not a grand master, Carmen Sanchez knew how to play. She had just finessed herself, a Fed, into a position of power in a purely state homicide.

"So she comes in with me."

She held out a hand and took the coveralls.

"And a set for me," a man's voice called out to them.

All eyes turned to see Jake Heron standing behind the perimeter tape at the edge of the front yard.

Carmen was tempted to let him stay where he was. He had been about to commit a felony to get inside the house before she stopped him. Then she remembered that he'd come through for her when she needed it. If he hadn't stood up to Williamson, she wouldn't be here at all.

"He's with me," she said. "An investigative consultant."

A job title she'd totally made up, but it had worked so far.

Sherlock Holmes . . .

The sergeant hesitated a beat before beckoning Heron, who ducked under the yellow tape to join them.

"Is the scene compromised?" Hall asked as he stepped into the thin white coveralls.

The sergeant shook his head. "Fireboard's gone. Vic was DRT."

Noting Heron's confusion, Carmen translated the cop-speak. "When there are obvious signs of death, rescue personnel don't work on the victim or transport him to the hospital—they don't want to contaminate the scene. He's declared DRT—dead right there—so they document their observations and leave the body in place."

After they were decked out in the latest CSI garb from elastic-capped head to bootied foot, all smelling of tangy plastic, they filed inside the house. Similarly clad Crime Scene techs took photographs as they went about their business.

Hall asked, "The unsub showed up today to get the gun and kill him in the process? Or bought it earlier and came back to clean house?"

"This was a return visit," she said. "They knew each other."

"How do you know that?"

Before she could answer, Heron weighed in. "He got Georgio from behind. I imagine illegal weapons dealers keep strangers in plain sight."

Exactly her thinking.

Heron continued, "I'm guessing he made an appointment to buy another gun—a pretext just to get inside and then . . ." He snapped his fingers.

Carmen noticed Heron wasn't troubled by the corpse and blood. Odd for a civilian.

An evidence tech approached. "We found a cache of weapons in a safe off the main bedroom," she reported. "Walk-in safe. Long guns, handguns, fully auto assault rifles, bump stocks, suppressors, armor-piercing rounds. And a case of that fucking .223 ammo."

While most bullets can be stopped by body armor, depending on distance from the shooter's weapon, the .223 rounds, based on those fired from assault rifles, are small and powerful enough to penetrate many ballistic vests.

"And a bunch of ghost guns," the tech added, then gestured toward the body. "That guy will not be missed."

Carmen understood the sentiment. She'd seen too much violence to mourn the loss of someone who peddled death for profit.

Heron asked, "Recover any computers or drives?"

"Negative," the tech replied, apparently under the assumption the white-suited figure addressing her was a homicide detective.

Hall said, "Maybe Georgio backed up his data to a cloud server."

Carmen laughed. "Gunrunners don't use iCloud. I learned that firsthand." At Hall's questioning look, she elaborated. "I did a stint in the FBI's Cybercrime Unit before joining DHS."

She didn't add that she'd been on desk duty with Cyber after getting shot in the bank job massacre.

Heron offered wryly, "And she was just as much of a hard-ass then as she is now."

Hall looked at each of them in turn. "You two knew each other back then?"

She didn't care to share, but Heron piped up. "That's right."

Involuntarily Carmen flashed on a memory. Christmas Eve four years ago, she and Jake Heron together, close together.

She forced the image away.

Heron himself said nothing more about the two of them and seemed to grow distracted as he took in their surroundings. "I'd keep looking. For electronics."

She began to regret letting him into the crime scene. She didn't appreciate his attitude or the cryptic remark. "You know something the rest of us don't, Heron?"

He shrugged. "Got a feeling you'll find something hidden. More electronics. That would fit his profile."

"A feeling," Carmen repeated. Despite her annoyance, she knew nobody knew more about the dark underside of the cyber world than Jacoby Heron. It was, after all, the reason she'd sought him out. She asked Hall, "You have EDCs?"

"No, but we can get one."

Electronic detection canines were trained like any other sniffing dogs, only they didn't locate drugs or explosives. They searched for phones, computers, chips, drives and other such items.

Hall put in a request for the specialized unit and, after disconnecting, reported that a dog-and-handler team was on the way.

That settled, Carmen dealt with the next issue. "I'm going to talk to Crime Scene," she said to Heron. "Don't touch anything. If you see something that may be relevant, let me know and I'll get a tech to collect it." She followed the statement with one of her patented don't-mess-with-me glares, emphasizing that she wouldn't appreciate any overstepping.

Heron wandered off. Hall stayed with her to question the Crime Scene techs about what they'd collected so far and what they'd observed.

There were marks consistent with someone wearing vinyl gloves, just like at the other scenes, so they wouldn't find the suspect's fingerprints. His DNA maybe, which would confirm it was the same perp as in Perris and San Diego but wouldn't lead them past that.

One of the techs interrupted her musings. "Hey, Agent Sanchez, you've gotta see this."

She and Hall walked into the living room to find the tech pointing at a Post-it Note stuck to a thick glossy magazine, *Concealed Weapons Roundup.* "Check it out."

Carmen edged closer to read the note. At the top was today's date. Below:

Ramirez — 8:30
Spider — 11

She and Heron had arrived around eleven fifteen.

She thought of how Selina had described him as Spider Tatt Guy. "His nickname is fitting."

Heron, who had returned from the kitchen, walked up behind her to read the note over her shoulder. "Another fact leading to our Points of Potential Intrusion, Sanchez," he said. "We're getting there. Slowly, but we're getting there."

CHAPTER 24

Fallow scrabbled over the rocks and through the sand as he crawled through bright-yellow wildflowers to keep low.

Dense, hot sunlight fell on him, and sweat stippled his forehead as he sucked in gulps of air.

He paused to swipe the droplets away from his stinging eyes. Then continued on, one hand gripping the shopping bag, the other supporting himself on the cracked-earth ground as he made his way toward his destination.

Dropping into a shallow canyon, Fallow heard distant sirens—the cries of the vehicles searching for him. A helicopter's blades thwapped the air high above, though that might have been for traffic. Its flight didn't seem urgent.

He'd had one hell of an escape. That lady cop had pursued him like a Fury from hell, then, outmaneuvered, skidding to a stop and racing to the school bus. Exactly as he'd planned. Fallow recalled her blazing eyes turning briefly his way in frustration.

He supposed no children were hurt or killed in the crash; that would have made the news.

Too bad.

Would have made the Push happy.

But the most important thing had been accomplished. He'd escaped.

He was pleased about the dognapping ruse.

That was clever, allowing him to waltz right by the cops—one of them undoubtedly the elite hacker who'd pried Georgio's message from the phone the bitch Selina had made off with.

He pulled out his new mobile and viewed the pictures he'd taken of the man and woman at Georgio's. He texted them to FeAR back in Anaheim, hoping he could identify them with facial recognition.

If so, a visit in the middle of the night would be in order.

Darkness crept into his thoughts, ushering in images of severed fingers. Perhaps he would remove those from the elite hacker and leave him alive.

The woman cop?

Maybe take out those fierce eyes of hers.

Then he changed his mind. After that car chase, she had to die. But he could certainly take his time and make a game of her death.

Her death would make up for the session he'd planned for the dishwasher lady, Emily.

The Push approved.

He stood and made his way to a six-foot-high chain-link fence. Ignoring the No TRESPASSING sign, he tugged at a section clipped by vandals long ago. He slipped through the opening and picked his way among the rocks to the shoreline, where cool blue water lapped in leisurely waves.

Lake Mathews, forty minutes west of Moreno Valley, is the terminus of the aqueduct delivering water from the Colorado River to Southern California—to the extent that the Colorado River still has any to give.

The local authority made the decision to keep the lake closed to the public—not popular on hot days, when the many acres of clear water beckoned, but there it was. The entire perimeter—fourteen miles—was fenced off.

From most people.

Not from Dennison Fallow.

Who found the place helpful in his avocation. It was also rich in personal history.

As he gazed, half-mesmerized by the glittering water, he recalled a conversation that had taken place four years and three months ago, unable to forget the familiar baritone voice.

"Dennison. I'm Charlie Benedict."

Fallow had slowly glanced around the man's office.

"Have a seat."

He lowered himself into the bare wood office chair across the desk from the brawny man with swept-back black-gray hair. He wore a white dress shirt and crisp blue jeans. A thin braided leather bracelet encircled his right wrist.

Not exactly shrink attire.

Nor was this a shrink office exactly. Oh, there were the typical certificates and diplomas on the walls and a few abstract and unchallenging pastel prints. Some official-looking medical or scientific books on a shelf. But most therapists had a couch or at least comfy leather chairs from which to spill your psychic guts. And always that box of can-I-make-you-cry tissue. But here? No.

Then again, the man was not a "therapist of last resort."

He was a specialist.

"You've been seeing Dr. Stillman at Santa Monica Psych."

"Not for real long. He's . . . my third doctor this year."

"He's one of the psychiatrists I consult with." The man handed Fallow a card with his name on the top, above a phone number and the words COMPULSIVE BEHAVIOR THERAPY.

Which explained why no Kleenex. Behaviorists didn't care much about dissecting your feelings. They wanted to change your actions and it didn't matter to them if you cried.

Mr. Benedict studied him, as the man absently spun his gold wedding band on his left heart finger. "Dr. Stillman said you feel these urges. The 'Push,' you call it."

"That's right."

"The Push makes you want to do bad things. Hit people. Humiliate them. And maybe to do more."

One thing about spiders: four hundred million years have taught them to be cautious.

And smart.

He remained silent. But Mr. Benedict said, "I'm not an MD, Dennison, but the California patient–doctor privilege includes *all* mental health professionals. You can tell me anything. It stays between us. What has the Push made you do so far?"

Only a brief hesitation. "Fights at school. Stuff like that. Bullies picked on me. I beat them up. Maybe I took it too far—I couldn't help myself. But at least they never bothered me again."

He smiled. "Funny how that works with bullies, isn't it?"

"But, you know, school. Fights like those? They were like . . . appetizers is all. I was more interested in . . . something different. The first time . . ."

"Go on."

"The first time I knew something really wasn't right with me was this girl . . . Katrina . . ." He fell silent.

"What happened?"

"I was maybe twelve or thirteen. She was walking home. I was too. We were behind the school. And she had her, you know, her period. Blood ran all down her leg. There was *a lot*. It made this big stain on her white skirt. I remember the red on the white. She freaked when she saw me. I laughed at her. Could not stop laughing. She started crying and ran off. See, with bullies, I was just fighting back. It was okay . . . but with Katrina, I hurt her for no reason. And it felt good."

"And the Push went away."

"Yes, sir."

Mr. Benedict's gray eyes bored into him. "And you wanted to experience that again."

"That." He swallowed and looked away. "Or worse than embarrassing somebody. Maybe . . . the blood. Maybe making someone bleed."

"What have you or your other therapists done to make you resist the Push?"

He nearly laughed. "A lot of talk, talk, talk. Meds, counseling, new age crap . . . Can I say that? Crap?"

"Isn't most of it? And your parents?"

"Oh, no talk from them." He scoffed. "They secured me."

"Secured. That's an odd word. Tell me."

"Every time I got into a fight, or my parents found me looking at those websites that have real footage of executions, murders and torture, or if some girl's parents called to say I was stalking their daughter, they'd lock me in the basement."

Mr. Benedict's brows furrowed. "Did that work?"

He didn't feel like talking about Hamlet and Ophelia and Prince Hal and his other eight-legged friends. "No."

Mr. Benedict jotted a few notes in a pad. He looked up. "You might think it's hopeless, but it isn't. I can help you. If, of course, you want me to."

"How?"

"Actually, you just gave me a clue."

"I did?"

Mr. Benedict didn't elaborate. "Will you let me help you, Dennison?"

"It's just I've seen so many people, counselors, shrinks . . ."

"But they weren't like me. My philosophy about my patients is that I'm going to fix them, or die trying."

A weird thing to say, he'd thought.

They'd shaken hands and parted ways. The next day, his therapy began.

And now, four years and three months later, Fallow felt his heart lurch at the thought of Mr. Benedict and his black-and-gray swept-back hair, his leather bracelet, his wedding ring.

He walked to the edge of the lake's shoreline and opened the plastic shopping bag. He lifted out Georgio's computer and a half dozen mobile phones he'd barely made off with before the fierce lady cop and her elite hacker partner arrived.

He tossed the electronics into the water, and they sank instantly, taking with them any personal information about himself and the pistol he'd bought a few days earlier.

Fallow watched the bubbles dissipate. The computer and phones were now at the bottom. He wondered if they had landed on the man's body, fifty feet below, enwrapped in chicken wire and weighed down by cinder blocks.

Fallow knew nothing about the reservoir's filtration system, but he guessed that tiny bits of flesh could get through. What would people in this part of Southern California think if they knew they were showering in and sipping water that contained residue of human remains?

Ah, Mr. Benedict . . .

Who worked so hard to save me as I grappled with the Push.

He gazed across the water for a long moment. Then, hearing no more sirens, returned to his car.

As he got into the front seat, his phone buzzed with a text from FeAR-15.

Pictures you sent of man and woman in Moreno Valley not clear enough. But have general description of them. I'll monitor security cams for better images.

Well, it had seemed like a long shot. Maybe FeAR would get a better photo of the pair.

And a name.

And address.

The lady cop especially.

Starting the engine, Fallow steered away from the water and made his way to the highway.

He was thinking of spitting spiders—in the family *Scytodidae*. They didn't build webs. They were hunters, known for their patience, willing to wait for as long as it took for a victim to appear. Then, after shooting them with immobilizing sticky goo, they'd watch the creature exhaust itself trying to escape before moving in for the kill.

It was important, he knew, never to hurry when the issue was life and death.

On the other hand, thinking about the Push a moment ago had, as usual, awakened it.

No, he wouldn't wait. He *couldn't*.

It was time to kill again.

CHAPTER 25

Jake considered the new information as he and Sanchez left Georgio's house. "He goes by Spider."

"Spider Tatt Guy," she said.

"Not very subtle—if you're inked with a black widow on your wrist."

"You think it's part of the Points of Potential Intrusion?"

"Don't know. Names can definitely be a form of intrusion. You ever been in a room and some supervisor refers to the men as 'Mr.' but you're just 'Carmen'?"

She scoffed. "You got a couple hours and I'll count the ways."

"Nicknames are often a way to put up barriers to intrusion. Or to let only certain people in. He didn't intend us to find 'Spider,' but we did. About the Point of Potential Intrusion? Yeah, I'd say the name is a piece of it. Has Mouse found anything?" Jake kept pace as they walked to the SUV, now dusty and dinged, parked along the curb.

"No."

Sanchez's assistant had already mined NCIC for references to the black widow tattoo, and now she was checking the name "Spider" for an alias cross-reference to somebody in the system.

With no luck so far.

They arrived at the vehicle and Jake wondered why federal agencies insisted on using gas-guzzling behemoths that screamed government issue. The intrusion of greenhouse gasses into poor planet Earth was hard to justify.

Besides, they were zero stealth.

Maybe that was the point. A suspect sees a dark Suburban with blacked-out windows pull up to his door and his sphincter instantly puckers. On the other—

Jake froze. Scanning the surroundings—force of habit—he'd spotted a man on a ridge about a hundred yards away. The figure hefted a rifle to his shoulder and aimed it their way.

Without thinking, Jake dive-tackled Sanchez to the ground.

She maneuvered fast and automatically, no doubt due to her tactical training. Using his momentum against him, she rolled him onto his back. Seconds later, she was sitting astride his stomach with her legs pinning his arms to his sides.

She put a palm on each of his shoulders, anchoring him in place. "What the hell are you doing, Heron?"

"Down! Shooter to your three o'clock."

He twisted to his side, apparently catching her off guard, and dislodged her. She tumbled beside him, so they were face-to-face, lying horizontal on the grass, inches apart, her right leg hooked over his thigh. Strands of her hair tumbled onto his cheek.

"Long gun," he huffed out. "On the ridge to the north. Male, I think. Dark-green jacket."

She sprang to her feet and peered over the hood of her SUV, left hand shading her eyes, her right hand on her sidearm. "Don't see anyone."

"Somebody was there." Jake stood too, scanning as he brushed himself off. "He must've realized I spotted him and left."

She continued to gaze at the ridge. "Nothing. How'd you make him? You're not military or law enforcement."

"Pen testing is all about threat detection. Weapon assessment is like a human algorithm. Body turning, stance, elbows and shoulders moving a certain way—they all set off alarms. Even if you can't see the gun or scope, you can tell it's there. Just the way he moved at first. And then I *did* see a weapon."

She finished surveying their surroundings and gave him a skeptical look. "You sure about this?"

Did she seriously think he would make up a fictitious gunman? "I'm sure I saw *someone*. And I'm at ninety percent he was holding a rifle."

"Well, who would it be?"

"Spider's the logical candidate."

"Coming back this way, after an escape like that? Not likely."

"Maybe that's the reason it was him."

She glanced at the ridge once more, where you could see the cell tower.

Heron continued, "Or maybe it was just a lineman. And it gave me a good excuse to jump you."

She regarded him in silence—he couldn't tell if she realized his comment was meant as a joke.

Though many a true word . . .

He pushed the unfinished adage down into his subconscious, where it belonged.

She trotted back to Georgio's place, darting glances toward the ridge, and returned a short time later. "The sarge will send units out. They'll look for somebody who fits your encyclopedic description."

"Sorry I wasn't in a position to whip out my camera for a photo op, Sanchez. I was a tad busy saving your life and all."

"There probably haven't been any cell tower lineman collared for doing their jobs lately. We'll bring him in for enhanced interrogation." She picked a corpse of dried leaf from her hair and flicked it away.

They belted in and she fired up the engine and pulled away from the curb.

"Before you tackled me, we were talking about his name. Something leading to a Point of Potential Intrusion, you said."

He nodded. "Why Spider? Might be misdirection, ironic, a name he used as a kid. Or maybe arachnids are meaningful to him."

"Yeah, they're creepy and disgusting." She shuddered. "They lurk in dark corners and jump out. They drop down from the ceiling into your hair. They build invisible webs that stick to your skin—or to their prey."

"They're silent hunters," he said, noting she seemed to suffer from a touch of arachnophobia. "You never see them until it's too late."

Sanchez maneuvered the SUV onto the freeway ramp. "Like how he used that damned white ball to distract Selina and then pounced."

"Did Hall have any updates about it?"

"Still researching." She paused. "Have to admit I'm impressed with his dedication."

"Hall? You told me he seemed . . . a bit overly interested in your sister."

"Yeah, well, if that motivates him to go the extra mile, I'll take it. To a point." Her dark brows drew together. "Lord knows we don't have much to go on from Georgio's murder. I told the techs to look for a white ball, but they didn't find one. Not surprised. He didn't need a distraction with Georgio." She briefly took her eyes off the road to glance at him. "Are we calling the suspect Spider now?"

"It's better than 'unsub' and 'Spider Tatt Guy.' And because it's what he calls himself, it forces us to remember the kind of predator we're dealing with."

"Don't need any help with that." She goosed the gas, blowing past a tractor trailer. "I'm still kicking myself for not catching up to him. If it weren't for that school bus . . ."

"He took a calculated risk, and it paid off."

Sanchez's phone vibrated. "It's Hall," she said, tapping the screen. "You're on speaker, Detective."

"Agent Sanchez, you two were right about the EDC. We brought one in, a black Lab, and it took her five minutes to find a hidden drive. A Seagate, three terabytes." He chuckled. "It was in a box of cereal."

"Any idea what's on it?"

"We didn't touch it. It's already bagged and on its way to the lab. And now that Captain Webster's on board in a big way, he'll order our cyber people to drop everything to handle it."

Sanchez said, "And send me the result ASAP."

"Sure, Car—Agent Sanchez."

Smiling, she disconnected. "Good call, Heron. That's *something*. Maybe it's got a list of his customers on it. Or Spider's real name. Or somebody who knows him. Be great if we could score the name of whoever wrote those encryption packages." She shook her head. "Weird. Hidden in cereal."

Reading something on his phone, Heron said, "Cap'n Crunch is always a popular place to hide disks and flash drives."

"Really?" Sanchez asked. "Why is—" Her voice froze. Then she snapped, "Hall said, 'Cereal.' He didn't give a brand name. How did you know what type?"

Okay, damn. That was careless.

"The hell is up, Heron?"

"Why don't you pull over?"

And pull over she did—dramatically, leaving skid marks on the asphalt and the scent of scorched rubber in the air.

She turned to face him. "Explain."

True, he'd slipped up. He should have been more careful.

On the other hand, the conversation that was about to occur was going to happen one way or another. This was as good a jump start as any.

"While you were on your car chase, after I called nine-one-one, I went back inside. Something I'd seen in the kitchen. The cereal box. There's an epic figure in the world of hacking—a guy nicknamed Captain Crunch. Real name's John Draper. He became famous in the seventies when he discovered that a little plastic whistle—a boatswain's whistle—given away as a prize in Cap'n Crunch boxes, made a tone that gave him access to AT&T trunk lines. He could make free long-distance calls."

"I'm not looking for a history lesson, Professor." Her eyes narrowed. "Get to the point."

First, she asks for an explanation, then she doesn't want to hear it. He cut to the end of what would have been an interesting lecture.

"A lot of old-school phreakers pay homage to Captain Crunch. Maybe Georgio would use a hidden external drive, not his computer itself, to keep his sensitive data. I saw the cereal box and peeked inside. There it was."

"If you'd already found it, why did you tell us to keep searching? Dammit, I had them call out a K-9 when you could have . . ." Her face flushed with anger. "Oh, no, Heron. Tell me you didn't."

She was taking this news about as well as he'd expected. "Even with Riverside Cyber on the job full time, who knows how long it'll take to get inside? We can't wait for actionable info, Sanchez. We need it now."

She closed her eyes and took a deep breath, held it for several seconds, then exhaled slowly. Apparently calmed, she opened her eyes and asked her next question. "What, exactly, did you do?"

"My gear bag—with the glass and the camera? I also have my pen test computer. A little one, thirteen inches. I isolated his encrypted data files on the Seagate and sent them to Aruba. Then I put the drive back. *And* made sure you found it. All good."

She was breathing hard. "No, *not* all good. The chain of custody is broken. Every single piece of evidence has to be accounted for at all times. Any moment it *isn't*, I mean, seconds, gives a defense attorney a shot at excluding it."

Heron squinted thoughtfully. "But *did* I break the chain of custody? All that Crime Scene knows is that they found a hard drive, right? I touched it *before* they found and logged it."

"A defense attorney is still going to make a motion to kick the drive out on its ass." Some Spanish words flew. He'd heard a few of them before. They were not complimentary.

But in a moment the anger faded. She stared out the windshield at the shoulder of the road, tiny whirlwinds of dust rising as cars zipped past. "All right. You could argue there's no chain-of-custody breach. But you still interfered with a crime scene."

"There are *two* things we can find in our hunt, Sanchez. One, evidence to *convict* him at trial and, two, evidence to *identify* him."

"They're supposed to be the same thing."

"But they aren't always, are they? If we don't find out who he is, we can't put him on trial."

She didn't answer.

"Right now, we need to find him. Whatever it takes. I don't see the problem," he muttered. "What's on the drive may lead us to where he lives or works . . . or to where the next victim is. If it does, well, won't we have plenty of other evidence to put him in prison?"

She gave a bitter laugh. "Please. You know the answer to that question. Which is a big fat 'not necessarily.' And if we don't, and he gets off on a technicality because of you and goes out there to kill somebody else . . . ?"

He was silent for a moment. Then he said, "Why does your imaginary defense attorney even have to find out what I did?"

"Because it's my job to tell them, Heron. Williamson, remember? Follow procedures and protocols. And follow the law. Anyway, they'll know soon enough. Your prints will be all over the drive."

"No, they won't. I wore gloves."

"*What?* I didn't know you had any."

"I always carry blue nitriles with my lockpick set."

After a few more choice Spanish words, she jabbed a finger at him. "If your little stunt screws this case up, if this 'actionable info lead' gets him off on a technicality, I can't protect you. Hell, I can't even save *myself*. We're both going down."

"Then will you tell them?"

She kneaded the steering wheel. Then slammed the car into gear and fishtailed onto the highway. Soon the speedometer nudged 80. "'Magic touch,' my ass. Working with you gives me heartburn."

"Glad I can return the favor," he said coolly.

Not bothering to add: after all you put me through four years ago.

Though, of course, he didn't have to. That subtext permeated the space between them, thick and toxic as an oil spill.

As he'd intended, the remark put an end to the discussion.

He took the opportunity to return to his phone, angling it so she couldn't see the screen. He used a sophisticated hacking program he developed years earlier to backdoor a website, bypassing the username and password request with ease.

He began to prowl through the servers. Navigation was a breeze; the IT personnel who'd designed the Homeland Security Investigations division of DHS had thoughtfully created a directory that sent him exactly where he needed to go in a matter of seconds.

CHAPTER 26

Carmen chanced a look at Heron, who had just put away his phone and was staring through the windshield with a stony expression.

He'd clearly never let go of that Christmas Eve, conveniently blaming her because he couldn't admit his own responsibility for what had happened. Seeing him now, it was clear the old Jacoby Heron was still there, stubborn and egotistical as ever.

She was about to break the heavy silence that had taken up most of their drive from Moreno Valley to Perris when her cell phone's screen lit up.

Unidentified Caller.

Most police-issued phones blocked caller ID, so she assumed someone from the murder scene wanted to talk to her. She put the phone on speaker and answered. "Agent Sanchez."

"It's Sergeant Radinsky."

The Moreno Valley PD patrol sergeant. Maybe his officers had located Heron's mystery rifleman—if he even existed.

"You're on speaker, Sergeant. I'm with Jake Heron."

A brief pause. "We didn't find any trace of anyone on the ridge, with or without a rifle. No footprints, no broken twigs, no dropped ammo on the ground. You sure that's what you saw up there?"

"Maybe a K-9 could get a scent?" Heron asked.

Carmen muttered, "I've already called out one K-9 unit, I'm not calling out another one for a ghost. Or a Verizon technician."

Heron lifted a palm with an expression that said, It's your funeral.

"Agent Sanchez?" Radinsky said before Heron could make one of his tactless comments.

"Yes?"

"Detective Hall would like to speak to you."

Her spirits lifted at the prospect of a development.

"Carmen," the detective said, this time not hesitating to use her given name.

"Go ahead. I'm here with Heron."

"I got the word on the white ball."

"And?" Heron said impatiently.

"It's a pill."

This made zero sense. "What?"

Hall chuckled briefly. "That's what a roulette wheel ball is called. I kept pressuring our crime lab to run more tests. They finally had a hit. It's Delrin—trade name for a particular acetal resin. Kind of heavy-duty plastic. And the one we recovered has the exact dimensions, smoothness and weight of the balls used in US casinos."

"Our boy's a gambler," Heron said. "A strategic thinker and natural risk-taker who calculates the odds before he makes a move."

"Well, he shouldn't have bet against Selina," Hall said. "He figured her for an easy mark and got his ass handed to him."

Damn straight. She and her sister might not be on the best of terms, but the self-defense lessons had stuck. Her respect for Hall kept growing too.

"Thanks for pushing the issue," she said to the detective. "Gambling . . ."

"Another fact for our PPIs, Sanchez. We're filling it in." Heron offered a smile, apparently done with his previous anger. "And we've got another lead."

"How do you mean, sir?" Hall asked the professor.

Carmen had a pretty good idea what Heron meant. She said to Hall, "We're close to Perris now. Isn't there a casino somewhere in town?"

Hall said, "Right. On West Fourth."

"We'll head over there now." She turned at the next intersection and steered toward the highway. "Never been inside, but I hear it's a pretty big operation."

They were only a few minutes out. Carmen said, "What do you think his connection with roulette is?"

Heron offered, "You could say a roulette wheel resembles a spider's web. Not sure if it's a PPI-worthy fact, but it's interesting."

Hall shared his thoughts. "I did a bit of research on roulette. I used to think it was all about chance. You know, place a bet on a number, then spin the wheel. Turns out there's a lot more to it. If you're strategic, you can do well. It's all about where you put your money, which is the only part of the process you control."

Unsure how this fit into the growing profile—and the hidden PPI she and Heron were so eager to establish—she stored the notion away for future use.

"Look." Heron pointed straight ahead. "There we go."

A brightly colored shuttle bus was traveling toward them on the opposite side of the road.

"What are you two looking at?" Hall asked.

"A casino shuttle," she said. "Possibly how he got through the roadblocks the other night."

She pulled into the parking lot. The casino sprawled over a massive campus that included a hotel, several restaurants and a parking lot with thousands of spaces.

"Bummer," she muttered, looking over the huge lot. "If he took the shuttle, he'd leave the SUV here, but there're acres of vehicles. It would take days to check them all out and run down the owners."

Heron said, "If my earlier guess was correct, he used dump wheels. The SUV will be stolen, or bought used with cash and a fake ID.

Even if we find it, I wouldn't be surprised if he emptied a gallon of oxygen bleach over the steering wheel and dash. So long, DNA and fingerprints."

She parked and they climbed out. "But there's some good news."

"What's that?" It was Hall.

"You want to tell him, Heron?"

He obliged. "You know the most common form of intrusion in current use?" When the detective didn't respond, Heron answered his own question. "Security cameras."

With her credentials, they could get the manager to show them footage from the day in question, both outside and inside the establishment, where they would probably find Spider at the roulette table. Nearly every square inch of casinos was under video surveillance.

All of it high-def.

And facial-recognition worthy.

"We'll be in touch," she told Hall and disconnected. She turned to Heron. "Let's go in and do a little intruding."

CHAPTER 27

Supervisory Special Agent Eric Williamson had a plan. Project X.

And currently that plan was going to shit.

He stared at the monitor on his desk, wishing he could be in Washington to plead his case rather than on a secure video call. His proposal had made it all the way up his chain of command only to stall at the desk of the largest obstacle, Deputy Secretary Stan Reynolds, second in command of the Department of Homeland Security.

Reynolds had been the *acting* Secretary for six months but was passed over when Congress failed to confirm him as the permanent leader.

Williamson had heard rumors about the horse-trading that went on in the smoke-filled back rooms of DC, but he'd never learned precisely what—or who—had torpedoed Reynolds. Since being denied the top spot, he'd become vindictive, seeming to take perverse pleasure in thwarting his subordinates. Williamson had met Reynolds twenty years ago when they were both young agents at Homeland, but the two had always seen things differently.

"I understand what you're trying to do, Eric," Reynolds said. "But what you're proposing is unprecedented."

That word again. "Unprecedented." Just because something hadn't been done before didn't mean the idea had no merit. Unless, of course, you were part of a massive governmental organization and worked under a bureaucrat who aspired to high office.

To put it simply, Stan Reynolds had a severe allergic reaction to whatever might jeopardize his flight path.

Williamson appealed to Reynolds' ambition. "Project X could revolutionize the way HSI operates. Our mission would advance dramatically—all under *your* watch. The only way to find out is to create a pilot program."

Williamson's belief was that because of the broad range of cases it pursued—more varied than any other federal law enforcement outfit—HSI was in a unique position to identify *all* threats to national security, which might include what seemed like purely local offenses with no obvious transnational ties. The serial killer Sanchez was pursuing now? Put him in a smaller town and life in the burg would be just as disrupted as if terrorists threatened an attack.

His goal was simply to stop bad actors from doing bad things. The resistance was frustrating beyond words.

Reynolds tapped the manila folder sitting on his desk. It contained the white paper study Williamson had submitted over a month ago. "Just not seeing it, Eric. Your plan would butt up against our brothers at the DOJ." He added quickly, "And sisters too, of course. Stepping on toes. Causing bad blood."

The plan was based on the premise that homeland security, lowercase *h* and *s*, was much more than terrorists foreign and domestic. Williamson wanted to redefine threats to America—its government and its people—which he saw as growing in number and size and complexity.

Just what he'd been speaking to Carmen Sanchez about.

He said, "You saw in the proposal I've worked out how to liaise with all the Justice Department groups, FBI, BATF, all of them. Major city police too."

Reynolds picked up the top page. "Even your executive summary sheet makes my head swim. So complicated, Eric. There's no way to justify a completely untried approach like this. I need more evidence before I can authorize funding and allocate resources."

The Deputy Secretary's chicken-and-egg logic seemed designed to quash any attempt at progress. He required evidence to implement the pilot, but the evidence could be gathered only by implementing the pilot.

Reynolds' expression darkened. "And when your proposal puts an agent like Carmen Sanchez on point . . ." He let the unspoken condemnation hang in the air between them.

Williamson had been wondering when her name would come up. "The project *needs* someone like her. She's a creative thinker."

Reynolds sipped from an oversize Starbucks cup. A straw was involved. "Maybe too creative."

"And a self-starter."

Slurp. "I've heard she *does* make up her own assignments from time to time."

He'd perhaps heard about the unsub known as Spider. How? Then he remembered Reynolds was the sort who considered it good management to cultivate spies at every level of the department.

This wasn't going at all how he'd planned. "I know she's unorthodox, but—"

"But so are you." Reynolds shook his head. "I'm sure it's why you recruited her from the Bureau. Peas. In. A. Pod. But this whole thing is too . . ." He glanced up at the ceiling, as if the word he wanted dangled in the air above him. "Risky."

They had finally gotten to the heart of the matter. Reynolds wasn't about to jeopardize his future prospects, even if the upside might be a big improvement. The status quo was his comfort zone.

Williamson had no respect for a leader without vision. Or without what Sanchez often referred to as "cojones." He'd had enough. Aware Reynolds had questioned his judgment, he decided to retaliate by questioning the man's leadership.

"Those who don't change stagnate, Stan."

The translation: "those" meant "you." Williamson added, "Nothing ventured, nothing gained."

"And nothing lost either," Reynolds snapped. So, it was gloves-off time. "You gave it your best shot, Eric, but Project X ends here." He narrowed his eyes. "And if you try an end run around me, your next assignment will be reviewing expense reports in the bowels of an admin building with no windows. Perhaps that will reinforce the importance of fiscal responsibility."

The gratuitously vicious comment surprised even Williamson. There was nothing more to say except, "I thank you for your time," maintaining his professional demeanor until the video call disconnected.

Then the volcano blew, and he fired off a series of expletives that had been stuck in the back of his throat for the past five minutes.

He considered his options and saw only one. Unlike his boss, however, Williamson wasn't risk averse. Just the opposite. His whole career had been what Camille, his prosecutor wife, called "juggling with blowtorches."

He stared at his phone, weighing the consequences that might result from the single call he was considering.

One good.

Many bad.

But his own words came back to him: Nothing ventured . . .

He reached for the receiver.

CHAPTER 28

Carmen looked all around, her senses overwhelmed by flashing lights luring gamblers to slot machines, jingling tones announcing payoffs and scented air wafting from the casino's ventilation system.

"You look like you'd rather be getting a root canal," Heron said to her as they made their way deeper inside in search of the management office.

"Never been big on gambling." She spotted a red-faced man pushing what was likely his last dollar into a machine. Widening armpit stains attested to his desperation. Maybe the HVAC perfume was pumped in to cover up the scent of sweating customers watching their children's college educations vanish.

Heron followed her gaze. "Having systems in place helps. You don't have to go broke if you stick to a plan." He paused. "My thoughts: there are two ways to approach any form of betting. You play to win, or you play not to lose."

She understood his meaning right away. "I've learned not to tempt fate. On the rare occasions I come to a place like this, I'm Ms. Conservative."

"You play not to lose." He lifted a shoulder. "Fine. You can have fun. But you never win big that way."

"I never lose big either. Sounds like you gamble, Heron."

"Me? No way in hell."

Carmen approached a man in a black jacket and tie watching the craps tables. His bearing marked him as a pit boss, and she figured he'd be a good place to start.

"I'm Agent Sanchez with Homeland Security Investigations," she said by way of greeting. "And this is my associate, Dr. Heron. We need to speak to the manager on duty."

She deliberately hadn't flashed her creds, assuming the casino staff would not appreciate her alarming the clientele.

The man inclined his head. "One moment."

As she'd anticipated, he hadn't questioned her—all casinos had procedures in place for dealing with law enforcement. He tapped his ear and spoke into a transmitter. Less than three minutes later, a slender man in a business suit strode briskly toward them. His bronze skin contrasted with the crisp white collar of his shirt and his glossy black hair fell in a single plait to the middle of his back.

He introduced himself. "Anthony Yanez," he said, inclining his head toward each of them in turn. "Follow me."

She recognized the name as Cahuilla, which must be the Indigenous nation that owned the establishment. They trailed Yanez to a nearly invisible door disguised as a mural set into the opposite wall. Once they passed through, the glitz and glamour gave way to an office space in muted beige tones decorated with Cahuilla artwork. The abrupt transition made the gaming area seem even more surreal by comparison.

He led them through a small warren of cubicles past a control room containing wall-to-wall video monitors, split screens and rows of panels that looked like they belonged in the cockpit of an airliner.

Yanez continued to his office and closed the door behind them. She displayed her creds, waiting while he looked from her photo to her face and back again before putting the leather case away. Hers was enough; he didn't ask Heron for an ID. "What can I do for you?"

Neither took the chairs he offered. She got straight to business. "We're investigating a homicide."

His eyes widened. "Someone in the nation?"

She should have anticipated the confusion. Since she was a federal agent, he assumed she was investigating a murder committed on tribal land. Haste had made her ham-fisted with her approach, and now he was worried about those he cared for most.

"It's unrelated to your nation," she said. "We believe the suspect came to this casino after committing a crime elsewhere and may have gotten on one of your shuttles to get past roadblocks."

His expression cleared. "Give me the time and date and we can check the videos. We store them all on a secure cloud server permanently."

She suppressed a smile. If Spider had come here for refuge or escape, he'd made a critical error. Casinos monitored every square inch of space except for the bathrooms. Catching cheaters and scammers required extra vigilance. And they never deleted recordings so they could track people they'd barred from the premises. If he'd been here, inside or out, they'd catch him on camera.

She hoped they could replace the composite sketch with a photograph she could run through facial rec. Or at least talk the press into putting up Spider's picture on the six-o'clock news and in digital editions of their papers and newscasts.

Heron, who had apparently been considering the time window they needed, answered Yanez's question. "Tuesday. As for the time—" But he stopped speaking.

The casino man's face fell. "Oh."

"What?" Sanchez asked.

"I can give you any day but that one." His face was awash with dismay. "Look. Please. This can't get out to the public. People would lose confidence in us. Only our cybersecurity company and the tribal council know what happened, and it needs to stay that way."

"We'll keep the information as limited as possible," she said. "But we have to know."

"We were hacked. A virus. All surveillance videos from that entire day were deleted from the server. Main and backup. I've been on the phone with the company that manages our cybersecurity and they've never seen anything like it."

"Of course," Heron muttered, his voice bitter.

She glanced at him with a frown. He didn't explain his fast, sharp reaction.

Yanez continued, "They tried to trace the source but couldn't. In the end, they managed to quarantine the virus and scrub it from the system, but not before the damage was done."

"Only security videos were gone?" she asked. "No betting records altered or credit card info stolen?"

Yanez nodded. "All things considered, we were lucky."

"You weren't lucky," Heron said. "You were targeted with a surgical strike. The intruder did precisely what was needed to accomplish their objective. Nothing more, nothing less."

"Are you saying the criminal you're investigating hacked in to erase his image from our system? An entire, multifirewalled server?"

"Not him personally. An associate of his—"

She cut Heron off before he revealed too much about the case. "Are there videos on the buses?"

"No."

She stifled a disappointed sigh. "We have a general description of the suspect and a composite drawing based on an eyewitness account. He likes to play roulette. Can we speak to someone who would have been in that part of the gaming area Tuesday night?"

Yanez moved to his desk and tapped the intercom button. "Send John Chacon please." After an affirmative response, he gestured toward a small conference table in the corner of his office, and they sat. "John is one of the pit bosses responsible for monitoring the roulette tables and the croupiers. I know he was on duty that day because, after the vids went dark, I had all the supervisors file reports documenting whatever they could recall about that day in case any complaints came up later."

"Contemporaneous notes," she said, grateful for his thoughtfulness. "We do the same thing with witnesses."

"Best I could do under the circumstances," Yanez said. "Mostly I wanted to catch anything that stood out to them. It's part of the pit boss psyche. They notice things."

A knock interrupted their discussion. "Come in."

A man in the same black suit all the floor supervisors wore entered, unfazed by the summons. More muscular and compact than Yanez, John Chacon was difficult to read. He stood quietly during the introductions and displayed no reaction while the manager explained their presence.

Carmen turned her cell phone toward him. "Did you see a man resembling this sketch playing roulette that day? He'd be six two or three, in good shape. Wearing a gray tweed sport coat, red shirt and tan cargo pants. He'd have on round glasses with brown frames and had light hair."

Chacon studied the sketch before responding. "Different clothes and he was wearing sunglasses. But I remember him from the tattoo."

The composite included a close-up of the black widow inked on his wrist. The pit boss, trained to watch people's hands at the table, had spotted the body art.

"Do you remember anything about his time here?"

"I noticed him when he came to the roulette tables," Chacon began. "*Poker* players wear sunglasses, not roulette players. I remember somebody was having a big run and there was a crowd around his table. Your man moved in to watch and I thought he was getting too close to one of the women in front of him. He seemed to be . . . sniffing her hair. I was about to have a word with him when he went to another table in the back. He sat there for a while, then started to play. Didn't see him after that."

Heron asked, "You said different clothing. What was he wearing?"

"Pink sweatshirt, white baseball cap and sunglasses. All from our souvenir shop."

Carmen asked, "Did he have a bag?"

"No. We always look for bags and large purses. We don't use magnetometers, so the bosses and dealers keep an eye out for anything that might hide a weapon."

"He would have changed in the men's bathroom where there aren't any cameras," she said to Yanez. "He could easily toss his old hat and glasses, but not the tweed jacket. I don't think he would draw attention by having anyone see him trying to cram his size 44 long sport coat into a men's room waste bin designed for paper towels."

"Fair point," Heron said. "Maybe he pretended to accidentally leave it on a hook in one of the stalls."

"And come back to pick it up later?" Yanez asked.

"No," Carmen said. "It was a toss-away."

"A what?"

"Our unsub is an organized offender. He plans everything. He bought the jacket with cash and if he got spotted, he'd chuck it. Can you check the lost and found?"

"Of course, Agent Sanchez." He led them from his office. They walked down a short corridor and into another room.

Inside, the place reminded Carmen of an evidence locker room, baskets and racks filled with hundreds of items left behind—in this case probably due to alcohol-induced forgetfulness.

There was no sign of a blue ball cap or tortoiseshell glasses, but a gray tweed sport coat hung on a clothing rack.

Yanez reached for it, but Carmen said, "Let me. It's evidence."

He stepped back and, without touching it, read the note attached to the hanger. "Brought in on Tuesday about midnight. Found in the southwest bathroom. The one right next to the gift shop," he added for her benefit.

Carmen snapped on plastic gloves and lifted the hanger. She had Heron take a picture of the garment with her phone, then sent the image to Selina.

Is this what he was wearing?

The response came in less than a minute.

Yes. Have you caught him?

Carmen was disappointed she didn't have better news to share.

Not yet but getting closer. How is all there? You okay?

She waited for the three telltale dots of a reply in progress. Nothing.

Her lips sealed tightly, and she stuffed her phone away.

"I'd like to collect that," she told Yanez.

Maybe they'd be lucky, and the lab could lift a partial print from a button. Or pull a hair with an intact follicle off the fabric. They already had Spider's DNA, but they might score an acquaintance's, or the clerk's who'd sold it to him, providing a new avenue of investigation. Maybe his brilliant hacker friend.

She gently squeezed the outside of each pocket. Experience had taught her never to plunge her hand into any concealed area of a garment. People kept knives, razor blades, needles and other pointy things hidden inside, and she had no time for a trip to the ER today.

Satisfied nothing would poke her, she opened the pockets to peer inside. Empty, except for a cocktail napkin, which she pulled and held pinched between her gloved thumb and index finger.

The white square had an italicized letter *D* on it. The typeface was unusual.

She used her free hand to pull out her cell phone and take a picture. "I'll send this to Mouse. Maybe she and Declan can run it down."

"Do you have a bag and some packing tape?" she asked Yanez.

He stepped across the hall to what must have been a storeroom and returned with a bright-yellow plastic bag, with the name of the casino on the top in blue above the bold red words: IT'S YOUR LUCKY LADY DAY!

It wasn't a sterilized evidence container but considering the garment's journey from Spider's back to the lost and found, she wasn't going to worry about cross-contamination from a commercial bag.

She replaced the napkin in the pocket, folded the garment, then carefully slid it inside the bag. After sealing it, she borrowed a thick indelible marker to write her name, the date and time and her initials across the tape. At least she could prove no one had tampered with the evidence after she secured it.

"I'm calling Detective Ryan Hall with the Riverside County Sheriff's Department," she said to Yanez. "He'll have somebody collect it. They'll also check all your parking areas for abandoned vehicles. We think he may have ditched his ride."

"Sure. You'll keep me posted about this? I don't want him to come back."

"He won't. Not after leaving the jacket and probably his SUV here."

She thanked Yanez and Chacon before leaving the management office. The visual and auditory assault that greeted them once again came as a shock to the system. She realized they must have soundproofed the employee areas to give everyone relief from sensory overload.

"Scrubbing an entire day's worth of cloud server video," Carmen said when they were alone. "But not the entire system."

"Which would've been easier," Heron added.

"Who the hell is backing him up?"

Heron dragged a hand through his hair, mussing it. "Wonder."

An odd comment. And a quick one.

"Wasn't asking for your date of birth and social security number, Heron. Just some off-the-rack speculation."

"Can't help you there either."

Her eyes lingered on his expressionless face. Then she said, "As long as we're in the area, I want to check on my sister."

"Sure."

As they walked toward the exit, the gift shop caught her eye, and she made a detour. Heron followed. She perused rows of mugs, T-shirts, key chains and refrigerator magnets before finding what she wanted. A display table in the corner held an array of playing cards, dice and other items that had been used on the floor of the casino and were now "retired" and made available for purchase. She picked up a small box and walked to the cashier.

She noticed Heron's curious expression.

"Souvenir," was all she said.

After paying they continued toward the exit, Carmen's senses once again flooded by the sounds and sights of a busy casino, a place that held a strange appeal for Spider. She sighed.

"What?" Heron asked.

"We're searching for PPIs, but the more facts we find, the less we seem to know about this guy, and where he's going to strike next."

CHAPTER 29

Christmas Eve, Four Years Earlier

Jacoby Heron was thinking of the special evening ahead.

As he sat in the ten-dollar Goodwill office chair and rocked back, eyes still on the computer monitor, Jake heard a sheet of rain slap against his windows, flung there by a relentless San Francisco wind.

He couldn't see out onto Sutter Street, a cousin of the tawdry Tenderloin, because the shade was drawn.

Even if he could peek out at the weather, he wouldn't be interested. His whole attention was on a three-by-two-foot screen in front of him, which showed the progress of software that would change the world.

> C:\JH\Banchee Routracing . . . Estimated time to connection: 4:20.

Jake was in San Francisco holiday attire, which was like San Francisco everyday attire, at least for geeks like him: gray shorts, no socks, a hoodie with the faded image of a superhero. The garment had been a gift.

From *her*.

So, he wore it frequently.

He'd donned it tonight in anticipation of their holiday get-together.

C:\JH\Banchee Routracing . . . Estimated time to connection: 3:43.

The program was Banchee 3.1—from the name of the Irish spirit whose eerie cry foretells death. The correct name is "banshee," with an *s*, but Jake misspelled it because script jocks like him always misspelled the names of their creations.

Banchee ranked among his best. It had taken months working eighty-hour weeks to perfect.

C:\JH\Banchee Routracing . . . Estimated time to connection: 3:27.

This was the largest of nine monitors in his studio apartment. The place was RadioShack on steroids. There were also dozens of boxes—the geek term for computers—and hundreds of boards, chips, wires, server racks, tools, hard drives, ancient floppy drives, virtual reality headsets and towering piles of Mountain Dew and Red Bull empties.

Jake's apartment, in other words, would *not* be the site of the festivities on this special holiday evening.

He cracked another Mountain Dew, which he guzzled simply for energy. He didn't savor the drink, the way he would the champagne he'd ordered for tonight. Like everyone serious about computers and coding, Jake rarely drank alcohol. You had to stay awake . . . and sharp.

But this would be a sparkling wine night.

The program ran silently, of course, though there was a soundtrack—the soft whir of the cooling fans.

C:\JH\Banchee Routracing . . . Estimated time to connection: 3:03.

From the cluttered desktop, he lifted a small velvet box.
His Christmas present to her.

A small gold rectangle, a reproduction of the very first micro-chip in history, made in 1958 by Jack Kilby, an engineer with Texas Instruments. The replica was two inches long by one wide and faithfully re-created the location of the transistors on the original. The chip, custom made by a jeweler in Sausalito, the artsy suburb north of the city, hung from the end of an 18K gold chain.

Soon, Banchee would finish the job and he could wrap her package and leave, to spend the evening in a home far less cluttered than here.

This Christmas Eve would be a good one.

Not like the ones he and his brother endured growing up.

On holidays Jake and Rudy were invariably left alone to play video games or watch TV. Their parents had to do their outreach work because that was a good time to recruit.

People alone in restaurants or movie theaters or parks on Christmas Eves like this, and Easters and Thanksgivings and New Year's Eves.

The lonely.

These were their prey.

Hi there, let me tell you about some people you'd like. We have a saying. Positive Thoughts Equal Positive Goals Equal Positive Rewards. You look like a positive person to us. Why don't you come to a meeting?

The "some people you'd like" was the group his parents belonged to and spent all their time with and money on, demanding its members put everything else in their lives second to the group, even their relatives.

The organization, a classic cult, was ironically called "The Family."

Now, on what would be a very different Christmas Eve, a happy one, the door buzzer sounded.

"Yes?"

"Grant Avenue Wines." The woman's voice clattered through the intercom. "Delivery of Moët . . . for Mr. J. Heron."

He checked the security camera and buzzed her in.

Moët . . .

He didn't have a clue about champagne. Rudy had recommended it, so he knew it would be good. Rudy had a real job.

A knock on the door.

He rose and, fishing a five from his pocket for a tip, he walked to it, looking back at the screen.

C:\JH\Banchee Routracing . . . Estimated time to connection: 1:03.

Almost there.

World changing.

He undid the locks and pulled open the door.

They rushed him.

Five or six of them, guns drawn, shouting commands. His shocked brain, on overload, took a moment to process their words, which came out in a jumble of angry, discordant noise.

One voice stood out in the confusion. The woman caught his attention because, unlike the others, she spoke calmly.

"Jacoby Heron, you're under arrest."

Imposing, grim and serious, she wore a blue windbreaker emblazoned with bright-yellow letters:

FBI

Carmen Sanchez

Near panic, he glanced at the screen.

C:\JH\Banchee Routracing . . . Estimated time to connection: 0:32.

No, not now!

He was so close. He turned back to Agent Sanchez. "Please . . ."

She leveled her large black pistol at him. "Hands where I can see them. You move, you're dead."

As calmly as if ordering a latte at Starbucks.

CHAPTER 30

Present Day

In the Eiffel Tower Inn, Jake stood by as Sanchez held out the silver dessert plate with a hopeful look in her eyes. Her effort to tempt Selina wasn't working.

"C'mon, Lina, you love crème brûlée."

The move made Sanchez seem oddly vulnerable, a supplicant placing her offering on the altar, praying it would be accepted.

Selina finally took the plate, on which sat a ramekin topped with caramelized sugar, and set it on the whitewashed French country–style café table in the corner of her room.

"You should eat it sooner rather than later," he said, breaking the awkward silence. "Your sister had them torch the top just right. It'll get soggy soon."

He *guessed* this was what would happen. Jacoby Heron had never eaten crème brûlée.

Though he supposed it was pretty damn good, since it was composed of two fancy-sounding French words and had been whipped up in the kitchen of a surrogate Parisian hotel—and was probably all the better since Sanchez had given the server detailed instructions on how much sugar to pour atop the creamy custard and how to apply the propane torch to turn it into a glossy tan glaze.

Selina eyed the dessert with a look Jake decided was more suspicious than intrigued. It certainly wasn't grateful.

"I have a few questions first." She turned back to Sanchez. "Starting with why you're really here."

Her older sister shifted on her feet. "Worried about you. Need to know you're okay."

Selina crossed her arms. "And?"

Jake looked from one sister to the other, trying to figure out what was going on between them. He sensed something akin to a pleading note in Sanchez's voice, and overt hostility in Selina's. The byplay gave him the sensation of walking into the middle of a movie.

A family drama.

"All right. I was wondering about that memorial next week," Sanchez said quietly. "Have you reconsidered?"

Like the sugar on the crème brûlée, Selina's features crystallized into a shell. "Here we go." She waved her hand, as if swatting away an irritating bug.

"It's important," Sanchez said. "He wasn't just our father. He had friends. His partner."

"Why should I honor him? Why should *anyone*? He abandoned us. Hell, I was just a kid. But you wouldn't care about that, would you?"

The defensive gaze in Sanchez's eyes was replaced by a flare of anger at the jab. Then it vanished.

"It's not about honoring him," Sanchez said. "It's about remembering the good parts of him. And putting the hard parts of the past to rest."

"I've put the past to rest. I've forgotten about him. Dredging up old feelings is the opposite of that."

A metric ton of baggage here, Jake thought, but he had no idea what had caused so much tension.

Sanchez, it seemed, had been holding back. She snapped, "Why can't you let it go, Lina?"

"Why can't *you*?"

The sisters glared at each other.

Standoff.

Jake, deciding a change of subject would ease the tension, addressed Selina. "Have you seen or heard anything suspicious?"

The young woman had no trouble firing a dark glance *his* way as well. "No. Why should I?"

"You kicked Spider's ass—and survived. He seems like somebody who doesn't like to lose. He might want to settle the score."

"How would he even find me here?"

Sanchez had paid cash for the room and registered using her middle name. Standard procedure for law enforcement. And, it turned out, for intrusionists as well. Jake was an expert in the art of anonymity.

"He's not like classic serial killers," Jake said. "We aren't quite sure what makes him tick. Stay vigilant. If you see *anything* your gut tells you isn't right—or even *sense* anything strange—call your sister." Noting her scowl, he added, "Or Detective Hall."

Now it was Sanchez's turn to aim a frown at him. "I'm sure he doesn't need any extra encouragement to keep an eye on her."

"Oh, really?" Selina rolled her eyes. "You're going to go *there*?"

Jake was treading through a minefield. He couldn't understand why Sanchez was worried about Ryan Hall. To his thinking, Selina and Hall had known each other less than one day. Eloping wasn't on the table. And the girl could do a lot worse than a young homicide detective who was not only intelligent and dedicated, but also carried a gun. With a maniac on the loose, she was lucky he'd taken an interest in her.

Then again, Selina wasn't his little sister.

Selina strode to the table in the corner and sat down in front of the rich French dessert. She gave Sanchez a pointed look and brought the heavy spoon down with a sharp crack, shattering the caramelized glaze. She took a bite and then pulled out her phone and began to text.

"Let's get out of here." Carmen's face was a mixture of sadness and anger. "We've got work to do."

A frosty nod between the sisters was their only farewell.

He barely made it inside the SUV before Sanchez revved the engine and accelerated out of the lot, heading onto the Ramona Expressway.

After a few minutes of silence he said, "There's worse intrusion between family members than between muggers and victims."

Sanchez said nothing.

He continued, "A mugger comes at you, your defenses instantly go up. It's fight or flight. But with family? You don't expect intrusion. And even if you do you tend to minimize the risk. Which lets the intruder stroll right in. By the time you recognize it, it's too late. You fight back, go overboard. There's a rift."

"You're saying I'm intruding on my sister with the memorial."

"I'm saying she sees it that way."

"Okay. But she's intruding on *me*, all that stuff about our father."

"I agree."

She scoffed. "What's that thing about two nuclear-capable enemies? Mutually assured destruction? Let's change the subject, Heron. I'm not in the mood— Oh, shit!"

Jake cut his eyes ahead.

A white Econoline van had veered into their lane, barreling straight at them.

Sanchez slammed on the brakes and jerked the Suburban's steering wheel to the right.

Jake gripped the dash as the van mirrored Sanchez's evasive maneuver, keeping them on course for a head-on collision.

An echo of the school bus incident.

Jake couldn't see the driver. Was it Spider, trying the same tactic here? And if it was, how the hell had he found them?

Sanchez steered the SUV onto the shoulder, gravel crunching under the tires as the vehicle shuddered to a halt.

The van did the same, coming to a stop, facing them, about thirty feet away.

There was a moment of stillness, and then the van's driver and front passenger threw open their doors, each of them putting one foot on the ground.

"What are they—?"

Sanchez never had a chance to finish the comment. Both men raised weapons, one a pistol, the other an assault rifle, and opened fire.

CHAPTER 31

"Get down!" Carmen threw the Suburban in reverse and stomped the gas pedal to the floor. A round penetrated the windshield, zinging past her ear as the vehicle lurched backward.

Heron ducked his head, clearly not understanding her instructions.

"All the way down on the floor," she shouted. "Get your ass behind the engine block."

He released his seat belt and crammed himself between the glove compartment and the floorboard. "It can't be Spider," he said over the cacophony of gunshots. "Who's after us?"

Two more bullets slammed into the windshield, one lodging in into the headrest where Heron's head had been moments earlier. The other smashed through the rear window.

The two assailants apparently hadn't expected them to survive the initial onslaught. They climbed back inside their van. The passenger, a White male in his early forties with a red face and wild eyes, was the one with the M4 rifle. The driver, who looked like he could have been his cohort's brother, held the pistol in one hand while he put the van in gear with the other.

Carmen expected them to flee.

She was wrong.

"They're coming after us," she called out to Heron. "Brace yourself."

She couldn't outrun them in reverse. Her best maneuver was a high-speed J-turn, something she'd practiced at the Federal Law Enforcement

Training Center driving track in Georgia but had never done with bullets flying and a civilian riding shotgun.

She continued to accelerate backward, twisting in her seat to look through the cracked rear window as she steered the SUV back onto the roadway. As soon as she had enough traction, she jammed on the brakes and spun the wheel hard.

The Suburban's tires went into a controlled skid, the heavy vehicle spinning in a 180-degree arc. The instant she saw the road stretching out in front of her, she took her foot off the brake and stomped on the gas. Smoke billowed up from the rear tires as she peeled away.

"Give me your gun," Heron called.

"No."

"Aren't you going to shoot?"

"No."

You never fired your weapon without checking the backdrop—where your slug would ultimately end up after passing by, or through, the perps you were targeting. Whatever you see in the movies, handguns are not particularly accurate, at least not in the chaos of combat, and here there were too many other vehicles that her rounds might hit.

A concern that did not enter their assailants' minds.

A fusillade of bullets tore through the back of the SUV, traveling past her headrest and blasting more holes in the windshield. She kept as low as she could, aware her seat offered small protection from the nasty .223 rounds she'd just been thinking about earlier that day, in the gunrunner's Moreno Valley home. She heard Heron, still hunkered on the floor, yelling into his cell phone.

"Gunshots. Perris, near the park, Ramona Expressway. We're federal agents. Two shooters in a white van . . . one automatic weapon. Maybe more."

She hadn't been able to call 9-1-1, but thankfully Heron had the presence of mind to get backup started their way.

"Put the dispatcher on speaker!"

Heron did and stuffed the phone in a cup holder.

The next two minutes were a frenzied exchange between the dispatcher, responding police and herself. She checked and assured them that all other nearby cars had pulled over or taken exits to escape the gun battle.

A lull in the assailants' target practice, and she heard the wail of sirens in the distance. This gave her an idea.

"Tell your units to go to lights only, cut the sirens. I don't want to spook them into rabbiting. I want them to come after us."

"Wonderful," Heron muttered.

She glanced to the north, a mostly undeveloped commercial zone. She asked Heron, "Where can I turn north in the next mile?"

He flipped through screens on his phone and glanced up. "Indian Avenue, a mile and change."

"I want to box them in," she told the dispatcher. "I'm turning north on Indian in two minutes. They'll come after us. Can your people set up stationary roadblocks on Indian?"

A new voice: "Agent Sanchez. This is Captain Dan Muñoz, CHP. We got four units north, heading your way now. They just passed March Air Base. And three cars coming in from the south. We can box them in."

She responded directly to the captain. "They have stop sticks?"

"Ten-four."

She couldn't let them take a bullet on her account. "Tell them these assholes have a shitload of ammo."

"Copy that, Agent Sanchez."

She had her own government-issued M4 .223 assault rifle, with a full auto mode, but it was locked in the rear cargo area of the Suburban. Exactly where they were currently taking fire. Driving while swerving to avoid incoming rounds took both hands, and she would give Heron her pistol only if she were hit and out of commission.

She could only imagine SSA Williamson's reaction to *that*.

Carmen listened while the lieutenant directed troopers to converge from several directions, shutting off escape routes. Everything was in place. The next sixty seconds would decide whether she and Heron made it out alive or not.

She skidded the SUV north on Indian, controlled the swinging rear end and punched the accelerator.

And there, before them, was the beautiful sight of a quartet of CHP black-and-whites—two blocked the highway and two were on the shoulder, cover for the eight officers who trained pistols and rifles in her direction.

She slammed on her brakes and jerked the wheel to the right, forcing the SUV into a sideways skid before accelerating toward the side of the road to give the troopers a clear shot at their pursuers.

The shooters tried to imitate her maneuver with their van, but as it approached a tangle of brush, an officer stepped out and slung a spike strip into its path.

The driver tried to veer to the side, but he couldn't—maybe because he was holding his pistol. The stop sticks shredded all four tires, and their van slowed dramatically.

Heron popped up from the floorboard, peering around his seat to look through the now-shattered rear window.

"Nobody's been disarmed," she yelled at him. "Stay down."

With one more glance at the van, now slowing to a stop, he did as she'd instructed.

A commanding voice boomed from a speaker in one of the CHP cars, ordering the occupants to exit the vehicle, raise their hands and walk backward toward the police line.

A tense sixty seconds followed.

Then the doors opened, and the two perps followed the instructions about raising hands and slowly moving backward toward the officers.

The pair did such a good job, Carmen suspected they'd done this before.

———

Five minutes later, both men had been cuffed and Mirandized, and the CHP lieutenant was standing with Carmen in the middle of the closed-off highway. His name was Quinn Lakowski.

A name as impressive as his biceps.

Carmen glanced behind him. Traffic was backed up for miles.

That situation wouldn't change anytime soon. White-gowned Crime Scene evidence collection techs were not finished processing the shooters' van. Every spent shell and fired slug had to be accounted for—and the passenger had been firing with a gun that spit out 750 of them a minute.

"Care to tell me who these yuck-a-pucks are?" Lieutenant Lakowski asked.

She'd had little time to process during the chaos. "We've got a few options to choose from. Not likely, but we're after a serial killer at the moment. Maybe you heard. Unsub. But goes by Spider."

"Yeah, the attack here in Perris last night. I saw the BOLO. That college girl. But this looks like drive-by gangbanger shit."

"I agree, it's not Spider's MO. I'm putting him at the bottom of my list. Another possibility: my colleague thinks he saw a man with a rifle sighting down on us in Moreno Valley."

"Thinks?"

"Can't be confirmed."

"Okay. I'll talk to him. Only he's a little . . . indisposed at the moment." The lieutenant pointed behind her. "He jumped out of your Suburban and ran over to the shoulder. This his first firefight?"

"Probably."

Lakowski tried, and failed, to hide a grin. "That explains it—he's behind those bushes, either barfing up his lunch or shucking his pants to drop a load in the dirt."

CHAPTER 32

Chef Renault Davide made his way to the annex in the back of his restaurant and sensed something different.

Not quite right.

He surveyed the large warehouse-like structure that contained his office as well as storage areas, the meat locker and the small but fully equipped kitchen used for catering jobs.

And then he saw it.

The fire door wasn't latched tight. He opened it and peered outside. Just the empty alley. Why was the door unlocked? The staff came in here to access the meat cooler or pick up staples. But they came and went through the kitchen, not by walking around the building to use the outside door.

A burglary?

Couldn't be. What was there to steal? Hardly inventory. A food thief would get far more from a meat wholesaler. The appliances? Not worth a jail sentence to walk off with some used food processors.

Anything else of value?

Knives were the most expensive utensils in any kitchen. His personal set, imported from Japan, had set him back over $5,000. The ones here cost less but were still pricey.

Chef Davide strode to one of the drawers and pulled it open. The chef's knives, nakiris, paring knives, santoku and cleaver were all present, but an eight-inch filleting knife was not in its usual place at the end of the gleaming row of steel blades. More expensive knives were still there, so it must have been misplaced.

His buzzing cell phone interrupted his search of the immediate area. "Oui?"

It was Pierre, his most important backer, a venture capitalist in Malibu.

Forgetting about the missing knife, he closed the drawer and continued to discuss a new restaurant he was planning. He walked to his office, which was an extension of the warehouse, filled with cartons of supplies, samples of oils, spices and vinegars that vendors had given him in hopes their products would be used in the restaurant.

He dropped into an old, comfy armchair, shipped here from his grandfather's farmhouse outside of Nice. "I will need to borrow au moins deux millions de dollars."

A laugh from the other end of the line. "Renault, you thinking it sounds like a less imposing sum en française?"

The chef smiled too and sat back to discuss details of the proposed venture.

He glanced up at a framed article from the *Los Angeles Herald*. Renault Davide was one of the featured individuals in a series devoted to success against the odds. The headline read He Calls Himself the Luckiest Chef in the World.

The title had been his idea, and the sentiment was true. Every day he woke up grateful to practice the art of pleasing discriminating diners with the best dishes he could conjure up.

For a moment his thoughts darkened. The open back door returned to his memory, and he recalled: the restaurant checkbook.

That was something a thief might go for.

He opened the bottom drawer quickly.

And felt the warm relief course through him. There it was! And no individual checks were missing.

Ah, the door had simply been left ajar by an employee taking a shortcut to their car. Or something similarly innocent.

Nothing to worry about.

Nothing at all.

"Pierre, pardon. Continuez, s'il vous plaît."

CHAPTER 33

Jake Heron's sneakered feet pounded the gravel lining the side of the roadway.

Needing an excuse for his illicit mission, he'd jumped out of the Suburban and made retching noises—as if traumatized by the shootout (and, in fact, while he didn't puke just then, it remained a distinct possibility).

Once he was sure the cops had heard him, he darted behind a stand of bushes, then made his way along the shoulder of Indian Road, going back the way Sanchez's SUV, trailed by the armed thugs, had come.

He scanned the area for the broken segment of guardrail he'd noted earlier, spotting it fifty feet ahead. He began to run, eager to get started before someone asked him what he was doing.

And stopped him.

While Sanchez had been occupied with driving, he'd managed a quick peek behind them. As the van had spun around the corner onto Indian, the two inside must have spotted the roadblock ahead and the patrol cars approaching from the rear. Jake had seen the driver fling something out his window. When the passenger did likewise seconds later, he realized they were jettisoning their cell phones.

What information was so valuable they couldn't risk being caught with it?

Logic told him it would probably include more than just their identity. Perhaps they planned to lie about who they were, but they had to know the cops would figure it out soon enough. Both men had probably been fingerprinted at some point in their lives. In that case, the identity of *others* they were involved with was likely the secret they wanted to keep. That, and potentially information about what they were up to or even financial arrangements that could incriminate their bosses—these two *had* to be hired muscle.

He finally found the driver's cell phone after traipsing through the high grass, where it had come to rest beside a battered and faded Coke can. He pulled a compact device roughly the size of a deck of cards from his pocket and powered it on. Sanchez would chew his ass for this, but at least he wouldn't be contaminating evidence by touching it.

And, if he worked quickly, she'd never know.

He held out the device, hovering it a few inches over the discarded cell phone. A button on his unit glowed bright red, then flashed blue. After about ten seconds, the light turned green.

One down, one to go.

Leaving the first phone in place, he stepped to the shoulder and with a stick marked an X in the dirt. He glanced to his left, where the police cars that had been following the pursuit were parked at the intersection of Indian and Ramona. The officers weren't looking his way. He trotted across the highway to check the opposite shoulder. It took him a bit longer to locate the passenger's cell and perform the same procedure.

He dropped to his knees behind a large, spiky agave plant and skimmed through the text that was scrolling up the screen of the device in his hand. In a few minutes he'd finished.

He walked to the shoulder and drew another X, then rose.

If he was lucky, no one had noticed his—

This thought ended abruptly when he turned toward the police roadblock to find Sanchez and a CHP patrol supervisor staring at him.

Shit.

He thought she'd be too preoccupied with the debriefing to keep track of him. He casually slipped the scanner into his back pocket and walked back to the pair.

The CHP supervisor, a lieutenant named Lakowski, asked, "So, Dr. Heron, you're consulting with Agent Sanchez here, she tells me?"

"That's right."

"And you're a professor. Like Indiana Jones in *Raiders of the Lost Ark*. But no whip."

"Exactly." He cast a look toward Sanchez, who showed no response to the joke.

The big lieutenant had former drill sergeant written all over him. Yet his voice was polite as he said, "One of my officers saw you sprinting down the road, sir. I'm a bit curious why."

How much of his efforts had they both seen?

Better to be honest.

Well, *somewhat* honest.

Jake waved in the direction of the high grass. "I saw the driver and the passenger toss something out of the van. Figured it might be evidence, so I went to check. Turned out to be cell phones."

Lakowski and Sanchez glanced to where he was pointing. The lieutenant said, "You could've told us so we could collect them."

"Thought it'd be easier to find them myself, rather than try to explain where they were. I marked both spots with an X on the shoulder." Jake glanced at Sanchez, thinking of Cap'n Crunch and Georgio's hidden Seagate portable drive. He added, "I never touched them."

"That's why you wouldn't listen to me and keep your damn head down," Sanchez muttered.

He didn't reply but, yes, it was. If he'd been about to be arrested and had incriminating information on his phone, he would have ditched it. He figured they'd do the same.

Lakowski seemed to believe there was nothing more to it. "Feeling better, Professor?"

Of course, the retching.

"I'm okay." The role called for a touch of his palm to his gut.

"Never been shot at before?"

Yes, he had. Several times. He said, "No, never have."

"Well, let's hope this is the last time." The lieutenant beckoned one of the white-gowned Crime Scene techs over. "Got a couple of phones to collect."

Jake pointed out where they lay.

Lakowski resumed his questioning. "I'd like to hear about the man with the rifle you saw in Moreno Valley. Could one of that pair be him?" He nodded to the shoulder, where the shooters sat handcuffed.

Jake wasn't going to go into his human algorithm modeling theory. He provided a description of the man by the cell tower in Moreno Valley, then added, "Didn't seem his body type was the same as these two. And the rifleman wore a green jacket. Dark. Like a soldier or hunter."

These two shooters wore cargo pants and Ts.

"And he was alone when Professor Heron saw him," Sanchez offered.

Her tone seemed to add: *If* he saw him.

The driver of the van began to shout. "You're all going to pay when the revolution comes! You're nothing more than tools of government!"

"So that's what this is about," Sanchez said in apparent recognition. "They're after me for an op yesterday."

She described the hostage situation in the Mojave Desert with the domestic terrorist Jason Powell, who had tried to blow up a corporate headquarters in Glendale.

"He's got a cult following." She jerked a thumb at the pair. "They must've heard I ran point on the takedown."

Lakowski asked, "What are they protesting?"

Sanchez said, "A tech merger that's going to end up with more data mining or something like that."

Jake followed the news of all corporate mergers and acquisitions—the bigger the company, the more risk of commercial intrusion. "Must be the DrethCo–Brakon merger," he said. "Brakon makes cheap laptops and DrethCo writes and sells code. But it's just meat-and-potatoes software—bookkeeping, education, inventory management. No data mining."

The driver of the van piped up again. "You're screwed, all of you! You sucked down the blue pill! And you don't have a clue what's going on!"

"Blue pill?" the lieutenant asked.

Jake said, "From *The Matrix*. The go-to antiestablishment dystopian movie. You choose the blue pill, and you accept the false reality being fed to you. You're complacent. You take the red pill to face the truth. And fight back against oppression."

The other shooter cried, "We're coming for you!"

"Well, no," Lakowski replied dryly, "you're not coming for anybody, son, at least not for twenty-five to thirty years."

Then he turned to Sanchez. "You'll have to make a statement."

"Sorry, Lieutenant. We've got to assume our serial doer is stalking his next victim right now."

Lakowski looked thoughtful. "You never discharged your weapon during the incident?"

"No."

"Neither one of you was injured?"

"Nope." Then Sanchez added pointedly, "Except for the puking."

Lakowski laughed. Then said, "Just get me an affidavit before the arraignment. Probably the day after tomorrow."

"That's a promise."

He handed her a card.

Sanchez smiled pleasantly to Lakowski, who walked back toward the suspects.

She and Jake climbed into the Suburban. Her smile survived one second longer. Then it vanished. "All right, Heron, now you're going to tell me why I shouldn't arrest you for evidence tampering."

CHAPTER 34

Four Years Earlier, Christmas Eve

"You move, you're dead."

Jake Heron stared at Special Agent Carmen Sanchez as she leveled her Glock on him.

His mind reeling, he realized the Feds had tapped the phone. It was how they'd learned about the wine delivery.

And who knew what else.

Sanchez issued another command. "Hands where we can see them." Still calm. Still completely in control.

Why now? When I'm so close.

He looked back at the computer monitor.

C:\JH\Banchee Routracing . . . Estimated time to connection: 0:11.

"On your knees!"

But I'm almost there!

Changing the world . . .

While Sanchez and two other agents covered him, the remaining two cleared the area. It didn't take long; the only separate place to hide in a studio apartment was the bathroom.

He held up his hands higher to show he wasn't armed. "Look, I need to type something into the keyboard. If I don't—"

"I'm not telling you again, Heron," Sanchez said. Her serenity was eerie. "Get down on your knees and lace your fingers behind your head."

"It's a security issue," he pleaded. "Lives are at stake. I've got to get to that keyboard."

Then he saw that Banchee was waiting.

C:\JH\Banchee Connection to target complete. Upload package Y/N?

He had only seconds to enter a command.

Sanchez noticed him staring at the screen. "You're not touching anything."

"Just one key. People will die if I don't."

One of the male agents scoffed. "Like we haven't heard that before. You hit a key and it bleaches the whole system."

Out of options, Jake flung himself toward his desk. He might get Tased, he might get shot, but at least he'd send the Banchee package where it needed to go.

But as he stretched out his arm and lunged for the keyboard, Sanchez rushed forward and swept his legs out from under him with some kind of martial arts move. He fell hard, breath knocked out of him, and pain radiated from his gut to the crown of his head. He ignored the agony and, gasping, pushed himself to his feet.

This time, no fancy stuff. Sanchez simply tackled him to the floor, scattering circuit boards and tools and clusters of wire everywhere. He landed on his back. For a few endless seconds, neither moved. She lay atop him, her dark hair spilling onto his face.

He smelled her shampoo or soap. Lavender.

And his computer issued a soft beep. He looked from her dark eyes to the screen.

C:\JH\Banchee Connection Lost.

"No," he groaned.

That had been his last chance. Months of work . . .

And all those lives . . .

Sanchez stood and another agent helped her roll Jake onto his belly. They cuffed him and pulled him to his feet.

"Jacoby Heron," Sanchez said, "you're under arrest for violation of US Code Title 18 Section 1030. And other charges relating to unauthorized access of confidential federal government data."

He had one final hope. "There's a file on that computer, it's—"

She pulled a card from her pocket. "You have the right to remain silent—"

"We don't have time for this bullshit."

She ignored him and finished reading his Miranda rights. "Do you wish to waive your right to remain silent?"

His eyes locked onto hers. "Listen to me. There's—"

"Are you waiving your right to remain silent?"

"Yes, I'm waiving my rights. There's a file on that computer. It's called Ironsights-26. Get it to your best cyber people, then have them call me, and I'll walk them through—"

"Where are the files you downloaded from the IRS servers?" Sanchez asked.

"That's not important now. You—"

"Where can I find them?" Again, that same smooth, unflappable voice. Unyielding as iron.

"In the goddamn file that says *IRS!* What matters right now is Ironsights-26. And a subfile called 'Nix.' Your best people. I can help them. I don't care if you arrest me—"

Another agent laughed. "We just *did*, Heron."

"But get that file to your—"

"Best people," Sanchez said. "I heard."

He *had* to make her understand. "It's vital."

Another agent said, "Don't believe him, Sanchez. He's got a self-destruct on it. You pull that file and it'll wipe the drive. You think we haven't seen this before, Heron?"

"You have to believe me."

Sanchez was looking down. The open box containing the gold transistor necklace had fallen to the floor. She picked it up and examined it. The card too, with the name "Julia" on the front. She cast a glance at Jake. "Your profile didn't include a spouse or partner. You seeing somebody?"

"She's my niece. It's her Christmas present. She's a computer science major at Stanford. Leave her alone."

"She's not on our radar." Sanchez set the card and necklace back on the workstation. "May not seem that way to you, Heron, but we only go after bad guys." Pointing at his desk, she addressed the other agents, "Cut in batteries to keep the boxes alive, then mirror it all and get it to Quantico."

"There's no time! Somebody needs to look at that file *now*."

Her penetrating gaze held his for what seemed like an eternity. Then she came to a decision. "Quantico."

"You have to listen . . ."

"It's Christmas Eve." Her tone brooked no argument. "I'm not in the mood to be played. Get him down to booking."

And with that, Jacoby Heron was whisked out the door.

CHAPTER 35

Present Day

"Now you're going to tell me why I shouldn't arrest you for evidence tampering."

Jake sat with Sanchez in the SUV parked by the side of Indian Avenue, after the Powell grunts' shootout. He dug his hand into his back pocket and held up the device he'd used to clone the shooters' phones.

She eyed it suspiciously. "Yeah?"

He explained what he'd done.

"Cloned them? You have five seconds to start talking." Sanchez gripped the steering wheel hard enough to whiten her knuckles. "Or my handcuffs come out."

"I wanted to know if they were working with Spider."

"Spider? We decided that didn't make sense. Didn't fit the profile. Something else is going on here, Heron. Out with it."

Traffic zipped past, summoning miniature cyclones of dust that whirled out into the wasteland to die.

"Four years ago," he finally said.

Her features settled into an inscrutable mask.

"That Christmas Eve," he continued, "when you nailed me for hacking into the IRS."

"You thought you were Robin Hood. You broke into the Treasury mainframe and moved the returns of crooked CEOs and other assholes to the Service's 'To Audit' file. And yeah, most of 'em got busted for hiding money offshore and in fake charities and diverting money meant for toxic cleanup. You nailed a bunch of bad people and you didn't line your own pocket. And it bought you some reduced charges by yours truly."

She was referring to the capital *F* Favor.

She added, "You did your time. You stopped hacking. You became an intrusionist. So why are you stealing data from the phones of two dyed-in-the-wool losers on a shitty road in a shitty part of the county?"

"There's more," he said. "So much more."

"I'm listening."

He began his story a month before that holiday night. He'd found a series of messages on the dark web encrypted with code he'd never seen. Brilliantly written code. He'd finally gotten inside the server of a hacker named Ironsights-26.

"He was helping a cell of separatists buy arms. It sounded like they were planning an attack. Domestic terror. The project was code-named 'Nix,' as in canceling something."

She frowned. Something familiar about the word, it seemed. But she gestured for him to continue.

"I could've sent everything to the Bureau anonymously. But there was something about this Ironsights . . . When I tried to get more details he'd block me with some new code he'd hacked together on the fly. He'd come after me and I'd block him. Then one day my screen goes blue and there's a message. It said, *'Game on,'* like he was challenging me to a duel.

"After that, I *had* to find him. For a week or more, we went at it, his skills against mine . . . he was doing things with script that *couldn't* be done—or so I thought. He kept taunting me, which only made me more determined to stop him."

Jake's gut twisted at the memory of his frustration. Of his humiliation. Of his failure.

Sanchez gave him a shrewd look. "He was leading you on for a reason."

"Wish I'd seen it as clearly as you just did. He knew if I'd done what I should have, handed my logs over to the Bureau, they might have stopped him. But he played me—played my ego. Just giving me enough of victory here and there to make sure it was just the two of us. And then, Christmas Eve." His eyes held hers. "I'd just hacked together Banchee 3.1, the most righteous exploit I'd ever written. The virus would find his physical location, lock him out of his own system, send me copies of all his files, including the Nix information. I'd send it all to the Bureau anonymously.

"I was so close . . . I had that window on Christmas Eve—after the traceroute found his server and before he realized it. But . . ." He shrugged. "You got to me first."

Her eyes were on a trio of bullet holes in the dash, equally spaced, as if they'd been planned with a ruler. "What you told us in your apartment, we hear that all the time in takedowns, Heron. Plots, conspiracies, naming names. People make shit up to give them a chance to wipe their drives. Or try to negotiate plea deals. You didn't tell us specifics. All you said was two words. 'Ironsights' and 'Nix.'"

"I didn't have any specifics yet."

"I didn't entirely blow it off, you know." Her eyes slid away from his. "That was my last operation with the Bureau. I had to transfer all my investigations to other agents when I left for Homeland. I wrote an after-action memo about what you told me."

He was surprised. "You did?"

She grimaced. "I sent it upstairs."

He gave a dark chuckle. "Upstairs," he muttered. "Where memos go to die." Then the smile vanished. In a soft voice: "January 4, a week and a half later. Chicago."

Her face showed confusion for an instant. Then her brow furrowed and her lips momentarily pressed tight. "Jesus. The International Trade Exhibition. Six dead, twenty-one injured. A separatist cult in Montana. They called themselves Nix. That's right."

He heaved a sigh. "All this time, I've been blaming you for not listening to me on Christmas Eve. But it was my own damn pride. I had to stop him myself. Solo."

Sanchez gave her head a rueful shake. "And I had to show everyone I could collar the infamous IRS hacker. That was all that mattered." Then she straightened. "All right, Heron. We're closing in, but there's more, isn't there?"

Well, he'd known she was good.

"Yeah, there's more. I didn't tell you everything when you asked me why I flew from Berkeley to San Diego, why I wanted to stay on the case. Aruba found the algorithm he used for his custom-made encryption on Spider's phone."

"The chemical symbols."

He appreciated her memory for detail. "They were nitrocellulose and nitroglycerin. Ingredients in modern gunpowder."

Sanchez actually gasped, "Ironsights-26!"

Jake nodded slowly. "Aruba confirmed it. Everybody who writes code has their own style. Tabs, white space, code grouping, included patterns, excluded patterns . . . a hundred different things that make your code uniquely yours. The script we found in Spider's phone matches Ironsights' perfectly. He doesn't go by that name anymore. Now his handle is FeAR-15. It's a combination of Fe, the atomic symbol for iron, and AR-15, the rifle. He likes weapons and he's into first-person shooter games."

"And you saw this case as another chance to bring him down."

A slow nod. "If those two in the van were working with Spider, then maybe they had information on their phones I could use to get to FeAR."

Sanchez indicated the cloning device. "But that wasn't it, right? There was no connection to the shooters and FeAR?"

"No. Everything was about Powell or them personally. Ranting about his conspiracies. And then your typical gambling and sex sites." He lifted his palms. "There you have it."

"So that hunch stuff outside San Diego PD was bullshit. You knew FeAR was working with Spider. You were just bluffing your way onto the case."

He gave her what he hoped was a disarming smile. "I love it when you hit nails on heads, Sanchez."

"You have any clues as to FeAR's ID? We should track him if we can."

"No. No name, or location. He's American and probably lives in the country somewhere. But nothing more than that. Aruba's got a dozen bots searching. No luck so far." Then Jake grew grave. "Oh yeah. One more thing I probably should share. I hacked into your HSI server."

"The fuck, Heron!" Her dark eyes were the widest he'd seen them.

"I'm doing you a favor. Clients pay me a fortune for that kind of pen testing."

"That's not funny. You just confessed to a felony."

A thoughtful look. "Doesn't count. You didn't Mirandize me."

"Because I don't have to unless you're in custody." She frowned. "And I'm thinking you should be."

"I didn't read anybody's email or access anything classified. I just needed to see your ping records. It would tell me if FeAR tried to hack into your servers. He didn't. You, Williamson, Mouse, everybody at HSI—they're all good. But I have to say, your firewalls are pathetic." He brushed his beard. "You really ought to talk to your IT security people about it."

"This isn't funny, Heron."

"If you want me gone, Sanchez, I'll jump on the next flight back to Berkeley. Just say the word."

She was absently watching the crime scene, where white-suited techs were placing little numbered squares like miniature sandwich boards indicating where evidence had been found.

After a moment he said, "It is *kind of* funny, though, isn't it?"

She cut her eyes to him.

"I mean, if Williamson knew I got inside and was prowling around HSI's files. Just thinking of his expression."

A beat of a moment and she laughed. Hard. "Your ass would be so gone, Heron. He'd collar you himself."

Jake too began laughing. It was infectious.

He reflected it had been a long time since he'd shared a laugh like this with a woman.

And he wondered why the gender qualifier had spontaneously come to mind and he hadn't thought the broader truth, that he hadn't shared a laugh with *anyone*.

Then the levity faded, and Sanchez raised the very question that was in the back of his mind. "But I don't get why a serial killer is using a world-class hacker to watch his back. How'd that happen?"

"FeAR is a mercenary but it's not like he advertises. Not even in the dark web. Spider knows people. And he's got to have some money. FeAR won't come cheap."

Sanchez massaged her shoulder. She must've twisted it in the shootout.

Or when he jumped on her, back in Moreno Valley.

The agent's phone chimed with a text. She read the screen. "It's Mouse. Declan got a hit on the logo from the napkin. It's from a restaurant in Irvine. Davide's."

"Maybe he was there to quote 'borrow a pen,' like he did with Selina. And find a new victim."

Then he was thinking: laughing aside, he had lied and he had hacked. Would she kick him to the curb, so he could Uber to the nearest airport, where he'd fly back to Hewlett College and ornery undergrads?

She put the Suburban in gear, then paused and turned to him. "We're heading for Irvine. You going to put your seat belt on, or what?"

CHAPTER 36

Concealed in a storeroom in the back of the restaurant, Dennison Fallow listened to the chef's end of the phone conversation.

"Oui, certainement."

Fallow strained to hear the rapid French from his hiding place across from the chef's office. As soon as the call ended, he could get to work on the man.

Anticipation always heightened the Push. He would have been here sooner but his near capture in Moreno Valley forced him to wait at Lake Mathews until the manhunt lost steam.

Unwilling to risk driving his sedan, he'd taken the time to switch it out at a car dealership in San Fernando Valley—the same place where he'd bought the Pathfinder he'd used for the attack on Selina and the dark Chevy Malibu he'd driven to Moreno Valley for the enjoyable task of slicing the throat of Alex Gregorio. The used car lot sold vehicles that were legally untraceable, and physically too if you never parked them at your house and wiped them for prints and scrubbed away DNA with oxygen bleach.

He'd exchanged the sedan, and some extra cash, for an old Ford Transit van. Naturally the only one available was white, and he gave his head a small shake, wondering if the dealer kept a supply of creepy kidnapper panel vans in case people like himself showed up at his lot.

Fallow bided his time while the chef prattled on. Surveying the area, he noticed a diagram of a cow on the wall, indicating different cuts of meat. The image took him back to a special day spent with Mr. Benedict, sitting on a park bench in Santa Monica, overlooking the Pacific Ocean.

Mr. Benedict's swept-back hair had ruffled in the breeze as he spoke. "The basement is the key, Dennison."

"It is? Why?" Fallow watched a Rollerblader, a young woman with dark hair who reminded him of bloody Katrina from middle school.

"A solitary space underground meant as a prison became a refuge from the Push because you couldn't act on it. You felt comfortable there, right?"

"I still do."

"Good. It means part of you wants to be cured. Now that we've established that, we can begin to work on the problem. I have a plan. It involves finding a substitute for the Push."

Even at a young age, Fallow knew people didn't always say what they meant. Did Mr. Benedict think the Push was like a drug and he was hooked?

"Like methadone for heroin addicts?" he asked.

"Exactly." Mr. Benedict seemed pleased he'd made the connection.

"What kind of substitute?" Fallow's heart sank. "At one of the psych units, we did pottery and planted herbs."

Mr. Benedict laughed. "And that was bullshit, right? Touchy-feely stuff."

Fallow, who never smiled, nearly did.

"You need something active," Mr. Benedict went on. "Something outdoors."

"I don't like sports. They made fun of me in gym class."

"What about hunting? Deer, elk, pheasant. Not for sport, for food."

The idea was completely alien. Other boys learned things like that from their fathers, but his own father would have nothing to do with him at all, let alone engage in activities with his son.

He looked down, afraid his next words would make Mr. Benedict think he was less of a man. "I've never fired a gun."

The response came quickly, with no trace of judgment. "I'll teach you."

Part of him longed for such an opportunity, but life had taught him to be skeptical. "But the Push . . . you know, it wants me to do bad stuff. Hunting isn't bad."

Mr. Benedict raised a brow. "A deer would beg to differ."

They started training that very day. Before teaching him to shoot, Mr. Benedict drilled him in the rules about respecting rifles, which were always treated as loaded, even when they weren't. The weapon could fire at any moment, even if it couldn't. You never pointed it anywhere you didn't want the bullet to go.

As for the mechanics of shooting, you never "pulled" the trigger. You zeroed your sight on the target and slowly applied pressure so that you were surprised when the gun went off. Jerking the trigger guaranteed a miss.

"Remember," Mr. Benedict said, "never hurry when the issue is life and death."

"I'll remember."

After a month or so of training and target practice Mr. Benedict decided he was ready and they hiked out into Deer Hunting Zone 14 in the San Bernardino Mountains. Within a half hour of arriving at the site, Fallow made his first kill, a whitetail deer, with a single round from a .270-caliber rifle.

"Nice clean shot," Mr. Benedict said. "Now, the big question. What about the Push?"

He took stock of his feelings. "I think . . . it's kind of sleeping." When Mr. Benedict smiled, Fallow added, "But it's not gone."

"Oh, this is just a start. We still have more work to do. Follow me."

The work, it turned out, was dressing the deer.

"Dress?" Fallow asked, as they stood over the carcass.

"It means gutting an animal and letting it bleed out. Then butchering it for the meat." Mr. Benedict regarded him. "If you can do it, you'll find using the knife will keep the Push away even longer." He gestured toward the deer at their feet. "But some people don't want to. It's messy. The blood, the organs, the smell . . ."

He looked from the animal back to the knife in Mr. Benedict's hand, the black blade with a narrow, shiny edge.

Fallow snapped back to the present as he heard the chef say, "A bientôt." He didn't speak French, but the ensuing silence told him the phone call had finally ended.

He watched the chef appear from his office and walk into the kitchen, carrying a clipboard and wearing a net over his thick black hair.

It reminded him of a spiderweb.

Fallow extracted a roulette pill from his back pocket. He rubbed it compulsively in his vinyl-gloved finger and thumb for a moment before rolling the tiny white ball along the floor toward the meat locker door at the end of the corridor. He stepped back into the storeroom.

The chef's soft-soled shoes prevented Fallow from hearing his footsteps, but he could see the shadow on the wall as Davide walked toward where the ball, which had bounced off the closed door, was rolling back into the corridor.

"Hello?" the man asked, walking past the room where Fallow waited.

He attacked from behind, wrapping his left arm around the chef's torso and bringing the knife to his throat with the right.

"No! Please . . ."

"Shhh," Fallow ordered.

Davide was a strong man, and he might have fought back but didn't. He stood completely still, trembling. "Money? I can—"

"Shhh."

The memory from a moment ago once again surfaced as Fallow thought of the question Mr. Benedict had asked him during that first hunting trip.

"If you can do it, you'll find using the knife will keep the Push away even longer. But some people don't want to. It's messy. The blood, the organs, the smell . . ."

After the pause, during which he had locked eyes with Mr. Benedict, Dennison Fallow had whispered, "Give it to me."

And held his hand out for the knife.

CHAPTER 37

Carmen pulled sideways Gs as she rounded a corner in downtown Irvine.

Red and blue lights strobed through the sky, each flash quickening her pulse. She pressed the accelerator harder.

"Ambulance." Heron pointed to an alley beside the restaurant.

She darted a glance. "They're not doing anything."

A pair of EMTs lounged near the back of the boxy yellow and orange vehicle, which meant they weren't urgently needed. Maybe the local police had gotten here in time and the potential victim was safe.

On the other hand, ambulances didn't carry corpses. They might be waiting for the Medical Examiner's transport van.

As soon as Mouse told her the source of the napkin, Carmen had called in a possible 10-64, assault in progress, in or around Davide's. Irvine PD and Highway Patrol from the Santa Ana barracks were dispatched.

During her warp-speed journey to the restaurant, the incident commander had called to advise her a tactical search was underway for the unsub.

And/or his victim . . .

She skidded to a stop near the other emergency vehicles. Her SUV drew some surprised reactions from the officers. The bullet holes from Powell's acolytes were impressive.

Carmen recalled that the result of a round perforating vehicular glass was referred to as "spidering."

She and Heron climbed from the vehicle and headed for the command post. She spotted the incident commander who had called her earlier. He was standing beside a CHP black-and-white, parked half-on, half-off the curb, giving instructions to responding officers. According to the printing on his car, the broad-shouldered man was with Southern Division's Special Services unit. His rank was captain.

Odd, though impressive, that someone that high up was here. Usually incidents, even homicides, are run by sergeants, or occasionally lieutenants.

Spider had caught the attention of the brass.

They walked up to him.

Sporting a trim mustache, Eduardo Torres, a distinguished-looking man in his fifties, was in an immaculate olive drab uniform with a blue tie. His tan shirt had railroad tracks on the collar, signifying his rank.

Carmen identified herself, then tipped her head toward Heron. "He's with me."

"You've been tracking this subject?" Torres asked.

"That's right. Since the attempted homicide in Perris."

"SWAT's clearing the place. Nothing so far. No bodies, no signs of a struggle." He gestured to a cluster of a half dozen men and women in street clothing, though several wore aprons. "Kitchen staff," Torres explained. "They didn't see any strangers enter the restaurant." Then he added, "But the chef who owns the place—the one who's missing—was in a separate building in the back. That's where his office is."

"What's his name?"

To Carmen, every victim was a human being and she wanted to know them personally, whether alive or no longer of this earth.

"Renault Davide. Guess he's a big deal. Been written up in the *Times*, the *OC Register*."

Judging by the glitzy building, with its facade of rich wood and polished glass, Carmen agreed that he must have some serious culinary talent. "Anybody see him today?"

"The hostess did. About an hour and a half ago he came in, they talked for a minute, then he headed to his office."

"The chef's phone?" Heron asked.

"Straight to voicemail. His car is still parked in the alley. Maybe he's inside but we don't know yet. The tac team hasn't finished."

Heron asked, "What's his number?"

"Like I said. He didn't pick up."

"Mind if I try?"

The captain read the number from his notebook while Heron typed it into his phone.

"Heron . . . ," Carmen whispered. They may have put the past largely to rest, but that didn't mean she would sanction him hacking into a cell carrier. "We can't—"

Heron looked up and said, "Phone's still inside." He put his own away.

Carmen could only sigh.

"You Feds must have a hell of a cyber team to work that fast," Torres said with an air of grudging respect. "And you've got paper already too."

Meaning a warrant.

Carmen was spared from deciding whether to come clean with the captain. He hadn't asked a question about the warrant. Just stated an assumption.

Not her job to correct him.

She wasn't pleased about Heron's hack, but now they knew the phone was inside. It meant Davide probably hadn't left the place voluntarily.

Torres' radio clattered. "Captain? It's McAvoy."

"Go ahead."

"Building and annex are both clear. No hostiles, no vics."

"Signs of struggle?"

"Negative."

"Keep me apprised." The captain disconnected.

"Vids," Heron said to Carmen in an undertone.

She turned to Torres. "We need to see the security footage."

"Guess it's okay." Torres gestured to a van with OCCSU printed on the side. "Usually they go in first, but here . . ." He shrugged. Meaning there was no specific indication of where the unsub had been. Or if he'd been here at all.

All they had was a napkin and a missing person.

"Who has access to the security system?" she asked the captain.

"Hostess, I guess. She's in her car. Pretty upset. I'll go get her."

He returned moments later, a petite brunette with red-rimmed eyes in tow, and the four of them walked into the dimly lit restaurant.

Carmen addressed her in a gentle tone. "We'd like to see the security footage."

The woman led them into a small office. Framed news stories about Renault Davide and his unlikely climb to the heights of culinary success adorned the walls.

The hostess dropped down onto a black desk chair, spun to face the computer and began to type.

"Don't bother." Heron pointed to a black box sitting on the floor. "It's a commercial cybersecurity system. I know it. A twelve-year-old could get in and delete the files at the same time he's playing *Fortnite*."

"It's guaranteed," the hostess said, frowning. "They said that . . ." Her voice faded as the screen filled with a snowstorm of static. She tried all the cameras. The same. "No . . . not possible."

"FeAR-15," Carmen muttered.

Heron turned to Torres. "What about street cams?"

"No city cams around the restaurant. I've got some officers canvassing residents and stores nearby in case any of them have security video. Doorbell cams too."

229

Torres took several radio calls from officers who had canvassed the streets around the restaurant, armed with the composite of Spider from the BOLO. No one reported seeing anybody resembling him.

Torres asked Carmen, "What's his game? Not sexual?"

"No. We aren't sure of his motive yet. We're slowly filling in the Points of Potential Intrusion. Nothing like I've ever seen."

"But it *is* national security? I mean, you're Homeland."

"That's right." She didn't share anything about her sister's involvement.

Which reminded her of the strained conversation she'd just had with Selina.

A dark pall descended over her, enlivened by a flash of anger.

Another call came in on Torres' radio.

"Captain?"

"Go ahead."

"Team Two. We're in the annex. You might want to ask one of the cooks to come over here."

"Copy that. Why?"

"I'm thinking somebody ought to shut off the pots."

The hostess blinked. "What pots?"

"Three big ones. I guess they got about fifteen gallons of stock each. They're simmering. I don't know if they should keep the flame on with nobody around."

The hostess said slowly, "That's funny. We're not using them for anything on the menu tonight. What's in them?"

"Hold on, ma'am." A few seconds later, the response came through. "Meat, and bones, a lot of them."

There was a gasp, and Carmen got to the hostess just before she hit the floor.

CHAPTER 38

Carmen eyed the massive stockpots sitting atop gas burners, set to low.

From each ring blue flames danced. The sight might have been cheerful under other circumstances but, considering what was simmering inside, the scene was straight out of a horror movie.

She stood beside Heron and Torres just inside the doorway of the annex, looking toward the small kitchen.

The Orange County Sheriff's Department Crime Scene team was inside, all decked out in level B hazmat suits. They shut off the flame and one began photographing the area while another assessed how best to remove the remains while preserving evidence.

The team opted for large forceps to remove the pieces of flesh and the bones. As a law enforcer for years, many of which included tactical work, Carmen had smelled the gut-churning odor of burned human flesh and singed hair.

It was a scent memory she wished would go away, though it never did.

But *boiled* remains?

That was different, very different.

And, oddly, it didn't smell as repugnant as she'd expected.

Which was horrifying in itself.

Torres whispered, "Jesus. I can't imagine . . ." He seemed nearly as shaken as the hostess.

The tech who'd been photographing the room approached and pulled down the Tyvek suit's hood. A tendril of curly brown hair escaped from the shower cap covering her head. She gave them her initial impressions. "Looks like he did the butchering someplace else. Outside I'd guess, because there's no obvious blood in here."

Made sense. Spider would want to spend as little time as possible inside the annex, in case somebody walked in.

"I found glove marks on doorknobs and drawer pulls," the tech continued. "But that's not unusual in a kitchen crime scene. A lot of the staff are gloved. But these had a few wrinkles in them, which means they weren't latex or nitrile. They were vinyl."

"What Spider likes to wear," Carmen said.

"I also found an empty slot where a knife used to be. Eight or ten inches long. If it matches the others, it's razor sharp. We should assume he used it and has it with him."

Like the others in the doorway, Carmen's gaze kept returning to the steaming pots, whose contents two of the techs were transferring to cutting boards that had become impromptu examination trays.

"You did everything you could," Heron told her. "This isn't on you, Sanchez."

The words, surprisingly moving, didn't absolve her of guilt.

The head of the CSU team, a tall, lanky woman, joined them.

Carmen turned to her. "Your team find anything we can use? Other than the missing knife?"

"No, the suspect was careful. Wore gloves and smooth-soled shoes or booties. No helpful prints." She regarded their troubled faces and added, "By the way, those aren't human remains in the stockpots."

Torres stopped talking midsentence and lowered his radio. "What?"

"It's beef. They've got a cooler with plenty of bigger bones stored. They look a lot like human tibias and femurs, radius and ulnas. But they're not."

"You're sure?" Torres asked. "We haven't tested anything yet."

"I'll do a rapid DNA back at the lab, but believe me, I've got four kids, and my husband doesn't cook. I know every cut of meat there is. The question is, Why the hell was your perp taking time off from murder to cut up beef and make stew?"

"Diversion," Heron said.

Torres raised a questioning brow.

"He kept us focused on those damn pots, *totally* focused," Carmen said. "Gave him a chance to get away and take the chef with him."

"So," Torres said, "it's a one-three-four."

The police code for kidnapping.

The Crime Scene tech said, "Which means he could still be alive."

She shared a glance with Heron. Spider didn't want a live victim. He just wanted to stage the death in a particular way, and he needed time to do it.

Torres' radio rattled once more, the sound reverberating through the small kitchen. He lowered the volume. "Torres. Go ahead."

"We've got a situation here. Figueroa and Seventy-Third." A pause. "Sir, you'll want to come see this for yourself."

Even through the radio Carmen could tell the cop was shaken.

"We'll need a hook-and-ladder from the fire department," the officer continued. "And request Crime Scene team too."

Had he witnessed something as disturbing as a dissected and boiled corpse?

A whisper. "I've never seen anything like this. In all my years . . ."

The answer, apparently, was yes.

CHAPTER 39

The body, hanging upside down and duct-taped into a ball, rotated slowly.

Carmen was a quarter mile from Davide's, in an alley between two office buildings, examining the scene with Heron and Captain Torres. She tried to suss out exactly how Spider had managed to create the grisly tableau.

He must have forced the man into his trunk and driven here, invisible to passersby. A dumpster concealed the alley from nearby roads. At gunpoint, Spider would have bound him with the duct tape, hands and ankles first, then forced him to lift his knees up to his chest as far as they would go and continued encircling the rest of the body.

Like a swimmer doing a cannonball from a diving board.

All the while Davide would be thinking: If I do exactly what he says he'll spare me. It's a kidnapping, not a murder. This is just about money.

But it wasn't about money at all.

Because Spider had then tied a rope around the chef's ankles, swung it over a rung of the fire escape about ten feet above the alley floor, then pulled, upending the poor man, and hoisting him into the air to dangle.

Had Spider watched his struggles, heard his muted groans, ignored his pleas for mercy? Had he smiled, taunted, laughed as he slapped the last piece of tape over the man's nose, suffocating him?

Carmen stared, thinking one thing, and one thing only. Regardless of what Heron said, she'd blown it.

Someone else was dead.

Heron was with her, a partner, but his level of responsibility wasn't the same as hers. She was a highly trained federal agent, a public servant. He was an intrusionist, an academic who worked to safeguard the privacy of companies and government agencies and individuals.

But those were abstract concepts. There were no human lives directly at stake in Heron's skirmishes.

Not like what they were witnessing now . . .

And yet, when she focused on Heron's eyes, she saw that, while on some absolute level, he was less guilty than she was, he nonetheless seemed filled with the same flinty dismay she felt.

She should have moved more quickly with the napkin.

She should have pressed Ryan Hall even harder to learn what the white balls were.

Should have, should have, should have . . .

They stepped away from the body to let the Medical Examiner and the CSU do their jobs, and she and Heron both gave statements to Torres. If the man was curious about what a team from Homeland Security Investigations was doing on a case like this, he gave no indication of it.

"Next of kin?" Carmen asked.

Torres said grimly, "The hostess told us he's got a partner. They've been together a few years. I'm on my way to talk to him now. Hate those notifications."

She had done her share. "Nothing worse."

Heron turned to say something, but suddenly he froze and gripped her arm. His alarmed expression made her reach for her weapon. "What?"

He pointed at a parking garage about five hundred yards away. "The rifleman."

She followed his gaze. "From the ridge in Moreno Valley?"

"He's gone."

She stifled an eye roll. "Come on, Heron. It's a quarter mile, and you're looking into the sun. How positive are you?"

"Eighty percent."

Torres asked, "You see your unsub?"

Carmen scoffed, "He's not sure what he sees."

Heron said, "A man in green, like camo. With a long gun."

Torres squinted. "You've got good eyes, sir." He turned to Sanchez. "Want me to send a uniform?"

She debated a moment. "If you don't mind."

Torres left to order a pair of deputies to search the structure.

"You know, Heron, there's good paranoia and bad paranoia."

"I saw something."

"You eighty percent saw something. Which means you twenty percent didn't."

As dusk settled around them, and the adrenaline left her system, she felt a yawn coming on and stifled it. But another one overtook her seconds later, hitting full force.

"I've got a thought," she said to Heron as they returned to the battle-scarred SUV. "I have to pick up another set of wheels from the fleet. It's a half hour from here. After that, my house isn't far. We can get some food. I've got a pull-out couch. Unless you want me to drop you at a hotel."

He didn't hesitate. "No, your place is good."

Five minutes later she pulled out her buzzing mobile and looked at the screen. "Torres texted. Garage is clear. No males in camo. No long guns."

Heron opened his mouth to say something, but she preempted. "I understand he can change clothes. I understand he can put his gun in a trunk. I'm going home. You coming with me?"

After a last glance toward the garage, he said, "Yes." They climbed into the Suburban. Together they surveyed the fire escape where Renault Davide had died. The Medical Examiner's van was pulling away.

Carmen said softly, "Heron?"

"I go to Dodgers games. See them a half dozen times a year. And I always get a hot dog when I'm there. I love those hot dogs. But I don't want to know how they're made."

Their eyes met, and she willed him to understand. "The stuff you and Aruba do is right on the line. Or maybe over it a little. What we were talking about before—information that'll lead us to him. Not information to use at trial. Get it. However you need to. Just don't tell me how you did it."

After a moment he said, "Dodgers. That's baseball, right?"

She laughed. "Yeah, Heron. It's baseball."

She fired up the big engine, slammed the Chevy into gear and skidded away from the scene.

CHAPTER 40

FeAR-15—a.k.a. Tristan Kane—absolutely *loved* first-person shooter games.

Call of Duty, Left 4 Dead 2, Halo and of course the foundational FPS, *Doom*, thirty years old and still holding its own. His favorite was *Grand Theft Auto*, where you got points for killing innocent people—and doing so in any number of ways, from the weapon-choice wheel.

Earlier this morning he'd burned two women to death, blown up a police chopper with an RPG, driven over a prostitute, then backed over her once more just to make sure, and machine-gunned down dozens of patrons and dancers in a strip club.

A delightful diversion.

Now he sat at his basement computer station in the Anaheim house, staring at the central, the biggest, monitor. Thinking: Move. It. Along . . .

He was bored and craved action.

Then as if obeying his request, the limousine appeared, driving north on Hidalgo Street, in Guadalajara.

FeAR leaned forward and typed on the keyboard. He could hit 130 words a minute with zero mistakes.

He sipped his Sleepytime herbal tea. Most hackers chugged Red Bull or Mountain Dew for the jolt. The latter soft drink did not, in fact, contain much more caffeine than any other leading brand. If you needed to stay awake during a marathon coding session, you took serious stimulants. Well, some did. FeAR-15 didn't partake. Coding and hacking provided all the excitement he needed.

On the screen, three motorcycle riders pulled alongside the limo and fired HK MP5 submachine guns into it.

Shards of glass, chunks of metal and a plume of blood sprayed from the shattered window.

Beautiful.

The action FeAR was observing was not, however, occurring in an FPS game. The execution was real, unfolding in real time.

Real bullets, ending real lives.

This was the culmination of a contract he'd had with a cartel. He'd been paid to find a choke point where they could take out a rival dealer. FeAR had hacked together a vehicle-recognition program, which had just successfully geotagged Señor Ortega's clearly nonbulletproof limousine. And sent his route, easily hacked from the car's navigation system, to the gunmen.

Success all around.

Even better than crushing prostitutes under your Furore GT.

Now back to the job at hand.

Spider-Clown's murder of the chef in Irvine.

The job had been completed, but there was a security cam across the street from Davide's. He wanted to see how the investigation was proceeding and to identify the lead detectives. The pictures Fallow had taken on his phone outside Alex Georgio's house in Moreno Valley had been too grainy for his facial-recognition software.

These images were much better. He studied them closely.

Clearly the Latina female with the long dark hair was in charge.

He captured her image and uploaded it.

Every human face has eighty landmarks, or nodal points. Things like distance between the eyes, cheekbone structure, dimensions of the jaw. FR software notes these and creates numeric code based on the sub-millimeter scale using 3D imaging. This yields a close approximation to the face, but the icing on the cake is the surface-tension skin-analysis algorithm, which produces a facial-rec image as unique as a fingerprint, but better. A fingerprint can only be matched using a database. Conversely, a facial-rec image can be compared to a massive bank of photos harvested from government and commercial records . . . and, of course the best—and most horrifying—invention of all time, the internet.

FeAR-15 ran the woman's image through a dataset containing sixty-two million faces.

His system labored away, flashing periodic progress reports on the screen.

Detection.
Alignment.
Measurement.
Matching.
Verification.

A pause as the cursor winked a dozen times.

Then out came the answer.

She was Carmen Sanchez, an agent with DHS' criminal operation, Homeland Security Investigations. FeAR sent a bot to scavenge more information about her.

Why a *federal* agent on a state homicide case?

He was about to log off and play some *Halo 2*, when he froze.

A figure had stepped out of the restaurant and walked to Agent Sanchez. FeAR studied him closely.

Was it possible?

Another capture, another facial-rec request.

99.978% match: Jacoby Heron, PhD, 449 W. San Miguel Ave., Berkeley, CA. 94702.

He now knew which 1337, which *elite* hacker, had broken the code he'd installed in Spider-Clown's phone.

And FeAR-15 couldn't help but recall the text he'd sent to Professor Jacoby Heron four years earlier:

Game on . . .

CHAPTER 41

Jake gripped the dashboard as Sanchez goosed her replacement car—a Homeland Security pool Dodge Charger Hemi—onto the Southern California beach town street.

She cut him a look. "You going to puke for real this time?"

"Happen to have any Dramamine?" he managed.

She made another turn and he saw her right hand automatically dip briefly toward the shifter. She liked manual transmissions, probably preferred to an automatic like this car featured.

As they continued west, Sanchez seemed to remember she wasn't in a car chase pursuit of Spider any longer and eased off the gas. A little.

The neighborhood was like a thousand other California coastal towns from LA down to San Diego. Old communities with an identifiable style, though not stamped from developers' cookie cutters. To Jake, an urban dweller whose ceiling was somebody else's floor, *any* stand-alone dwelling was both appealing and had a nearly supernatural quality about it.

Sanchez pulled into a driveway, brakes squealing, and parked behind a hard-driven white Jeep Wrangler. He could only imagine what she did with an off-road vehicle.

In Moreno Valley, she'd left him standing in an acrid cloud of smoke from scorched rubber, tires screeching as she roared off in pursuit of Spider. She'd steered the Suburban with a deft and sure touch, not easy considering the vehicle handled like a whale.

He climbed out and surveyed the property, which was covered with a wide variety of foliage. "You've got everything. Catalina cherry, Mexican blue palm, cypress, paloverde, bishop pine, desert rose, scrub oak, deer grass, sycamore . . ."

The list went on.

She laughed. "Heron, you sit in a dark room and hack for fifteen hours a day."

"Usually twelve. I'm slowing down."

"How do you know about plants?"

"Physical pen testing. First step . . ."

She nodded. "Surveillance."

"You get as close as possible to the facility. Can't very well army-crawl over asphalt without being seen. Somebody will pick you up with glass or on radar. Instead, you move through the densest foliage you can find. Need to know what makes noise and what doesn't. The poisonous ones too." Another appraisal of the yard.

"I remember what you told me at Georgio's. You'd cut all this back, right?"

"To the property line. A little over if you can get away with it. You want to be able to see them coming, Sanchez."

"I'll take my chances." She worked the two dead bolts and a single keypad lock to open the door.

Once inside, she entered the alarm code.

Ten digits.

She knew her way around security, though he made a note to buy her a present—one of the nearly unpickable chain locks he had on all his doors.

Sanchez flicked the light on, revealing an orderly, sparse living room with comfortable, if mismatched, furniture. Mission-style oak-and-green-leather chairs, a glass-topped end table and a French provincial one with carved feet at the bottoms of the legs, the long black leather pull out couch that would be his bed, a marble-topped coffee table.

The house had two bedrooms. The one to the left as you entered was Sanchez's. She pointed to the other one. "If you want to wash up."

She walked into her room, tugging off her jacket and body armor. Before he turned away, he noted her T-shirt had risen and he could see a shiny scar on her back. He knew enough about injuries to recognize it as an exit wound. He understood that abdominal wounds were among the most painful and deadly of gunshot injuries.

She glanced back and saw him looking. "You should see the other guy."

She turned away and pulled off the T, revealing a black sports bra, before she kicked the door farther, but not all the way, closed.

Was she flirting?

Of course not.

Jake stepped into the guest bedroom, currently in use as an office and storage area. The small space had no sleeping apparatus. He dug through his gear bag and extracted clean jeans, underwear, socks and a black T. He took a fast shower, dressed and returned to the living room.

He walked to the mantel, where two dozen family photos sat in frames. His eyes rested on a picture of Sanchez with a ruggedly handsome man. They were at a shooting range, both wearing olive drab fatigues. They had been caught unawares by the photographer but had turned his way and seemed to have quickly slipped smiles on their faces.

Sanchez walked into the living room, wearing blue jeans and a Lakers sweatshirt. She continued into the kitchen.

Jake peered through the pass-through in the wall and found himself looking at a butcher block with ten black-handled knives.

He was thinking of the chef Spider had murdered. The Crime Scene tech had mentioned a missing knife.

The chef had been suffocated, not stabbed, so why had Spider taken it, which they assumed he had done?

What was next on his gruesome agenda?

Sanchez was foraging in the refrigerator, which wasn't nearly as empty as his. Jake believed he'd cooked a meal two years ago but couldn't swear to it. Sanchez, on the other hand, had dozens of appliances and implements and two overburdened spice racks. He recalled her giving the server expert directions on browning the crème brûlée she'd ordered for Selina at the Eiffel Tower Inn.

"I've got turkey, tamales, chorizo, peppers that aren't psychedelically hot. Then fresh tortillas from a local mercado, jicama slaw—no, scratch that. Just checked the date." She chucked it in the trash. "And chardonnay. Not oaked."

The "oak" part must have been important for her to mention it. Not a drinker, he recalled relying on his brother to recommend a brand of champagne for that Christmas Eve celebration with Rudy and Julia that had never occurred.

Moët . . .

Odd the memory came back, but even stranger: he was jolted to find that after their heart-to-heart, the sting was gone when he thought of that Christmas Eve.

She opened the screw-top bottle and poured.

He sipped. Good. Sweet and rich.

Sanchez assembled a platter. "Let's do the patio."

He helped her carry the food, plates, glasses and utensils out onto a flagstone semicircle with a black wrought iron dining set. She switched on white-and-yellow Christmas lights strung from trellises and scrub oak.

They sat and filled their plates from the dark red serving dishes and ate.

He looked around. "You've got twice as much property as the other homes here. Why don't you expand the house?"

"Because that lot's not mine. It's an encyclopedia lot."

He lifted a brow.

"Decades ago, nobody thought this part of the state was worth anything. Thirty miles from LA? Now, it's an easy commute. Then it was a trek. The Encyclopedia Americana gave away Huntington Beach parcels with the purchase of a set of the volumes. There were five or six hundred of them."

She flicked a glance at the overgrown lot beside her. "That's owned by somebody in Iowa or New Jersey who doesn't even know it exists. Lucky for a privacy freak like me. Oh, and that was my ex, by the way."

She'd seen him looking at the picture on the mantel.

"We weren't together that long."

He sipped.

"You going to ask me what happened?"

"Not my business."

It wasn't.

On the other hand, he *was* curious.

"What's the opposite of intrusion?" She wrapped turkey and salsa and a green pepper in a flour tortilla and took a robust bite.

"Opposite? There are two. First, entities or people entering your life in a positive way. My definition of 'intrusion' is negative. A harmful or unwanted incursion into somebody's space. But companies merge successfully, peace accords are signed, mentors help their protégés, people become lovers. I call those 'alliances,' not intrusions." Another taste of the wine. "The second opposite of intrusion is indifference."

She considered this for a moment. "You don't get intruded on because nobody cares enough to intrude on you."

"That's it."

Her knowing expression suggested *this* was what the marriage had devolved into.

But who had ignored whom?

They finished the meal and took the plates inside. She filled the dishwasher while Jake walked into the living room to view the other pictures on the mantel. The Sanchez family. It was easy to deduce the cast: her mother was a striking woman with long hair—black in the earlier pictures and silver in the later. Then some images revealed her gaunt face beneath a head wrap with a few wisps of gray poking out from underneath. In all of them she was beside a distinguished-looking man, often in a suit.

Of all the qualities that Sanchez's father radiated, confidence was the most visible, followed by adoration, when his gaze was focused not on the lens but on his wife or daughters.

Several photos were of the family outside a church—the girls and their mother with a kerchief or scarf covering their heads. A smiling priest stood in the center.

Some shots featured only the sisters. In playgrounds, at the beach, dressed in stunning gowns at their respective quinceañeras. There were a few of the sisters and their father alone, smiling in a listless way and looking diminished—after Sanchez's mother had died, presumably. There were a few of the girls together, several years old. The only recent ones were Sanchez with some women friends at a resort on a beach, and a few of Selina alone. They appeared to be downloaded from the internet. He assumed Sanchez had sent them out for printing and framing. A sad effort of a reminder of her sibling.

Sanchez joined him, cradling a wineglass and the bottle. She topped them both off and sat on the couch.

Jake picked up a clipping, presumably soon to be framed—an article about Selina from the local edition of the major daily, the *Los Angeles Herald*. Selina had won a gymnastics competition recently. The story described how she was so talented that she won both athletic and academic scholarships at her college.

He turned and noted Sanchez's eyes, cast with sadness, reading the article too.

Jake sat in a recliner across from the sofa. "We were interrupted by those two assholes shooting at us." He nodded toward the article of her sister, drawing her attention back to their previous discussion.

"Oh, Selina and me. You want to know why the room temperature drops about fifty degrees when we're together?"

He lifted his hand, the universal sign meaning "Only if you're comfortable."

Apparently she was.

CHAPTER 42

Jake Heron was careful not to intrude here.

He waited, silent, as Sanchez seemed to steel herself before speaking.

"Our father was an investment adviser."

She sipped more wine, then eased back onto the couch, gripping the glass with both hands, as if it were a life preserver.

"Wasn't in a big firm, just a two-person partnership handling work for families mostly. A lot of them were friends. He was successful, worked hard. Studied the markets, but then he made some bad investments for clients. No wrongdoing, no Bernie Madoff scenario. And nothing dicey like crypto. He thought a particular fund would skyrocket. But it tanked. A half dozen families lost their life savings. He was devastated. He would have covered the losses himself, but he didn't have that kind of money."

She took a deep breath. "About two weeks after the fund went belly-up, he left a note saying how sorry he was and what a failure he'd been, and he killed himself. Jumped out of his office window."

"I'm sorry. So *that's* what Selina meant about not forgiving him. She feels he abandoned both of you."

"And even worse, it was two days before her seventeenth birthday." Her voice caught. "We were both devastated. But I understood. An aging widower, who'd ruined a half dozen lives, choosing not to live with the sorrow. I forgave him. Maybe because I've investigated similar cases and learned to put myself in the mindset of someone desperate enough to take their own life."

"But your sister didn't have your life experience," he said gently. "She was young."

"I tried to help her understand. Reminded her how Dad was never the same after Mom died. I hoped it would make her feel better, but she saw it as confirmation of his selfishness. He only cared about his own pain, not ours."

Sanchez's wineglass came in for a landing on the coffee table.

After a lengthy moment during which only the placid ocean—maybe two or three blocks away—could be heard, he said, "You know what I see?"

"What?"

"The first kind of opposite? Alliance. It can morph, change colors like a chameleon. Sometimes it turns into intrusion—that's her anger against you. But it can swing back the other way. That happens a lot. I'd give it some time."

She smiled. "My God, Heron, you're a hacker, trespasser, pen tester *and* headshrinker."

He rose, poured himself some more wine and looked at a picture of the sisters together, posing in front of a Mesoamerican step pyramid. They were hugging and their faces beamed with broad smiles.

Jake turned back to see Sanchez on her side, head on the pillow—*his* pillow—breathing deeply, eyes closed.

Smiling to himself, he unfolded one of the blankets she'd brought out for him, and covered her. He then walked into her room, where he started for her bed and stopped. It was perfectly made and topped with a half dozen carefully arranged decorative pillows.

No.

The security specialist then walked to the alarm panel, hit the ARM button for the windows and doors. Noting where Sanchez had stowed her weapon—the top shelf of the coat closet by the front door—he made a circuit of the house and peered out each pane of glass. He saw no threats, nothing out of the ordinary.

In the living room he found a commemorative throw pillow and picked it up. An embroidered likeness of a white-stone step pyramid set against a blue sky graced the front. The words "Chichén Itzá" and "Hecho en México" were neatly stitched beneath the structure. He recalled the photo of teenaged Carmen, who had obviously kept a souvenir of her family vacation to visit one of the architectural wonders of the world.

He returned to the overstuffed chair and reclined it as far as it would go before covering himself with a blanket. He was soon asleep, his head resting on the back side of the colorful pillow, taking care not to provoke the wrath of any Mesoamerican gods.

CHAPTER 43

Sometimes things didn't go as expected.

Dennison Fallow had begun the busy day with a memory of Charlie Benedict, the compulsive behavior specialist, who was devoted to saving his patients.

Or die trying . . .

And now, near midnight, lying on the futon in his basement bedroom of the Anaheim house, kneading the leg that still ached from the bitch Selina's attack, he was thinking of the man once again.

He looked up to see Macbeth hard at work in the corner, building a web. He was a spider in the *Uloboridae* family, so the construction was triangular, like a pizza slice. Ophelia, a nursery web spider, was carrying her loosely wrapped egg sac in her mouth. The name gave her story away. She would create a web to be the brood's nursery and would stand guard for a week after they made their appearance, through their post-hatch molt.

A cobweb spider named King Lear, family *Theridiidae*, busied himself in another corner. His webs weren't elegant. They were messy tangles designed not for shelter but to catch prey. Black widows are in this family and make the same sort of web, but Lear wasn't one of those. He was a *Parasteatoda tepidariorum*, a common house spider. Harmless to humans. As are 99.999999 percent, and then some, of all arachnids.

Then there's the brown recluse.

If the Push, which Mr. Benedict had been so determined to deal with, were a spider, it would be a recluse.

The creature was in the family *Sicariidae*, from the Latin word for "assassin." Six-eyed and small, they were armed with a tissue-destroying venom otherwise seen only in dangerous dermonecrotic bacteria. Of all the spiders on Earth, only brown recluses and black widows were considered "medically significant." The impressive tarantula? Mostly it just tickles when it strolls over your arm.

The recluse's initial bite was painless, but soon the venom began to eat away the skin, leaving excruciating sunken lesions, like shallow wells. Sometimes bites led to sepsis, gas gangrene, kidney failure, coma and, occasionally, death.

The assassin spider . . .

By the time people realized they'd been bitten by a brown recluse, the toxin was already inside the body, attacking the blood cells and internal organs.

There is no known antidote for a recluse bite. Doctors can only treat symptoms and make referrals to cosmetic surgeons to repair the terrible scarring.

Or watch their patients die agonizing deaths.

Bites often occur because brown recluses are small, drably colored, and easily missed in their favorite hiding places—people's clothing.

But they aren't native to California. In fact, they're never seen here.

And that, Dennison Fallow thought, was just a shame.

The Push . . .

Mr. Benedict's regimen for his patient hadn't worked out quite as Fallow had expected.

The hunting trips had satisfied the Push.

Until they didn't.

Until they had the *opposite* effect.

And it was no longer enough to aim at a deer's shoulder and let the gun fire itself under the soft pressure of the trigger.

The Push demanded more.

A memory came to mind.

The shore of Lake Mathews, a hot afternoon four years ago.

Charlie Benedict was gazing across the expanse of the glittery water that was so appealing yet strictly off limits, even for waders. But Mr. Benedict explained that he came here often and knew how to avoid the guards.

Fallow was at the SUV outside the cut section of the chain-link fence. He was quietly honing the knife he'd used to dress his first deer a month earlier.

He was reflecting on just how Mr. Benedict's treatments worked out.

To use his own analogy, the man managed to turn a methadone cure into . . . a raging heroin addiction.

The Push was back and stronger than ever. The hunting trips had merely made the Push hungrier.

It consumed his soul.

Gripping the knife firmly, Fallow had walked up behind Mr. Benedict, whose eyes remained on the water.

And then . . .

That memory faded as Ophelia, the nursery spider, scurried across her web, drawing him from his reverie. His eyes grew heavy as he looked on while she tucked her egg sac into the gossamer strands.

In his basement, under the watch of several resourceful spiders, Dennison Fallow dozed off, sinking back into the memory of that day at the lake, and the blood and screams and thrashing of limbs that grew more and more still under the piercing and slashing.

In just a few minutes, picturing the body lying face up, dead eyes staring at a bright sun, Dennison Fallow slipped into a peaceful sleep.

IV
THURSDAY

CHAPTER 44

Carmen thrashed and struggled inside the spider's web, desperate to escape from the sticky threads.

Completely immobilized, she sensed the approach of the monster that had spun the trap, drawing ever closer. A warning buzzer began to blare, sending her hammering heart into overdrive.

Her eyes flew open, and she realized the buzzing had come from her cell phone's alarm, set to awaken her at six thirty every morning—though occasionally the same alarm had reminded her to *get* to bed at that same time for some sleep, if she'd been up all night wrestling with a difficult case.

Years of being on call had accustomed her to instant alertness upon waking. Heron, on the other hand, had probably not been rousted from sleep very often in his ivory tower. He squinted and groaned. Then lurched from the recliner where he'd apparently spent the night and looked around, orienting himself and scanning for threats, it seemed.

Oh, that's right, she recalled. He wasn't just a professor. He also made a living army-crawling toward government facilities and assessing risks.

And spotting men in green fatigues holding long guns.

Requiring him to tackle her . . .

She pushed the memory aside.

"Morning," she said and shut the alarm off.

He grunted once more.

"Coffee?"

"Please."

She rose and made two Keurig cups. She dumped sugar into hers, remembered to stir—she often forgot—and left his black.

She carried them into the living room, where Heron was stretching and wincing. The chair must've been torture. Why hadn't he slept in her bed?

"Hungry?"

"I could eat, if you are."

"Business first." She opened her computer and logged on. "Got an email from Captain Torres." She read the message in silence.

"Care to share?" Heron prompted.

She summarized. The Crime Scene techs discovered a booklet taped to the chef's body after they cut it down. It was a book Davide had written, titled *La Belle Cuisine et La Belle Table*. It was about food plating, the art of displaying a meal. Forensic analysis had revealed no trace evidence on the booklet itself.

"He always leaves a token," Heron said when she finished. "The shovel with Kemp, the rope with Selina."

"I couldn't figure out why Spider didn't do what we *thought* he did—stab Davide to death and butcher him. So I asked Mouse to find out if binding and hanging upside down is a documented COD. That's—"

"Cause of death. Got it."

"She found mentions during the Inquisition, but you know where it's most common?"

He shook his head and massaged his neck.

"Spiders."

"Interesting."

"Here's what Declan found. 'Spiders in the *Uloboridae* family have a hunting style that's unique among arachnids. They don't have venom, so they catch prey with their silk, then wrap it tighter and tighter and hang it. They pierce the body with a tubelike structure, dissolve the interior with digestive fluids and suck it out.'"

Heron grimaced. "Think I'll pass on breakfast."

She couldn't resist needling him. "You sure? I make a mean soft-boiled egg."

"Maybe later. So he took a victim who prepared food for a living—and then Spider prepared him like a meal. That's a pretty sick joke."

The thought hit her with the force of a physical blow. "No, it's not a joke, Heron. The tokens are messages. This is part of the PPIs."

He caught her enthusiasm. "There must be something about the victims' lives that's motivating him to kill. What's in your notes about Kemp and Selina?"

She found her notebook and opened it. "This is from Kemp's son, Michael. *'Semiretired. No stalkers. Kemp didn't post much. Famous developer. Lately made news for doing urban renewal and environmentally friendly projects.'* You thinking what I am, Heron?"

Apparently he was, because he stood and picked up the framed article about Selina from the mantel. "This was published two weeks ago. Kemp was written up too, his son said. Google 'Kemp, affordable housing, environment.'"

She did and read the results of her online search. "He's featured in last week's *Los Angeles Herald*. And Renault Davide. In the restaurant, there were some articles about him too. Mounted on his wall."

It took only seconds for related keywords to bear fruit. "The Orange County edition of the *Herald*. A feature about his rise to the top, part of a series on business success stories. I think that's it, Heron. His victims are people who've been successful."

"And murdering them in a way that relates to their success. The PPIs are coming together. He's using the *Herald* to find them. The next victim will be in the paper somewhere. Written up in the past couple of weeks, probably."

"I'll get Mouse and Declan on the job." She typed the request and sent it off.

Her doorbell chimed, startling both of them. She tapped an icon on the phone still in her hand and a view of the front porch came up. "Delivery. A package I ordered."

Their eyes met and she knew he was thinking about that Christmas Eve when she had pretended to be with a wine delivery company to get access to Heron's building for the takedown.

The moment of tension dissolved, and they both laughed. Then, rising, she cocked her head. "That necklace, the gold computer chip? I saw your niece's picture in your office. She was holding it up."

"Julia." His smile was wistful. "She sent that photo to me when I was at Club Fed. My brother, Rudy, found it in my office after your Crime Scene people left."

"She'd have graduated by now."

"Valedictorian." He seemed immensely proud of her.

Carmen asked, "Was her commencement speech about privacy?"

He laughed. "No. She had a double major. Art and cybersecurity. She talked about Georgia O'Keeffe."

She walked to the door and retrieved the parcel, then brought it inside and handed it to Heron.

"What's this?"

"A present."

"You shouldn't have."

"Yeah." She slid him a smile. "I really should."

CHAPTER 45

Tanya Hilton was terrified.

Her fear was an omnipresent force that invaded her mind constantly. Like it did now, as her feet pounded on the treadmill, its odd whirring sound reminding her of human breath.

An overwhelming sense of dread kept her awake at night, discussing the matter with Mr. Alonzo, who really didn't care one bit but at least *appeared* to listen. His purring gave the semblance of sympathy, and was, in fact, more of a response than she got from some men she'd dated.

Her big fear was this: That the rest of the world—including her friends and family, especially her hypercritical mother—would come to realize what Tanya knew in her heart. That the twenty-eight-year-old SoCal girl, bottle-blonde and bubbly, was a complete fraud.

Someday everyone would see through her act and say, "Phony. You can't trick us anymore. Pay back the money. We're not falling for it."

When the doubts hit, Tanya came to her club and ran.

The treadmill's whizzing breath exhaled faster, as she pressed the up arrow on the control panel.

She looked around, pleased to find the spotless place nearly empty. At this time of day, midmorning, there was just one other jogger.

She'd been lucky to get where she was. True. But she also worked hard as hell on her website and blog, *TheNew-U*, to do some good for people. In fact, she sometimes joked she worked her ass off—because that's exactly what the site was devoted to: losing weight.

No matter her success, insecurity plagued her, and Tanya Hilton believed in her heart she didn't deserve the half million dollars she'd made by giving advice cobbled together from various fitness resources. Generic advice anyone could find for themselves.

TheNew-U diet was absurdly simple: you counted calories and allowed yourself X number per day depending on your weight and your goal. You did not deviate from that number.

No cheat days. No "poor me, I've dieted all week and deserve a steak dinner, loaded potatoes and a hot fudge sundae."

How simple was that?

Her blog, podcast and YouTube channel had taken off. The audience loved the easy-to-follow advice and her boot camp delivery. The story of a five-foot-tall Barbie look-alike talking about calorie counts and her own journey resonated with people. Lots of people. They—

Wait . . . What was that?

A shadow from the corridor that led to a part of the gym she'd believed was locked—some old, deserted rooms used for Pilates, which had fallen out of favor here.

A shadow.

Tanya was paranoid about something else too.

Her fame, such as it was, brought with it risks.

Too much attention. The possibility of stalkers.

Especially after she was written up in the newspaper—an article on the top influencers of the year.

The word had stunned her. She'd always thought of influencers as eighteen-year-old girls selling a particular brand of makeup to other eighteen-year-old girls, who didn't know that all makeup was identical.

But "influencer" she was to the newspaper, and that meant to the public.

Including some visitors to her site, who were clearly interested in something other than losing weight.

She quickened her pace yet again, thud, thud, thud . . .

The shadow again, somebody hovering just out of sight in that corridor, which was about thirty feet away.

But then she laughed.

The shadow turned out to be a club attendant, a tall well-built guy collecting discarded towels. Most members tossed their used ones in the hamper. But some were pigs. They left them lying around on machines or dropped them on the floor.

See, nothing to worry about.

She finished the run and made a show of placing her towels in the hamper.

The attendant smiled at her courtesy. She nodded.

"You need more?" he asked.

"Thanks."

Tanya, currently unattached and always alert to possible dating material, assessed the attendant with a practiced eye. Not a bad-looking man, in even better shape than she'd thought at first, with a nice smile.

She took the pair of clean towels he offered, studying his thick red hair and bright-green eyes.

He rolled the container with the dirty towels away.

Now, a swim.

She walked through the double doors into the room that held the Olympic-size pool and was assaulted by the odor of chlorine. She set the towels and her phone on the floor near one of the plastic loungers along the deck.

Thirty, forty laps and she'd be done.

And as always happened, the insecurity and doubt would have been deflated, thanks to the exercise.

Then back to her home webcast studio, coffee with skim milk, one piece of whole wheat toast and two scoops of peanut butter. And, of course, the purr-meister Mr. Alonzo.

CHAPTER 46

Fallow thought the Del Aire health club attendant's uniform was a little silly.

The cargo shorts had roomy side pockets, but also showcased his pale, though muscular, legs. The shirt was kind of blousy for him. He liked his clothes fitted. And it seemed odd for an attendant to wear a long-sleeved shirt. Unfortunately there had been a few newscasts warning the public about the killer with a spider tatt on his wrist. So he had to keep it hidden.

But the outfit served its purpose. Tanya Hilton had bought his identity 100 percent. To her, he was a gym employee. Part of the woodwork. Invisible.

He now carried a stack of towels into the pool area.

No one had seen him at the chef's murder scene in Irvine, so he still looked the Irishman with red hair and green eyes.

He watched Tanya in her white one-piece suit, platinum hair in a ponytail, dive into the water and swim freestyle to the far end. One other woman was present too, doing laps on the opposite side.

While Tanya and the second swimmer were facing away, Fallow plucked her phone from her towel and walked quickly to the pool's edge to dunk it. He put it back where she'd left it, scooping some pool water around the device.

He tried to turn it on.

Nothing. It had shorted out.

She'd think, Oh hell, I must've splashed it when I jumped in.

Paying no attention to the swimmers, he carried another stack of towels to the corridor that led to the women's locker room. This was a variation of the rule that nobody paid attention to someone in a safety vest carrying a clipboard.

It hadn't been easy to find a scenario where Tanya would be alone and accessible. FeAR had used his formidable skills to find out the mini-internet celebrity lived in a concierge building and had several dead bolts on her door—which Fallow didn't have the skill to pick—and a real-time security camera monitoring service.

But the hacker had also learned about the club.

Spider tossed the towels into a bin and walked up the corridor to the storeroom halfway between the pool and the women's locker room. Here, he changed from the attendant's outfit back into his street clothes.

He removed from his pocket an object wrapped in paper towels. It was the eight-inch filleting knife he'd taken from Renault Davide's restaurant. A weapon from one murder that he would leave behind at the next, linking the two crimes.

Tanya's death would be the same as the other victims—something to do with an aspect of their lives. But in her case, it would be particularly appropriate.

The idea for her demise had been inspired by the book he'd read and reread as a boy, locked in the basement. His only entertainment during his imprisonment was a worn volume: *The Complete Works of William Shakespeare.*

Tough going at first but, once he'd gotten used to the language, the stories in the plays kicked ass. Some more than others. *The Merchant of Venice* was his least favorite. He didn't like the way the playwright portrayed the main character, but he'd been fascinated by the grisly plot. If a borrower didn't repay a loan, the lender could take payment in the form of a pound of flesh carved from any part of the body of his choosing.

And he happened to be in possession of a knife made for that express purpose.

The weight-loss guru was about to cut a few pounds.

CHAPTER 47

Jake had left the Bay Area so quickly for the flight to San Diego he'd forgotten his hairbrush. He caught sight of himself in the mirror and finger-combed his unkempt locks into some semblance of order.

Sanchez was only slightly better put together than he was. He didn't think he'd ever seen her fuss over her appearance.

She certainly hadn't that Christmas Eve.

He finished cleaning up in the guest room and returned to the coffee table, where she was online, plowing through the *Los Angeles Herald* digital edition. She shook her head. "Successful people written up in the past two weeks? Only about two hundred of them. And that's just lifestyle stories. If we expand to hard news, the list is endless. Mouse and Declan? No luck either."

She sat back. "We need something else. Another element for the PPI . . ." She shook her head. "I'm thinking of the serial actors we studied at Quantico. Ted Bundy, John Wayne Gacy, Jeffrey Dahmer, Gary Ridgway, Mikhail Popkov—the Russian who killed over eighty. And Pedro López and Luis Garavito . . . South Americans. Together, their body count was over six hundred."

"Seriously?"

"Probably more," she went on. "Different brand of justice down there. At first Garavito was sentenced to eighteen hundred years in prison. It was reduced to twenty-two when he agreed to tell the authorities where the bodies were. He may already be eligible for parole." She ended the morbid tally. "More coffee?"

"Definitely."

She asked, "They make Red Bull coffee?"

"I don't think so. But there's definitely a market."

She stood and walked to the kitchen, returning with two cups. Her cup was halfway to her lips when she froze. "Geography," she muttered.

He sipped the refreshed coffee. "Go ahead."

"Those killers I mentioned fall into two categories based on where they pick their targets. One is transitory, traveling to find their victims. The other is place specific, sticking close to home. Ted Bundy was the first type. Ridgway was the second."

He considered this. "Then Spider's a combination. Southern California, but no single town. San Diego to Perris to Irvine."

"What do those cities have in common?" She began to pace.

"Looking for details for a PPI?"

A nod. "I took a course on geographical profiling at Quantico. Investigators do a lot of work with interactive maps and satellites."

"Good. Keep talking." He grabbed his laptop and opened Google Earth.

She pointed a long, slim finger at each of the locations in turn. "San Diego, Perris, Irvine." Then closed her eyes. "Oh, shit, Heron."

"What?"

"Focus on the names of the cities." She gestured at the screen. "Take another look at them . . . in the order of the crimes."

And then he saw it too. "S-P-I. He's spelling his damn nickname. There's our Point of Potential Intrusion! The next victim will be in a 'D' city." He glanced back at the screen. "Plenty of 'Dels' and 'Deserts.'"

She said, "Some 'Diablos' too. Now that we're getting to know him, that sounds like the sort of joke he'd go for."

"I don't know how funny he is, modeling his MO on arachnids who dissolve their prey from the inside out."

"We need some help on this one." She tapped the speed dial for Mouse.

"Hey, Carmen."

"On speaker with Heron. Fast search. *LA Herald* last two weeks. Lifestyle profiles of successful people who live in a town starting with the letter 'D.'"

"The Spider case?"

"Yes. And we have to assume he's already got somebody in his sights."

"I'll get Declan on it. Stay on the line."

Jake heard her reciting instructions to her assistant, whom he pictured as an eager and tireless young intern—assuming, for no particular reason, he was pale and skinny, with Coke-bottle glasses.

"Borrow yours?" Sanchez held out her free hand, and he unlocked his phone with his thumbprint and seven-digit PIN and handed it to her.

She placed a call.

Jake couldn't hear more than a faint responding voice, but it was clear the person on the other end was someone with Highway Patrol, and Sanchez was explaining that the serial killer going by "Spider" might strike somewhere in the Southern California area soon.

Her face revealed relief at what was obviously good news, probably that she wouldn't have to fight for tactical officers.

Jake was getting quite the lesson in interagency politics on this case.

She disconnected and handed him back the unit.

"Of course," she muttered, "that assumes we can find—"

"Got a possibility." Mouse's voice rattled from the speaker. "Declan got three hits. Two of them are out of town and won't be back for at least a week. Not sure about the other one, but you can give it a shot. In Del Aire. An influencer. She has a weight-loss blog and website. Got written up in the *Herald* as a rags-to-riches success story. Tanya Hilton, 2248 Beach View Drive, Unit 4C."

"Heron, call Tanya to warn her," Sanchez said to him. "I'll get deputies started to her place."

While he worked his cell phone, Sanchez disconnected and called back the CHP officer to arrange for their units and local PD to get to Tanya's address immediately.

The woman's phone was unlisted but that was a minor speed bump for Jake. Ten seconds later he was making the call.

"Hello, you've reached . . ."

He waited through the recording and left a message. "Tanya Hilton, I'm calling from the Department of Homeland Security. We think your life may be in danger. When you get this, call 9-1-1. If you're home, lock your doors. If you're out, get to the nearest police station. And—"

Sanchez began, "Tell her to—"

Just as Jake added, "Stay around people."

"Just what I was going to say. You're thinking like a cop, Heron." The ghost of a smile played across her face. "Now let's move."

CHAPTER 48

In the storeroom of Del Aire Health and Fitness, Fallow set the chef's filleting knife on a table and extracted the Leatherman multitool from his pocket. He opened one of the blades and began making a peephole in the Sheetrock to give him a view of the hallway Tanya Hilton would walk through at any minute.

The largest of the blades bored through the drywall easily. The device was quite amazing. There were nineteen different tools on it—an awl, scissors, file, screwdrivers . . . helpful in getting access to victims, removing lock plates and stripping electric wires, for instance.

But the Leatherman was much more to Fallow than a practical implement in his avocation. It had great sentimental value to him—a person who felt very little sentiment.

He thought back to that hot Saturday afternoon when he and Mr. Benedict were on the shoreline of Lake Mathews in Riverside County.

Mr. Benedict, looking out over the water.

Fallow, gripping the deer-dressing knife.

And the Push, alive and strong.

Methadone becoming heroin.

He had walked up behind Mr. Benedict and stopped.

Mr. Benedict asked, "Are you ready, Dennison?"

"I am."

Mr. Benedict stepped aside, revealing a man in his forties, in jeans and a work shirt, light blue with sweat stains under the arms. Thick strips of duct tape bound his hands and feet and covered his mouth.

"Go ahead. Watch him. I want you to watch."

As the man screamed to the extent he could scream and thrashed to the extent he could thrash, Fallow grasped a hank of his hair and pulled his head back. He wanted to do this right, as Mr. Benedict had taught him. Bracing himself, he plunged the blade into the side of the man's neck just below his left ear and quickly drew his arm sideways, slitting the throat.

And then more slashing and stabbing.

Muted gurgles, jerky spasms and blood everywhere, everywhere, everywhere . . . spewing in rhythmic spurts from the arterial bleed.

When it was done, he and Mr. Benedict tidied up, wrapping the man in chicken wire and affixing cinder blocks to it. Then they rolled him into the lake. After that they scooped up water with paper cups and rinsed the blood off the rocks.

"Let me ask you a question, Dennison."

"Sure."

"How do you feel?"

He didn't recall anyone asking him that question in a way that suggested they really cared—not like the shrinks and counselors would ask, as a formality at the start of a session.

He thought hard. It was important to describe to Mr. Benedict *exactly* how he felt.

"I guess comfortable," he replied. "At peace."

"I was hoping that was the word you'd use. You got close a couple of the times we'd been together. Shooting the deer, skinning them. The elk. But there was something missing."

"That's right," he said. "I wasn't really . . . fulfilled. But now it's all good."

"And why do you think that is?"

It was an important question and he answered thoughtfully. "Because today I was finally able to do what you've been telling me. The Push appeared. And I didn't fight it. I gave in."

Mr. Benedict smiled. "You embraced it, and now you've achieved your potential. Sounds corny but it's true."

Fallow looked down at the watery grave of the man he'd just murdered. His first victim.

With every slash and stab of the knife, he'd merged with the Push, consummating the union like a couple on their wedding night.

All his trials were over with. All the struggles.

Mr. Benedict's plan was brilliant. From a young age his protégé had been conditioned to resist the Push and find substitutes for those urges to humiliate and hurt and—ultimately—kill.

So Mr. Benedict had shown him one of those substitutes—hunting—that let him break through the inhibition and accept what he really was: a man made to take lives.

The basement was the key.

Mr. Benedict understood that Fallow had been locked away in the basement only because he resisted the Push. The very act of resistance gave it more power over him.

Which meant that all along he *needed* to embrace it so he could control it.

It was merely a question of Mr. Benedict's wearing him down until he could come to this place mentally and make his first true kill.

And as it turned out, the plan was not only about some unorthodox therapist saving a troubled patient at all. Mr. Benedict had identified Fallow as somebody he himself needed.

Charlie Benedict, it seemed, was one of the West Coast's most talented professional killers. He'd served in the military, then become a mercenary, honing his deadly skills in conflict regions around the world.

When those jobs no longer satisfied his needs, he'd taken his savings (in gold and diamonds mostly) and moved back to Southern California, where he'd been born. Eventually he met a woman who understood him. A woman with underworld ties. After their marriage, he began hiring himself out as a "fixer" for cartels, gangs and other organized crime operations.

Mr. Benedict had found it useful to work with an associate, and he sometimes recruited them from a very odd place: a Santa Monica psychiatrist who specialized in sociopathic behavior.

Dr. Stillman had formed a symbiotic relationship with Mr. Benedict, receiving a generous finder's fee for referring patients with antisocial tendencies to him.

Mr. Benedict, in turn, played the role of a specialized behavioral therapist. He carefully screened each candidate to determine whether there was any potential to assist him with his work.

None had proved as promising as Dennison Fallow.

"Once in a lifetime does a killer like him come along," he'd told Dr. Stillman—and shared the phrase with Fallow, who had felt an unprecedented sense of pride.

After completing the hit at Lake Mathews, which had been ordered by a gang leader, Mr. Benedict had told Fallow, "I come here a lot. I've sunk over two dozen corpses in the lake. This place is comforting to me."

Fallow agreed.

"If you're ever troubled, Dennison, you can come here and stand in this spot and remember that there, fifty feet down, is your first kill. It represents your giving in fully to the Push."

"I will."

The two had driven to Mr. Benedict's house, a large ranch in Hollywood Hills. There they'd sat outside and had a meal, cooked by his wife, an attractive woman with sharp, cool eyes.

After dinner, he followed Mr. Benedict to his den. There, the mentor took something from the desk drawer and handed it to his protégé.

A velvet pouch.

"A graduation present."

With trembling hands, he took the soft material and undid the drawstring. He removed the multitool.

Staring at it brought to mind a passage from—of course—Shakespeare. *Hamlet*, in fact.

> This above all: to thine own self be true,
> And it must follow, as the night the day,
> Thou canst not then be false to any man.

Now, in Del Aire Health and Fitness, he would be true to himself again.

Fallow—decidedly in Spider mode—looked through the peephole, noting that Tanya was delaying her death by swimming a few more laps.

Well, let her enjoy her last few minutes on Earth.

CHAPTER 49

Carmen studied the white stone condo fronted with palm trees and succulent plants. Tanya Hilton lived in housing typical of that owned or rented by SoCal people in their twenties.

A stepping stone for bigger things.

She glanced at Heron. "You get an answer yet?"

"Still straight to voicemail."

Thinking of what he'd done with Chef Davide's phone, hacking to find the location, she asked obliquely, "You think . . ."

"Tried," he said. "It's off. No signal at all."

Two LA County Sheriff's Office vehicles arrived, parking beside the three town police cruisers already on the scene.

Carmen and Heron stood on the sidewalk in front of the building. Two more officers joined them, these from the Del Aire PD. Carmen thought they looked young, but their eyes were confident and quick, and she realized they had the situational awareness of military veterans. Given what they had perhaps seen overseas, a serial killer in a Southern California suburb would not unnerve them.

There had been no answer at Tanya's door, and the super had let the two officers inside—no warrant needed for a welfare check.

"Unoccupied," one of them said. "Just her cat. And not a lot of food left down, so she wasn't planning on being away long."

His partner said, "We knocked on some doors. Nobody's seen her this morning or knows where she is."

"The woman next door told us Tanya is currently between boyfriends. But she does the usual—shopping, bicycling, hanging out with friends for coffee."

Another officer approached. She too carried herself like a combat veteran. You could tell. Upright posture, wary eyes. "I checked two blocks around for her listed vehicle. Her car's not here."

Heron brushed his beard with the back of his hand. "So she could be anywhere . . ."

The officers gave Heron a curious glance, but Carmen didn't explain who the guy in the black clothes was.

She turned and gazed at a gathering crowd of spectators, locals standing shoulder to shoulder, keeping back as if behind nonexistent yellow crime scene tape. Mostly retired folks, young mothers and a few people in their twenties, probably remote workers like Tanya.

Heron's phone buzzed and he looked at the screen. "Aruba." He accepted the call. "On speaker with Carmen."

"Got something," Aruba said. "I saw some of Tanya's emails."

Once Carmen okayed their furtive tactics, she wanted results, worried they wouldn't reach the D-city victim in time.

Worse, she again recalled the Crime Scene inventory from the restaurant. The missing filleting knife. Impossible to know for certain, but she had to assume Spider planned to put it to use.

Aruba continued, "She emailed a friend about her plans for the day. They were going to get together. Hold on, I'm still mining them."

Carmen's eyes were on one of the spectators—the young brunette looked frightened and upset. She must have heard the police were looking for Tanya.

"Got some more," Aruba said. "Tanya's into pottery, and there's an art show she wanted to go to with her friend. They're supposed to meet there in ten minutes."

Carmen glanced at Heron, who asked, "Where?"

"Someplace called Oxnard."

Carmen pulled out her phone quickly and connected with someone from her contacts list.

The response was brisk and efficient. "Ventura County Sheriff's Office. Is this an emergency?"

"Yes." She identified herself. "I need officers at any art fairs in and around Oxnard. While you're there, hit Ojai too. Possible Two-Four-Zero." She rattled off Tanya's personal information and vehicle description. She finished by sending a copy of Spider's composite sketch to the Sheriff's Office's main email address.

"Copy that, Agent Sanchez. And we'll have local PD respond as well."

"Thanks." She hesitated, then added, "The more units the better."

"Ten-four."

She disconnected, slipping the phone away.

Heron, a Northern California boy, asked, "Oxnard, where is that?"

"Sixty or seventy miles north, up the 101." She turned to one of the Orange County deputies and the city police officers. "Radio your supervisors—the subject is in Ventura County. Tell them you can all stand down."

CHAPTER 50

Fallow's phone was muted, of course.

He stood in the storeroom of Del Aire Health and Fitness, peering through the peephole, waiting for Tanya to appear in what he'd come to think of as the "Death Corridor." A tad dramatic, but he liked the imagery.

Glancing at the phone's screen, he read:

Police took the bait. Found the emails I loaded into her system. Standing down in Orange County. Response shifted to Oxnard. You're clear. Don't waste it.

He texted back simply,

K

Working with a "leet" hacker was certainly a benefit, even if he sometimes scared the hell out of Spider. For all he knew FeAR didn't even *own* an assault rifle, and his gunplay was limited to his beloved first-person shooter games. But his malware could wreak catastrophic damage on every aspect of your life.

Still, the arrogant prick didn't have to add, "Don't waste it."

He considered the question of the other swimmer. Tanya didn't seem to know her, so he was betting they wouldn't leave together.

He suddenly tensed.

A shadow in the corridor. Yes, It was the second swimmer, toweling her hair as she walked to the locker room.

He relaxed. Tanya would be alone in the Death Corridor.

And three minutes later, there she was.

His right hand gripped Davide's filleting knife as his left pulled the roulette pill from his pocket.

The plan was simple.

He'd roll the pill and pick up one of the towels. While Tanya watched the ball, he'd step out and slap the terry cloth over her mouth, then drag her into the storeroom.

Duct tape would secure the towel in place to mute the delightful screams as he bound her hands and feet.

And started to work.

She was twenty feet away.

He eased the door open.

Then fifteen, ten.

Five . . .

He rolled the pill, and it made its lovely little clatter like it was spinning on the wheel, slowly decelerating, about to determine someone's fate.

He saw her pause, then walk toward the noise and stoop down.

Now—

A man's urgent shout stopped him in his tracks.

"Tanya Hilton?"

She straightened. "Yes?"

"I'm Jake Heron. I'm working with Homeland Security. You're in danger."

"What?" she gasped.

Fallow froze.

How had this happened?

Through the peephole he glanced up the corridor. He recognized Heron from outside the gunrunner's house in Moreno Valley. He was the hacker FeAR had told him about, the one who cracked the code in the phone he'd lost to the bitch Selina.

Heron had somehow figured out FeAR had faked the emails about her going to the art show in Oxnard. And they'd learned she was at the health club. Talking to neighbors maybe. A Post-it Note. Didn't matter.

His only concern now was escape.

He had one play.

Drawing his Glock, Fallow stepped from the storeroom.

Tanya screamed and the hacker pushed her to the floor.

Without a moment's hesitation, Fallow lifted the gun, drilled three rounds directly into Heron's chest, then turned and charged through a nearby emergency door. An alarm began to blare, a jarring sound that did not at all match the beauty of this fine autumn morning.

CHAPTER 51

Carmen rushed to Heron and dropped to her knees, examining his inert form.

"Talk to me, Jake." She deliberately used his first name.

No response.

A part of her mind registered that Spider was getting away, but she pushed the thought to the background. But there were other officers in pursuit. The focus now: Her partner was down. She tugged his shirt up to expose his belly and chest, looking for blood.

His eyes fluttered open. "Uhngh."

She lifted the hem of his shirt high enough to see the torn material where the three rounds had penetrated the ballistic vest's outer covering.

He had laughed when she'd opened the package delivered to her house in the morning, cracking jokes about her choice of a gift for him: the body armor.

You shouldn't have . . .

He wasn't laughing now.

Neither was she. When they'd arrived at the club, she had explicitly directed Heron to remain outside and watch the perimeter so he could alert her if Fallow tried to slip in or out through the side door.

Next, she hurried to the main entrance and pushed inside, flashing her creds at the receptionist, who registered wide-eyed shock at the presence of a federal agent. After learning Tanya was probably in the treadmill room or at the pool, Carmen had hustled the receptionist out the front door to safety.

The two had barely made it outside when the sound of gunfire alerted Carmen to the fact that Heron had disobeyed her orders to stay outside and *watch*.

She'd rushed back inside to find him lying on the floor, unresponsive. Now that he'd come around, she couldn't tell how badly he was injured, and opted not to berate him about his foolhardy behavior.

"Felt like I took a fastball in my right pec," he managed.

She pushed him back down when he tried to sit up. She noted with relief that none of the three slugs had gotten farther than the outer covering of the vest.

Law enforcement professionals didn't refer to ballistic vests as bulletproof. Nothing stopped every kind of round. She'd gotten Heron a level-IIIA vest after learning Spider had bought a firearm from Alex Georgio—and the shootout by Powell's fanatic followers in the white van. He needed the same protection she wore.

But there might be other injuries; bullets from a pistol travel at over 800 mph. "I need to check you for cracked ribs. At the very least, you'll have a nasty bruise. Worst case, a piece of your rib snapped off and punctured a lung."

"I'm okay," Heron said. "Tanya?"

"She's fine. My main concern is you."

Sometimes people went into shock a few minutes to a few hours after an injury. Just because he was alert and talking didn't mean he was safe.

"Like I said, I'm good." He quirked a brow at her. "Tell me you got Spider."

She tore the Velcro straps open, lifted the front of the vest, and slid her hand underneath the dense layers of tightly woven fabric. "He made it to his car and took off. Local PD and CHP are in pursuit."

Tanya Hilton was alive due to Carmen's sharp eyes and experience. Back at the apartment, she had grown curious about the particularly distraught woman at the police line, who had turned out to be Tanya's friend.

She explained that she'd seen Tanya get into her car with a gym bag earlier. She told Carmen that Tanya was obsessive about her workouts and went to her gym at the same time every day. Mid-morning to avoid the crowds.

Carmen began to suspect the emails about Oxnard were bogus, and Heron had confirmed they were the sort FeAR could easily gin up. Carmen made certain there was a lot of noise about the troops going to Oxnard—FeAR would monitor police channels to be sure he'd fooled them. Then she and Heron sped to Tanya's club.

She now probed along his chest and abdomen again. When he cursed, she couldn't tell if it was out of frustration or pain as she palpated his upper torso. She said, "I don't feel anything crunching in there, but you should get checked out."

A CHP sergeant crossed the room to join them. "I notified the dispatcher that the scene is secure. The paramedics staged on the perimeter will be inside shortly."

The sergeant bent to examine Heron's vest and the slugs. "Mushroomed on impact. But they're nine-mil Luger jacketed hollow points. Seen a million. We'll collect 'em and send 'em to the lab. Maybe we'll get a hit and put a name to the shooter."

The Bureau of Alcohol, Tobacco, Firearms and Explosives maintained a database with ballistic information regarding all weapons used during the commission of a crime.

She hated to burst his bubble. "He bought it from an Alex Georgio in Moreno Valley."

"That prick? The superstore of ghost guns. He ran into some problems, right?"

Carmen said, "The unsub we're after now? Did a Joker on his throat."

A grunt. "So, every cloud . . ." Then he added, "Crime Scene got the brass from the hallway but I'm guessing this guy wore gloves when he loaded the mag. So no prints."

"That's affirmative, I'm a hundred percent."

Heron sat up. "Can you turn up your radio?" he asked the sergeant.

They listened to bursts of communication consisting of ten-codes, call signals, unit designators and other police jargon she doubted Heron understood.

The gist of the dispatches was clear. "Sounds like they're having trouble chasing his car."

"Damn traffic lights," the sergeant said. "Suspect keeps getting green lights and our guys are getting all reds. Not like on TV, you know. *We* have to follow regulations, which means slowing down or even stopping completely to make sure the intersection is clear before they go through it."

She knew the police had other options. "Helicopter?"

"Air unit's on the way. ETA is under ten minutes, but we could lose him by then."

Heron dug his phone out. "I don't believe this guy catches every light while your units don't." He began thumb-typing. "Someone's messing with the traffic control system."

As if in confirmation, the dispatcher broadcast an alert that the signals were malfunctioning.

Carmen was about to ask Heron what he was doing on his phone, then hesitated. In this case, plausible deniability might be best. She listened to the radio traffic as police attempted to cut off Spider's escape.

A couple of minutes later, a pursuing officer announced that the traffic signals were functioning normally again.

"Thank God for that," the sergeant said.

Carmen noticed a bead of perspiration trickling down the side of Heron's face as he continued to work his phone. So divine intervention hadn't been involved in fixing the stoplights.

She leaned close to him. "You're reversing FeAR's hack."

He nodded, keeping his eyes on the screen. "Making a hot dog, Sanchez."

The victory was short-lived. Less than a minute later, troopers and local PD were reporting the same malfunction with the traffic lights again.

"All units, expand bull's-eye perimeters," the sergeant said into his radio, pulling her attention away from Heron. "We need to contain the subject until we get a visual on the vehicle again."

"They lost him," she whispered to Heron. "Do something."

But he was already thumb-typing once again.

The sergeant issued more orders. "Subject may attempt a 215 or a 459."

She worked with the CHP often enough to commit their radio codes to memory. The sergeant was warning his officers Spider might ditch his vehicle and carjack someone or break into a house to hide until the hunt settled down.

"Got back control," Heron murmured. "I'm trying to reinforce the firewalls before he can penetrate the system again."

"Chopper?" she called out to the sergeant.

"Six minutes."

Too long, too long. The squad cars *had* to get closer.

Heron finally looked up from his phone. "Locked his ass out. He won't be getting back in."

The sergeant looked his way, scanned the civvy clothing. "What are you, like CIA cyber? How did you access LA Traffic mainframe?"

So he'd been paying attention after all.

"DHS has its own cyber platform," Carmen said. "We have access to a lot of sites."

Completely true.

Completely evasive.

The sergeant returned to his radio, then spat out an obscenity. "The lights are normal, yeah, but they lost him."

Heron glanced down at his phone again and the color drained from his face.

"What?" she asked. "The gunshots?"

He shook his head. "No, not that. It's that the son of a bitch traced *me*. And he sent a text to be sure I knew who he is." He dropped his voice. "The names of six victims from the Chicago bombing."

The Nix attack by the DomTerr cell Heron had missed because he'd been chasing his nemesis—this same hacker.

She could scarcely believe it.

"He signed off with two words." Heron angled his phone so only she could read the screen.

Game on.

Carmen wondered, again, why a world-class hacker like FeAR was helping Spider. "Can you trace him?"

"No. He's vanished. Burned his own system." Heron's shrug ended in a wince.

Spider's escape brought a fresh worry to her mind. She needed to warn her sister to stay vigilant.

She tapped in Selina's number and waited.

Answering the phone with the word "Hey" could convey a cheerful greeting or impatience. Selina's version when she picked up was solidly in the second camp.

"Hi." Carmen was relieved to hear her sister's voice, but the chill, though not surprising, still stung.

"You calling to tell me I can get the hell out of here?"

"Just checking on you."

"So you haven't caught him yet."

"No. Why I'm calling. He's still at large. Stay put and if you go to the lobby to get a soda or something, keep an eye out."

"I've missed three classes. I'm not going to miss any more."

"One more day, Lina."

A pause. "I've got to take this call. It's Ryan."

And she disconnected. In movies you always hear a dial tone when somebody hangs up. It doesn't work that way. It's silence. Like now. Dead silence.

Carmen put her mobile away, reflecting that her sister said it was "Ryan" calling. Not "Detective Hall."

Was there actually another caller at all?

"She all right?" Heron asked.

Feisty and cold as ever, Carmen thought, but said, "She's fine."

Heron said, "I don't think Spider would have attacked Selina if he knew her big sister was a federal agent. He made life exponentially harder for himself. He's an organized offender. They do their homework. How did he miss that?"

"If you look at Selina's social media, there's nothing about me. I told her never to mention me or include pics of us together. Partly because I lock up really scary people and I don't want them tracking her down for revenge, partly because I might need to go undercover and I don't want any connection to my real identity out there."

Heron struggled to his feet. Carmen had been about to help him, but he managed on his own. "When I was ten, I got a hand-me-down Compaq LTE laptop from my uncle. Best present I ever got. Until this." He tapped the vest.

She responded with a faint smile.

His phone buzzed with another incoming text. "It's Aruba."

"Did she manage to run down FeAR?" She kept references to hot tubs at bay.

"It would take another Banchee attack to do that." He brushed at his beard absently as he read. "She cracked the encryption on Alex Georgio's Seagate drive. The one from the cereal box."

Cap'n Crunch . . .

Carmen had forgotten about the evidence Heron had tampered with in the gunrunner's kitchen.

She sensed her comment about loving hot dogs but hating the process had come back to bite her. Whatever Aruba found had been obtained without a warrant. But was now fully in a frame of mind that said: Find the bastard now. Worry about trial later.

Carmen knew Jacoby Heron wasn't emotional, yet the dismay that suffused his face was unmistakable. What had Aruba found?

Without looking up, he said, "You know how we keep saying Spider's not acting like a textbook serial killer?" His eyes drifted up to meet hers. "That's because he isn't."

CHAPTER 52

Jake summarized Aruba's discovery for Sanchez. "She found a URL to an underground website Georgio was on. So was Spider."

He dug into his kit bag, pulled out his laptop and hooked up a wired secure router—never, ever, ever Bluetooth, of course.

"The URL is H8ers.org." He spelled it and said, "Hackerspeak for 'Haters.'"

"A site devoted to peace and harmony then," Sanchez muttered sardonically.

"I'm going online now. There's a passcode but Aruba snagged it in about three minutes."

"Without putting the economy of Japan at risk by hijacking their supercomputer?"

"Not at all," he said, typing. "She used the Norwegian Central Banks."

Sanchez clapped her hands over her ears. "I don't want to hear this shit, Heron. Hot dogs!"

A moment later, the site came up. What they saw stunned them into silence.

H8ers

"Revenge should have no bounds."
—William Shakespeare

The H8ers are a community devoted to waging WAR on the Lux—life's lottery winners in the name of justise and freedom and because its just so goddamn cool. Remember our motto:

H8 Rools!

Lux Wall of Blame

Send in pix and deets on your fave Lux. They've been lucky in life, nows the chance to cut em down to size! Maybe they'll lose it all with one spin of the roulette wheel—and our favorite arachnid will pay them a visit!

CLICK HERE

Chat Rooms

CLICK HERE

Videos

- Los Zetas Decapitations and other fun and games
  This is your head on drugs!
- Car Crashes of the Rich and Famous
  Pass the champagne . . . Oh shit . . .
- Celebrity Suicides
  No Acadamy Award for you!
- Revenge Porn (deep fakes allowed)
  Dumped by some bitch? Lets take a look at her—and we mean everything!
- Epic Fails Online
  Laugh your ass off at the LWP's— Losers Who Post

CLICK HERE

The Trolling Corner

Send us email addresses, X, Facebook, Insta, Snap, Threads, Discord, Reddit handles, ANYTHING and let the H8ers get to work at the fine art of cyberbullying.

CLICK HERE

Resources

- **Where to find personal info 4 doxing**
- **How to SWAT and not get CAUT**
- **Using body image as a weapon**
- **Staying anonimus online**

CLICK HERE

Members: 479
Currently Online: 277
Contact us at: info@H8ers.org

"Disgusting," Sanchez said.

"And the spelling and grammar mistakes are typical for a group like this," Jake said. "It's clear they spent more time online than in school." He read the page a second time. "I've seen plenty of virtual attacks but glorifying them like this is next-level shit."

He clicked through to some of the internal pages. In the chat room were dozens of people bragging about their trolling and cyberbullying exploits. He didn't bother watching the videos, having seen similar horrific images when he hacked into various sites to dismantle them.

"All websites, chat rooms and social media platforms attract some of this—people who bully and threaten and slander. But this." He sighed. "I've never seen a site *devoted* to them. That's their whole point."

He clicked on the WALL OF BLAME.

There, members had posted hundreds of comments and photos of blogs and articles about success stories—maybe of people they knew, maybe from the news—including from the *LA Herald*. The targets varied but most were those who had capitalized on an opportunity—perhaps winning a scholarship or an award, which gave them their first break.

"Lux," Sanchez said. "As in 'lucky ones.'"

293

Realization dawned. "It's reverse schadenfreude—*unhappiness* at the *good* fortune of others."

Sanchez continued reviewing the posts. "And they didn't seem to read the articles. The people they've put on the wall worked like hell to parlay their good fortune into success." She tapped the screen. "'One spin of the roulette wheel.' Explains the white ball. And Spider's love of the game. And look at all the members." She now pointed to the bottom of the site. "Hundreds! Who are all these people? Where do they come from?"

"Your classic trolls," Jake offered. "Mostly single males between sixteen and twenty-five. Wouldn't call them men. They live with their parents. Spend most of their time in the bedroom or the basement, either gaming or browsing chat rooms and boards. Usually unemployed, or underemployed in menial jobs, which they resent. They think it's always somebody else's fault they don't have money or a hot date every Saturday night."

"The victims . . . on the Wall of Blame. Let's check it out."

But Jake was already searching that portion of the site. "Look."

All four targets were among those listed.

Walter Kemp, who'd initially financed his real estate company with a loan from his father.

Selina Sanchez, who'd won scholarships because of her talents as a student and a gymnast.

Renault Davide, who had been able to start his restaurant because he'd been selected to attend a top cooking school.

Tanya Hilton, who became an online success when her blog took off.

Lux . . .

"There's SWATing and there's tormenting someone until they kill themselves, but this is one for the books. Members submit somebody's name for death—and the site director plays God, deciding who dies. I wish I could say I was shocked. But the level of online hatred is off the charts. Look at their motto: 'H8 Rools.'"

Sanchez's expression reflected his own outrage. "Williamson and I talked about this a couple of days ago—at Powell's takedown in the Mojave. Online discourse keeps devolving. And it's all anonymous, so everyone feels free to spew hate and spread lies. I suppose it's not surprising that murder at whim was the next progression."

Sanchez said urgently, "But now. The next victim. We know he's following the spelling of his nickname. S-P-I-D so far. An 'E' city is next. Let's get to the victim before he does."

Jake downloaded the list of names on the Wall and ran a search of where they lived or worked.

But of the 340 individuals mocked and denigrated on the Wall of Blame, none were in a Southern California city beginning with "E." There were, however, plenty from around the world. Members nominated people in El Paso, Essen, Edinburgh, Essaouira, El Nido, Edmonton, and Exeter.

Sanchez said bitterly, "There's even one from Patagonia: El Chaltén. But nothing near here."

Jake asked, "Think he's taking a break?" They looked at each other. "Never mind. Of course he isn't. We need to get into their servers and the email account. Info@H8ers.org."

He felt her eyes on him.

Jake laughed. "Hot dogs, Sanchez—a hack is the only way in."

"Hot dogs," she muttered and waved her hand, silent permission to push the boundaries of the Fourth Amendment yet again.

"I can't do it from this box." He gestured toward his laptop. "Aruba?"

He nodded and typed on the keyboard.

A moment later he received a secure email. "She's online and looking at the site now." He gave a faint laugh. "Aruba never gets emotional—"

Sanchez gave him a coy look.

"Okay, yeah, like me," he admitted. "She told me to give her the word and she'd burn down the whole site and send a virus to infect everyone on it."

"Look at that," Sanchez whispered.

In the few minutes since they'd discovered the site, the membership had grown from 479 to 534.

"Hate sells," Jake muttered.

A window popped up. He read the message. "Aruba says the site's protected by a security bundle she's never seen. I haven't heard of it either. It's called Labyrinth. A maze of different routes and false leads. She's tried all the standard tools. No joy."

Sanchez stared at the screen. "There's a difference," she said distractedly.

"What?"

"Between a labyrinth and a maze. A maze has multiple routes and dead ends. You have to choose which way to go. A labyrinth is unicursal. There's only one way to the center. If you enter a labyrinth, you'll get to the middle eventually. A maze could trap you forever."

He raised an inquiring brow.

A wistful look crossed her face. "My father would read to Lina and me in the evenings. We all liked mythology. The Minotaur always fascinated me. A creature—half-man, half-bull—on an island off Crete. Daedalus, the guy who made the wax wings? He built a labyrinth to imprison the Minotaur. It was called a labyrinth but technically it *was* a maze." She glanced away from the screen. "Did she say how hard it'll be to crack it?"

"No. She'll send out some pings to see where they lead. And even if she gets through Labyrinth, she's got to traceroute the proxies."

"So there's no way to tell where the site originates?"

"No." Jake brushed his beard with the back of his hand. "It could be anywhere in the world."

CHAPTER 53

Man, if I'm lucky, she'll come down here. If I'm lucky, she'll come down here. If I'm lucky, she'll—

"Hey, dude, you're talking to yourself."

Oh, shit. Trey snapped his mouth shut.

"Sorry, man," he said to Poley.

He didn't want to piss Poley off and get kicked out of the club. He and Doobie were the newest members.

They all hung out in the half-finished basement of the house Poley's mom was renting in Anaheim, in the middle of Orange County.

In shorts and sandals and a hoodie, Trey stretched his lanky form across the couch, which reeked of stale Doritos, spilled beer, and pot. The last odor was courtesy of Dylan, who had earned the nickname Doobie because he always smelled like he'd just smoked a joint.

Trey passed the time doomscrolling on his phone while Doobie synced a new joystick to the video monitor so they could do multiplayer games.

The setup was cool, and Trey wanted to send some selfies from here but none of the members of the H8ers allowed into the inner circle were permitted to text. And he never did, ever, because the rule came straight from the cold-eyed fuck who sat on a swivel chair in front of the five monitors, staring and typing, staring and typing, and taking a ten-second break sometimes to sip tea.

The dude creeped Trey out.

When Poley had first let him into the basement, Trey had walked up to the guy and introduced himself. The man had said nothing but kept 'boarding.

Poley had explained, "You can call him the Admin."

"Cool."

The Admin didn't wear T-shirts or hoodies. He wore dark suits, like Trey's father wore when he was on trial, especially for sentencing. This made him even scarier for some reason—a hacker in a suit.

Despite his uneasiness about the hacker, Trey still considered himself one of the luckiest people in the world—pretty funny because the clubhouse and the H8ers.org website were all about trolling the Lux, the lucky assholes out there who had the breaks people like him never got.

No texting.

And no muttering to yourself out loud.

Lucky . . .

Because like Doobie, he'd stumbled on the site a few days ago and thought he'd died and gone to heaven.

While other boards and sites had plenty of trolls, H8ers.org was all about trolling itself. No other purpose. He joined up and got even with an ex—well, a girl he'd *wanted* to go out with but had pretty much ignored him. And he doxed a boss too, well, an ex-boss.

And then a miracle happened.

He'd gotten a secure email from the owner of the site—Poley—who had seen his IP address and noticed he lived nearby. Did he want to come over and hang out at the H8er's clubhouse? Maybe volunteer to do some work?

Oh, man, yeah. He got his skinny ass here, on his skateboard, in twenty minutes.

Same with Doobie, who lived even closer.

The two went on food runs and took out trash. Sometimes they watched the Admin totally dominate at FPS games, racking up the highest kill/death ratio they'd ever seen. He'd let them do some gaming too, though on boxes that looked like they belonged in ancient Rome or wherever.

And then there was Poley's mom.

Man, if I'm lucky she'll come down here. If I'm lucky she'll come down here. If I'm lucky she'll come down here.

This time he was careful not to say it out loud.

"Hmm." Poley was reading a text—since he was in charge of the site he could text and do whatever he wanted. He was a heavy dude, about twenty-five—six years older than Trey and Doobie. "Looks like he's safe."

Some shit show had just gone down. Spider—the H8ers' so-called fixer—had nearly gotten a Lux named Tanya in Del Aire, but the police found out in time and saved her. Which was bullshit, in Trey's opinion, because she was hot, like the first girl to die in a slasher film, and it would've been cool to see pictures of her body.

Trey and Doobie had watched the Admin hack all the stoplights in Orange County so Spider could get away, which worked okay, it sounded like.

"And that cop is alive," Poley said. "The guy Spider shot."

The Admin glared at Poley through his thick round-framed glasses. "It wasn't a *cop.*" His tone was pure ice. "I told you that. Remember? It was the *hacker.* Heron."

Poley reddened. "Well, *like* a cop is all I mean."

"A hacker is the opposite of a cop, wouldn't you say? That's not a question for you to answer. It's called rhetorical. Look it up sometime." The Admin turned back to the screens, scanning. "And the police band traffic out of Del Aire? They're using the name Spider. They scored it."

"Shit," Trey said. "How?"

The Admin didn't answer. He was reading another window. "Oh, fantastic," he spat out.

Poley grabbed a handful of popcorn from an open bag on the table beside him and walked closer.

"Back away." The Admin shot him a scowl. "Crumbs."

Poley didn't seem to care and hovered nearby, munching as he stared at the screens. "What is it?"

The Admin pointed to the home page for H8ers.org. "They found the site too."

"They got Spider *and* the site," Poley said around a mouthful of popcorn, drawing another chill glance from the Admin.

Trey couldn't believe anyone had gotten to them so fast. "Are you sure?"

The Admin sighed. "Would you understand if I said my script logged a cluster of Internet Control Message Protocol pings that were unique, deriving from certain tessellations of layered proxies that I recognize?"

"I . . ." His brain seized like a bad car engine. He tried again. "I, uh—"

"Hush." The Admin dismissed him with a wave, then started muttering to himself. "Had to come from Georgio. Asshole must've had a backup device at his place in Moreno Valley." He squinted at the screen. "Yeah, that's it. I can see the signature. A Seagate drive. Spider missed it when he was there. And Georgio must've written the word 'Spider' somewhere. A Post-it or something. People think computer data will sink you. A pen and paper are a hundred times more dangerous."

Trey could see both the Admin and Poley were righteously pissed.

Poley flopped down in the armchair, shoveled in more popcorn. "So what does this, you know, mean?"

"It means we move faster. That's all."

Poley grunted and gave Trey a smile with bits of chewed popcorn in his teeth. "All good, dude. Just life in the dark web fast lane."

When Trey got the invite to come to the H8er's clubhouse, Poley had led him into a bedroom in the back of the basement and climbed back onto the bed, where he'd been playing games on his phone.

It felt like a weird job interview.

"Trey, Trey, Trey . . ." Poley had been eating bite-size doughnuts at the time.

"How do you like our club?"

"It's cool. Like, the best."

"Have you posted anybody's story on the Wall of Blame?"

Trey felt a shiver of excitement. "Not yet. But I will. Got some major assholes in mind. There was this coach in tenth grade and—"

"You know, Trey, it wouldn't be good for you to tell anybody where our base of operations is."

"I never would. Like really. And I know to only do games on my phone. Never morpegs."

Someone in a multiplayer online role-playing game could be traced.

Poley studied him closely. "You know what happens, Trey? When we pick a name and Spider pays them a visit?"

"Yeah, sure."

"Does that bother you, Trey?"

"No, sir." He'd beamed. "I think it's cool. Those fuckers, the Lux? They deserve it."

Poley had eyed him again and then said, "Welcome to the H8ers."

And offered the bag of doughnuts. Trey hadn't been hungry, but he took one anyway, ignoring the Cheeto-colored fingerprints in the chocolate.

But now the memory vanished, and Trey was back to the present, very much so, because the door opened and down the stairs she came.

Mom . . .

Trey's heart stuttered, seeing her appear—from her fuck-me shoes to her long hair and every luscious curve in between.

Poley's mother usually wore skintight yoga pants and crop tops that showed off her tanned belly—never any frumpy T-shirts or sweats, and her perfume sent his hormones into overdrive.

She was so clueless about what they were doing that the Admin didn't even bother to hit Alt-Ctrl-F6 to switch to an innocent window when she came downstairs. It was like she didn't even know what a computer was. Like a lot of women.

She was carrying a cooler of soda and some bags of chips. More doughnuts too.

Trey leaped from the couch to help, knocking into Doobie, who cursed.

He smiled at her, and his prayers were answered. She smiled back—the woman he'd made love to five times already. Though on each occasion he was alone in his shower.

Would it ever happen for real?

Well, he'd been lucky to be picked by the H8ers. Maybe he'd get lucky again.

There was no shame in being a *little* bit Lux.

She turned to her son. "How's it going, honey? Everything good?"

"Sure, I guess." Poley didn't, of course, tell his mother anything about the mess in Del Aire with the slasher film girl still alive and their fixer on the run.

"You boys comfortable down here?"

Not looking up from the screen, the Admin said, "We're good."

Doobie dug through the cooler, apparently not happy with the selection. But Trey kept his eyes locked on hers and said, "Thanks for the, you know, stuff."

"You're very welcome, Trey."

OMG, she remembered his name.

"When you're through, could you collect the trash and take it outside?"

"Yeah, totally."

"And don't forget to separate the recycling."

"For sure. I'll do a good job too."

Another smile.

Trey checked that his T-shirt was pulled down enough to cover his crotch as he watched her climb the stairs.

Poley got a text. "Spider's safe. I'll tell him to go to the next one on the list." He typed a reply, then glanced at Trey and Doobie. "Want to see who it is?"

He saw his own excitement reflected in Doobie's face. They walked to the computer and stood behind the Admin, who muttered, "The side. Stand to the side, not behind me."

They moved to flank him.

The Admin's fingers flew over the keys.

A picture appeared. A pretty woman in her twenties with her hair in a cascade of long braids held a certificate. Trey couldn't read the printing, but she was showing it off like she'd just won a prize. She wore a pantsuit, which was a problem with professional women. You never saw anything good.

Like a lot of the Lux on the Wall of Blame, she had a bullshit expression on her face: a confident smile.

An expression that would be very, very different when Spider caught her.

CHAPTER 54

Natalie Jackson took her first sip of piping-hot brew, fogging the lenses of her red-framed glasses.

As the words on the page blurred, she leaned back in the overstuffed armchair and took in the sounds and smells of her favorite café. She loved the place because no one minded if she ordered only a single cup of coffee and nursed it for an hour. Or two.

Her glasses cleared and she returned her gaze to the thick stack of printouts and handwritten notes clutched in her hand. The conclusion they were leading her to didn't seem possible. She was an engineer. Maybe a *young* engineer, but her elite education had solidly grounded her in fact. Graduating in the top 1 percent of her class at Howard University had resulted in a scholarship to Stanford, up in Silicon Valley, where she'd earned her master's degree.

Now she was in Southern California, coding freelance, while considering which of the IT firms relentlessly recruiting her she'd choose to work for.

One of these companies had hired her two weeks ago to write some code. She liked the place—it did a lot for education. And she also was impressed with the number of Black women engineers the company employed. So she wanted to do a good job with the assignment. And Natalie thought she had.

But the code was of a different mindset.

Okay, start over at the—

"Hey there."

She jumped, nearly dropping the papers, and looked up into the dark-brown eyes of the man who'd approached her table from behind. Good-looking, and in his early thirties, he wore tan slacks and a navy-blue sport jacket. So, a businessman of some sort.

Responsible, social, of some means. And because his shirt was a garish green, she decided he had no shortage of self-confidence. A first hurdle, if a low one, had been cleared.

On the other hand, he could be a psychotic killer, for all she knew. But engineers always reserve final judgment until all the facts are in. And so Natalie did this now.

He gave her a disarming smile, complete with dimples. "Could I borrow a pen?" He held up a newspaper folded to show a partly completed crossword puzzle. "Ran out of ink."

"I've got a spare." She reached for a black leather shoulder bag slouched in the chair next to hers and tugged it into her lap.

"May I?" He gestured toward the empty seat, waited for her nod of approval and sat.

His gaze never wandered below her neckline. Was it because she was in a loose-fitting black sweater and baggy jeans, or was he actually a . . . *gentleman*?

She rooted through her purse, eyes down. Hot guys didn't normally approach her. She knew she gave off a mussed, nerdy vibe but that was just her. Makeovers didn't last very long. Was he interested? She couldn't tell—a testament to how long her dry spell had been.

He slipped out his phone, checked the screen for a message, sent one and set the unit on the table beside hers.

"There's one here *someplace*." She shot him an apologetic smile and kept rummaging.

He leaned in close. "Is that a pen, or a lipstick?"

He'd spotted it before she did. She lifted out a ballpoint and offered it to him with nervous fingers. This guy had her totally flustered.

"You twist the end." She showed him. "I can't use the clicky-top kind. I end up constantly clicking them without thinking. Drives everyone around me nuts, you know?"

God, I'm babbling . . .

He slid the pen from her grasp. "Thank you."

When he put his hand out, his shirt cuff slid back a bit, showing two black lines on his inner wrist. She couldn't seem to stop her inane chatter. "I see you're into body art. I got some new ink yesterday," she said, tugging up her sleeve to reveal a unicorn head on her forearm.

"Nice." He admired the tattoo.

She wondered if he'd show her his, but his attention turned toward the crossword where there appeared to be only one empty line. He must be the type who wouldn't be satisfied until he finished what he started.

Like her, in a way.

He twisted the pen and focused on the crossword. "Hmm, ten letters. 'Quick board meeting.'" He showed it to her.

Adept at puzzles, she figured it out instantly. Should she tell him the answer?

He solved it before she could make up her mind. "'Quick board meeting'—'Speed chess.' Clever."

She smiled as he jotted the letters.

The dark eyes cut back to her. "Finished it. Now I can die in peace."

She knew what he meant, but his turn of phrase was a tad unsettling.

He picked up his phone from beside hers and held out her pen.

"Keep it." She waved him off. "I've got a million more."

"Nice of you. I'm new in the area. Maybe I'll see you here again."

He left the café, the bells above the door tinkling in his wake.

Natalie forced her attention back to the documents. Her boss expected the new code she'd written to be finalized and debugged the day after tomorrow. But seemingly with a mind of its own . . . a persistent bug remained, and she just couldn't fix it.

She spent the next half hour poring over the papers and scribbling in the margins. Then checked her watch and, startled to see how much time had passed, stuffed the papers into her bag.

"Heading out?" the slim male barista called to her.

"If I don't get back to feed him, my dog will eat the sofa like he did last month."

He beckoned her to the counter. "You've got a rescue golden retriever, right?"

"Pooh Bear. Right."

He held out a dog biscuit. "Here, take a peace offering."

She thanked him and tucked the treat in her pocket before heading out.

The weather was exceptional. A made-to-order Southern California day. She walked two blocks in the direction of her building, through a deserted neighborhood.

She ambled along the sidewalk, wondering if she'd ever see Hot Guy again, and turned the corner.

Natalie stopped suddenly.

There he stood, dimples on full display, as if he were waiting for his date to arrive and looking forward to a very special evening.

CHAPTER 55

Carmen nearly broke the sound barrier getting to Lake Elsinore.

In the passenger seat Heron was pale. She really *would* have to get him some Dramamine before their next drive.

After Aruba failed to crack Labyrinth, she and Heron tried a new approach to finding the E-city victim. Realizing how many Southern California cities had two-part names like San Diego and Los Angeles, they compiled all the potential victims from the H8ers.org's Wall of Blame, expanding the search to include cities with an "E" at the beginning of either part of their names.

Natalie Jackson lived in Lake Elsinore. Her ranking as a potential target went to the top slot when Declan found she'd been written up last month in the *LA Herald*, a story about her receiving an honor from a women-in-science group. The article mentioned a scholarship to attend Stanford, making her a Lux and qualifying her for a place on the Wall.

They'd tried to contact her, but the call went straight to voicemail. A receptionist at Natalie's place of work informed them she was out for the day.

Carmen reported the threat to the Riverside County Sheriff's Office's Lake Elsinore station, and deputies were dispatched to Natalie's apartment.

As they neared the town, Heron inhaled deeply and said, "Social media." He pulled his computer from his gear bag and typed frantically while she drove.

He swiped through Natalie's Facebook and Instagram pages. "May have something."

Natalie had posted dozens of selfies at the same café in downtown Lake Elsinore. She also took pics of the fancy designs the baristas put in her coffee using frothed cream or chocolate or caramel or sprinkles.

Heron swallowed audibly, apparently struggling to control his churning stomach, but stayed on task. "If she keeps to the same schedule according to the time stamps on the posts, she's probably there now."

She agreed. "Let's call the place."

"No need. We're there." He pointed to an intersection. "Around the corner to the right."

Carmen skidded around the corner, jerked the steering wheel to the left, and sent the car careening into the café's parking lot.

Checking their surroundings, she unbuckled her seat belt and flung open the door. "Call dispatch, get backup started this way. I'm going inside. Stay here. I mean it. You've been shot at enough for one day."

The café wasn't busy, and clearly neither Natalie nor Spider was present. She strode straight to the counter, past three people in line, flashing her ID to avoid any potential protests.

She turned her phone's screen toward the young, highly pierced barista. "Have you seen this woman today?"

"That's Natalie. You just missed her." A frown. "She okay?"

"Was she by herself?"

"Some guy was chatting her up, but he left before she did."

Carmen flashed the artist's composite. "This the one?"

The barista squinted. "Could be."

A sickening wave of dread washed through her as the details of her sister's attack rushed back in vivid detail. As did the slowly revolving body of chef Renault Davide.

"Any idea where she went?"

"She was headed back to her apartment."

"Would she drive?"

"No. She always walked."

"Which way?" Carmen knew the address but hadn't studied a map of the area.

He pointed to the street in front of the shop. "Four blocks north. That's left. Please, let me know—"

Carmen bolted from the café and nearly collided with Heron, who had apparently decided to join her inside.

"What the hell, Sanchez?"

She didn't have time to chew him out for yet again ignoring her orders. "Natalie's headed to her apartment." She danced around him and started to run "Call 9-1-1 again. Have them alert the deputies who are headed to her apartment."

She didn't wait for an acknowledgment. Her assumptions might be wrong, but she couldn't take the chance. She ran two more blocks, then rounded a corner at a dead sprint.

And saw Spider.

She took in several things at once, noting the jet-black hair that altered his appearance. He wore yet another distracting shirt, this one bright green.

But Carmen's main focus was on the woman struggling against him as he pulled her backward into an alley.

Natalie thrashed and clawed at her neck as Spider tightened a cord around her throat, stifling her screams and cutting off air to the lungs and blood to the brain.

Without slowing down, Carmen barreled at them on an intercept course, pulling her Glock from its holster. "Stop, federal agent!"

Spider's head snapped toward her. "Shit."

Taking advantage of her attacker's momentary distraction, Natalie kicked his shin. He gave a yelp. It was the same leg Selina had targeted. Natalie tried to break free, but he pulled the cord harder, yanking her back against his chest.

Where was his gun?

Carmen pounded to a stop a few yards away, her pistol's sights trained directly at him. "Let her go and get down on the ground."

He loosened his grip on the cord but kept it wrapped around his captive's neck. Natalie sucked in a noisy gulp of air while he darted a glance over his shoulder at the alley behind him. "I'm leaving, and I'm taking her with me."

She tightened her trigger finger a fraction, looking for a clean head-shot. "That's not going to work. It never does. Don't make it any worse for yourself. Step away from her, put your hands behind your head, and interlace your fingers."

He dropped the cord and took a few steps backward, still dragging Natalie in front of him. "You may as well put your gun away. You can't shoot an unarmed man."

"I'm sure as hell not going to let you take her and leave."

"Then I guess we've got a problem."

He had to know backup was coming. He was stalling for time, but why?

Without warning, he gave Natalie a vicious shove, sending her sprawling to the pavement. As Carmen rushed toward Natalie, Spider turned and ran.

Natalie lay still. Had her skull cracked on the asphalt?

Carmen registered that Spider was repeating a successful tactic. He'd stabbed a Good Samaritan, overturned a school bus, and shot Heron, all distractions to effect an escape.

She faced a dilemma. Her training and her compassion demanded that she help Natalie, but the cop in her screamed that a killer was getting away. A killer who would take more lives. A killer who might come back to finish what he'd started with Selina.

She holstered her weapon and pulled out her cell, tapping as she raced after Spider.

"Nine-one-one, what is your emergency?"

"Send an ambulance to an alley off Montrose, half klick north of Broad Street. There's a woman . . . she's hurt." She'd gasped the last few words as she ran flat out.

"What is the nature of her injuries?"

"I'm a federal agent, and I'm chasing the suspect on foot . . . we're headed south on Montrose. Just get EMS to her, stat."

"We just got another call here. Is this the same suspect?"

"Right. I need backup too. SWAT if you have it."

Carmen disconnected. She figured the call taker had enough information to get help where it needed to go. Meanwhile, she had to save her breath if she was going to catch Spider.

Her phone vibrated in her pocket. The call center was trying to reestablish contact. She kept running, arms and legs pumping, closing in on her quarry. He'd had a head start, but she was leaner and faster, and he occasionally favored one leg—surely thanks to the one-two kicks by Selina and Natalie. His bulky muscles slowed him down too.

Of course, those muscles would also make him a strong adversary.

She got closer, thought about her weapon, but knew that all kinds of shit got activated when you shot a fleeing suspect in the back. Besides, winded from the run, she couldn't accurately control her shot and might hit an innocent bystander. Heron's intrusion approach to criminal investigation, the PPIs, had given them the why. But not the who. She needed Spider alive to learn who was behind the H8ers.

Closer . . . closer. Finally, she calculated the distance between them, and launched herself onto his back, bringing them both crashing to the ground. She deliberately used his body to cushion her fall, letting him take the road rash and the direct impact with the hard surface.

He howled with pain, rolled over and started throwing punches.

Fine with her. The Systema training included ground-fighting techniques. She had experience with large male adversaries and had learned to leverage her lower body strength, her speed and her fast reaction time to protect herself.

With a big guy like Spider, she decided her best course of action was to let him exhaust himself trying to land a punch. It was a dangerous tactic. If he managed to connect, he could easily knock her unconscious.

Her death would soon follow. And if he weren't armed now, he soon would be—with her Glock.

Most street fights lasted under two minutes, which was about all it took to drain the average person's reserves of strength, adrenaline and rage. Spider was no exception, and his fists began to flail rather than swing at her.

She chose her moment and drove her knuckles directly into his Adam's apple. Eyes wide with shock, he clutched his throat and flopped on his back. She pounced, jumping on his midsection and using her legs to pin his arms.

An image of Heron similarly trapped beneath her in Moreno Valley flitted through her mind. She discarded it.

Spider wheezed and sputtered. She'd tried to modulate the blow, but he still might suffocate if his windpipe was compromised. The irony that he'd attempted to cut off Natalie's air was not lost on Carmen.

Well, karma could be a bitch . . .

But by the time she heard sirens approaching, Spider had recovered enough to gasp a few hoarse obscenities. She wanted answers but knew her questions would have to wait until he was Mirandized. Unlike on TV, real interrogations didn't take place on the street after a scuffle.

A half dozen deputies rushed to surround them. One deputy pulled Spider to his feet and slapped bracelets on him before his partner searched him.

"No ID," the second deputy said to Carmen. "No wallet or credit cards. Weird."

Really? she thought angrily. Well, a fingerprint might get them a name.

The first deputy told Spider, now in his custody and therefore his responsibility, that EMTs would check him out.

After another coughing fit, Spider turned to Carmen. "Bitch."

"Enough," the first cop said. Then he asked her, "You want to meet us at intake?" He double-locked the cuffs. "We got a preliminary statement from the victim while the paramedics treated her. For booking we'll charge him with abduction, assault, battery and resisting. And we'll throw in obstruction because why not?"

The deputy had just engaged in metaphoric leg lifting, marking his territory, making it clear their case took precedence, what she—a Fed—was after him for. Fine with her. Spider could rot in a local jail cell until they got an ID. The US attorney and state prosecutors could duke out who had first crack at him. Meanwhile she'd reach out to Hall—and Captain Webster—as well as Étienne in San Diego to report the collar and to make sure they filed more charges on him before his arraignment.

"I've got to pick up my associate back at the café," she said. "We'll meet you there."

She focused on Spider, staring him down. Willing him to talk.

He stared back. Not with anger. Not with fear. But with a completely flat expression.

She suppressed a shudder. Those eyes were fathomless voids. A thought appeared suddenly: The man had no soul.

CHAPTER 56

The good news just kept rolling in, Tristan Kane, a.k.a. FeAR-15, the H8ers' site admin, reflected, the thought dripping with his finely tuned sarcasm.

He faced an array of monitors at his desk in the basement of the Anaheim house, the H8ers headquarters, in a state of disbelief.

He'd finally gotten the 360 on Carmen Sanchez and learned that Poley—rocket scientist that he was—had picked Sanchez's own sister, Selina, for the second target from the Wall of Blame.

Un-fucking-believable.

While the authorities would have searched for the girl's attacker anyway, Poley had guaranteed that Carmen Sanchez, a former FBI turned DHS agent rumored to have the tenacity of a honey badger, was on the case.

And she'd brought in the master intrusionist, Game-on Jacoby Heron.

A true 1337, as he'd told Spider-Clown.

As elite as they came.

Kane heard Poley across the room arguing with Trey about whether Wolverine's claws were pure adamantium or an alloy of steel and vibranium.

"No, man," Trey said, frustrated at Poley's apparent ignorance. "Dr. MacLain was trying to make Captain America's shield and—"

"You're a dolt."

Kane was certain Trey didn't know what the word meant, but he seemed to grasp that it was an insult and shut his mouth.

The third village idiot, Doobie, skinny and floppy haired as Trey, was giggling as he watched TikTok videos of goats fainting.

Trey was, in fact, correct about the claws, but Kane had no desire to join the inane discussion.

A text chimed on his phone, bringing more bad news.

Fallow arrested. Lake Elsinore. Victim alive.

Kane sucked in a breath and calmed his voice. "Poley."

The young man joined him, accompanied by a package of Nantucket cookies. He chewed and asked, "You know anything about Wolverine?"

"Don't react," Kane whispered. "Fallow got arrested in Lake Elsinore. The target survived."

"Fuck me! What happened?"

So much for not reacting. But Fool Trey and Fool Doobie, engrossed by the swooning goats, hadn't heard Poley's outburst.

"You should get over there now," he told Poley.

"Like, sure, I guess," Poley said.

"Like, good."

The searing edge of his cutting remark was lost on Poley. How nice it must be to live life in subtext-free oblivion. The young man trooped up the stairs while Kane sat forward and began hacking code together. Minutes later, he uploaded the new scripts along with some he'd written a long time ago. He fired off a few secure texts, then stood and stretched.

"Man, I'm sloppy," he said, surveying his workspace.

"No, dude," Trey assured him. "You're cool."

Trey said this because he was a whiny sycophant.

And because he was envious. Kane knew the little turd suspected him of sleeping with Poley's mother.

Which he was.

"I've got an errand to run. Do me a favor, both of you?"

Doobie's head went up and down like a bobblehead dog. "Totally, man. Yeah. Whatever you want."

"Use some of this." He nodded to a spray bottle on the floor. It contained oxygen bleach and would not only remove chocolate stains but fingerprints and DNA—one of the few cleaners that accomplished the latter. "And scrub the whole workstation."

Doobie blurted, "You want us to use paper towels?"

He was really asking that? "Paper towels would be perfect. Don't forget the chair. And unplug the keyboard and the mouse. Clean those too."

"Sure," Trey said. His eyes were bright.

Kane pulled on his black Armani suit jacket.

He bent over the main keyboard and simultaneously pressed Alt, Shift and the backtick key—the one below the tilde on the far left of the number keys. An awkward combination no one would make by mistake.

He watched lines of code fill each monitor, like the Atlantic Ocean pouring into the torn hull of the *Titanic*.

"Hey, you guys want some takeout?" Kane was amused by their reaction. Surprise, bordering on shock. "Pizza sound good?" he asked, assuming that would be the sort of food these two liked.

Trey gave him a powerful grin. "I could totally go for some pie."

Doobie beamed. "Yeah. I'm all over pizza."

Which, for some inexplicable reason, brought a chortle from both of them.

"I'll go pick a couple up. Plain, pepperoni?"

"Yeah." From one of them.

Which didn't really answer the question, but no matter. Their future would contain many things, but pizza of any variety would not be one of them.

Trey's eyes were on his shoes. "Thing is, man, I'm a little low on coinage."

Doobie admitted he too had no money because he'd blown it all on weed.

"No worries," he told them. "It's on me."

More astonishment. "Yeah?"

Kane picked up his backpack, zipped it closed. "Totally."

CHAPTER 57

Imprisonment was nothing new to Dennison Fallow.

He'd done time in the basement as a child.

And he was familiar with incarcerated characters from Shakespeare, who used prison as a dramatic device. Falstaff, Malvolio, Cordelia . . . Elizabethan crowds flocked to the plays, though their justice system often involved "not being," as in Hamlet's musing, "to be or not to be," since the executor's axe and hangman's rope saw a lot of action.

He thought of jail as he sat in the back of Deputy T. Gregory's cruiser, being transported along Route 74 from the botched murder of Natalie Jackson to the lockup.

Botched . . .

Thank you, Poley, he reflected. I'm here because of you. FeAR-15, Tristan Kane, had told him the young man had picked Selina Sanchez as the second victim because she "was totally hot in her leotard." Her relationship to Carmen Sanchez wasn't evident from a basic online search, which was all he'd done.

Mr. Benedict had taught Fallow not to cut corners when there were issues of life and death.

"Dive as deep as the knife you're going to use," the man had said.

Worse yet, Agent Sanchez had recruited the cyber warrior, Jake Heron.

Fallow should have had plenty of time to throttle Natalie, but Sanchez had gotten there just in time. And now he was on his way to jail, like the two princes, sons of Edward IV, tossed into the Tower of London by Richard III In the 1400s, where most scholars believe they were murdered.

These thoughts put in mind the memory of a day very different from the joyful time with Mr. Benedict when he'd made his first kill standing beside his mentor on the shore of Lake Mathews.

Far from it.

Fallow had received a phone call as he happened, coincidentally, to be cleaning his beloved multitool.

"Dennison?" Mrs. Benedict's voice sounded strained.

"Yes."

"I'm afraid I have some bad news."

She proceeded to tell him Mr. Benedict was dead.

"No," he'd moaned, sinking to the floor.

His mentor, the man who taught him to embrace the Push.

To achieve his full potential.

Fallow came close to tears.

The police had informed her Mr. Benedict was shot in what looked like a professional hit, which baffled them since they had no clue he was a hired killer. She'd feigned ignorance when they interviewed her, but told Fallow she suspected a cartel had taken out a contract on her husband.

If Fallow ever found them, they would die.

And *that* visit would last a long time and occur where it would be impossible to hear their 120-decibel screams.

The police car glided along a scruffy stretch of highway, land east of the mountains separating Riverside from LA. They passed commercial space, then construction, then industrial, then cleared land, waiting for developers, or . . . waiting for nothing whatsoever, destined to remain heat-cracked dirt, dusty and oil stained, forever.

Deputy Gregory glanced at the rearview mirror, eyeing him through the plexiglass divider.

Fallow held his gaze until the deputy looked away. Probably to pay attention to the road, but maybe because he suspected his prisoner was the heir apparent to the Riverside Prostitute Killer, a.k.a. the Lake Elsinore Killer, convicted of torturing and murdering twelve women and suspected in a half dozen other deaths in the nineties.

Then his thoughts returned to the days following Mr. Benedict's death.

The devastation.

The depression.

And anger. Raw fury.

Fallow had wanted desperately to find out who murdered his mentor. He'd asked the police but had to be careful, lest he raise suspicions. In any case, they were useless. Mrs. Benedict knew nothing. Dr. Stillman had left the state—wise, considering his part-time gig matching lethal clients with mob bosses and terrorist organizations.

Ah, Mr. Benedict, dead at the hands of an unknown killer.

And Natalie Jackson was still alive.

At *his* hand—because he had failed.

He turned his attention to the front seat, where Deputy Gregory had pulled out his phone, which had pinged with an incoming text.

"Huh?" The officer's brows drew together as he glanced at the small screen.

Fallow said, "That's a photo of your house."

"*What?*"

"You're about to get a call. Put it on speaker."

"The fuck are you—"

His words were cut off by a ringtone.

He put the phone to his ear. "Who the hell is this?"

Fallow reminded, "Speaker."

He hesitated and then tapped the screen.

A voice said, "Listen carefully, Deputy Gregory. We don't have much time."

"Who the fuck are you?"

The answer was FeAR—Tristan Kane, initiating one of their contingency plans they'd set up together in case Fallow was ever arrested.

"You see where I am?" the voice continued without answering. "Outside your modest split-level home, which could use a coat of paint, by the way."

The deputy paled. "If you hurt a single hair—"

"Hairs have no sensation," FeAR said calmly. "I can, however, hurt the *rest* of someone's body. And both your wife, Sara, and your daughter, Kelsey, have very nice ones. Your son too, but that doesn't interest me."

"Oh, God. No. Please . . ."

"Now that I have your attention, here's what's going to happen." A sigh. "Are you listening?"

"All right, all right." He somehow sounded both terrified and resigned.

"You're going to do exactly as I say. Take the next right onto Sixteenth Street."

"But all our vehicles have GPS. Anyone who takes another route on a prisoner transport has to explain why."

"You wanted to avoid the traffic jam."

"What traffic—"

"Look."

Ahead in the distance, brake lights flared red as traffic slowed. Apparently a crash had occurred at an intersection about a half mile in front of them.

"Did *you* do that? How?"

Fallow, who had already benefited from FeAR's ability to hack a traffic control system, knew better than to question him.

"Quiet. Does your car have door handles in the back?" FeAR asked.

"I—"

"Does your car have handles?" he repeated softly, which made the words far more menacing.

"Yes, but there are no locks. I control that from up here."

"Unlock the doors."

He did.

"I see you're almost to Sixteenth. Make the turn," FeAR ordered.

Deputy Gregory made the turn.

"In a few minutes you'll go left on Howell Avenue. It's a logical route to get you north, around the accident. Make the turn at less than five miles an hour. Your passenger will open the door and step out. Then you speed up to the limit, forty-five. And when you see a solid tree, ram it, head-on. At that speed, the airbags will protect you. Get out, open the back door, and lie down on the ground."

"How can I explain crashing my patrol car?"

"Tell them you swerved to avoid a kid on a bike. There was no time to brake. After the collision you were worried about fire and got your prisoner out. Then you fainted. When you came to, he was gone. You're near Howell. Slow down."

He did.

FeAR said, "She looked so cute."

"What?"

"Your daughter on her way to school today. Those gray tights, the green skirt and the sweater with a llama on it. You know, only really pretty girls like her could get away with a top like that."

A tear coursed down the deputy's cheek. He now seemed desperate to make the getaway work. He said, "There's going to be a major investigation. My cell phone records will show I was texting or talking right before the accident."

"No, they won't," FeAR said matter-of-factly. "Are you ready?"

Fallow knew FeAR had directed the question at him. "Yes," he called out from the back seat.

The car was approaching Howell. It was a left turn, so he scooted to the right door, twisted, and gripped the handle.

"I'm turning," Deputy Gregory said to Fallow. "Please don't let him hurt—"

He didn't hear the obvious conclusion of that sentence as he pulled the handle, pushed the door open and stepped out. Even at under five miles an hour, it was an awkward maneuver without the use of his hands. He wobbled like a newborn giraffe but managed to stay upright. He scurried to a stand of bushes, keeping out of view of nearby houses.

Then, following the script, Deputy Gregory gunned the engine. Ten seconds later, the car bounded over the curb and slammed straight into a sturdy oak tree. Fallow hoped it didn't really catch fire, which would arouse suspicion as to why the deputy was extra crispy while his prisoner had miraculously escaped the same fate.

But no. Not a single flame, only some steam from the cooling system.

Fallow was pleased by the escape plan. He thought of the *Cyclosa*, a type of spider that travels by ballooning. For a quick getaway, it climbs as high as it can, then reclines on its back and shoots silky strands into the air. The threads meet overhead and form a triangle that serves as a parasail, carrying the creature away.

A large engine roared, and he turned to see a black Cadillac Escalade speeding toward him. The driver brought the SUV to a fast stop and clambered out. He wore a black suit, white shirt and dark tie. FeAR had told Fallow someone named Luciano would be dispatched to collect him if anything went wrong. From the driver's curly black hair to his Italian shoes, he looked like a Luciano. His barrel chest and sausage-like fingers screamed hired muscle.

He said nothing as he used a universal key to remove the cuffs.

Free from the restraints, Fallow hoisted himself into the rear seat while the driver wedged his bulk behind the steering wheel and drove from the crash site, keeping the vehicle at the speed limit.

With his eyes focused on the road, Luciano lifted a backpack from the front passenger seat and passed it back to him. "Here, Mr. Fallow," he said in a heavy Brooklyn accent. "There's a burner phone inside. Keys to some new wheels too. Where we're goin' now." His dark-brown eyes met Fallow's in the rearview mirror. "Couple other things you're going to want. In the bottom."

He unzipped the bag and found the phone and keys, pocketing both. The pistol too, a Glock 17, the bigger model, and two full magazines. A baggie held a dozen pairs of the clear vinyl gloves he preferred to wear. And a small white cardboard box. It rattled when he lifted it out. He removed the lid.

Luciano said. "You want any more of those, I know a guy who knows a guy who can get 'em for you cheap. Just say the word."

Dennison Fallow rarely smiled, but he came close now.

Inside were a half dozen small white roulette-wheel pills.

CHAPTER 58

Carmen wanted to hit something. Hard.

Their perp—the man who had taken two lives and tried to take two others in the past forty-eight hours, including her sister's—had escaped.

She and Heron were still in Riverside County, in the foothills of the Santa Anas. They'd booked a suite at the unglamorous, but convenient, Avanti Inn. Jake had checked in—using, of course, one of his intrusion-resistant anonymous credit cards issued to fictitious people by offshore banks. Perfectly legal, as long as you paid the bill.

They weren't alone. Natalie Jackson was with them. Fortunately, she'd sustained only minor injuries. The young woman, obviously tougher than her somewhat delicate appearance conveyed, had refused transport to the hospital.

Carmen thought the killer had probably moved on, but her protective instincts had kicked in, and until the psycho was snagged or bagged, she would keep Natalie close.

For her part, Natalie could absolutely not get her head around the fact that she'd been targeted because she'd *earned*—not been given—a scholarship and had gained a measure of success in a business where men tended to predominate.

"It makes no sense," she muttered, straightening her mussed hair and then shoving her red-framed glasses higher on her nose, a habit Carmen had noticed from the moment they'd checked in.

Heron said, "None at all. They're just a bunch of troubled little boys. Who happen to also be very, very dangerous."

Natalie took the ballpoint pen from the bedside table and began to click it, absently and compulsively, until she seemed to catch herself and stopped. She dropped the implement deep inside her purse.

Their review of the attack had already borne fruit. The Crime Scene techs who had collected the intended garrote told Carmen it was a coaxial cable. Natalie's background as a computer engineer made it clear why he had chosen that method of execution—once again the cause of death was calculated to echo something of the victims' lives.

Most significantly, the arrest at Lake Elsinore had finally put a name to the man who called himself Spider. He'd been too smart to carry an ID to his intended murder scene, but he couldn't hide his face anymore.

Carmen had texted his picture to Mouse, who had uploaded it to the world's largest face-rec database. A rapid AI scan through more than ten billion publicly available images gleaned from the internet resulted in a hit.

Spider was Dennison Montague Fallow. A curious name—made even stranger because court records show that he changed his middle name (his father's, James) to the present one.

Armed with the new information, Mouse quickly located his residence, a single-family home in Santa Barbara. Carmen debated whether to file an affidavit for a search warrant herself or leave it to one of the police detectives. Given their situation, she decided not to take a half day away from the investigation when she could review the return of the warrant and inventory after it was served.

Mouse had scoured Fallow's past, unearthing school psychologists' reports and juvie offense records for peeping, bullying and assaults that ultimately resulted in his expulsion from public education. He was then homeschooled. He had no trouble with the law after he turned eighteen. A deeper dive revealed he was a call center operator—Carmen and Heron shared raised eyebrows at that. He'd have access to plenty of personal information about customers—that was, potential victims.

Their eyebrows went up even higher when they learned his parents had died in a bizarre murder-suicide scenario. The case report from the investigating agency had concluded his father had laced their evening cocktails with poison.

"There's no way Fallow grew up in a normal, stable environment," Carmen said.

"Agreed," Heron said. "Murder-suicide is the ultimate form of familial intrusion. The Fallows must have been off-the-charts dysfunctional for a long time."

"According to the police report, Fallow was their only child and inherited the house." She considered the implications. "He still lives there."

She called Santa Barbara police and asked them to search the place, then pull out and set up a stakeout. It would nearly be impossible for an organized offender like him to take the chance of returning home. But she was determined to cover all eventualities.

She then asked Mouse to have Declan run the Homeland Security Investigations obscure relationship system, which searched through massive databases to find connections among people and incidents that weren't apparent on the surface.

It didn't take long for results to come in. She perched her laptop on a rickety coffee table. "Heron. Look."

Among the incident reports Declan had found were three unsolved missing persons cases. A cross-search in the obscure relationship system revealed that all three had purchased appliances from American General.

They might have made calls about their products—calls that Fallow could have taken. She directed Mouse to follow up with the company.

She was pacing back and forth across the gaudy carpet of the hotel room, now a makeshift base of operations. The Sheriff's Office had offered them space at one of their facilities, but she and Heron needed room to think . . . and to do things that may not technically fall within proper procedure.

Things that involved Aruba.

Heron glanced at his humming phone. "It's her."

He tapped the screen. "You're on speaker with Carmen and me. Natalie Jackson is here too."

"I'm going after the badger in its burrow," Aruba said. She had been attempting to trace the H8ers.org website back to a physical address— trying to crack the Labyrinth security package.

Carmen and Heron exchanged glances. "Any luck?" she asked.

"FeAR-15 is supposed to be hot shit. Well, I'm pretty hot too."

Heron chuckled. "No argument here."

Carmen pictured a swimsuit model pounding away on a keyboard. Or sitting in a hot tub.

Stop it, she told herself.

Aruba continued, "I tried to brute force my way into the site and got borked. Any thoughts on a righteously clever password? I've tried the obvious shit. 'Labyrinth,' and 'Greek, Greece, Minotaur, myth, Crete, Minos, maze, mythology.' Probably forty others."

Carmen thought back to her childhood obsession with mythology. "'Hesiod,'" she suggested. "The first man to write down Greek myths, around 700 BC."

That didn't work.

Heron asked Carmen, "Who did you say built the labyrinth?"

"Daedalus."

"The wax-wing guy," Natalie chimed in.

"Right."

Heron said, "FeAR created *this* labyrinth. Maybe he identifies with Daedalus."

Aruba responded within seconds. "Nope."

"Icarus, his son, right?" Heron asked. "His solo flight didn't end well but that might be the word."

"Nope," Aruba repeated.

Carmen gazed at the ratty curtain—drawn to prevent anyone seeing them from the parking lot. "The one who killed the Minotaur and escaped from the labyrinth was Theseus."

Another fail.

Aruba added, "And by the way—"

Heron said, "You're using the Greek alphabet too."

"Exactly. Forwards and backwards, upper case, lower case, and combinations of the languages."

Yep, Carmen thought, those two are definitely on the same page. Then an idea hit her. "Theseus couldn't defeat the Minotaur alone. He needed a woman's help. Minos' daughter gave him a ball of yarn to help him find his way out." She took a deep breath. "Ariadne."

A brief pause.

"I'm in." Aruba's voice displayed no emotion.

"Can you ping their location?" Heron asked.

"I'm tracerouting through the proxies." Aruba was hitting the keyboard so hard Carmen could hear clacking.

They waited for what seemed like an eternity before Aruba's voice came back on.

"Got it. The site's run out of a single-family house in Anaheim. Texting you the address now."

Carmen glanced at it. "We can be there in thirty minutes. Orange County SWAT in ten."

CHAPTER 59

Trey's nuts shriveled to the size of peas and headed north.

From the moment the SWAT team took a battering ram to the basement door of the house in Anaheim and charged in, shouting, no *screaming*, commands and pointing their weapons at him, he'd been in a state of terror.

A federal agent lady who scared the crawling shit out of him came in next. She was so eager to get her claws into him she didn't even haul his ass to a police station but shoved him into a chair in the garage, after the Crime Scene dudes—in their white moon suits—searched it.

The agent brought back childhood nightmares of Maleficent. She sat across from him and pulled her chair so close their knees touched. And some hacker, name of Heron, stood behind her with crossed arms.

He could've totally used a wingman, but they'd separated him and Doobie. Trey had two problems. First, Poley had threatened him not to talk. Second, Maleficent was goddamn asking questions he legit didn't know the answers to.

And they clearly didn't believe him. Could his situation suck any harder?

Agent Sanchez wanted to know about a dude named Fallow, but Trey had no clue who that was.

He fired up his gray cells, desperate for any scrap of information to get her off his back. "You mean Spider?"

She pounced. "Yes. Now tell us. Where. Is. He?"

"I don't know him, like *know* him. I never met him. I heard about him is all."

"Okay."

Cops said that all the time and it didn't mean okay. It meant your ass was lying.

She looked at him like he was a fly not even worth brushing away. He tried again. "I'm telling you, I don't know! Honest. I was here a couple days is all. And he was never here when I was. I swear."

"How would you like to spend the next fifteen years in a federal penitentiary, Trey? I'm not talking Club Fed either. I'll make sure you're in a place where we put cartel assholes, gangbangers, murderers. A place where they eat soft, pasty boys like you for lunch." She leaned in close. "Sometimes literally."

Oh, Jesus . . .

He wasn't sure what would go first. Would he puke or pee his pants?

"Who's in the cast?"

"The—"

"The H8ers," Heron said. "Who ran the website out of here?" He wasn't as crazy as her. Longish hair, short beard, he seemed like a pretty okay dude.

Trey wanted to talk to *him*.

"Poley was in charge of it."

"Who's he?" Now Maleficent was at him again.

"He lives here with his mom."

"His real first name?"

"It's Napoleon, but everyone calls him Poley."

Witch-lady said to Heron, "Then the name on the rental agreement was fake." She turned back. "Tell me more about this Poley guy."

"I don't know more." He raised his hands. "I swear."

"You join a club whose purpose is to troll people, and you don't know anything about who's running it?"

"Like I said, a couple days is all!"

Puke, pee or cry?

She was frustrated or acting frustrated. "You really don't have a clue about him?"

"No. I swear on . . ." He didn't know what to swear on. So he shut up.

The agent said, "Witnesses saw a woman, brown or auburn hair, forties. She was here a couple of times. Who's she?"

"That's Poley's mother. She didn't know what was going on. She thought we were hanging out, playing video games."

Now Heron leaned closer. "What about FeAR-15?"

"About . . . who?"

"Poley may have been in charge of the site, but FeAR ran the technical side."

Another gray cell fired. "Oh, him. I only knew him as the Admin. He didn't want any names used. He's a scary fuck."

The agent lady and Heron looked at each other. Could he use that kind of language talking to cops? Well, it was out now.

"What do you know about the Admin?" she asked him.

"Keyboards faster than anybody I've ever seen. Drinks tea. Plays FPS games like nobody I've ever seen. Wears suits. Insults, like, everybody."

Heron asked, "Where is he?"

"Dude told us to clean his workstation and he left to get us some pizza. And he just booked."

And maybe it was *him* who dimed them out to the cops. Cold. Totally cold.

Agent Sanchez looked at Heron. "So our friend here destroyed evidence."

"Not. Good." Heron looked toward the ceiling briefly, then down once more. "That's obstruction, right?"

Maybe the computer guy wasn't so okay after all.

"Sure is. And a whole other charge." She shook her head. "A bad one."

Nuts shriveling again.

Oh, man . . .

Agent Sanchez glanced at her phone before narrowing her eyes at him. "You're telling me you *didn't* know Spider went out to kill people on the Wall of Blame?"

"No! Really! Not a clue."

She showed the screen to Heron, who read it, then looked Trey up and down.

What was that? Was Doobie talking, giving him up?

Fucking sellout.

She turned back to him. "Is that the story you're sticking with?" She held up a hand. "Before you answer, you should know that lying to a federal agent is a felony. More people do hard time for that than for the crime itself." She let that sink in. "So. I'm a federal agent. And you're lying."

Heron shrugged. "Cut and dried."

Trey kept replaying what Poley told him would happen to him if he told anybody anything about the H8ers.

But the time for that was over.

His shoulders slumped. "I knew. Doobie and me both knew what was going on. Hell, *everybody* who went onto the site knew. That's why we were there." Tears now. "We were just so tired of it all."

"Tired of what?" she asked.

"Everything. We got shit on so much. All the H8ers. This was a way to get even."

Heron said, "You're online a lot, I'll bet."

"Yeah, I game. I pretty much live on Twitch."

"And you go to the chans," Heron said. "4chan, 8kun, the others."

"Yeah, that's where I heard about H8ers."

He leaned forward. "*When* did you hear?"

"I don't know. Last week maybe. Look, I was just . . . Poley saw my IP address. He knew I was nearby. Asked me here to hang out. You know, clean up, make food runs. I was here, yeah, I knew maybe what was going on. But I didn't do anything."

"It's still conspiracy," Maleficent said, like it made her happy to say the word. "Do you hear that sound, Trey? It's like a loud roar."

He tilted his head, listening hard, but couldn't make out any noise. "What do you mean?"

"It's the sound of your buddy stepping on the gas of that bus he just threw you under." She pointed toward the front yard, where other officers had taken Doobie. She lifted her phone, which would have the fucker's statement.

"He's out there cutting a deal for himself. You'd better spit out whatever you know, because whoever talks first and gives us the best information wins a get-out-of-jail-free card. The other loser gets a one-way ticket to a cell and a roommate with a record for 817s."

"Jesus," Heron muttered.

"Eight seventeens?" Trey's voice cracked. "What's an 817?"

She didn't answer. "Do you know what prison is like? They never totally shut out the lights. You never get any privacy. You can't even take a crap in peace. There's no quiet. No space. Your cellmate farts, and you smell it. He snores and you hear it. He comes on to you, and you pretend you like it."

More tears. A lot of tears.

Agent Sanchez said, "FeAR. Spider. Poley and his mother. What are they driving?"

"I don't know anything else!"

Trey couldn't hold it anymore.

It was pee, dribbling from crotch to socks and pooling in his shoes. And he'd worn light-blue jeans. Figured.

Agent Badass didn't bat an eye. "I see you're taking us seriously."

"I'll do whatever I can." He resorted to begging.

"You have *any* deets?"

"Deets . . . details?"

Agent Sanchez lifted an eyebrow. Impatient.

"No, ma'am! Doobie and me, we were like . . ." He remembered an earlier thought. "Flies. We were like flies, nothing. Nobodies."

Her look suggested she agreed with the assessment.

"Somebody wiped the servers," Heron said. "Was that you?"

"Man, I can't even finish *Mario Kart*. Wiping servers? Forget about it. The Admin—that FeAR guy. He typed something before he left. The screens filled with lines of code and stuff."

Agent Sanchez turned to Heron. "He knew we were coming."

Bile climbed the back of Trey's throat, burning its way up. He swallowed hard. Not wanting to add to his humiliation by vomiting on Agent Badass' shoes, which would probably be another felony.

"I got nothing else. Seriously."

Sanchez gave her head a disgusted shake and rose. She walked to the door. Heron gave him an assessing look before leaving the room behind her.

"Wait!" Trey called, his voice cracking. "What'd he say? You have to tell me!"

"Oh, your buddy, Doobie?" Sanchez gave him a shrug. "I don't know. We haven't heard from the team outside."

"What?"

Maleficent said, "Doesn't matter. We got what we needed from you." She closed the door.

Now, the stench of the urine oozing in his pants overwhelmed him. He leaned forward and puked on his own shoes.

Fan-fucking-tastic.

Pee and puke.

His only saving grace was that Poley's mom wasn't here to see him like this. He wasn't sure why she had gone, or where she and Poley had gotten to, but he hoped she wouldn't be too upset by what had happened in her basement.

Most of all, he hoped she was safe.

CHAPTER 60

Fallow relaxed in the back seat as Luciano drove expertly, just two miles above the limit, never weaving, never honking.

They could have arrived far sooner. Lake Elsinore and the surrounding environs in Riverside County were not that big. But Luciano was taking a complicated route to get to their destination, all the while scanning for threats.

Fallow was thinking about what lay ahead.

Like Natalie Jackson.

Still roaming the earth, alive if traumatized. And maybe a goose egg on her head.

He was about to ask how much longer the drive would take when Luciano called over his shoulder, "Fifteen minutes."

Fallow compulsively rolled a roulette pill in his fingers. His heart rate was up. His legs felt bouncy.

The Push reared its head once more. The downside of embracing his nature was that if he didn't kill with some regularity, it affected his equilibrium—physical as well as psychic.

The SUV made several broad turns and headed to the foothills of the Santa Anas. The mountains had always seemed to Fallow like a footnote to the City of Angels. Filthy, scruffy, littered with gravel and grapefruit-size rocks and boulders. It was as if the entire uninspired range was crumbling. This was not the Rockies.

Luciano piloted the Escalade to the front of an extended-stay inn. It was the sort of place where the deluxe suite—if they had one—was under a hundred a night.

And for damn sure no guest had ever arrived in a $100,000 limo.

"Ain't the Ritz, sir. But you'll be, like, invisible. You know what I'm saying?"

He nodded. Then climbed out silently, slung his newly acquired backpack over his shoulder and took stock of his surroundings. There were no other residences or commercial or retail structures nearby.

The gleaming, bulky vehicle glided away and Fallow skirted the pale-blue one-story building, grit scraping under the soles of his shoes.

At room 149, he paused and looked around.

No one noticed because there was no one *to* notice.

He rapped.

Three times. Not soft, not loud.

No secret pattern.

The voices inside quieted. Fallow looked toward the peephole and a moment later the dead bolt and the chain offered two different types of clattering as they were undone.

Strange to see Poley and Jennifer, his mother, in a context different from the basement of the rental house in Anaheim, though the rooms here weren't much better. A bit cleaner, a bit brighter.

And, sadly, surely lacking in his favorite accent in the basement—spiders.

He walked inside.

Jennifer looked him over as he dropped the backpack and sloughed off his jacket.

"Anaheim?" Fallow asked.

"Raided. They picked up the two losers."

Trey and Doobie.

Fallow got a bottle of water from the minibar and drank most of it down. Then, as he and Jennifer exchanged glances, he was aware that another topic had just been placed on the agenda.

She said to her son, "Poley, go do some errands."

"But we don't need—"

"Now."

He grimaced and cast a chill look toward Fallow, an odd mix of disgust and anger. The young man heaved a dramatic sigh and stalked to the door.

"An hour," she called after him.

Poley tried to slam the door behind him, but since it was mounted to a hydraulic self-closer, he couldn't get any speed. It simply clicked shut.

Fallow crossed the room, took Jennifer in his arms and kissed her hard. Her mouth hungrily sought his.

She broke away to take his hand and lead him to the bedroom. "Better than a futon in a basement," she whispered, pulling him onto the bed.

And better than an office chair in a call center, by yourself.

She unclasped his belt and worked his pants off.

He lay back and closed his eyes.

Dennison Fallow couldn't help but reflect that Jennifer was as talented at this skill as she was at her true profession.

CHAPTER 61

Ten Days Earlier

"What's the story with that crazy man, Jason Powell?" Gerard Dreth asked from the back of his limousine.

Solid, thick-haired Luciano—driver and minder—steered the black stretch Escalade into the Santa Anas. He answered in what Dreth had come to think of as Brooklynese, "Keeps ranting about conspiracies and world domination, you know what I'm saying? Threatening you, threatening the company. He's on Discord, 4chan, Substack and some others. He's banned from Facebook and Twitter—or X, or whatever. Serious media hasn't picked him up. Yet."

He grunted by way of acknowledgment. The fifty-year-old CEO of DrethCo Inc. outweighed his bodyguard by forty pounds, little of it muscle. He didn't play tennis, he didn't golf, he didn't run. He sat on his ass and invented things, then sold them and figured out what to do with his money. Or extorted people, who then gave him loads of cash, and then he figured out what to do with *that*.

He scrubbed a hand across his face and realized he hadn't shaved that morning.

Not good.

Dreth always wanted to look put-together for meetings. Physical appearance communicated power or weakness.

He wondered if the person he'd come to see would care.

Luciano said, "We had eyes on Powell, but we lost track of him somewhere in the Mojave. Our sources tell us he bought guns and explosives. He keeps yapping about blowing up the Glendale HQ. But word is the Feds are on him and getting close."

Dreth shifted his focus to a more immediate concern. "You're sure about this person?" Meaning the impending meeting.

"Forget about it. Vetted 'em myself. I'm talking deep dive. Solid. And from what I hear, you're getting the best in the country."

Best was important to Gerard Dreth. It was the standard he set in his own life. From computer programmers to his bespoke worsted suits to Kathy, the obedient and beautiful wife, twenty years younger, he cultivated only the best.

Luciano pulled into a parking lot. A dark-green Range Rover—an expensive model—sat facing nose-out in one of the parking slots. There were no other cars.

Luciano consulted a complicated scanner. "Clear. No transmissions. We're good."

Dreth climbed out. "Wait here."

"You got it, boss."

He walked to the Rover and stopped about ten feet from the driver's side as the door opened and the person he'd come to meet stepped out.

In her mid-forties, she was tall and lean, athletically built. Abundant auburn hair. Her jacket and sleek pencil skirt, both black, were very nearly as nice as his suit.

"Gerard Dreth."

An attractive and, yes, sexy woman like this he might otherwise have pulled into a brief but tight embrace, even on first meeting her.

One look at those laser-ish eyes, though, told him not to take liberties. He released her hand after a quick shake.

"I'm Jennifer," she said. "I understand you want me to kill someone."

341

Jennifer studied him.

Dreth was a large man—well over 250 pounds. His hair was perfectly trimmed but he hadn't shaved, which was curious. He'd likely forgotten. He was, she'd learned, a ruthless businessman, but he probably had never met a professional killer.

Much less hired one.

They stood together, both looking into the field. She nearly smiled, noting a spider spinning a web.

Thinking of Dennison Fallow.

"I've looked into you." Jennifer always did her research. Hours of it, *days* of it. Every hit was organized with military precision—from the initial planning to the diversion, to the invasion, to triage, to evac.

"You founded and are CEO of DrethCo, a private company. It makes unglamorous software—"

"Well—" he began to protest.

She repeated bluntly, "Unglamorous software. No shoot-'em-up games, no cute apps. You've never been in any trouble criminally or, I should say, been caught doing anything criminal. The only news the company's made lately is the acquisition of Brakon Computing. Hardly got any coverage outside the business press. But there's a conspiracy nut named Powell who says you're demonic. I can't figure out his gripe. Data mining?"

Dreth grimaced. "Data mining is used chewing gum. *Everybody* does it. And AI is scavenging for every last bit of remaining details on our lives. There's no profit margin left. But this isn't about Powell."

He explained that someone working for the company had become a problem. "They found some shit they shouldn't have and could do the whistleblower thing. Fuck up the merger. Fuck me over. Big time."

"You need them gone. But in a way their death can't lead to their job, you or the company."

"In a nutshell."

"You have what I asked for?" Spoken in a tone that said it wouldn't be good if you didn't.

He gave her a thumb drive with all the details on the target he'd been able to pull together. She pocketed it.

"Give me forty-eight hours to put things in motion, then I'll meet you here again to brief you. And I'll need half the fee transferred beforehand."

The price for the hit was two million. Which he thought was a bit steep. But then again, murder was definitely a sellers' market.

He said, "All right. You have a Bitcoin vault?"

Jennifer let out a derisive snort. "Crypto? You can't be serious."

———

Two days later, Jennifer met the portly CEO in the same parking lot in the stark Santa Ana Mountains.

"I've put together a three-level strategy," she began. "At first, it'll look like the target's the random victim of a serial killer. Cops just love them. But then they'll run the case and, if they're halfway smart and they probably are, they'll discover that the serial killing's a cover, to hide what's really going on."

"Which is?"

"The killer's working for an organization devoted to hate."

"Hate? There is such a thing?"

"You'd better believe it. The online world is filled with jealous ass-holes who can't stand to see other people succeed. Nobody gave *them* a leg up. Envy becomes hate and they lash out anonymously from dark corners of the web. That's what we'll exploit."

She pulled out her phone and tapped the screen. "My son and a computer expert I use created a website. H8ers.org." She handed the phone to Dreth.

"'H' and 8. Haters. Clever."

"Look through it. See, they target people who've had some luck in life and become successful."

"Jesus. It already has hundreds of members."

"And it's growing hourly. Trolls send in newspaper clippings and posts about people like your target. Success stories. They're posted on a page called the Wall of Blame." She tipped her head toward the phone. "Because the trolls blame these so-called lucky people for getting the breaks they should've had."

Dreth caught on quickly. "And one of them takes it a step further than trolling. He kills."

"Exactly. We'll have six victims. Your target will be one of them. The cops will easily buy the H8ers motive—because first of all, they'll be smug they saw through the serial killer ruse. And second, because all cops are convinced that *everything* having to do with the internet has to be evil. Finally, they'll see the site, all the members and think, Oh, it has to be real."

The plan was already underway. Her son had used a fake identity to rent a house in Anaheim, converting the basement into a clubhouse for the H8ers and the location of the website's servers. He had also identified two complete losers, Trey and Doobie, who would be invited into the inner circle. When the police inevitably closed in, Tweedledum and Tweedledee would spill their guts, verifying to detectives that H8ers was real and its purpose was to kill targets on the Wall of Blame.

The CEO frowned. "How do you know the cops will find the rental house?"

"We'll lead them there. Leave clues at each scene linking the crimes together. The police will see that every victim was mentioned in the *LA Herald.*

"The victims will be in cities that begin with letters that spell out the nickname of the hit man from the site." Jennifer now examined him closely. "You understand that for this to work, there have to be other victims. Innocent. How are you with collateral damage?"

He waved away the question as if it bored him and asked, "Who's the hit man?"

"Somebody I've used before. I need him to mimic being a serial killer, and he'll be great for the role, considering he really *is* a card-carrying sociopath."

"What's his name?"

"Dennison Fallow."

"And he's good?"

"The best. He was personally mentored by my late husband."

And there was nobody better at planning and carrying out murders than Charlie Benedict.

CHAPTER 62

Present Day

"Do I really have to stay here?"

Jake sympathized with Natalie Jackson but held his ground. "Yes. Too risky to leave."

Sanchez added, "In the past, the perp's left town after an attack, successful or not, but until we get him, you need to stay out of sight. You're a danger to him, an eyewitness."

A neighbor had taken her dog to his apartment, so she was taken care of. What concerned Natalie the most was her job.

"I've got so much work to do for my client."

"You'll have to do it here," Sanchez said.

"I guess." The woman did more glasses shoving, then she sat on the suite's couch and pulled her computer toward her. She had her own router and Heron noted that she had to type the password in, presumably every time she used it. Much wiser than storing it in cache.

Jake watched Natalie coding. In addition to JavaScript and C++, she used a language he'd never seen. Maybe she'd hacked it together herself. She definitely knew her way around script.

A loud knock punctuated the silence. Sanchez rested a hand on her gun, checked the peephole, then opened the door to a Highway Patrol officer. He carried a paper bag marked "Evidence" and a box containing what looked like deli-wrapped sandwiches and drinks. He handed Sanchez the evidence bag. "From Lake Elsinore PD. They found something the perp dropped in the take-down." He set down the box. "And we got a call from DHS, Long Beach."

"My office," Sanchez said.

"Someone named Mouse? She asked if we could get you guys some food and put it on your tab."

"Thanks. We can use it."

"This Mouse—that's her real name?"

"Might as well be."

"She said somebody in the office, Declan, placed the food order. She hopes you like it."

After the officer left, Jake handed out sandwiches and chips. Among them was tuna and tomato, his favorite. His chosen beverage too. Red Bull. A nice coincidence. There was coffee for the women.

Jake took several long hits of the drink. He needed the caffeine. Sleeping upright in a chair was not really sleeping. He couldn't imagine what tonight would be like, tossing and turning in agony, with the eggplant-colored bruises from the gunshots radiating pain. The aspirin he'd taken brought minimal relief, but he needed to be sharp and wouldn't even consider popping anything stronger.

Sanchez looked through the evidence bag.

"Anything helpful?"

She pulled out a clear plastic baggie with an evidence card attached. It contained a computer printout.

"A letter to the *Herald*." She read it to them. "'I'm a member of the website H8ers.org. They kill people who's'—misspelled—'who's names are posted on the site. The killer's a psycho. I don't know his real name, but he goes by Spider. I don't know anything more about him. He's going to kill six people. You have to stop him. I'm not giving you my name. He'd kill me if he saw I wrote this. I'm leaving until he's caught. Maybe leaving for good.'"

Natalie stared at the letter. "You know what that means?"

Jake did. If Fallow was in possession of the letter, he had found the traitor within the club and killed him before he could send the note.

Sanchez asked Natalie, "Do you remember him following you before he made initial contact?"

"No. He was just there. Like from out of nowhere."

"Did you see him with anybody else?"

"No."

"He didn't say anything about where he was going later?"

Again: "I'm sorry. No."

Sanchez was a solid, comprehensive interviewer and, obviously taking pains to keep Natalie at ease, she asked dozens of questions about the incident.

The woman clearly wanted to help but had nothing useful.

One aspect of Jake's business was the psychology of intrusion—which included recognizing post-traumatic stress from victimization.

Depending on a variety of factors, the fallout could range from blithe denial to withdrawal into a nearly catatonic state. And every victim of intrusion suffered some degree of amnesia.

He could see that Natalie fell somewhere in the middle. She might hold a key that would lead them to where Fallow planned to strike next, but that clue was locked deep within her. The best way to bring out those facts was not to ask directly about her experience.

Something might occur to her, but for now it was vital to move the case forward. He tried a different tack. "Sanchez, let's look at where we are."

He opened his laptop and, as he and Sanchez reviewed the major elements of the case so far, Jake typed their conclusions into a Word document.

- Victims mentioned in articles in the *Herald* newspaper.
- Victims murdered in ways that reflected jobs or lifestyles and because of their "luck."

- H8ers.org created to target people who have had some luck getting ahead.
- Victims attacked in cities with letters sequentially spelling out the killer's nickname, SPIDER.
- Attacker is Dennison Fallow, part-time call center operator for American General Appliances.
- Fallow owns house—his old family residence, inherited after his parents died. Santa Barbara. Search warrant executed. Nothing relevant found.
- Anaheim clubhouse rented by individual running H8ers website. First name Napoleon, a.k.a. Poley. Last name unknown. Name on lease was fictional. Cash paid.
- Located house by cracking password to site servers.
- Administrator of site, formerly Ironsights, now FeAR-15. Location unknown.
- House rented and site established recently, last few days.
- Two underlings, Trey and Doobie, left in house after principals fled. Confirmed the site and motive for killings.
- Private server. Wiped before raid. FeAR used his own bleaching program. No data recovery possible.
- Whistle-blowing letter addressed to *Herald* re: Spider and the site. Never delivered. Written by member of H8ers. Dead now? No other details.
- Victims:
  - *San Diego*: Walter Kemp, real estate developer
  - *Perris*: Selina Sanchez, student-athlete
  - *Irvine*: Renault Davide, chef
  - *Del Aire*: Tanya Hilton, fitness influencer
  - *Lake Elsinore*: Natalie Jackson, computer programmer
  - *R City?*

Jake found himself sitting beside Sanchez in a similar pose to hers: arms crossed, leaning slightly forward.

He supposed she was *thinking* the same thing he was. If Fallow hadn't fled the area and was intent on killing a sixth victim, he might end his identifiable pattern of using his nickname to select the location of his next kill.

Which meant that the next attack, if there were one, might be in any city or town in the LA area, from A to Z.

It seemed Sanchez had been thinking similar thoughts when she whispered, "Where the hell are you, Fallow? Where?"

CHAPTER 63

Dennison Fallow lay back in the motel bed. Stretched. Heard a bone pop.

The timing had worked out well—sending the puppy Poley out on his errand for an hour. After fifty or so minutes with his energetic and uninhibited playmate, Jennifer, he was spent.

His mind segued to the first time he met her.

Mr. Benedict had shared few details of his personal life with Fallow during the weeks of his training. Fallow had spotted the wedding band on his hand the day they'd met, but had not been introduced to his wife until the night of his "graduation" after the stabbing at Lake Mathews.

The couple's Hollywood Hills home was set in the middle of a cleared lot, so Mr. Benedict had an unobstructed kill zone in case of attack. They parked behind the house and were joined by the cool-eyed Jennifer. Fallow thought she was a hottie for a woman who was older than he was—fifteen years or so—but he didn't think anything more of her at the time. That stuff, the *close* stuff between two people was good but it wasn't an obsession to Fallow like it was to some people. He liked touching flesh, yes, but mostly to obey the Push, which meant ripping or cutting or compressing skin until its owner stopped moving.

He had seen her at the house a few other times, briefly, before she called to deliver the news of Mr. Benedict's death.

Then nothing more.

Until a few months later, when Jennifer sent a text. She had taken over her husband's business and wanted to hire Fallow to assist on some contracts. He was moved that apparently Mr. Benedict had spoken highly of him.

The job went well. She was as skilled as her husband, but better in one regard: she shoved weighted corpses off her thirty-eight-foot boat into the Pacific Ocean. Lake Mathews might run dry at some point, giving up Mr. Benedict's dead. That would not happen if you sank the bodies a mile deep.

Several more hits followed.

One night, after they killed a government contractor turned whistleblower, they found themselves at the dead man's kitchen sink, washing off the blood and . . . one thing led to another.

They ended up on the floor of the desert cabin where the victim had been holed up.

Two hours later they'd finished cleaning away the blood—which, being slippery, had enhanced their liaison—and set fire to the cabin, then returned home.

What followed was not dating. They never went out socially. But occasionally one of them found themselves in a certain frame of mind and the other was happy to accommodate. After the always robust coupling they went their separate ways.

Now, in the extended-stay inn, Jennifer emerged from the bathroom. Water droplets beaded on her bare skin. Her body was firm and toned. Killing is a physical profession; one needed to stay in shape. They both worked out four or five times a week. Nothing fancy. Weights, kettles and battle ropes. Fallow had never been on an exercise machine in his life, yet he had plenty of muscle.

He muttered, "We have to assume the cops know who I am. I never carry ID on a job, but they took photos. Their computers will put a name to my face."

She crouched over her gym bag. "That won't be a problem. You'll be gone before they track you down."

He watched her dig through the boxes of ammunition, yellow and green, and from underneath them remove a black thong. She pulled it on.

"Where's he looking?"

He was speaking of Tristan Kane, FeAR, who was in the process of finding some distant safe houses where they could lie low until the heat died down. The man lived in the dark web, where you could acquire anything on God's earth, including hidey-holes that authorities would never find.

A knock at the door. Instantly Jennifer's pistol was in her hand, thumb flipping off the safety. She had a Kimber Micro 9 she could tuck almost anywhere due to its compact size. The special edition rose gold finish was sleek, sexy and lethal. Pure Jennifer.

"It's me," came the voice.

Unfortunate Poley.

Without pulling on any more clothing, she let him inside and walked back to the gym bag, crouching once more. She grabbed jeans, a black blouse and a matching lace bra.

Her son's gaze lingered as she dressed.

Fallow noted that she put on her clothes slowly, a reverse striptease.

Mr. Benedict was the only normal one in the family, if you counted a professional killer among the normals of the world.

Poley was sullen and, after a glance at the damp, rumpled sheets, cast a resentful look toward Fallow. Who didn't care. No one liked Poley. Not even his mother. He did what he was told. He created websites, he beat up people Mom wanted beaten up, he stole what she needed him to steal, and he could drive a boat and was efficient at wrapping bodies in chicken wire and sending them to sleep in the cold Pacific Ocean.

His brain, however, was not stellar—selecting Special Agent Sanchez's sister as a target, for instance.

"No word from FeAR?" he asked Fallow.

He didn't answer. Because if there had been word, he would have shared it.

Jennifer opened a screw-top bottle of wine and poured a glass. A key difference between her and her husband, Fallow reflected. Mr. Benedict never drank liquor during the twenty-four hours before a job and twenty-four hours after, in case follow-up was necessary.

He supposed, though, she was entitled to a little anesthetic. This particular job, so carefully planned, had required some stressful retooling.

Well, he too was dismayed.

Goddamn Sanchez, goddamn Heron . . .

And after being busted he could never go back to his home in Santa Barbara. They would have surveillance.

It was 3,204 square feet of colonial suburban home, though Fallow used only 934 of those feet to live in.

The basement.

Where his friends Desdemona III and Caliban IV also lived. He'd enjoyed naming one Henry V and, being the third generation, he became Henry V, III, which kind of made him Henry VIII. A few spiders might be the same ones he'd grown up with. Some can live for decades (the record being held by a trapdoor spider in Australia, who was part of a scientific study—the clumsily named "Number 16" lived to be forty-three).

Neighbors probably wondered if it was difficult for him to continue to live in the same house where the tragedy of his parents' deaths had occurred several years earlier.

But, no, he would tell them. He'd gotten over the bizarre and horrific murder-suicide. Records showed that Fallow's father purchased poisonous chemicals from scientific supply houses. The chemicals were mixed into the daiquiris he and his wife had as their traditional beverage at cocktail hour.

Their prolonged and agonizing deaths—basically dissolving from the inside out—made the police wonder why the man had selected those particular substances: sphingomyelinase D, hyaluronidase, alkaline phosphatase and esterase.

Fallow could have told the detectives those were the chemicals that made up brown recluse spider toxin.

But he didn't.

Jennifer's phone buzzed.

She took the call and listened.

"Good."

She disconnected, re-safetied her rose gold pistol and slipped it into the pocket of her leather jacket. "Let's move. FeAR arranged for a private jet and he found some good safe houses in the Caribbean and Central America. We can hide out there for, say, a year." She looked from her son to Fallow.

Poley said, "Whatever." And hit the snack basket above the minibar.

Fallow took more pleasure at the news. Central America was home to the goliath bird-eating tarantula, with a leg span of eleven inches. He returned Jennifer's gaze. "Works for me."

CHAPTER 64

Where? Jake Heron was thinking, echoing Sanchez's previous question.

Where are you, Fallow?

Sitting in a moderately comfortable chair in their suite, he didn't bother to refer to the map he'd downloaded, with nearby "R" cities highlighted in red. What good would that do? He'd given up on the idea that Spider—Fallow—would attack the sixth victim there. He would assume they'd figured out the city name plan and attack somewhere else altogether.

So the answer had to come from a very different source: deductive work by Sanchez and himself.

He continued to study the bullet points they'd pulled together a half hour ago, though his efforts had yet to produce any results.

Sanchez had reinterviewed Natalie Jackson, who still could recall nothing to assist them.

He leaned forward and had another bite of sandwich and a hit of Red Bull. He'd have to thank Mouse's associate for ordering what amounted to his favorite meal. He wondered if Declan was a computer nerd, like himself and Mouse and Aruba. Maybe—

"Heron?" Sanchez's voice contained a whiff of urgency.

He set the can down. "Hmm?"

"Something's not right."

Natalie stopped keyboarding and looked up too.

Sanchez was standing behind him, looking at the computer screen over his shoulder.

"Intrusion," she whispered.

He replied dryly, "Heard of it."

"Your article. It said there were two ways investigators could use intrusion in solving cases. Your Points of Potential Intrusion. And the other distinction. Intrusion for its own sake and intrusion to further a different crime. We assumed the H8ers are intruding into the lives of victims as a goal, but what if it's the second type? They're planning something else and the attacks are secondary. Maybe to misdirect us."

"Why do you think that?"

"Look at your list." She pointed to the Word document on his computer. "First, the password. That led us to the H8ers' clubhouse in Anaheim."

He swiveled to face her. "It was too easy."

"Exactly. Wouldn't FeAR—"

"—come up with a random eight or ten alphanumeric password, or graphics like his chemical symbols, that would take weeks or months to crack?"

She nodded. "Even with Hot Tub Woman and her Japanese computer working full time."

"Sanchez. It was one night."

The agent pursed her lips. "In Italy. At midnight. Overlooking a scenic mountain. I'm just saying."

He jumped to the next logical conclusion. "Our friend with the incontinence problem—"

"Trey." She rolled her eyes. "The one among us who really *does* puke."

"What he told us about wiping the servers. FeAR *knew* we were coming. He slapped on an easy-to-guess password because he *wanted* us to crack it. And they set up Trey and Doobie. Invited them to the house."

She nodded. "To conveniently give us all the gruesome details of what the H8ers were up to. So we'd stop looking for anything else."

"And the roulette pills. Why would he leave them at the scenes? The only reason was to direct us to the theme of the site. The Lux. The lucky ones."

Another hit of Red Bull. "And murdering people who lived in cities that spelled out his nickname. You ever hear of killers doing that?"

"Outside of a bad thriller movie? No. There are rituals, but nothing like that."

"Let's look at the big picture," Jake said. "First, it looks like we're after a serial killer. But then we figure out it's not that at all. The serial killing is just meant to misdirect us. We keep digging and find more clues. They lead us to what we're supposed to believe is the *real* crime: there's a sick website targeting victims for their success. We take it down. We arrest the two losers and put out an APB for Fallow, who's fled the country. As a practical matter it's case closed."

"We don't say that, but, yeah, you're right."

Sanchez picked up the evidence envelope containing the letter found on Fallow at his arrest, the one intended for the *Herald*, written by the anonymous H8er giving away Spider's name and the URL for the site. "We assumed Fallow found this in some member's possession. But what if he wrote it himself?"

"Of course," Jake said. "He had it ready to go in case we *didn't* figure out about the H8ers on our own."

Natalie asked, "But what *is* the real crime, the third one?"

Sanchez responded with a close variation of the words Jake himself had been about to utter: "A professional killing. Somebody needs one of the six victims dead for reasons . . ." She shrugged. "That we don't know yet."

Jake considered the possibilities. "So which of the six is the real intended vic?"

Sanchez pointed at their chart. "Walter Kemp, the real estate man?"

"Mostly retired, doing some community-oriented development. Nothing controversial there."

"And when we were at San Diego PD headquarters, Kemp's son, Michael, told us his dad had no enemies. Renault Davide, the chef? Tanya Hilton, an influencer? Can't see any reason to use such an elaborate scheme to kill either of them."

"Selina?" Jake said, about to dismiss her too as a target. But he frowned as he looked to Sanchez. "We eliminated her . . . but mostly because we didn't think she'd be attacked in revenge against you. We didn't consider that she might have been targeted because of something else about her life. You mentioned her job, but we didn't go into it."

Sanchez was nodding slowly. "You're right. Just because she was a low-level, part-time employee doesn't mean she didn't stumble across something she shouldn't have."

"And you don't know the name of the company?"

"No. She probably told me. But only in passing. And it was a while ago." Concern grew in Sanchez's eyes. "And if she's the target, then she's still at risk. Fallow will circle back to come after her again." She picked up her phone and, instead of Selina, placed a call directly to Detective Hall. They had a brief discussion, during which she explained their new theory.

After she hung up, she told Jake, "He's getting a patrol officer stationed outside her room."

Both Jake and Sanchez looked at Natalie Jackson. "And how about you?"

"*Me?*" She let out an amused laugh. "Nobody would want to hurt me. I'm a geek. I code. I compile. I debug."

"We never asked about your job," Sanchez said. "Who do you code for?"

"A software company. You've probably never heard of them. DrethCo Inc."

CHAPTER 65

Jake glanced at Sanchez, then rolled his chair closer to Natalie.

"Oh, we've heard of it." He kept his tone understated.

Sanchez added, "The merger with Brakon Computing. It's been on the news."

"Has it?" Natalie's eyes widened behind her red-framed glasses. And up they went higher on her nose. "I don't watch TV. Or read the papers. Or do much else, other than code. My mom tells me I have to get out more." She closed her eyes briefly. "That's why I made an idiot of myself with . . . him. Fallow. At the coffee shop, you know. You don't meet a lot of possible dates when you're banging out JavaScript and C Plus Plus twenty hours a day."

How true, thought Jacoby Heron.

Then she asked, "But why do you think *I'm* the target?"

"We don't, not necessarily," Sanchez said. "But it's worth looking into. Tell us what you do for DrethCo."

"Either of you know anything about software?" she asked them.

"I code a bit," Jake said and pursed his lips.

Sanchez stifled a grin.

"My specialty is biometrics and kinesis analysis. I've been writing code for their educational software, K through twelve. And I head up the age-verification program."

Jake was intrigued. He told Sanchez that determining the age of visitors to websites had long been a holy grail of IT. Home pages absolutely had to keep youngsters away from inappropriate content and software that collected data or asked for credit card info.

He said to Natalie, "Tell me about yours."

Like most coders, she grew animated when talking about her work. "My script uses a combination of facial and cranial analysis, retinal scans and keyboard profiling to estimate the age of the user. It's ninety-nine percent accurate."

He blinked. "Unheard of."

"I'm good." Her smile faltered. "Only there's a problem. A glitch I can't fix." A glance at Jake. "If you know coding, you'll appreciate this—I could be dealing with a mandelbug."

Jake told Sanchez, "A bug that's so complex or chaotic, it's nearly impossible to analyze and repair. Named after a physicist who worked with fractals." He scanned the lines of code on her screen. "This is what you're working on now?"

She gave a humorless laugh. "Now. And every other waking minute of my life."

"What's the problem?"

"For some reason the bug *reverses* my code when the program runs."

"Reverses?"

A frustrated sigh. "I have no idea what's going on. It's resistant to every patch I write."

"Can I see?" Jake asked.

She pushed the big laptop closer to him.

He hunched forward and squinted at the screen, on which was the shell: the C: prompt, pulsing on a black background. He assessed what programs she was running, easily recognizing them. He began to keyboard.

"Whoa," Natalie whispered. "He *does* know code."

After three or four minutes, he pointed to lines of software, incomprehensible to most of the world, but a glowing beacon to him. He turned to Sanchez. "I traced the bug to this. It's a barrier to the company's inner servers. It's so righteous we call it a Ballistic Firewall."

Natalie said, "Yeah, that's where my debugging ends. But I'm not authorized to get through it. And I asked the supervisor, he just thanked me for the work and said they didn't need me anymore. But I couldn't let it go. I kept trying to get in anyway." She shrugged. "I wanted a full-time job there. So I had to make sure my code was clean. But I kept getting borked."

"When did that happen?" Sanchez asked.

"I don't know. About two weeks ago."

"Not long before the H8ers site went live." Jake felt a puzzle piece snap into place.

"You think somebody in the company saw me trying to penetrate the firewall and . . . wanted to hurt me? Jesus! I mean, Mr. Dreth? He's a dirty old man, but killing someone? No, he wouldn't. Impossible."

Jake knew the worst intrusions were carried out by those we're convinced would never intrude. He told the two women as much.

Sanchez stared at the raw code on the screen as if trying to read a foreign language. She said absently, "You think that's the key, Heron? Whatever's on the other side of that wall?"

"One way to find out." Jake turned his eyes toward her, expecting resistance, if not an outright order of prohibition. She'd already let him step over the line with his hacking twice today, and that was to find people who were at risk of immediate death. Hacking a corporation's main server? Maybe she'd had enough.

Sanchez was motionless for a long moment. Then she rose, stretched and said, "I'm going to send some texts." With a glance at Natalie's computer, she added casually, "Make me a hot dog, Heron." And she walked into the bedroom of the suite, pulling her phone from her pocket.

He began keyboarding once more.

Natalie moved close and watched, rapt, as he pounded out lines of code. There were some helpful programs on a thumb drive in his gear bag, but it would have taken too long to find and load the software. And Jake had learned that it was usually better to hack together exploits like this on the fly, since he could improvise better. He had long felt that writing commercial software was like composing a pleasant but predictable symphony, but hacking was akin to playing jazz.

Twenty minutes later, he was in. He loaded a cloaking program to disguise his presence, but these efforts never lasted long. His time inside the servers would be limited. He went to the most recent files and the ones that had been reviewed with the most frequency. He copied them, created an encrypted container on Natalie's laptop and dumped them in. Then he backed out, shredding all evidence of his presence.

He called up the documents and looked them over fast.

Then, hardly believing what he was seeing, read them again.

He sat back, motionless, his shoulders slumped.

"Dr. Heron," Natalie said urgently. "Are you okay?"

He called out to Sanchez, "You need to see this."

She returned and studied him. "Heron. The cliché about seeing a ghost? That's your face right now."

As if it were an explosive device, he slowly turned the computer toward both women.

Sanchez leaned down. Her hair dipped near his cheek and the inevitable smell of lavender wafted. Jake read the document yet again.

CLASSIFIED: NOT FOR DISTRIBUTION

DrethCo Inc., Level Three Marketing Plan for the LEAP Project.

Beneath were three pages of dense text. After Natalie had finished reading she gasped. "*That's* what I've been working on?" Sanchez too sat back, her face revealing shock.

Jake looked at her. "You know what this means?"

A nod. "We've got a problem. A big one."

CHAPTER 66

Jennifer Benedict was recalling her conversation with FeAR from twenty minutes earlier.

He had imparted far more than the locations of safe houses in the Caribbean. He had also shared details about his hack into local law enforcement comms and nearby hotel security cameras. He had learned that Sanchez, Heron and Natalie were in the Avanti Inn in Lake Elsinore. The threesome had used a credit card trick to hide their identities at check-in, but FeAR's automated license plate scanning program placed them at the Avanti. And the inn's computer registered only one check-in that day.

They'd been assigned room 118.

Jennifer was on her way there now, accompanied by Fallow and Poley, who was behind the wheel of the SUV.

She would never leave a contract hit unfinished. No one would be heading to any safe houses until Natalie Jackson was dead. Once that was done, she could disappear for a while, then reemerge with a new identity. That meant leaving parts of her past behind, as she always did after a major job, and this had been her biggest one to date. She always tidied up loose ends—the mark of a true professional—and this time was no exception.

Part of it was the money Dreth was paying her. Murder, to her, was a business, after all. Like making toothpaste or writing commercial books. But there was her professional pride too. Like her husband, Charlie, she had never failed to fulfill a contract.

She glanced to her left, at Poley. He was competent behind the wheel, though she wished he'd concentrate a bit more on the road and less on the Doritos he was shoveling in.

As they rode in silence, her thoughts drifted to the past, when her son was born. She'd decided to call him Napoleon, imagining he'd become a brilliant, if ruthless, leader. It did not take long for her to realize the boy was no Bonaparte. No, he was a Poley, through and through.

Being honest with herself, she regretted the affair that had brought her only child into existence. If Poley had been Charlie Benedict's true son, he might have turned out like Dennison Fallow.

A part of her had always wondered whether her husband knew the child wasn't his.

And if that was why he had embraced Fallow in a way he never did Poley.

Her pregnancy was the unexpected by-product of an affair with a married hedge fund billionaire. She decided to convert what could have been a disaster into a windfall. Jennifer played the game out to the tune of $6 million over four years before her former lover got divorced and she lost her power over him.

The hapless billionaire perished in a freak car accident two weeks after sending the last blackmail fee to her secret account.

Men. Truly the weaker sex.

"There's the inn," Fallow said, pulling her back to the present.

"Drive past it," she told Poley.

There was no police guard at the place. Which made sense, since they'd assume Fallow had left the area to hunt for his next victim. And parking a cruiser would have drawn attention to the inn.

She said, "Pull into the gas station next door, go around back and drive over the grass to the lot behind the motel."

"Huh? Why?"

Sighing, Fallow said, "There are cameras covering the front lot of the inn."

"Oh. Yeah. Sure."

The black Acura SUV they were in was a dump vehicle. Jennifer didn't care if the plates were recorded—it would go up in flames soon—but she didn't want the clerk to notice three armed individuals exiting a car in the front lot.

Poley turned into the station and drove to the back, then rolled over the grassy strip separating the gas station from the motel. The tires dropped over a high curb into the inn's lot with a resonant thud.

"Shit," Poley muttered. "You think the axle's broken?"

Fallow whispered, "It's an SUV, Poley. That's what they're made for."

"Sure, I guess."

"There." Jennifer pointed to a space under a stand of oak trees. "Park facing out."

He backed in and cut the engine.

She checked their surroundings and saw no one, then consulted some texts from FeAR before gesturing toward the back of the motel. "The window to the right of the back door? That's theirs, one eighteen." She turned to her son. "We'll keep watch out here while Dennison goes to the window to take out Natalie. As for the other two, Sanchez and Heron"—she glanced at Fallow—"incapacitate them. Killing a Fed will take things to a higher level and we don't need that kind of attention. Some well-placed rounds will take them out of commission forever. With hollow points, the surgeons will never be able to repair the damage to their knees and ankles."

The man nodded, apparently eager to get started. She gave him a slow perusal, admiring his hard muscles. Heat pooled low in her belly. After this was over, she'd take him back to the hotel room bed, send Poley on another errand and enjoy herself before the trip to the private jet terminal.

Her son interrupted her wayward thoughts. "Hey, what if one of us breaks into the building and, you know, knocks on their door. And that distracts them, then Spider, *blam*, shoots them."

She struggled for patience. "Because the police would know somebody else was part of the plan. Dennison is a solo killer. He uses FeAR for information, but he doesn't take any backup on a job. Remember?"

"Oh, yeah. Right."

Honestly. That son of hers . . .

"I'll go cover the left side," she said to him. "You stay near here. We only shoot as a last resort. If there's no other way out. Understand?"

"Sure, I guess."

If he said that sentence once more, she'd scream. "Let's go."

All three climbed out.

Poley took up position close to their SUV and she and Fallow walked together toward the window. She would continue on to the other end of the lot and keep an eye on the driveway to the front.

The scent of recently poured asphalt and pine and faint diesel fumes surrounded them. After Fallow fired all seventeen rounds in his Glock, the air would be redolent with the sweet and heady odor of smokeless powder, a fragrance Jennifer preferred over any perfume.

They had gotten no more than twenty feet from the SUV when they stopped cold.

Jennifer sucked in a breath.

Agent Carmen Sanchez was pushing out the back door of the motel, weapon in hand. There was a millisecond pause as she blinked. Then she aimed her Glock directly at Jennifer's face.

"Federal agent," she said, her voice deadly calm. "Get down on your knees, hands on your heads."

CHAPTER 67

Jennifer's shock became rage, which morphed into icy calculation.

Sanchez's face revealed no surprise at seeing Spider in the company of a woman holding a compact semiauto. Somehow, she and that fucking hacker had realized Natalie was the true intended target and Fallow was coming to finish the job. She'd come here to look for threats but hadn't expected to walk right into them.

"Knees," Sanchez repeated. "Hands on your heads."

But the agent was alone, which meant she and Heron had just figured out the real plan minutes ago. Backup would be on the way, but Jennifer had a window here. Maybe she could salvage the situation.

For an instant, none of the three moved, the only sound traffic passing by. A jet bound for John Wayne.

Then a gunshot from behind them. And a shriek. "Oh, shit!" Poley's voice cracked.

Sanchez turned her attention toward the new threat. Only for an instant.

It was enough.

Fallow dived to the right, behind a nearby car, drawing his gun, and Jennifer fired two covering shots toward Sanchez—to keep her down—and sprinted back to Poley, who was hunkered behind a battered white pickup truck.

She knew her son hadn't fired at Sanchez in an effort to help Mom and Fallow escape. He'd accidentally pulled the trigger of his LCP getting it out of his pocket, nearly shooting himself in the leg.

For once his incompetence had paid off.

Jennifer raised her rose gold Kimber and peered from behind the truck, searching for a target.

Sanchez spotted her first and blasted two rounds at her. They slammed into the front fender of the truck. Poley yelped in fear.

Jennifer scooted to the other side of the pickup, popped up and fired six shots toward Sanchez, forcing her to dive behind an old green dumpster.

The metal container rang fiercely under the slugs' impact.

Damn, so close . . .

Sanchez didn't stay down for long. She stood to let loose a barrage of return fire. Jennifer hadn't expected the move and just missed being hit as she dropped hard to the asphalt, losing skin on a palm.

From the right side of the parking lot, Fallow fired several times—toward the dumpster and then into room 118, though Jennifer suspected Sanchez and Heron had moved Natalie from the room for her safety.

Beside her, Poley jumped up and fired blindly. His rounds landed in the back wall of the motel, nowhere near Sanchez. He ducked immediately and continued to whimper.

Then the agent was on the move, sprinting toward Fallow. Rather than firing at him, Sanchez was shooting suppressive rounds toward Jennifer to keep her pinned down.

The tactic worked. By the time Jennifer chanced another peek, Sanchez was out of sight.

An instance of passion tainting judgment? Had Sanchez gone after Fallow because he'd attacked her sister?

Or had she assessed that Jennifer was burdened by an inept associate and posed the lesser threat?

Jennifer wasn't sure about the first, but the second was definitely the case.

Another glance. No Sanchez, no Fallow.

The contract had gone to shit. There was nothing to do now but escape, forgoing the rest of the fee. If they didn't already know her identity, they soon would, and she had to get her go bag and flee the country to one of FeAR's Caribbean safe houses. Dennison Fallow was on his own.

But even as she stepped toward the driver's door, SWAT arrived.

A massive tactical vehicle screeched into the lot, disgorging a six-person team, in full combat gear: Nomex hoods, body armor, ballistic helmets. They fanned out like a black swarm.

Sanchez was busy chasing Fallow and apparently had no radio, so she couldn't explain to the SWAT team exactly what was happening. They were assessing the situation and clearing the lot. Then two shots rang out from the direction in which Fallow and Sanchez had disappeared. Three officers ran in that direction.

The remaining three and the commander continued through the lot, clearing it—soon they would find the mother and son.

It was too late for Jennifer to hide her gun and claim she was a guest caught in a crossfire. Tactical officers were pros. They would detain and search everybody at the scene. And even if they couldn't prove she was behind the plot to kill Natalie Jackson, she'd just discharged a weapon at a federal agent. For that alone she'd end up behind bars so long she'd be in dentures and diapers by the time she left supermax.

She judged angles and distances.

She had to make her move now. More cops would arrive any minute.

"What do we do, Mom?"

She looked at Poley, with his nose running and his hands shaking so hard he could barely hold his weapon.

"Don't you worry, honey. Mommy always takes care of you."

An announcement from a bullhorn cut their conversation short. "Anyone in the parking lot, this is a police operation. Come forward with your hands up."

Poley whimpered again.

"We'll be okay. We've got surprise on our side. We'll split up—"

"No!"

"Just for a few minutes. Look. There." She pointed to a grassy field behind them and to the left. "Down the hill, see it? The grocery store. GreenFresh. See the lights?"

"Yeah." He sniffed up some snot.

"I'll keep them busy here. You get to the parking lot. Carjack some wheels and drive to the corner there." She nodded toward the light. "I'll meet you. We'll head back to our motel. Get our go bags and fly to one of FeAR's safe houses." She smiled. "Just the two of us. You can do that? Jack a car? For me?"

He wiped his nose. "Sure, I guess."

"Your gun. Remember, keep your finger off the trigger until you're ready to shoot."

"Yeah, I forgot before."

"It's all right."

She looked around. The tactical officers were getting close.

Jennifer turned back. "There may be a cop or two in the field, but they won't be expecting anybody to be going in that direction. If you see anybody in a uniform, shoot them."

Panic strained his voice. "I . . . I don't know if I can."

She patted his shoulder. "That's okay, honey. Then just shoot *toward* them, scare them. So they have to hide. Can you do that?"

He nodded. "Sure, I guess."

Jennifer looked down and brushed some crumbs off his *Fortnite* T-shirt. "You ready?"

"Mom?" He gave her a plaintive look.

She smiled and hugged him. "Go. I'll meet you at the corner."

He turned and began to scrabble away behind the cars.

When he was at the crest of the grassy hill that led down to the grocery store, she inhaled deeply. A debate. It didn't last long. She pulled out her cell phone and tapped the screen.

"Nine-one-one, what's your emer—"

"There's a man with a gun behind the Avanti Inn," she said in an urgent whisper. "He's headed to GreenFresh Grocery. He's shooting people!"

"Ma'am, we have units at that location. Can you provide a description?"

"White male, twenty-two years old, six feet tall, heavyset, wearing jeans and a gray T. He said he'd kill every cop he saw. Please, you have to stop him. And wait, yes, there are two or three other men with him. All running toward the grocery store. Hurry!"

A keyboard clacked in the background. "I've advised the officers at the scene. What's your name, ma'am?"

Jennifer disconnected and watched the SWAT team react as the message was relayed to them. The supervisor and two of his people sprinted toward the hill leading down to the grocery store, leaving only one in the parking lot.

Perfect. They would converge on the hill where Poley and the mythical "two or three others" were.

Leaving her free to get into the SUV and take off.

Jennifer Benedict glanced toward where her unfortunate son was galloping toward the safety she had promised him.

Sorry, honey, she thought, so sorry. If only you hadn't turned out to be . . . *you*. Then immediately turned her attention to how best to get to the SUV and leave everyone in her rearview.

CHAPTER 68

Fallow sprinted toward an abandoned warehouse across the two-lane street from the Avanti Inn.

Cars skidded out of his path, their drivers honking in anger, but he ignored them and kept going.

The warehouse offered the perfect opportunity to ambush Sanchez.

Jennifer had ordered him to wound rather than kill and he'd liked the idea of Sanchez's torment—both physical because of the shattered bone, and emotional as she wasted away from boredom.

But he decided it was easier and safer to kill the bitch and be done with it.

He twisted to fire a few shots her way, then put on an extra burst of speed, darting inside the warehouse before she closed the fifty-foot gap between them.

He climbed onto the loading dock, the only entrance he could find, and disappeared deep into the warren of the warehouse's interior. Dim and reeking of mold. In the back, he found cover behind a pile of construction debris. Catching his breath, he turned to face the loading dock doorway.

And waited for Special Agent Carmen Sanchez . . .

Once he'd learned her name, yesterday, he'd asked FeAR to dig up what he could. Mr. Benedict had taught him to know his enemies. FeAR found a news story from years back about her getting shot in the line of duty. She'd been an FBI field agent in their LA office, but also was a member of their enhanced SWAT team.

There was no reported reason why she'd left the Bureau to join Homeland, and he wondered what the exact nature of her current assignment was. There seemed to be a lot of secrecy and little documentation about Homeland Security Investigations. But she was decorated, she closed cases that resulted in successful convictions, she'd run up against tabloid-worthy mob bosses and renowned terrorists . . . and exchanged their designer custom suits for orange jumpsuits.

FeAR offered to do some further digging, but he told him not to bother. He knew what he needed to know.

She was what Mr. Benedict would have called a worthy adversary. He would not underestimate her.

Especially after their mixed-martial-arts match earlier near the coffee shop where he'd first targeted Natalie Jackson.

He glanced out the door once more and noted Sanchez had been slowed by traffic. She hadn't sprinted across the street like he had. She was being smarter—more cautious—showing her badge to the cars and gesturing for them to stop. Only about half complied. To avoid getting waffled, she'd been forced to take it slow.

He looked around at the piles of trash from unfinished demo work. Pale sunlight slanted in through shattered windows high in the ceiling.

A hulking piece of rusty machinery towered nearby. Probably too heavy to waste money hauling away. He couldn't tell what kind of equipment it was, but it would serve his purpose. He could hide behind it and be protected by solid iron yet have an easy shot at Sanchez in silhouette. Just like the paper targets on the range where Mr. Benedict took him to practice marksmanship.

He rushed around the side of the machine and crouched down.

Would she follow him in?

Of course she would. Another cop might not, but Carmen Sanchez was after the man who had tried to strangle her sister with a multicolor gymnastic rope. Nothing would stop her.

Except a hollow point slug in her forehead—his new target of choice.

Fallow rested his elbows on a rusty metal bar, its iron scent reminiscent of blood.

Any second now, Sanchez would appear in his kill zone. He felt like the wolf spider, the one who didn't build a web but who hunted, lying in wait to ambush prey.

Seconds passed. A full minute. He grew concerned. She should be here by now. The traffic couldn't have delayed her this long. Maybe she was trying to sneak up to the door. Maybe she was waiting for backup, although she seemed like the type to rush in.

Where the hell was she?

A faint tapping sound drew his attention to the left. He spun, aiming his gun that way. No one. He glanced down and saw a small white ball bounce twice more and then roll toward the far wall of the room along the concrete floor.

In the same instant, he registered that it was a roulette pill and that apparently there *was* another way inside other than the loading door.

He started to turn fast.

Sanchez spoke from behind him. "Drop the gun, Fallow. It's over."

As a fan of Shakespeare, who deployed irony with expert precision in crafting his plays, Dennison Fallow, watching the pill roll to a stop, could appreciate the concept now—as it kicked him hard in the ass.

CHAPTER 69

Carmen was prepared to drop Fallow where he stood if he so much as twitched.

He made no move, apparently considering his options. To make sure he had none, she took him through the full felony takedown procedure.

"Open your hand and let the gun drop." She didn't tell him to toss it or place it on the ground, which might give him a chance to point it or throw it at her. He had to know action was quicker than reaction, but she was in the superior position since her weapon was already trained on him and he was facing the other direction.

After what seemed like an eternity, he shook his head in what appeared to be some odd mix of amusement and resignation, spread his fingers wide and let the gun clatter to the floor.

"Interlace your fingers behind your head and walk backward toward my voice until I tell you to stop."

She watched as he backed up. When he'd distanced himself far enough from the weapon on the ground, she gave him the next command.

"Turn around in a complete circle. Slowly."

Hands still behind his head, Fallow rotated on the spot. When he faced her, he gave her a smirk that promised retribution.

She met his gaze and upped the ante with a look that said, *Bring it on, asshole.*

When his back was to her again, she said, "Get down on your knees."

He complied.

She remained where she was, muzzle two degrees off target. Cuffing him would involve holstering her weapon. She could hold her own in a ground fight against him, but she wasn't interested in going another round with Fallow. He was powerfully built, fast and desperate.

Besides, there was a certain indefinable appeal to shooting him in the head two or three times.

Before entering the warehouse, she'd taken sixty seconds to call the County Sheriff's Office's dispatcher to provide her location and relay her situation to the tactical personnel at the motel. She reported the female shooter too. She thought of Trey's interview and decided the woman was probably Poley's mom—obviously more involved than just a mother who brought snacks and soda to the basement. The initial shooter in the parking lot was likely her son.

She pulled her jacket aside, revealing the shield clipped to her belt, and waited.

Moments later, a detachment from a tactical unit moved in, weapons raised, scanning as they made second-by-second threat assessments.

"Here!" Carmen called.

They joined her, one of them scooping up the weapon on the floor and clearing it, while another two covered Fallow.

"Agent Carmen Sanchez with Homeland," she announced. "I've got Title 18s on this prisoner."

There would be state charges too, but at times like this it was never a bad idea to push out your chest with the US Federal Code to establish your cred.

The team leader gave a hand signal and the two operators closest to Fallow pulled his arms behind him, secured him with cuffs and double-locked them.

"The others?" Carmen asked. "The female and second male shooters?"

The leader said, "No report yet. All we know is shots fired."

"Where do you want him, ma'am?"

"I don't have a transport vehicle. Where's the nearest police lockup?"

"Riverside County, Lake Elsinore. Fifteen minutes."

"Can you take him there?"

"Sure, Agent Sanchez."

"And make sure there's a rear guard. Last time, the bird flew off."

A pair of tac team members escorted him from the building. She followed, blinking in the late-afternoon sunlight.

A cluster of gawkers with their cell phones out recorded the impromptu perp walk. Fallow made no attempt to hide his face, marching straight ahead, expressionless.

Flashing red lights drew Carmen's eye as she neared the motel. Paramedics were working furiously on a figure lying on a gurney. She diverted her course to check it out.

A man in full uniform with enough brass on his collar to mark him as a commander approached her. "You Agent Sanchez?"

"I am."

"Can I ask, the hell was this all about?"

"I'll give you a rundown, Commander, but first, the other two perps?"

"We got 'em both." He shook his head. "And this is one for the books. The main doer is Jennifer Benedict. She's got a half dozen aliases, but we never knew her real name. She's a pro, hired killer in big demand on the West Coast. She took over her husband's business after he got tapped a few years ago. Charles Benedict."

"That answers a few questions." She added the new intel to the growing list of facts. "My associate, Dr. Heron." She jerked a thumb toward the inn, where he was with Natalie in a locked storeroom. "We figured out there was a kill team hunting the woman we stashed at the inn." A brief laugh. "About two minutes before the shooters showed up."

The medics were still working on the young man who'd been hit. "So that's her son, Poley?"

"Yeah. We were moving in, so she sends her kid running toward a grocery store to escape or jack a car or something. And get this. She calls it in, reports him! Drew off most of my people."

"Her own son?" Carmen couldn't fathom a mother sacrificing her child to save herself.

She recalled Heron's observation that some of the worst intrusion occurred between family members.

"I know, right?" The commander gave a disgusted shake of the head. "He sees us and starts to shoot. Poor schmuck. He missed everybody by a mile. But we had to drop him. And Mom? She makes it to her SUV but barely gets it in gear before a sniper takes out two of her tires. I don't know who the shooter was, but it was a hell of a shot, four hundred yards."

"Not one of your people?"

"Naw, but believe me, around here it's always so quiet, when something like this happens, LEOs come out of the woodwork and suddenly we got traffic cops, narcs, MPs from Air National Guard on the scene. I think we had a school resource officer. Everybody, and I mean *everybody*, with a badge wants in on the action."

CHAPTER 70

Jake Heron stood beside Sanchez and her boss, SSA Eric Williamson.

The big man, broad shoulders challenging the seams of his suit jacket, had driven here from Long Beach for a debriefing. He'd made good time, though Jake could not picture the man hurrying for any reason.

The three of them were in a new Avanti Inn room; Crime Scene was busy in 118. Someone—Fallow most likely—had fired several shots through the window in a futile attempt to kill Natalie, who wasn't in the room at all. Heron had taken her inside the utility room.

"The story," Williamson said. "And make it complete because my next call is to the AG in Washington. And notice? I didn't add the word 'Assistant' to that job description."

"You know magic?" Jake asked him.

Williamson's expression tightened with impatience. Then he relented. "Yeah, I know magic. I give my kids twenty dollars, they go to the mall and it disappears. What's your point?"

Jake said, "Misdirection."

Sanchez took over. "It's what happened here."

She explained how their initial focus on catching a serial killer had misdirected them from what was supposed to appear to be the real crime: Fallow murdering people whose names showed up on the H8ers. org website. And that, in turn, was supposed to misdirect them from the real mission—to kill Natalie Jackson. "She was digging into an illegal project Gerard Dreth was trying to put together."

Williamson's face tightened. "The hell was it? Had to be huge for him to go to all this trouble."

"Huge? How about massive?" Sanchez offered.

Jake said, "Look." He typed some commands and the screen came up.

DrethCo Inc. and Brakon Computing, Inc., present . . .

The Learning Excellence Assistance Project

Williamson whispered, "DrethCo and Brakon? The merger." He paused. "What that guy Powell was ranting about?"

Sanchez nodded. "Learning Excellence . . . They call it LEAP. Brakon makes inexpensive laptops. They're giving away tens of millions of them to students around the country. K through twelve. DrethCo writes the code they're preloaded with."

Jake began scrolling through various lesson plans. Williamson squinted as the pages flipped past. History, geography, math, science, art. There were video lectures, quizzes, even virtual field trips to national parks, museums, classical concerts, historical sites, natural resources.

From time to time "recommended links" would pop up.

"Educational websites with links," Williamson said. "The problem?"

Jake said, "The pop-up links." He hit one, then another. They led to kid-friendly games, cute-animal videos and the like.

Sanchez said, "Natalie's assignment was writing programs that use biometrics to make sure students wouldn't see inappropriate content."

"Only someone kept reversing her code," Jake said. "So the software didn't block *children*; it blocked *adults*."

Sanchez pointed to the screen. "We're adults. We see kittens and puppies and G-rated pirate games. But when youngsters start clicking on the pop-ups, there are no safeguards. It's shit like this."

Jake clicked links to override the system and they suddenly found themselves watching brief videos of personable, attractive people like you'd see in any online ads—only they weren't selling anything. One was delivering a lecture about how it was everyone's responsibility to resist the authoritarian state. A woman said that *The Hunger Games*— the book and movie about a dystopian, dictatorial world—was a true story. Sites saying that American democracy was a threat.

"Lord."

Sanchez muttered, "Poisoning the kids' minds. From kindergarten through high school."

Williamson asked, "Wouldn't internet providers spot a COPPA violation?"

The Children's Online Privacy Protection Act made it illegal to data mine anyone under thirteen.

"But nobody's stealing anyone's data," Jake explained. "It's the opposite. They're *giving* the kids information. COPPA algorithms will ignore it." He clicked some more. A racist site popped up.

"Some parents will see the links," Williamson pointed out.

Jake wondered if he should tell the supervisory special agent that he'd done a bit of hacking. He glanced at Sanchez, who inclined her head in tacit approval.

"I found a memo about that on the DrethCo servers. The company calculates it'll lose five percent of its audience at most because of adults. A lot of parents are completely unaware of what their children do and see online."

"And will any kid complain and risk getting their computer taken away?" Sanchez said. "I don't think so."

Jake offered, "Brainwashing. That's what the program is all about. Clients are paying millions to get the kids messages like that."

Sanchez said, "It goes deeper. Stuff that encourages the kids to act out. Strength is revered, especially in the form of violence. Worse, the kids are instructed on how to make crude bombs, fashion other weapons, synthesize drugs and avoid detection."

Several ads were devoted to promoting political and social anarchy. Williamson muttered, "Targeting unformed, receptive and curious minds. Fueled by hormones too. Who are the clients paying Dreth to get this bullshit to the kids?"

Sanchez explained, "Conspiracy theorists. Separatists. Heads of cults looking for recruits. Silk Road businesses selling guns and drugs."

Heron added, "Foreign states too. I ran one of my traceroute programs and whaleboned through their proxies. The server's based in eastern Europe. It's a government address. I've written about Nazis' use of intrusion in the 1930s. Hitler believed whoever controlled the minds of children, controlled the future. Exactly what's happening here."

Williamson gazed at the screen as if it were radioactive. The big man said softly, "You know what this means?"

Sanchez said, "Jason Powell, our crackpot, was right all along. The merger is a national security risk." She looked toward Jake. "It all makes sense now. He shouted about choosing the blue pill or the red pill. Complacency or the truth."

Williamson didn't inquire about the reference, but seemed to get the gist. "Who've you rolled up?"

Sanchez rattled off a list of arrestees. "Jennifer Benedict, the hired gun. Her triggerman and our serial killer, Dennison Fallow. A.k.a. Spider. Two nobodies in Anaheim. They were window dressing for the misdirection."

Jake grimaced. "The site administrator? FeAR-15. He's a ghost now. I'm trying to find him." He felt a twist in his gut. "Haven't had much luck in the past. Maybe this time will be different."

Williamson waved at the computer, his face a mask of frustration. "Brainwashing kids is despicable, but you won't do much time under Title 18 for that. Anything to connect Dreth and Brakon to the killings?

They have to go down. We can expose this, but if they go free, they'll just find some other project like LEAP."

Sanchez said, "Only if we flip Jennifer or Fallow."

Williamson scoffed. "They're pros. You know how hard it is to turn them."

"True," Sanchez said. "But, speaking of magic, we've got one more trick up our sleeve."

CHAPTER 71

Federal agents conducted interviews, but Carmen would call this what it was . . . an interrogation.

And she had never been so eager to start one.

She had let the suspect stew in an interview room of the local Sheriff's Office satellite station for the past hour, while she'd pitched her case for handling the session herself. The county and state had jurisdiction too. Technically you could say they had *more* jurisdiction, if there was such a thing, since the shootout at the Avanti was a bucketful of state offenses mostly. But given the far-reaching implications of Dreth's plot, the senior officials in the Sheriff's Office and Highway Patrol decided to let her have at him.

Carmen now found herself in that *place*, that hard-to-define mindset before a one-on-one with the suspect, as she watched him through the two-way mirror, her forehead nearly against the glass.

"All the scarier 'cause he doesn't look scary," the stocky, blond Sheriff's Office captain said.

True. Fallow was in his flat-affect mode again, giving nothing away. He didn't bounce his knee, rub his hands together, or pick at his cuticles. None of the signs of disturbance she was used to seeing. He was facing life behind bars and he displayed no emotion. He was, in a way, as dead on the inside as his victims were on the outside.

The captain said something else. She didn't hear.

A few deep breaths.

Then she stepped into the hallway, stowed her weapon in a lockbox and entered the room.

He turned toward her. The brown contact lenses were gone and he was back to his natural hue. The irises were chips of ice. His hair was still dyed and the contrast of pale-blue eyes and jet-black hair gave him an unsettling look. It put in mind some of the images of spiders she'd seen in the past few days.

"Hello, Dennison." She sat across from him.

No reaction. Other than studying her.

His hands were cuffed but not shackled to the metal fixtures on the table. She wasn't concerned about this. She'd taken him once and, while he was a remorseless killer, he was not foolish enough to attack an officer in an escape-proof facility.

She began her carefully constructed plan of attack. "Dennison Fallow. An interesting name. Fitting, since you've had a rather interesting life. Made for good reading over the last hour."

His gaze hardened. He clearly didn't like any mention of his past. Good.

Then his expression became calculating. "Where's your shadow, Agent Sanchez? The elite super hacker, Jacoby?"

"Jake's doing a debriefing with my boss. It's just you and me."

"Oh, he's not hanging with his friend, FeAR-15? They go way back, you know. Best of buds."

Carmen squinted. "Right. FeAR-15. What's his real name again?"

Fallow's look said, Nice try. He remained silent.

Carmen had brought a yellow pad, a manila folder and a zippered pouch. She set them down, opened the pad and clicked a pen to readiness.

There was a world of information she might ask about—the murders, the education conspiracy plot, his connection to Jennifer Benedict—but Carmen would steer clear of all that. The mere mention of those at the outset would slam doors shut.

She would ease into the present by looping back to the past.

"You've had a history of trouble, Dennison."

Always the first name. It's like sitting taller than your subject.

Interrogations were about power.

"Starting in elementary school. Middle school. And things didn't improve when you were homeschooled." She tilted her head. "What kind of lessons did your parents teach you, Dennison?"

Only the faintest flicker of reaction.

She would reveal just enough to convince him she had access to detailed information about his background, but hold back most of what she knew.

Subjects tend not to lie when they're unsure if they'll be caught. It's a psychological failure to them and gives the interrogator more power. With a subject like Dennison Fallow, any ground taken was a major victory.

She shook her head. "You were expelled from the public school system. The homeschooling . . . well, whatever happened there, you kept beating up kids in the afternoon and following girls home. No, you had a rough time with school, didn't you? Until . . ."

She let the word linger.

He waited, gazing coolly.

". . . until you started a new course of study. Your postgraduate lessons. In tradecraft. You learned about clear gloves, spraying down everything you touched before a job, the disguises—but subtle ones. The ones that work. No wigs or fake mustaches. Contacts and hair dye. And clothes—like the bright-red shirt you wore when you met my sister, the bright-green one with Natalie. They drew attention away from your face. Toss-away outfits. Like the sport coat in the casino. Toss-away *cars*—like the SUV you left in the parking lot there. That's smart stuff, Dennison. Who was your professor for *those* studies? Maybe a Mr. Charles Benedict?"

Another flicker in his eyes.

She was on the right course.

"You've agreed to waive your Miranda rights, but I don't think it's because you plan to give me information. No, you're not the chatty type. You think you're smart, so you'll let me do the talking and you'll find out what I know. Isn't that right?"

He'd recovered from his surprise and gave her a look that bordered on arrogant. "You're wrong, Agent Sanchez. I'm *happy* to talk. In fact, I've got quite a few things to say. Things you'll find . . . enlightening."

She was supposed to ask, what? He was trying to exert control over her, so she didn't pursue that thread. This would be a small but important loss for him and tip the balance ever further in her favor. "We know about your call center job at American General. You've been named operator of the month several times."

"I try to be helpful." He tried for an air of nonchalance but fell short of the mark. Instead, he seemed incrementally more concerned.

"Just cross-referencing some data, Dennison. Three of their customers have gone missing in the past year."

He cleared his throat. "That right? How sad."

"And their phone records all show they spoke to you about warranty claims."

He'd be wondering how she'd pieced it together, unaware of Declan's obscure relationship search program at HSI.

"Three out of thousands." Unable to raise his hands, he lifted his shoulders in an exaggerated shrug. "I take a lot of calls. Must be a coincidence."

"I'm curious about a woman you spoke with yesterday. Emily Halcomb. About a dishwasher warranty."

"Doesn't ring any bells. But the calls are recorded"—he added wryly—"for quality assurance and training purposes, or so they say. Which means you know damn well I got her call."

She was getting under his skin. "I also know that at the same time you took the call, you googled her name and address and social media sites."

He slouched and gazed up at the ceiling. "You know what I'm thinking, Agent Sanchez?"

"What's that, Dennison?"

"If only I'd had five minutes more with your sister . . ." A leer.

His attempt at deflection—and rattling her—failed. Carmen laughed. A genuine sound. "She would have wiped up the pavement with you."

Anger suffused his face.

Handing her yet more control. She kept up the pressure. "Let's get back to Emily. We found something interesting in your bedroom at the Anaheim house." She paused for dramatic effect. "Her name and address on a Post-it Note. A doodle too. Of a woman missing both index fingers. Were you planning to visit her, Dennison?"

"I don't make service calls."

"Not true, Dennison. You *did* call on those three customers who are missing. We're reopening those cases. And now that we have you, that puts the investigations on the front burner. Your social media and search engine history, security cams, doorbell cams, witnesses, DNA. The works."

She decided she had bombarded the landing zone sufficiently. Now it was time for phase one of her assault and she used a favorite interrogation tactic, abruptly changing subjects to keep him off balance. "You saw the paramedics working on Poley outside the Avanti Inn. You haven't heard but he was declared dead on arrival at the hospital. It's tragic, really, because he was set up."

That got his attention.

She made a show of opening the zippered pouch and sliding out a digital recorder.

"This is a recording of a 9-1-1 call made while he was running out of the parking lot behind the inn."

She pushed PLAY.

"Nine-one-one, what's your emer—"

"There's a man with a gun behind the Avanti Inn. He's headed to GreenFresh Grocery. He's shooting people!"

"Ma'am, we have units at that location. Can you provide a description?"

"White male, twenty-two years old, six feet tall, heavyset, wearing jeans and a gray T. He said he'd kill every cop he saw. Please, you have to stop him. And wait, yes, there are two or three other men with him. All running toward the grocery store. Hurry!"

"I've advised the officers at the scene. What's your name, ma'am?"

The call was disconnected.

Carmen pressed STOP. "I'm sure you recognize Jennifer's voice."

Fallow's eyes became wary.

She pressed her advantage. "What kind of mother would do that to her own son?"

What had been a flicker of emotion in his eyes became an angry spark.

She hadn't learned everything about Fallow's childhood, but the school psychologists' and juvie court reports left no doubt about his hard upbringing. Changing his middle name too, from his father's, was a flare.

"Jennifer set him up, Dennison." She softened her tone.

Now, phase two.

She told him, "Set him up . . . the same way she set you up."

Interrogation is like a dance, and Carmen Sanchez had her choreography down cold.

His head gave an almost imperceptible shake of denial.

"I'm afraid so, Dennison. I'm sorry but it's true. We got into Jennifer's phone."

This was the up-the-sleeve trick she'd told Williamson about. Heron had cloned Jennifer's phone, the same way he'd cloned the phones of the two Powell fanatics who'd shot up her vehicle. The "magical" part was that it would normally take weeks to suck incriminating data from a mobile. But Heron's little device had done so in seconds.

And the contents were revealing indeed.

"This is what we found in her text history." She slid a sheet of paper from the manila folder and pushed it toward him. His eyes widened a fraction as he looked at his own picture.

He fidgeted in his chair, clearly uncomfortable.

Some of the texts suggested they were sleeping together. But Fallow would know Jennifer was hardly the sort to keep a photo of him on her phone for sentimental reasons.

"She sent the picture to a virtual dead drop site on the dark web—think Craigslist for paid assassins—along with a promise of a quarter-million-dollar fee . . . for, that's right, for murdering you."

A second sheet appeared. "It's authentic, Dennison. I've sworn to that in an affidavit." This too she proffered. "While you were headed to a city beginning with 'R,' Jennifer would be on a flight somewhere far away, with a new identity."

He looked at her, refusing to acknowledge the truth.

So she spelled it out for him. "The sixth victim, the R victim, was supposed to be you. Jennifer and Dreth had to make sure the police closed their investigation, which would only happen if you were captured or killed."

She watched to see if he arrived at the next inevitable conclusion. Seeing no response, she led him directly to it. "They couldn't allow you to be arrested. Why do you think they arranged for your escape last time?"

Another baleful look.

"Dead men tell no tales," she went on. "From the beginning, you were always meant to be the scapegoat."

Fallow started to cross his arms, a significant defensive kinesic—body language—move. But the handcuffs prevented it. He lowered his fists to the tabletop with a loud metallic clank. His face was devoid of emotion with the exception of movement in his eyelids and the corners of his mouth, which told her his thoughts were unspooling fast.

Maybe he'd guessed from the beginning that Jennifer was a highly dangerous woman to have an affair with, but seeing proof of her deadly intent against him was a shock.

Still, Carmen could tell he wasn't ready to give in. Some defiance—and perhaps some subconscious attraction to Jennifer, as unlikely as that seemed—kept him silent.

She moved on to the final phase of the interrogation, saving the best for last. "Jennifer Benedict is a paid killer. Why would she hire someone else for a job she's perfectly capable of doing herself?"

His mouth flattened into a hard line. "Exactly."

"Because she intended to be long gone when it happened. No one would connect your death with her. Not through ballistics, or DNA, or other forensic evidence. Her hands would be clean and she'd have an alibi."

Timing was critical at this point in the discussion. Carmen waited a full minute before delivering the final blow.

Phase three.

"It's the same reason Jennifer hired someone for another hit."

Fallow's eyes, no longer filled with disdain, locked with hers. He waited in silence.

"Did you know text messages are permanently archived, Dennison? Even on burner phones. Once we have the number, we can access every bit of communication sent or received through the device. We dug into her archived messages and found a series of texts sent to the same dead drop site two years earlier. It included another picture of a target. This hit cost more than you, though. Double. A half million."

Slowly she withdrew a third printout and slid it forward.

At first, he kept his eyes on hers, then finally lowered them to the photograph.

His shoulders slumped and his face radiated pure dismay.

He was now a font of emotion.

The man Jennifer had hired a hit man to assassinate was none other than Dennison Fallow's mentor, and her own husband, Charles Benedict.

CHAPTER 72

For years Dennison Fallow had watched female spiders devour their mates.

He'd known from the beginning the danger Jennifer posed.

And he wasn't really surprised that she'd sacrificed her own son to help her escape capture.

Or that she'd set Fallow himself up to die after Natalie. After all, there *was* a cold logic to it.

But Mr. Benedict . . .

The man who had instructed him in the art of the hunt. The man who had taught him to embrace his true nature. The man who had saved him.

He thought of Shakespeare's line from *Hamlet. What a piece of work is a man, How noble in reason, how infinite in faculty, In form and moving how express and admirable. In action how like an Angel, In apprehension how like a god . . .*

There was no one like Mr. Benedict.

His icy facade melted. He wanted to shout at Agent Sanchez. Wanted to scream that she was wrong. Wanted to rail against the betrayal that shook him to his core. But her reasoning made too much sense.

Jennifer would know the spouse is always at the top of the suspect list in a murder investigation. How better to avoid suspicion than to use the services of another pro?

"Jennifer used him, Dennison," Sanchez said quietly, all judgment gone from her voice. "Just like she used you and everybody else."

He wouldn't give Sanchez the pleasure of seeing him waver. He was strong. He had the Push with him and he leaned into it now. Think. What would Mr. Benedict have done if he'd known his own wife was plotting to have him killed? And why had she done it? Was it for money? Ambition? Power?

Or was it simply, like Fallow himself, like a billion spiders, in her nature?

Jennifer Benedict clearly had a Push too.

Sanchez interrupted his musings. "She's going to prison. Attempted murder, shooting at me tonight? In California that's life in prison. There's your revenge, Dennison. Except . . . she still has some cards to play. She could flip on Dreth, buy herself a shorter sentence. The woman who killed your mentor might be out on the street in a few years again. Living the good life. Is that what you want?"

Of course not. But he hadn't heard anything that sounded like an offer yet. He raised a questioning brow at Agent Sanchez.

"You've got assault and homicide on your ticket, Dennison. Your life is in our hands. But what you do in the next five minutes can make a huge difference in how you spend the rest of your days. You give me Dreth and Brakon and the location of your call center victims. I'll talk to the prosecutors. Won't be a country club but it'll be better than a box in Pelican Bay."

He could give her what she wanted. He could dime out Luciano, the driver, who was obviously hired muscle. And he and FeAR had lifted emails from Jennifer's computer, which led straight to Dreth and Brakon. The email messages were insurance they'd taken out for precisely this situation—if Jennifer tried to burn them. He had copies in a go bag buried near the Santa Barbara beach.

But that involved confessing.

Maybe he could beat the rap. All he needed was one "not guilty" on the jury. And Fallow had a way of looking at people that often made them change their minds.

How much did Sanchez really know?

She had some evidence, but did she have proof? He studied her closely, until her steady gaze forced him to look away, still unable to tell if she was bluffing. He decided she would do better at poker than roulette.

"You keep up that stone face, Dennison, I walk out the door and have a chat with Jennifer." A shrug. "Frankly, I'd rather offer a deal to you." She smiled. "We've had quite the few days, haven't we? The back-and-forth." She cocked her head to one side. "Do spiders dance?"

He didn't even have to think. "Male jumping spiders. A mating ritual. And they drum out a message with their legs. The females can feel it in the ground."

A chuckle. "Mating. Not quite the back-and-forth I was thinking of between us. You know what Jennifer will do? She'll claim it was your idea. That you forced her to go along with it."

If the situation weren't so grim, he would have laughed. "She's a professional assassin."

"An assassin who'll wear a Laura Ashley floral print dress to court and pin her hair up like a schoolmarm and cry for the jury. And you'll be fucked. You want to take that gamble?" She gave her chin a thoughtful tap. "Of course, that was our first lead to you—the casino. Go ahead, if you want to try your luck. Spin the wheel."

A moment passed.

And he decided he wouldn't take that bet. In light of what he knew of Jennifer as well as everything he'd learned about arachnids, her behavior made perfect—and sickening—sense. Male spiders were aware they would die after mating but were still driven to reproduce.

With Jennifer, the sex had been good but, whatever the species, those were famous last words.

Fallow was suddenly very tired. "Some male spiders come up with ingenious ways to stay alive so the female doesn't eat them after mating. Sometimes they wrap up a bug in webbing and give it to her as an offering, in hopes she'll let him get away. But my favorite is the spider who wraps up a pebble, disguising it as an insect, and while she's unwrapping it, he escapes."

"Are you saying you'll cooperate?"

"I'll give them all up. Jennifer. And Dreth. And Brakon. I've got some hidden evidence. It's solid."

"And FeAR-15?"

"His real name's Tristan Kane. He's gone. Left the country. A safe house in the Caribbean somewhere. I really don't know more than that."

"Thank you, Dennison." The agent smiled once more. "Let's go. There's a transport van outside. It'll take you to main detention in Riverside for intake."

Two officers entered, standing by while she recuffed his hands behind his back. On the way out, she stopped to retrieve and holster her weapon before escorting him through the rear exit into the parking lot.

He saw the Riverside County Prisoner Transport van and mused, "I wonder if I'll have any friends in my cell."

"Friends?" Sanchez's brows furrowed. "Crimes like yours, Dennison? You'll be in solitary—for your own protection."

A smile tugged at the corners of his lips. "I don't think so, Agent Sanchez. I have a feeling I'll find some in my cell. In fact, I'm counting on it."

CHAPTER 73

He smelled the sweet scent of Hoppe's cleaner as he lay in the dusty earth in the foothills of the Santa Anas, watching Agent Sanchez and her prisoner leave the back door of the local police lockup for a short walk to an idling van.

He was peering through a Nikon scope mounted to his Nosler hunting rifle, the crosshairs resting between the two.

They'd be fifty-four yards away when they reached the kill zone. A shot at that range was nothing for the 6.5 PRC—precision rifle cartridge—which fired faster and flatter than the famous 6.5 Creedmoor. The PRC was beginning to steal the thunder from the ancient Winchester .308 too.

He'd learned about weapons from his father, with whom he'd gone hunting several times a month during season. They had no interest in firing scatterguns at birds. His goal was to take deer for the venison and for the rec room trophy. A single shot. A single kill.

He controlled his breathing, the key to good marksmanship.

He was being careful, keeping his finger out of the trigger guard until he acquired the target.

Then it would come down to a simple shot of less than a hundred yards.

Nothing . . .

It didn't matter where he hit the body. The jacketed hollow point round, traveling at three thousand feet per second, would enter and destroy every organ, vein and bone in its path. A chest shot would bring death before the body collapsed to the ground. Hitting the lower abdomen? Dying would take a bit longer, and it would be amusing to watch the medics assessing how to stanch the blood and to gingerly collect the organs that had been blown out of the exit cavity.

Breathe in, breathe out.

They were close to the kill zone now.

Inhale, exhale . . .

Safety off.

Slide his finger from the guard to the trigger, which he didn't dare caress.

Not until he had a perfect sight picture.

Sanchez and the suspect were nearly to the van.

Now.

He began to apply pressure.

In the same moment, he felt a presence behind him—the surrounding sound had dampened ever so slightly and the cold barrel of a gun touched the back of his neck.

A low, male voice uttered a single word. "No."

He froze, silently cursing himself. He'd been so focused on his quarry that someone had gotten the drop on him. He contemplated his options and concluded he had none.

A man's hand reached around and grasped the forestock, raising the muzzle upward to point harmlessly at the sky.

He lowered his head and let his beloved rifle, a gift from his father, be taken from his arms.

———

While Jacoby Heron never carried a weapon, he was well aware of their workings from his job. He kept his finger off the trigger of the rifle but kept the muzzle pointed in the man's general direction.

"Turn around."

The would-be shooter complied.

With a shock, he recognized the mysterious rifleman—the man formerly in green, now it was desert camo—who'd been dogging them for days. At Moreno Valley and in Irvine, at the parking garage, where his 80 percent sighting now became 100.

Not a cell tower lineman at all, the rifleman was Michael Kemp, son of San Diego real estate developer Walter Kemp, Dennison Fallow's first victim.

"That's what you passed off as a gun?" Michael asked in a disgusted voice.

He was looking at the stubby black halogen flashlight Jake had pressed against the back of his head as if it were an old-time six-shooter.

Michael had apparently been tracking Sanchez and himself in hopes they'd lead him to Spider and a clear vista where he could take a shot.

"How did you spot me?"

Jake didn't tell him it was simply situational awareness, standard fare for a physical pen tester who had made enemies in his job as an intrusionist.

"You're the sniper who shot the car's tires at the Avanti Inn."

"Yes, sir."

They'd met at the SDPD and Jake didn't recall how he'd been introduced. Michael might not either and could believe he was talking to a law officer.

"I didn't know who she was," Michael said. "But I saw her with a gun and she was escaping. I didn't want to shoot her. I just didn't want her to get away. The police could figure it out later. Who was she?"

"They were working together—she and the man who killed your father."

"The news, on TV. They said Dad was just a random victim." Michael wiped his eyes.

"He was. To make it look like the real target was random too."

"The woman I saw you with tonight, the one with the long braids and red glasses, she's the real target?"

"Yes," he said simply. "A computer programmer who'd found some things her boss wanted to stay hidden."

Michael said, "You saved her."

"We did."

"And the asshole who killed my father?" A nod toward the prisoner van.

"He's not getting out. We have plenty of evidence."

"He'll be alive. My father isn't. Besides, he might escape from prison."

"Highly unlikely."

He didn't bother to add that he knew from personal experience jailbreaks were much rarer than consumers of popular entertainment believed.

"Let us get justice for your father. He wouldn't want you ruining your future by taking the law into your own hands."

Michael nodded slowly. Then he stiffened as he looked toward the prisoner transport van and watched Sanchez and a uniformed officer help Fallow inside. The doors slammed shut. Jake noticed there were two officers in the vehicle, and a second marked car behind it. No chance of another escape.

Michael watched the van drive off. "I fired my rifle to take out the tires of that woman's car. That's got to be a crime. The police will arrest me."

"Not if they don't know who you are." Jake looked around. Saw no one. "You've been a mystery man since I first saw you on the hillside in Moreno Valley. You can stay a mystery man."

Michael's eyes widened. "You'd do that for me?"

Jake worked the bolt to empty the gun of bullets and pocketed them. He handed the rifle back to Michael. "Go on, get out of here."

They shook hands and the young man walked down a shadowy path and vanished, his camo blending with the floor and walls of the dusty canyon.

CHAPTER 74

Carmen Sanchez eyed Heron, whose overly innocent expression and casual backhanded brush of his beard didn't fool her for a hot minute.

"Who was that walking away?"

Heron waved off the question and changed the subject. "I'll explain in a minute. First, tell me if you got anything out of Jennifer. I had to leave the viewing area to take a call from Aruba, and the uniform at the front desk wouldn't let me back in without a federal agent or a cop to escort me."

"Jennifer's a piece of work. Like I figured, she started by playing the victim. When I wasn't buying what she was selling, she tried to cut a deal."

"I've been on the receiving end of your interview tactics. I'm sure that didn't go well for her."

"The dominoes are falling, Heron. Fallow's rolling over on Jennifer and Dreth. What he doesn't have on Brakon, Dreth will probably fill in if we shave a few years off his sentence." Carmen swept her hair aside and regarded Heron.

He returned her steady gaze. "Yes?"

"I wonder how you're feeling."

He tapped the body armor under his black windbreaker. "Bruises still hurt some but nothing serious. Why do you ask?"

"Not what I mean. You got Jennifer's phone data *legally*. Without hacking. I was worried you'd break out in hives."

"Made my palms sweat," Heron said, deadpan. "But it was kind of fun. Almost better than making hot dogs."

Someone who shot at a federal agent was bound to end up on the wrong end of a search warrant. It had taken a local federal magistrate five minutes to approve Carmen's application and affidavit, which included permission to use a "civilian expert," as well as law enforcement, to examine her electronics.

A trick up our sleeve . . .

Carmen grew serious. "That's the way it ought to be, Heron. Let the system do its thing. It works."

"Understood."

Of course, his agreement to do the right thing in the future didn't mean much. Their time working together was done.

No reason for them to see each other again after he gave an official statement.

She wondered how she felt about that.

Drew no conclusion.

Although one more matter remained between them.

"Now the question you're avoiding?"

"Question?"

"Answering a question with a question, Heron. Shame on you. Tell me who that guy was you were having the oh-shit-here-comes-somebody conversation with?"

"Michael Kemp."

"Walter Kemp's son." She struggled to fit him into the picture. "The hell was he . . ."

Understanding dawned. "He was carrying something."

A brief pause. Heron said, "A long gun."

She pulled her phone from her pocket. "So, he's the rifleman. The reason you jumped me in Moreno Valley."

"I wouldn't quite put it that way but, yes, it was him."

"And he was at the garage in Irvine too. He was following us, hoping we'd lead him to Fallow. Shoot him to avenge his father." She eyed him. "But you talked him down?"

Once again, Heron absently brushed his beard with his knuckles. "I went to prison for a cause. And some of the worst CEOs I targeted are still inside. My sentence was worth it. But Michael going away for killing Fallow would have been a total waste of his life."

"You let an armed man, one who admitted he intended to commit murder, walk away?"

"In a word, yes."

"It's a crime, Heron. Under the circumstances, he probably wouldn't get a long sentence, but it's still punishable." She looked in the direction that Michael had disappeared and lifted her phone.

"Wait," Heron said. "There's something else you should know."

"Which is?"

"He's the one who shot out Jennifer's tires."

Sanchez lowered her head and rubbed her eyes. "Two illegal shots and the slugs could have hit an innocent bystander."

"I got the sense he knew what he was doing."

Despite Heron's confidence, she knew bullets often went astray. But this time, nobody had been injured. California Penal Code 246/247 made it a crime to willfully discharge a firearm at an occupied house or car.

Michael Kemp was clearly guilty.

And yet Carmen Sanchez was not thinking of him, at the moment, but of Jacoby Heron.

If he could take a step *away* from the line separating right from wrong, by getting a warrant for Jennifer's phone, well, she could take a step *closer* to it, by letting this one slide.

She put her phone away.

"You know, Heron, I'm still pretty shaken up from the firefight. I can't seem to remember a single thing about our conversation here."

He nodded, straight-faced. "Funny how that can happen."

CHAPTER 75

Carmen had no clue what Jake Heron was up to . . . often a troubling sign.

He'd been feverishly texting on his cell phone during the drive to the Eiffel Tower Inn in Perris to see Selina. She figured—unreasonably, she admitted—that he was communicating with Hot Tub Woman, which somehow increased her annoyance. The fact that she was annoyed at all annoyed her further.

The tires screeched as she braked to an abrupt stop in front of Selina's room at the back of the inn. The protection detail squad car Hall had ordered earlier was gone.

Heron continued to concentrate on his phone, abstaining from his usual remarks about her driving as they climbed out.

Carmen's mood did not improve when her sister greeted them with eyes narrowed in suspicion.

"You don't call first?"

Nice to see you too, Carmen thought, but made no comment. She wasn't pleased to be here either. She tipped her head toward Heron to indicate their impromptu visit was, for reasons he had not yet explained, his idea. "We'll only be a minute," she said, hoping the statement was accurate. Completely spent from the near-constant adrenaline rush of the past few days, she had no energy left to spar with her sister.

Selina had been packing to leave. A safe house was no longer necessary. The "serial killer," who wanted to murder her for no good reason, except as a Lego brick in a broader wall of misdirection, was in custody, as was his employer, Jennifer. Gerard Dreth, the ultimate perp, knew they were onto him and had lawyered up. In any event, Selina was the least of his problems.

Carmen wondered if Ryan Hall was on his way to help with the move, since this would be his last chance to have an official excuse to cozy up to Selina. Then she realized that, as Selina hadn't requested a ride to her apartment from Carmen, the detective might have offered to drive her.

Aware she had no say in her sister's love life, Carmen turned her attention to Heron, who had been cryptic about why he wanted to stop here on the way back to the Long Beach field office. She figured he wanted to question Selina about anything she might have observed during her interaction with Fallow in the Wicked Brew Coffee Shop that could lead to his Moriarty—Tristan Kane, FeAR-15, who was still MIA.

When Carmen had asked Heron about the purpose of the detour, he'd answered with a noncommittal "I'm not sure yet."

The hacker now surfaced from his phone long enough to give Selina a brief smile before tucking the mobile away and replacing it with his small pen-testing laptop, which he dug from his ever-present gear bag.

He seemed to be making a meal of navigating to a particular file.

Finally, he looked up and eyed each sister in turn. "While we were hunting Spider down, I was running a separate investigation. Involving both of you."

It was the last thing she expected to hear. Selina looked equally surprised—which meant he hadn't enlisted her help with whatever he was up to.

"Sit, sit." He gestured to a pair of white-and-gold rococo chairs.

The sisters exchanged glances but did as he suggested.

He sat on the neatly made bed directly across from them. "It's about your father."

Selina tilted her head in wary confusion.

"I got to wondering about his death," Heron went on.

Carmen bristled. She couldn't believe the man had the cojones to meddle in their family business. Especially when he knew the mere mention of their father caused so much strain. "You took it on yourself to stick your nose into our affairs—to *intrude*—without our consent."

"*Would* you have consented?"

She and Selina responded in unison. "No."

"Well, then," Heron said as if that explained everything. Before she could launch another attack, he offered, "I had Aruba do some research."

Now curious, Carmen reined in her anger and held her tongue, waiting to see where this was going.

Heron regarded the laptop once more, then closed it with a snap, as if something he had just read confirmed a suspicion. Then his eyes did another slow sweep of both sisters' faces.

"According to what she found, I can tell you with ninety-nine percent certainty that your father didn't kill himself."

Selina's hand flew to her mouth.

Carmen's mind reeled. "But, you mean . . ."

"That's right," Heron said. "He was murdered."

CHAPTER 76

"Impossible," Carmen whispered.

Selina's response was more colorful. "What the actual fuck?"

"I got suspicious when I saw those pictures in your bungalow," Heron said to Carmen. "The family photos on the walls and the mantel."

This comment drew a brief side-eye from Selina. But Heron's overnight visit was a topic for another time. If ever.

"A few of them were taken at church. You two and your mother wore lace handkerchiefs. I'm not much of a churchgoer but I looked it up. That's a Catholic thing."

"They're called mantillas," Carmen said. "What's your point?"

"Head coverings haven't been required since the seventies, so I assume your family was observant."

"That's right," Carmen told him, flooded with memories of Sunday mass, Selina's baptism, confirmation dresses and Easters and Christmases. The mantillas were reserved for special services.

"Then your father was devout as well?"

"Yes," Selina said. "He was a lector, a lay reader, a few times a month."

Heron paused as if to choose his next words. "And suicide is a mortal sin in the Catholic faith, isn't it?"

Selina said bitterly, "Making what he did even worse."

"But," Heron said slowly, "I couldn't get past the way he looked at you two in those pictures after your mother died. You were his world."

Did Heron's voice catch? Yes, Carmen decided, and his troubled expression made her suspect that something about his own childhood made it difficult for him to witness deep family love.

He was looking at Carmen when he said, "You told me he made some bad investments for clients who lost their life savings. But no one died, no one ended up on the street. I looked up his bio and CV. He was a professional all his life. Financial advisers make innocent mistakes all the time. That's why investors are warned about the risks. What happened to his clients didn't seem like a reason for suicide."

Carmen had felt the same at the time, and the detective within her had immediately examined the facts, in parallel with the Orange County detectives and the medical examiner. But the case for suicide grew stronger. First, murder was the only alternative COD, but Roberto Sanchez had no enemies either of his daughters had ever heard of. Then there was the note. Handwritten and authenticated by a forensic handwriting expert. Carmen recalled that, though her mother had died some years before, her father had never fully recovered from the loss.

Finally, like all law enforcers, she'd been trained to deal with individuals contemplating self-harm and knew the decision to take one's life could occur impulsively and as fast as a finger snap.

She might have delved further, but chaos had descended after her father's death. There were the funeral plans to make. The estate had to be settled. And several clients who had lost their savings brought suits that Carmen, as executor, had to hire lawyers to defend. On top of that, she became the legal guardian of then seventeen-year-old Selina, who was overwhelmed with grief. Caring for her became Carmen's full-time job, in addition to her *real* full-time job at DHS.

She tried to reconcile the new information. "But, Heron, the note . . ."

"Forced to write it."

Not unheard of. People had been coerced to sign contracts, powers of attorney, even deeds—witnessed by those working with the coercer.

Made to write his own suicide note. She closed her eyes for a long moment, imagining his anguish as he put pen to paper, knowing he was about to die.

Had this person, whoever he was, told their father he would hurt his daughters if he didn't write the note? Yes, of course, that's what would have happened.

She was getting ahead of herself. This was all speculation. And based on what? "Intrusionists don't make guesses. They identify PPIs . . . Tell me about those, Heron."

Selina frowned but Carmen chose not to get into the weeds of intrusion theory just then.

"Emails, Sanchez. Aruba found some emails of your father's from back then."

"Aruba?" Selina asked.

"I'll tell you later." Carmen gestured for Heron to continue.

"Carmen told me your father died two days before your birthday," Heron said to Selina. "And a few days before *that*, he made an online reservation for three people at a restaurant in Laguna Beach. Cantina de Flores."

"Mom's favorite place." Selina darted a glance at Carmen. "Where we always went for special occasions. We kept up the tradition after she died."

"He also emailed the manager. Said he was surprising his daughter on her seventeenth birthday. He put in a request for a small tres leches cake and a cluster of balloons. He meant it as a surprise for his older daughter too, so if Carmen happened to come in, the manager wasn't supposed to say anything. Your father wouldn't—"

"—have killed himself after doing that," Carmen cut in. "Absolutely not."

Selina gasped. "We never knew." And let out a strangled sob.

Carmen reached out to hold her sister's hand. For once, Selina didn't shy away.

Heron said, "I see that look, Sanchez. And you're right. All this only gets us so far. There's more. Do you know what a hash is?"

She thought back to her stint in the Cybercrime Unit before she left the FBI. "Turning words and phrases into random strings of data. Hashes are the basis for generating passwords."

"I ran your father's name through the most popular hash generators on the dark web. Aruba sent out search bots to see if she could locate that hash. She did. On a hidden site." He gave her a meaningful look. "Similar to the one Jennifer used."

"Dios mío . . ."

"What?" Selina asked.

"He's talking about a murder-for-hire site."

Selina paled. "Who would hire a . . . a hit man to kill Dad?"

Carmen had the same question. "Did Aruba come up with any names?"

"No. She's still looking. If there's anything more, she'll find it."

Fugaku, Carmen thought.

One point one quintillion . . .

The sisters regarded each other. Everything they had believed about their father's death, including what had appeared to be his abandonment, was shifting like sand under their feet. Couple this revelation with the devastating news of his murder, by persons and for reasons unknown, and everything took on a surreal quality.

Selina's phone buzzed. She checked the screen, then wiped away tears and cleared her throat before answering, "Hey." She listened briefly to a man's voice on the other end, then said, "Now's good . . . sure." She disconnected. "My ride."

All three stood.

Suddenly Selina stepped forward.

Carmen lifted her arms to accept her younger sister's embrace.

But Selina walked past her and hugged Heron fiercely, clearly startling him. Tearful, she whispered, "Thank you, Jake. Thank you!"

She returned to the bed and began tugging at the zipper of her battered gym bag.

Eyes welling too, Carmen whispered, "Te quiero, hermanita . . ."

The look Selina gave her was complicated. The source of her despair had proved to be wrong, but it had consumed her nonetheless, derailing years of her life. Despite what Heron said about the prowess of the killer, and Carmen's efforts to investigate the suicide, Selina might be thinking that if her older sister had not been focused on her new job at Homeland, she could have tipped to the very facts Heron had just shared.

And their father's murderer would not have escaped.

Painfully aware of all this, Carmen could not stop herself from approaching her sister.

Selina retreated. "Not yet, Carm. Soon, I think. But not yet." Her voice was firm but no longer angry.

Carmen swallowed the lump that had formed in her throat and walked to the door with Heron. He opened it. She glanced over her shoulder. "If you want to talk, Lina, I'm here."

Selina gave the faintest of nods and returned to the uncooperative luggage.

Outside Carmen and Heron climbed into the HSI pool car. She didn't fire up the engine but sat gripping the wheel, staring forward at a pair of hummingbirds, their wings invisible as they hovered to squabble over the rights to a crimson California fuchsia.

"I don't know what to say, Heron." She too felt a sudden urge to fling her arms around him in gratitude but knew that, of course, she never would. Probably. "What you did . . ."

He looked away, spending a bit more time than necessary stowing his laptop in his bag. "You're going to pursue it."

"Technically I can't." She rattled off the reasons. "A family member. A local homicide case. No federal jurisdiction."

He scoffed, though with one of his rare smiles. "Isn't that exactly where we started, with Spider?"

"True." A pause. "But there're no solid leads. All we've got is hacked emails from HTW."

"From . . . oh, Hot Tub Woman. Really, Sanchez."

Carmen continued, "With Spider, we had multiple murders, the perp operating in real time. This? A solitary hit a few years ago? And talk about fruit of the poisonous tree? Aruba's hack into an email server is Superfund toxic. Can't use a single line of anything she found. All I have to work with is that someone hired a pro to murder our father. No clue who, or why. Nothing else to go on."

"About the size of it."

She started the car and put it into gear.

As she pulled out of the lot Heron said, "Sanchez, you're a cop. Go do cop stuff and find the son of a bitch."

Which was, oddly enough, exactly what she was thinking.

CHAPTER 77

He had a new handle.

The online name FeAR-15 was gone. Tristan Kane didn't merely delete all traces of the past operation, he shredded them. If you deleted anything on a computer, you simply moved it to another part of the device, where it was ripe for the picking. To get rid of something permanently, you shredded it, you overwrote it thirty-five times with random characters and then you shredded it again.

That was what had to happen with the events of the past few days and all evidence of them, so Kane had left behind the remnants of his shredded life in Southern California.

Adios, FeAR-15.

But, of course, no hacker, troll, or phreaker could become notorious in the dark recesses of the internet without an identity. And he loved the new one he'd come up with.

DR-one.

It was in keeping with the new weapons of the times. His handles had evolved from a single-shot long gun to an assault rifle to, what else? The standard for death and destruction in the modern age.

A drone.

It was one of his preferred weapons in the first-person shooter games he loved.

Carmen Sanchez and Jake Heron were mopping up in Lake Elsinore, where they would inevitably find various links to him. Had the plan gone as Jennifer intended, Natalie would now be dead, the pathetic pair of Trey and Doobie would be spilling their guts about the H8ers and their targets, the Lux, and Dreth and Brakon would be doing their world-domination thing or whatever they were about.

And Dennison Fallow would be dead.

Instead, Kane had implemented plan B, which involved a hasty flight from a private airstrip.

Trinidad and Tobago, the twin-island nation in the Caribbean Sea off the coast of Venezuela, changed hands more than forty times before 1800, and things didn't get much more stable after that.

But the white-sand beaches appealed, as did the exotic drinks and the ubiquitous steel drum–laced calypso.

And it was out of the way. T and T was not along the standard Caribbean cruise ship routes and was harder to reach than the classic destinations closer to the US.

Tristan Kane could live like a king—no, better, like an oligarch—with his money in an account in a Trinidad bank that was particularly skilled at keeping such accounts secret.

He'd learned about the bank from Jennifer, whose nest egg had just been transferred into his account, bringing his total fortune to $16 million. It had taken some time and effort, but the forged authorization signature and hacked access code had allowed the transaction to go through. Jennifer certainly wouldn't need the money where she was going.

The Trinidad police force was small, another plus. While generally ethical, its upper ranks included two senior officials who were $100,000 richer thanks to Kane.

Finally, close proximity to Venezuela meant he could vanish into that country if the need arose. Contrary to popular belief, the nation did in fact have an extradition treaty with the United States, but the price of getting it ignored was well within his budget.

Indeed, life was going perfectly.

He sipped his tea and reflected on the latest project.

The crew that made up the H8ers were gone. Poley was dead. Trey and Doobie in custody. Carmen Sanchez had arrested Fallow and it appeared he was cooperating. Dreth and Brakon had both been criminally charged—which had suddenly catapulted activist Powell into the spotlight. He would have been hailed as a hero if not for his rambling manifestos and fondness for high explosives.

And then there was Jennifer, the true mastermind.

Their failure to fulfill the contract on Natalie wasn't of any concern to him. He'd done his job and been paid—and he'd tormented Jake Heron in the process.

Kane, DR-one, checked his email on his heavily firewalled laptop. Plenty of lucrative offers to choose from. An assassination here, some extortion there, shutting down the entire surgical ward of a hospital—all the power, backup generators too—just to kill a politician having heart surgery. That would be fun . . . and a stroll in the park for him.

Decisions, decisions, decisions . . .

CHAPTER 78

Jake sat in Sanchez's office in the Long Beach field office, his laptop open in front of him.

On the screen:

C:\JH\Banchee Routracing . . . Searching for target

The program was Banchee 4.0, the new-and-improved version of the software he'd hacked together a few years ago in an attempt to find his nemesis, the hacker Tristan Kane, a search interrupted—forcibly—on that Christmas Eve a few years ago.

Banchee was prowling through billions of connections, searching for a potential match with Kane's previous online profiles.

Needle. Haystack.

"Where are you?"

"What's that?" Sanchez asked.

He realized he'd spoken the words aloud. "She's not having any luck finding him."

"She. You mean HTW?"

Jake cut her a look. "Not Aruba. I mean her." He nodded to his computer. "A banshee is a female spirit."

"Oh."

Was there a faint smile accompanying the word? He couldn't tell.

She typed on her own keyboard and, with a sigh, pointed at her screen.

"They're back in business."

He rolled his chair next to hers and looked at her monitor. At the top of the screen he read:

H8ers

**"It is impossible to suffer
without making someone pay for it."
—Friedrich Nietzsche**

**Welcome to H8ers 2.0! They tried to shut us down
but were not going anywhere!**

H8 Rools!

"There's a new admin," Jake said. "Maybe one of the members took over."

Below those lines, the contents were basically the same—from the violent websites, to the doxing. A Wall of Blame too, though there was a warning that violence was prohibited. Cyberbullying and trolling, however, were encouraged.

Her face was a mask of dismay. "Look." She pointed to the lower left part of the screen.

Members: 2,324
Currently online: 988

"What was it last time we checked?"

"Half that."

As they watched, both numbers rolled up.

"The original site was bogus," Sanchez said. "Window dressing to fake a motive for killing Natalie. Fallow, Jennifer, Poley, FeAR . . . none of the principals believed the message."

"Well, plenty of people buy into it now."

"They created Frankenstein's monster. It's got a life of its own."

Jake scrolled through some postings. And found the members continuing to post about the Lux, the lucky people they blamed for stealing their chance at success.

"Hate," Sanchez muttered. "The new normal."

A woman's cheerful voice came from the doorway. "Hey there."

Jake pulled himself away from the swelling numbers.

She was in her mid-twenties, wearing jeans and a stylish black blouse and orange sneakers. Hair in a tight bun, she had intense blue eyes that darted around the room, settling on the monitor. A quizzical look, then a smile of greeting. She was the essence of energy.

Walking Red Bull.

Sanchez said, "Mouse. Meet Jake Heron."

"My other boss!" She surged forward and clasped Jake's hand, pumping it up and down enthusiastically.

Sanchez gave an amused eye roll.

Jake finally managed to disconnect from Mouse's firm grip. "Thanks. For everything. You get *any* sleep the last couple of days?"

Her response, like her work, was delivered at warp speed. "Tried sleep once. Didn't work for me, so I gave it up."

"And your assistant. I want to thank him too. We couldn't have done it without him. Declan." Jake looked over her shoulder into the other cubicles and offices visible through Sanchez's door. "Is he here?"

He was confused when neither of the women responded, but merely regarded each other with a quizzical look. Mouse finally said, "He doesn't know."

Sanchez echoed, "He doesn't know."

Mouse explained, "Declan's not a person, though he may dispute that. It's a large language model. An acronym for Decoder-EnCoder Language-based AI Network."

As an intrusionist, Jake was more than aware of—and alarmed by—AI. He kept current on the subject and incorporated it into his course. Large language machine learning models came in three varieties. Decoders, like ChatGPT, generated language. Encoders analyzed and understood language. Other models were a combination of the two.

Declan was an impressive example of the third type. His—well, *its*—ability to order Jake's favorite meal in Lake Elsinore was not, as he'd thought, a coincidence. Declan probably knew as much about Jacoby Heron as he himself did.

"You hacked it together yourself?"

"Pretty much." Mouse added, "Originally it was 'Declann' with two *n*'s for '*neural network*,' but he objected. He said that wasn't a real name. Wouldn't listen. Made a big hairy deal about it. Threatened to go on strike." Her eyes widened. "He was all 'Open the pod bay door, Hal . . .'" She gave her head a small shake. "I had to tweak the code a bit. Remind him who was in charge."

Jake could only laugh. "Well, thank him for me anyway. From what I know about large language models, he'll understand—and appreciate—it."

Suddenly serious, Mouse looked at Sanchez. "The boss wants to see you." Her gaze shifted to Jake. "You too. He said it's important. And he hopes you two can make it down the hall to his office without getting into a shootout on the way."

CHAPTER 79

Carmen tried for an air of confidence as she strode into SSA Williamson's office with Heron close on her heels.

When Mouse said the boss wanted to see her, Carmen suspected he'd learned about some of their forays outside the lines. Until his request was extended to Heron, which had thrown her completely.

Would making hot dogs be on the agenda?

Bringing to mind another topic altogether.

The stunning bombshell that her father had been murdered.

And her new self-appointed mission to find the killer.

Cop stuff . . .

How would she broach the topic with Williamson?

Should she broach it?

Her boss would say he was sorry for her loss and upset that apparently a murder had gone undetected . . . and then hand the whole thing over to CHP or Orange County Homicide, or the Bureau if it looked like the killer had crossed state lines.

Which would not be good enough for her. Or Selina.

As they walked into her boss' office, the big man regarded her thoughtfully. "Something on your mind, Sanchez?"

Dammit, why did he have that uncanny ability to read her?

A beat. "No, sir."

A glance at Heron, as if hoping *he'd* spill. But he said nothing.

Williamson gestured for them to sit. "I don't have much time." He waved a hand at his desk. "Crime awaits. So I'll get to it." His eyes targeted Heron. "I'm not sure how much you know about DHS, but it's like a big umbrella that includes agencies like the Secret Service, FEMA, the Coast Guard, TSA and Cybersecurity to name a few."

Why was her boss giving Heron an overview of the org chart?

"Homeland Security Investigations is a subsidiary agency, with eight divisions of its own. Agent Sanchez and I are assigned to the National Security Division. At the moment."

Now he had her full attention.

"Most people don't know that HSI has its own Office of Intelligence. They compile, analyze and share information about potential threats to national security. For months now I've wanted to create a section that's nimbler and more forward-looking, and house it there. With expanded jurisdiction. The threat doesn't have to be directly transnational."

"Collection and analysis aren't enough," Heron said. "You want to go proactive."

Williamson appeared to consider the description of his objective. "In a word, yes. Agents identify a threat and move. Fast." He lifted an eyebrow. "With supervisory permission, of course."

"Of course," Carmen added.

He sat back. The chair groaned. "I drew up a plan and budget for a new section composed of a hundred agents and analysts. Two in each state."

So this was the mysterious Project X.

"My good friend Stan Reynolds gave the proposal a hard pass," Williamson said.

She turned to Heron. "Deputy Secretary of Homeland. And a certified—"

A glance from Williamson lopped off the last word, but she was sure Heron got the idea of her opinion of the man. Hers and everyone else's here.

"He contacted me on a video link." Williamson's scowl left no doubt about the tone of the conversation. "Never saw anyone so happy to deliver bad news."

She noticed the corners of his eyes crinkle.

He set his palms flat on the desk. "And then a certain person in Washington received a briefing about how you two uncovered the true motive behind the DrethCo–Brakon merger."

When her boss didn't name the "certain" person, she assumed that information was on a need-to-know basis.

"This . . . individual found out about my proposal and got a copy, which concluded—in my brilliant prose—that we're facing, let's call them *unusual* threats. Risks to the country that are in a different category from, say, your average terrorists. I called it the 'New Geometry of Threat.' And it needs stopping." Williamson couldn't hide his smile. "Reynolds found *himself* on the receiving end of a video call, inquiring why he put the kibosh on my ideas. Long story short, Project X is greenlighted."

She could think of very few people with the juice to override Reynolds.

"You're a disrupter," Heron said to him. "Which makes you dangerous to those in power, but also vital for survival. Institutions that can't adapt and evolve are doomed to collapse under the weight of their own bureaucracy."

Williamson looked impressed. "Who said that?"

Carmen jerked a thumb at Heron. "He did. In one of his articles. It was about complacency as a form of intrusion."

Carmen enjoyed Heron's blink of surprise and brief smile. She wondered if Aruba had ever read any of his work. Maybe she'd ask him.

She forced her attention back to her boss and the hurdles he'd overcome to accomplish his goal. "Congratulations, sir. You got your section."

Williamson chuckled. "In a way." He sat back in the chair and looked out the window at the ever-busy docks. "My grandfather . . . he was a circuit court judge in Illinois. Every Sunday after supper he'd sit on our front porch and whittle. Had a penknife. Sharp little thing. Kept it like a razor. And he'd pick up branches in the backyard and whittle away. Didn't make anything, just kept whittling till there was hardly anything left of that branch."

"That's what Washington did," Carmen guessed. "Instead of a hundred-person section, sir, what did you end up with?"

"Got whittled down to a toothpick. One agent."

"In each state?" Heron asked.

"In the country. Rapid response team. First to identify a threat. First on the scene to analyze it. First to neutralize it."

"Team?" she asked. "But you said one agent."

"They also approved a civilian consultant to partner with them." His eye swayed to Heron.

"What?" she asked.

Heron remained stone-faced.

"They can save money on benefits, health insurance, pension. Penny saved and all that." A broad-shouldered shrug. "Federal government, you know."

The two of us? Carmen was thinking.

"Oh, there'll be support, of course, if you need it. Tactical, forensic, admin. Though you may have to arm wrestle when it comes to resources."

Not a big deal. She'd wrestled before.

Then another thought occurred. A curious one, but she had to ask. "What will you call your toothpick? 'Project X' sounds like a one-season TV series."

Every functioning component of the federal government had a name, usually consisting of an uninspired description converted into three initials.

"Hadn't worked that out yet." Williamson looked at Heron thoughtfully. "What is it you call yourself again?"

"An intrusionist."

"Intrusion Investigations," Williamson said thoughtfully. "Vague enough to give us a lot of latitude about what kinds of cases you take on, but serious sounding." He glanced at each of them in turn. "Works for me."

Carmen shook her head. "It always ends up as an acronym, like TSA, BATF. Our initials would be I-I. It doesn't sing."

"Not that I'm necessarily on board with this," Heron said. "But you could shorten it. Since it's the same letter twice, how about I-squared? You could write it mathematically, with a lowercase I and a squared symbol, like i^2."

"Only a professor would come up with that," Carmen said dryly. "Which is why it's probably the last acronym in the entire alphabet-soup-obsessed government that isn't already taken."

Williamson brightened. "I like it."

Frankly, she wasn't concerned about the name as much as the mission. "So, how does this look in practice?"

"I'd handpick each case for you to investigate based on reports from other agencies, federal or local, red-flagged financial transactions, chatter."

"There's a problem, sir." Carmen threw Heron an apologetic glance before continuing. "If he decides to get on board, how could he work on classified cases?"

Heron himself supplied, "That felony thing."

"You wouldn't be the first. We've granted limited access clearances under special circumstances in the past. In fact, a few of them were hackers who changed to white hats. And remember, I have a friend in a high place. A very high place."

Carmen wondered if the DrethCo–Brakon case report he was talking about ended up in the Oval Office.

Then she decided that more was going on here. She'd learned to read her boss. He wasn't the type to rush rolling out a new program. Especially when that program could either elevate or capsize his career. She rested her hands on her hips. "What just hit the fan?"

He smiled that she'd caught him.

Williamson's response was deliberately vague. "Okay. There's a situation and I'd like you both to take point." He glanced at Heron, then back to her. "But I can't go into further details until I know if you're in. I'll have to expedite the authorizations and have Heron approved as a civilian contractor." This time, he gave Heron a pointed look. "I won't waste time or government resources—or my breath—unless you're on board."

Carmen found herself looking toward Heron. At the beginning of this investigation, he told her he was done with her after it concluded. They'd come a hell of a long way since then. He no longer owed her any favors. She had no leverage to use. Would he be up for another consulting gig? Would he ever want to partner with her again?

Before he could answer, Mouse appeared in the doorway. "Sorry to interrupt, but Jake? Something's happening with your computer. Laptops simply should *not* be making sounds like that."

CHAPTER 80

A banshee's wail.

That was the noise Mouse had heard and it now made Jake Heron's heart pound.

He'd programmed the software to make the sound when it had succeeded. The most beautiful words he'd ever read appeared on the screen.

C:\JH\Banchee Connection to target complete.

He tapped a key and the laptop went silent.

"It . . . *she* found FeAR?" Sanchez asked. "Was that some sort of alert?"

"That's exactly what it was." He entered a series of commands and read the results. "He's in a hotel in Trinidad. Makes sense. It's near Venezuela—playground for bad boys and girls. He's got a new handle. DR-one."

"Drone," Sanchez said. "Clever."

"Even got his room number." Jake found himself whispering. He was not entirely present. Memories were—yes—*intruding*.

Six Dead as Domestic Terrorists
Bomb Chicago Trade Expo

He was breathing fast, his heart staccato. Only his hands remained steady as steel.

She frowned at her phone. "The FBI has a legal attaché at the US Embassy in Port of Spain, Trinidad, but any serious investigations are run out of the Bureau's Miami field office." She sighed. "That's a lot of hoops to jump through and word could get back to him."

Jake agreed. "He'll have an early-warning system. And he'll be bulletproof down there. He'll have a few local cops and magistrates on the hook. And a charter plane company on speed dial to get him to Venezuela or Colombia."

He asked, "On the basis of the DrethCo case, could we get a warrant to freeze his bank accounts?" He gestured at the screen, which revealed dense financial statements. "He's got sixteen million in an account in International Bank of Trinidad. No other money Aruba can find. He can't bribe anybody without money."

"We can. But it takes a court order to freeze assets."

"Then we'll expedite the process. Lock down the funds, get the order after."

"Banchee can do that?"

"Easy."

She shook her head. "No good. He'll just tell some bank official to unfreeze it."

He remembered the faces of the victims' families at the funerals in Chicago. He hadn't been there in person. He'd watched it on the TV in the cellblock in prison.

A new idea took shape. "What if the money isn't frozen? What if it disappears?"

She pursed her lips. "And how would that happen?"

"It could be transferred from the account. Cleaned out."

"We can't seize somebody's assets extrajudicially. That's not a hot dog, Heron. That's a chorizo—a damned felony."

He thought fast. "Sanchez. You bust a drug dealer with a million in cash. What happens to the money—I mean before he goes to court?"

"It's impounded. And released if the defendant's found not guilty or confiscated if he's convicted." A laugh, as she obviously understood what he was getting at. "Yes, this is exactly the same. We move his funds temporarily to a holding account we control. The only way he can get it back is to surrender for trial. Yeah, like that's going to happen." She turned to the door. "Mouse!"

An instant later, her head appeared in the doorway. "You shouted?"

"What's our impounded funds routing and account number?"

"I'll get it."

She returned in less than sixty seconds. With a long glance toward Heron and a smile, Mouse handed a sheet of paper to Sanchez, who set it down in front of him.

He typed in the information. Then a few more keystrokes. "It's ready to go." The screen glowed with a prompt.

C:\JH\Banchee Connection to target complete.
Upload package Y/N?

Jake moved his chair closer to hers. Their knees brushed. Suddenly he could smell a hint of lavender.

He looked at her. "You do the honors."

"Me?"

He thought back to Christmas Eve, the night they met.

He nodded.

She gave him a smile and hit *Y*.

On the monitor came the message

C:\JH\Banchee upload successful. Notices sent . . .

A minute later:

Transfer of Funds complete. T. Kane balance in all accounts: $0.00.

"We got him, Heron." She gripped his arm.

Despite what the H8ers preached, revenge is a tawdry pleasure, since it owes its existence solely to tragedy.

But this was something different.

It was justice.

His hand momentarily closed on hers.

"There's one more thing, Sanchez. I'm going to shut down his phone service, but I want to send a message first." He typed. Then looked up. "I'm sending it in the names of the six victims in the Chicago bombing." He had these memorized.

"What's the message, Heron?"

He hit Return.

Onto the screen flashed the words:

Game Over.

ACKNOWLEDGMENTS

Writers keep odd hours, have odd thoughts and even odder conversations. Their families, who are on the front lines of all the mayhem, deserve special recognition. Jeff finds constant support from sister Julie, Madelyn and Robby, Katie and Kyla, not to mention Monti and Blush (as long as he feeds them on time). Isabella has the unswerving support of her husband, Mike; her son, Max; and her writing muse / dog, aptly named Buddy. Our gratitude includes, of course, a hugely understanding group of extended family and friends.

We are fortunate, too, to have an outstanding publishing team at Thomas & Mercer. Senior Editor Megha Parekh, who shared our vision; Charlotte Herscher, who helped shape it; and the editing team who polished it to a shine, including Miranda Gardner and ace copyeditors, James Gallagher, Sarah Vostok and Robin O'Dell.

Finally, our heartfelt thanks to our agents, Deborah Schneider, Liza Fleissig and Ginger Harris-Dontzin, a.k.a. The Dream Team. When we approached them with the idea of a partnership, they swung into action and brought our goals to fruition.

ABOUT THE AUTHORS

Photos © 2010 Niko Giovanni Coniglio and © 2016 Skip Feinstein

Jeffery Deaver is the award-winning #1 international and *New York Times* bestselling author of the Lincoln Rhyme, Colter Shaw and Kathryn Dance series, among many others. Deaver's work includes forty-seven novels, one hundred short stories, and a nonfiction law book. His books are sold in 150 countries and translated into twenty-five languages. A former journalist, folk singer, and attorney, he was born outside Chicago and has a Bachelor of Journalism degree from the University of Missouri and a law degree from Fordham University. He was recently named a Grand Master of Mystery Writers of America, whose ranks include Agatha Christie, Elmore Leonard and Mickey Spillane. For more information, visit www.jefferydeaver.com.

Isabella Maldonado is the award-winning and *Wall Street Journal* bestselling author of the Nina Guerrera, Daniela Vega and Veranda Cruz series. Her books are published in twenty-four languages. Maldonado wore a gun and badge in real life before turning to crime writing. A graduate of the FBI National Academy in Quantico and the first Latina to attain the rank of captain in her police department, she retired as the Commander of Special Investigations and Forensics. During more than two decades on the force, her assignments included hostage negotiator, department spokesperson, and precinct commander. She uses her law enforcement background to bring a realistic edge to her writing. For more information, visit www.isabellamaldonado.com.